Sutherlin Alliance

Copyright © James Spix, 2001. All rights reserved. No part of this book may be reproduced or transmitted in any form or by any means, electronic or mechanical, including photocopying, recording, or by any information storage and retrieval system, without permission in writing from the publisher.

Bedside Books
2389 South, 300 East, Salt Lake City, Utah 84115
www.american-book.com
Printed in the United States of America on acid-free paper.

Sutherlin Alliance

Designed by David Beaty, BEATYDv@aol.com

Publisher's Note: This is a work of fiction. Names, characters, places, and incidents either are the product of the author's imagination or, are used fictitiously, and any resemblance to actual persons, living or dead, events, or locales is entirely coincidental.

Library of Congress Cataloging-in-Publication Data is available upon request.

ISBN 1-930586-86-8

Spix, James, Sutherlin Alliance

Special Sales

These books are available at special discounts for bulk purchases. Special editions, including personalized covers, excerpts of existing books, and corporate imprints, can be created in large quantities for special needs. For more information e-mail cln@american-book.com or call 1-800-296-1248.

Sutherlin Alliance

By James Spix

To Sandy, with all my heart, who makes even the toughest roads worth traveling.

Prologue

On the edge of this solar system, a black, two-kilometer long monolith appeared from the grasp of space and slowed. The gently rounded edges glimmered from the distant sun, reflecting the smooth surface against the stars. Grooves, marking the links between thick panels of steel, sparkled as the faceless vessel came to a stop a million kilometers from the system's life bearing planet. It was a green world with a thick forest that supported a wide variety of plant and animal life.

The seemingly dead object rotated on an invisible axis, positioning itself so that the one edge directly faced the planet. Light cracked the smooth exterior, splitting the length of the vessel into a pair of black slabs held together by one relatively small rear section. Giant pillars pried the two sections away from each other, exposing a tight web of steel conduits. They stopped a quarter of a kilometer apart.

The ship lay silently in space. The light, which had so recently marked its only movement, dimmed as time passed by. After an hour the light was all but gone, with only the distant glimmer of the sun to slightly illuminate the webbing inside.

Another hour passed. A spark of bluish-gray light ran along one of the long conduits, giving the metal a dim glow of the same color. The same spark disappeared into the upper section, then reappeared along another conduit. Additional sparks lit up more conduits adding to the growing glow. Static energy built up, sending blue bolts of lightning between the split monolith.

Space cracked with a dull blue flare of light. A pulse the size of the vessel's opening radiated around the outside of the ship and hid the web innards. The blinding light continued to increase in intensity until the final moment, when the pressure became too great. In a kilometer long beam, the pulse raced towards the planet.

The red and green atmosphere of the target planet was taken without resistance, the vibrant colors flashing away to a pale brown before lighting up into an aura of reds and blues. Like the very star that shined against the surface, the waves of air that had blanketed the life below rose out in giant arms of dark flame.

The air itself took to space in walls of flame that resembled the appendages of the creatures that it so recently protected. The same flame burst down onto the surface, roasting the vegetation and scarring the ground into a thin, black soot.

The last of the air reached out in the vacuum of space, dissipating the fire as it reached out for thousands of kilometers. The last of the protective shell that held the surface intact was gone in a second. The sudden release of all that was life freed the vacuum to take what it wanted from the surface. Down to the last ash of choked out life, space claimed the surface until it was nothing more than a well-defined piece of rock floating in the vast emptiness of its surroundings.

In a mere heartbeat, the once-alive world was suddenly no more active than the chair that the attacker sat upon.

Chapter One

The battle group crashed back into real space with the harsh flash of distant starlight forcing the bridge's blast shield to dim against the blinding light. A million stars fell into their appropriate visual location for this part of the galaxy and began to shine as they were supposed to. Six ships emerged from a hyperspace star jump, rapidly approaching a seven planet star system. The lead starship, measuring some 670 meters in length, slowed down, allowing the five smaller ships to fan out in an attack wing formation. Its cylindrical nose section rotated a few degrees to her port side to align with the fourth planet from the central star. The second third of the starship was made up of a 125-meter horizontal plane with a smaller flattened plane above and below. The last third were four half cylindrical drive sections. Weapons emplacements bristled along all but the drive section as well as numerous docking ports and a highly visible dual landing bay.

The trailing star ships, appropriately nicknamed hammerheads, looked more like cruisers that had been pieced together from spare parts. The drive sections, which fanned out in a flattened octagon, and the lengthy 95-meter necks were nothing unusual. The command module and landing bay made the difference. The head of the ship was simply a quarter moon on the front and above the neck. Six docking racks with their fighters safely attached were visible on the underside of the neck and directly behind a large heavy assault cannon. A second dual barrel cannon was mounted on the top of the neck along with the bulky long-range communications array. Various lighter gun emplacements, shield generators, and power modules bubbled up on each section.

By themselves the Riordan manufactured LT-6000 destroyers were formidable. Grouped together behind the massive Kolbstar heavy cruiser and its five squadrons of fighters, there were few forces that could put forth a stronger defense. The battle group had both the firepower and ground forces to take almost any target and occupy it for any amount of time.

This was the basis for the Alcon Empire's Imperial Navy. Battle groups of four to six star cruisers grouped under sector task forces, controlling countless star systems across the galaxy. Few could doubt the intimidation factor that this kind of power brought with it.

On the bridge of the cruiser Valiant, the white lights of standard running flashed off and were simultaneously replaced with the dull read of battle readiness. The bridge crews sat with attention drawn strictly to their tasks along the two sides of the bridge, each station of three officers indented slightly into the bulkhead. A center row of communications and helm officers faced each other running lengthwise along the bridge. Above it all on a darkened transparent deck were the command officers.

In the center of the arc of five officers and their slightly elevated status panels sat Captain Gulf Merrill. A Kolb by birth, the typical Alcon Empire naval officer stood just less than two meters in height with an average build, as did most in service of the Empire. Unlike his ground troops and security personnel, officers and pilots seldom faced situations in which a strong build was necessary. Like most captains he used his position to refuse the use of the deep black cap, allowing his thick, gray splashed black hair to be seen by all. The sight of hair among those in the navy announced that you were one of command.

Merrill ran a scarred hand along his smooth cheek in an anxious fashion. As was the case in an ever-growing empire, small rebellions periodically arose. Most captains would prefer to take on a new conquest, giving his technology the avenue of surprise. With rebellion situations, the opposing force had firm knowledge of Imperial technology and tactics. This raised the odds that he would lose more of his force to unfriendly fire.

Even the reputation Merrill had for his usually cruel handling of unruly civilians did not help him in some situations. The documentation on rebellions throughout the recorded history of the galaxy was there for every captain to review. The sheer determination of an upset man or woman could give them an edge that could only be countered with swift and deadly retribution. Or so he chose to think.

The history of the Badlands task force had been a bloody one. More rebellions had sprung up in this region on the edge of the galaxy than in any other. Pirate attacks and illegal smuggling operations were also more frequent out here. That prompted the use of officers that would otherwise not have a place among fleets in charge of conquering new territory; officers with the same attitude towards rebels as Merrill's.

He had seen his fair share of dirty combat in his years of service. Trips to the surface had left him with a distorted mind and scarred body. He had lost much of the impetuous drive that had thrust him into those scarring situations. As a result, he was more cautious and reserved when it came to his command. Though he would go to any length to see a victory through, he would not go in blind.

Merrill did have an ace up his sleeve this time, which helped him in this area. Long-range sensors had detected a large armed vessel in the system giving the captain the incentive to ask for additional help from his task force commander. The help joined his group in the form of two destroyers with the registered names of Black-

Chapter One

hawk and Nightwing. The names alone meant nothing unless you knew which squadron was attached to the duo.

"Devil squadron is standing by," the chief communications officer said from the right.

Devil squadron was the ace fighter group of the Alcon Empire. Twelve pilots and twelve fighters with a greater reputation than any full battle group in any of the Empire's fleets. Their mission success was a staggering one hundred percent with over 1200 star fighter kills and seven starships captured or killed. In their twenty years of service only eight pilots had lost their lives and another twenty-five had retired or moved on to fleet command positions.

Merrill considered it both an honor and a privilege to have the squadron under his command. This however was not the first time he served with them. Before his command of the Valiant he had served as Nightwing's master during the first badland campaigns, the start of which had coincided with the formation of Devil. This time around, things were much different. It was an honor more so to direct the squadron into battle than it was to simply house them.

He also held himself in high regard. He was the first captain to have this type of request granted. Until now only task force admirals had been honored with a granted request such as this. He felt that his reputation gave him the leverage to receive what he wanted from the third fleet. He also felt that if he could prove his worth he could gain the greatest honor among ship commanders.

The command of a task force.

"Status," Merrill requested in his familiar raspy voice.

The ship's first officer spun around, his entire station turning with him. "Approach vector will bring us up from behind the fourth planet's only moon. We will be cloaked from long-range sensors until we peek from the southern hemisphere. Shields are at maximum and all gunners are in position. All three intrusion squads are standing by in their transports."

Excellent, he thought to himself. This was the ideal approach. Hidden from sensors by the shadow of a moon his group had every advantage a captain required. Just thousands of kilometers out, his bi-wings had the added edge of appearing around the moon and dropping within weapons range before the cruiser had a chance to dump it's alert fighters.

"Bring up the tactical screen and send the mission parameters to Devil squadron."

Lieutenant Wes Barger grimaced within the cockpit of the boxy Ioline H-90 Bi-Wing fighter. The rough looking pilot ran his gloved hands over his face then back along his thin red hair, pausing to grip the back of his neck. He did not like the idea of being placed under the command of a renowned killer of women and children. Captain Merrill had a reputation for bringing the iron fist down on villages that opposed local Alcon rule, leveling everything both inanimate and alive.

Barger was a connoisseur of the past. He had an affinity for sorting out legend and fact on the history of the fifty-year-old Empire and the 250-year-old Galactic

Council. Much of the formation of the Empire under Councilman Alcon had been shrouded in secrecy surrounding an unpublicized incident in one of the many Galactic Realms. Most soldiers and pilots left that part of history for security.

Barger was the exception. He was especially interested in the history of Devil squadron and its former commanders. The task force Admiral had been a destroyer captain in its early years, as was Merrill. It was in those early missions before Devil proved itself and was transferred to another fleet that the infamous reputation of Merrill first surfaced. Due to sealed files surrounding one particular mission, the captain's most hated actions became legend. He never learned exactly what happened.

What troubled him more than being placed under Merrill's command was the fact that Devil Squadron had been brought in to deal with what appeared to be an older model Kolbstar light cruiser. From the long range scan only the silhouette was shown. The outline resembled that of a simple rectangle with five engines extending aft and two piers shooting forward. In its entirety, the cruiser was not much larger than the destroyers and had just a bit more firepower. The only danger Barger could foresee would be the three squadrons of twelve fighters each that the large landing bay could hold.

The young but vastly experienced Lieutenant scratched at his boxy chin, a bad habit of his that appeared whenever a twinge of nerves struck him. Devil squadron's usual tours of duty took them to the outskirts of the empire, where they acted as point for larger battle groups. They typically dropped into a known hostile system, effectively eliminated the bulk of resistance, then retreated out ahead of the main assault force.

Now he was reduced to clean up duty for a less than effective local government. It was known throughout the fighter corps as mop up duty. Ground troops and fighter pilots shared similar contempt for one another, each feeling that they had to clean up after the other. It was missions like this one that gave pilots the benefit of the argument. Not only did Devil have the duty of strafing ground targets, but they also sometimes had the dubious honor of landing and tying up loose ends.

"I don't like this, skipper," Barger said into the headset that hung above his chin.

"Looks like a routine mission to me, two," the squadron's captain responded. "A couple passes and we'll be on our way home for chow."

Barger raised an eyebrow. It did appear to be an open and shut mission. He still did not like the mission parameters though. As ordered they were to disable any and all fighter opposition, then enter the atmosphere and take out ground targets. If Captain Merrill's reputation was correct, the ground targets would be the fleeing families of the pilots they just vaporized.

"You're set, sir," a woman's voice echoed down the docking tube which connected the fighter to the Blackhawk.

Barger looked straight up into the eyes of the squadron's very masculine crew chief, Loma Cole, who was responsible for keeping the fighters up to spec. "Thanks, Loma."

Chapter One

She gave him a brief salute before shutting the canopy and sealing it from the outside. Normally the pilot was responsible for sealing his own canopy, but the two held special interest in each other. Even as the clear canopy darkened with the dimming of the docking tube he could still picture her climbing back up into the ship.

Cole was a Barlon with an average lifespan of two hundred ten standard years. She was in her middle years when she had first joined the Galactic Defense Fleet and served in transport maintenance. When the Galactic Council transferred the defense fleet to the Alcon Empire she was transferred to fighter maintenance: a serious promotion for years of dedicated service. It was only natural given her talents as an engineer that she was the first choice for Devil squadron's crew chief.

She had been Barger's first friend in the squadron and had seen him through ever since. He never flew into battle with a worry about his fighter as long as she was on duty. She was one of only a few he trusted with his life. Another was an artificial life form that was plugged into his console.

"Sadler," Barger said openly.

Dual whistles emanated from a small, removable device attached to the control console. Sadler, his personal companion was the electronic brain inside the device. With the mass manufacturing required to supply the Imperial navy with fighters, onboard computers were limited to simple tasks. To assist every pilot with more complex requirements, such as power regulation and navigation, each was given a companion after exiting the naval academy.

"Get me running, buddy."

Sadler whistled in the positive. Power instantly raced through the electrical veins of the fighter, lighting up the dormant controls and igniting the four Holmes reactor engines. Freed to prepare himself, Barger strapped himself in and slipped the thick, gray helmet over his head. Once on, all but his eyes were shielded from view. In combat even his pale gray eyes would disappear as the blast shades darkened.

"Two, this is lead."

Barger finished sealing his helmet to his gray flight suit before answering. "Two up and running," he answered through the slight echo in his helmet.

"Captain Merrill wants two full passes of the cruiser on the first run so I want you to take two flight. As soon as you're set relay the order to Nightwing."

Any normal Imperial squadron was made up of six fighters that were paired off in flight. Devil and Varlet squadrons were the exceptions. Because Devil was frequently called upon to be the lead group in any offensive they were divided into two flights of six. One flight on advance and one in reserve. The combination proved most effective.

Wonderful, he thought to himself. "Sadler, secure a channel to three." Once his companion had completed its task his earpiece cracked as it switched from an open to a secure channel. "Three."

"I'm set, two. What is it?"

"We're staying with two flights. Lead wants me in front of two flight so you need to split off one of your guys and swap with me."

"Copy that, two. Let lead know that I'll send him eight."

"Thanks three."

"Uh, Wes."

Barger rested his head against the padded chair. Whenever his friend, flight officer Alder Kirkland called him by his first name outside of social meetings he knew he was in for an earful. "Shoot, Alder, and don't tell me you hate rebel chasing. I feel the same way and don't need another opinion in my head."

"It's more than that. It has to do with the rumors that were spreading when we received our current orders."

"About Merrill," Barger interjected. "I've heard them myself and I'm still hoping they aren't true. I didn't join the fighter corps to shoot at defenseless kids."

"Neither did I. I'm starting to believe that the Sutherlin Alliance has appropriate motives."

Panic attacked him with Kirkland's treacherous words. Barger's eyes shot to his communications status, verifying that the two were the only ones occupying this channel. He relaxed once his stabbing worries were put to rest. "Keep that to yourself, Alder. Talk like that and you'll be on the receiving end of a Devil attack and not a part of it."

He gripped the loose grips of the flight controls and squeezed. "Look, Alder. Despite its flaws the Empire is doing the right thing. The galaxy hasn't had a single governing body in over two hundred years. If Emperor Alcon hadn't began the push from the core systems, we still wouldn't have the trade lanes that have allowed both our worlds to prosper." He knew he was pushing a load. Cadets had been fed that same line for years.

"You sound like a rookie, Wes. Don't feed me that line unless you truly believe it."

Barger sighed. He should have figured that his friend would see through that garbage. With all the two had been through together, Kirkland knew him too well. Neither had really believed the propaganda that was fed them. "Just do your job, three," he said evasively. "And leave the debating for the politicians. If we still have any."

Anticipating his next thought, Sadler deactivated communications and snapped an inquisitive whistle. The question posed by his companion scrolled out across his communications board.

"I don't know, Sadler. Maybe Alder is right." Maybe the alliance is more than just a disorganized rebellion.

Barger had never objected to Kirkland's open feelings about the growing rebellion, though he would never admit to it. As a good soldier he apposed any opposition to the Emperor. Privately though, the thoughts of dissension were creeping in on him. The sealed files on the formation of the Alcon Empire, the punishment attacks on semi-loyal systems, and the supported actions of captains like Merrill all pointed to a less than meaningful purpose in the Emperor.

He often wondered if his growing distrust of the Empire would lead anywhere. His skills and ability to follow any order to the end had brought him to his position in

Chapter One

Devil squadron. It would not be much longer before he made Captain. In another two or three years beyond that, he might even have his choice of posts. If he could hold on that long, he knew exactly where he wanted to go: back to Eriam, the planet of his birth and a home that he had not seen in seventeen years.

His other choice was not one he wanted to look at. As much as the door to an honorable future was in reach, the escape pod of desertion was also at hand. It had happened before. The price paid for such an action provided the doubts he should have had anyway. Deserters were written off as dead and a hefty price was placed on the head of the deserter. In nine out of ten cases the soldier or pilot was returned to the Empire in a bag.

"Stay sharp," lead's voice rang out. "Were coming up over the moon. We launch in two."

Running and locking lights dimmed all along the neck of the Blackhawk. In response, the fighters' engines flared to life, throwing shadows across one side of the ship. The backlight gave Barger his first look at the wing configuration of his fighter. As was customary, he closely examined his craft from the cockpit to check the work of their crews. If the brief inspection failed, which it seldom did, the pilot could halt his launch. An unsafe craft was a dead craft.

The Bi-wing was made up of three parts; the command pod, drive pylons, and generator wings. The command module pod was just a cube with sharply sloping angles coming to a small nose in the front and more relaxed angles forming into a snubbed tail. The canopy was open, giving the pilot a large field of vision in the front, which offset the limited peripheral vision that most fighter pilots had. The lower half of the pod held four laser guns that, because of the limited space, lacked a tracking extension on each barrel. While this did give the guns a slight power increase, they were only truly effective at a closer range.

The drive pylons, which extended out from either side of the pod, were each made up of one Holmes reactor core and a jut that connected the wing to the body. The reactor-based engine provided the fighter with much more power than the standard ion propulsion that most other fighter crafts used. This also drew on more power that the reactor panels attached to the wings provided. The combination gave the Bi-wing formidable speed, maneuvering, and firepower while in space. The drag caused by the cumbersome wings reduced the fighters maneuvering capabilities while in atmosphere, but it retained the superior speed and was still considered the superior all around fighter.

Held to the body by the two juts, the wrap around wings provided both power regeneration and extra shielding. The thick photocells could withstand several direct hits before their ability to absorb energy would overload. The design was that of a thick, rectangular sheet pushed inward at the edges from the jut to where the leading edge hid half the engine. To allow for a steady intake and exhaust both the forward and after angled in plates were grooved out, causing the plates to appear more as arrows than triangles.

Had the wings been angled in any further, Barger would have felt like he was in a cocoon. As it was he felt more like a pack animal with vision guards that kept him looking forward. He never understood why the pilots were given such large canopies when they had no view to the left or right.

"Lead to flight. Thirty seconds to launch. Targeting data coming in from the advance probes."

The tactical display located just below the holographic targeting system lit up. A dark gray area hugging the side of the central point on the screen represented the moon. Lined up next to the white speck that was Barger were five green dots. A larger green target surrounding him and the rest of the flight was the destroyer. Four more similar formations were spread out behind them with an even larger target representing the Valiant.

Ahead of the Alcon battle group was a single red dot. The Kolbstar light cruiser sat motionless just outside the orbit of the forth planet. It would remain a pale red until he was close enough to receive weapons fire from the cruiser. At a bright red he had better be a good pilot or he would be a dead one.

"Launch...launch...launch."

On command Barger pushed forward hard and rotated the grips forward. The docking clamps automatically rattled and broke free. By rotating the grips the bi-wing's engines ignited with full force. At the same time the fighter jerked down and away from the Blackhawk at a sixty-degree angle. In the blink of an eye, the fighter was rocketing towards the lunar surface, leaving the rest of the flight behind.

Barger eased back on the grips and pulled the fighter out of its dive a few hundred meters from the surface. He slowed even further as he banked to his right. The slight alteration in course allowed him a brief view of both the Blackhawk and Nightwing. As expected, one flight was grouping up in the lead while two flight was dropping towards the surface after him. Standard procedure for Devil squadron was for the lead flight to attack the target head on. Two flight would then come up from a different approach and hit any aggressors to one flight.

"Two, I've got your right," Kirkland said as it dropped in off of his right wing. He was as good if not better in formation flying. Showing off his skills as he usually did, Kirkland pulled to within a few meters before rolling out to his assigned spot in the formation.

"Keep 'em low and keep 'em tight. I want to see scrape marks on your bellies when we get back. Five, you've got intercept duty. If we get missile threat I want you on it."

"Copy that, two."

The flight of six fighters hugged the lunar surface reaching no further than ten meters of altitude. Lunar dust billowed up under the pressure of each fighter's four engines. Each pilot companion ran its own terrain following style, allowing each pilot to monitor the first flight as it approached the cruiser. The two flights were more than a thousand meters apart before any response was detected.

"Power build-up, lead," Barger said.

Chapter One

"I've got it, two. She's raising shields. Damn thing only registers five hundred."

One pass should do it, he thought with growing concern. With such weak shields either she was a decoy or this attack was unwarranted.

"Coming up," lead said. "Ten seconds to firing range. Still no sign of powered up weapons."

"Two flight. Break terrain following and accelerate to attack speed. Fifty seconds to first pass."

Even from this distance, the bright amber laser fire was clearly visible. Twenty-four continuous streaks of light began to trace the cruiser along the port side. The ship's shields flared up in brilliant splashes of orange and green, sending sparks of fading energy out into space. Even before the last bi-wing passed over the bow, the strafing run began to penetrate the shields, splashing fiery red across the hull.

Still there was no sign of a response. The port docking bay was dark. Power readings from the laser batteries were negligible, just enough to keep the weapons on dormant standby. If there had been gunners on standby, their weapons would not be hot before two flight reached them. This was a turkey shoot.

"This isn't right," Barger mumbled to himself.

"What was that, two?" asked Kirkland. "Please repeat."

"Nothing. Ten seconds to target. Break off for strafing run."

Barger pulled into a tight turn, banking around the backside of the cruiser. He let off a shot to test its shields and was surprised to find his linked fire crash into the engine housing and tear up the armor. The old, fatigued hull split apart around the point of impact and atmosphere streamed out into space. A series of internal explosions tore through the engine housing quickly followed by a tear of fire bursting from the side of the starboard engine. For all intents and purposes, he had just succeeded in scoring the shot of a century. In one shot, he had crippled one of the four engines with secondary explosions severely damaging the other three.

Flashes from the trailing fighters inflicted similar damage, ripping large holes in the side of the vessel. Atmosphere vented from every opening, indicating direct hits through both the outer and inner hulls. The last two fighters managed to squeeze off another shot before the speedy craft pulled up over the bow. Both linked blasts ripped off the armor directly in front of the bridge, exposing the lower deck. Both the bridge and deck below it were then sucked out into space through the growing tear.

In one pass, twelve fighters had effectively crippled a star ship beyond operation. On an inspection pass, Barger carefully looked for escape pods, but found none. He thought for sure that after the shields fell the crew would have scrambled for escape. Surely they knew that a boarding party would be on its way.

"She's dead," he said. "No power readings of any level."

"Very good," A harsh, raspy voice rumbled over the squadron frequency. "Intrusion team has been dispatched. Proceed with the rest of your mission."

"As ordered," lead responded. "Two, break flight and proceed to the surface. Make one pass over the capitol and take out any weapons emplacements."

"Two?" asked Kirkland.

"Keep it down, three. Take five and six and follow us in on the first pass." Kirkland mumbled something harsh under his breath. Barger did not blame him a bit. It was evident that the cruiser was no threat and not a decoy. If he had any theory at all, he would have pegged the ship as a converted cargo ship or even an economy starliner. He shivered with the last thought. If the latter of his theories was correct, then Devil squadron had just killed a few hundred passengers enjoying a vacation.

Two flight dropped into the atmosphere in groups of three. Controls became sluggish against the thick air and growing gravitational pull. Sadler compensated by increasing power to the resistor engines. The pair of anti-gravitational pods caused the power drain to double. The drain was matched only by the elevated level of energy the photocells generated. He lost no power to either his engines or weapons, though the drag on the two wings was evident.

Barger passed through the high level clouds, billowing them out around the two engines. A layer of condensation built up on the canopy. Heater strips along the creases activated, burning off the layer of water. The drops of moisture remained for a moment, altering his view as he dropped from the layer of clouds. For that moment he witnessed six identical capitols. In that moment, he fantasized about that size of challenge.

In reality, the city was a mere four square kilometers in size, and the imperial capitol building was nothing more than a three story building in the center of the town. At a closer distance, Barger noted the Alcon flag still flying over the building and a ground vehicle that resembled that of an older model troop transport. A single, abandoned laser turret was mounted atop the capitol building.

"No threat indicators or defensive signals," Barger relayed to one flight. "Beginning first pass."

Dropping to three hundred meters he spun his bi-wing upside down and made a visual scan of the city. Two armored soldiers stood in front of the capitol, both staring up at the passing fighters. A block away was the combined spaceport and military base. A single passenger shuttle sat at the end of the landing pad. Both fighter hangars were wide open and empty. Gun emplacements were void of both personnel and turrets. As far as he could tell, the town was barren of all but a handful of ground troops and a few hundred civilians who were just now making their way out to see what the disturbance was.

Barger's open channel crackled to life with a confused voice. "Unidentified Imperial flight, this is ground control. Please...intent...uh, what are you doing here?"

Holding back a laugh at the lack of protocol, he answered the bewildered operator. "Ground control this is Devil two. We have disabled your orbital defenses and are now determining ground threat. You are ordered to contain all air traffic." All one of it.

"Understood Devil two. Can I ask what orbital defense you are referring to?"

"The Kolbstar light cruiser."

Chapter One

"You've got to be kidding me. That thing has been out of commission for six months."

Barger switched off the open frequency and leveled out his flight. There were no ground emplacements, fighters, or fleeing rebels. The starship was abandoned to decay in space, its shield response nothing more than automation. And an obvious civilian had hailed him instead of an imperial officer. What was going on here?

"Two. Status."

"Surface is secure, lead. Only two troops spotted outside the capitol building. They look like they're wearing second generation armor."

"Understood." The channel fell silent as lead relayed the report to Captain Merrill.

Barger manually plotted a return course to the Blackhawk. He scanned the atmosphere for air pockets that might slow or hinder his ability to exit the planet's grasp. A long arc gave him the best chance of a hasty escape. The bi-wing lacked all the necessities for a smooth flight in heavy gravity. He would be thrilled to get back into the zero-g environment.

When the squadron captain came back on, he lacked the determination he had had before they launched. "Swing around and commence strafing run."

"Sir?"

"You heard me, two. Level the space port and capitol building then return to the Blackhawk."

"Copy that," Grumbled Barger as he erased his exit vector.

This was why he hated serving in the Badlands task force. In his mind, the fighter corps was never meant to enact some twisted vengeance on unarmed, defenseless civilians. Now he was faced with the choice he had before he launched on the mission. Would he break formation and abandon this way of life in order to retain his personal honor?

Barger moaned, rejecting his personal beliefs. "You heard him, flight." He flipped on the channel to the capitol's control tower. He heard whispers between the nervous tower operator and someone else who was with him. He decided that this brief warning would be the only way he could live with himself. "Follow me for one strafing pass. Make your shots count." Cause I don't wanna do this again.

Chapter Two

"Devil squadron has returned to their ships, sir," the communications officer said. "The intrusion team has secured the cruiser. They report no sign of activity. There appears to have been a skeleton bridge crew. Six have been accounted for floating outside the hull breach."

Captain Merrill crossed his leg, pleased that such a simple mission had been made even easier with the precise skills of the Devil pilots. "Pull the intrusion team off the ship and send them to the surface. Make sure they understand that any Alcon personnel remaining on the surface are to be removed and brought back here. Have the civilian population informed that a fresh garrison will be detached to secure the city."

The slender officer turned back around, stopping as she cupped her ear. She turned back in a flurry. "Admiral Fallon demands your attention."

Already? Merrill straightened his black shirt, making sure that the breast flap was even across his left breast. He had nothing to worry about. He had completed his task in just under twenty minutes with no casualties and a harsh sense of fear placed against the citizens bellow. If anything, the Admiral should be congratulating him on his success.

A small circle of beveled metal embedded in the floor directly in front of him flashed up a hazy image of Admiral Galt Fallon. He was adorned in the same all-black officer's uniform with a red sash tight around his waist. A wisp of gray hair streaked back from his right ear through the jet-black. It had a much more regal look then Merrill's gray hairs had. He often wondered if the slightly older officer colored it to retain his majestic look.

"Admiral, what a surprise. I had not expected you so soon."

The admiral's response came behind a deep, but intensely clear voice. "A virtue of my position I assure you, Captain Merrill. This however is the time I had expected you to complete your task. Was the use of Devil squadron an added benefit?"

"I have not received any ground reports as of yet, but early passes over the city have produced acceptable results. The destruction of the capitol should place considerable pressure on this sector."

"Did you experience any rebel resistance?"

"None, sir. As expected, if the alliance had been here they left some time ago. The cruiser that was reportedly in their possession was abandoned here six months ago and had only a fraction of the personnel the reports led us to believe. I did receive a report that the city was all but barren of our troops, let alone rebel forces. I'm not sure that this demonstration will serve more than as a show of strength in this area."

"No matter. The report will be leaked that our scouts spotted alliance occupation of the capitol along with a heavily armed cruiser in orbit. Once you scuttle the cruiser and level the capitol you will deposit captured alliance fighters and equipment around the debris. The next freighter to enter the system will confirm our report and strengthen our position. If our spies have been diligent, then the alliance will increase activities and give away their position in a vain attempt to clear their name."

For the most part the Sutherlin Alliance had limited their activities to attacking Imperial convoys and bases. A report that they had occupied a capitol city, forcing a violent response to protect the citizens, could do their cause considerable harm.

"Be sure that the garrison you leave behind keeps the citizen population in order. Make it known that if a single person admits to seeing Imperial fighters strafing unarmed targets, then the entire city along with its populace will burn. To ensure their loyalty, remove their youth and send them through forced academy enrollment. Any bravery should be quelled before it surfaces."

His orders were nothing new for Merrill. His and the Admiral's agenda were similar in regards to the Alliance.

"Do you wish for me to proceed to the Gresham system once I am done here?"

The image of the admiral waved momentarily from a fault in the transmission. Once clear, he responded. "As planned you will continue to the Gresham system and stage your ambush of the Alliance. As you are well aware, a good number of attacks have occurred during freight transfers at the Gresham station. Intelligence has yet to place Alliance operatives during the raids, but we do know that stolen property has been used during Alliance assaults on the outer rim territories."

Again this was covered territory. Merrill knew everything he needed to know before his current operational tour had begun. Most of his information came directly from fleet command, and was then verified from the Admiral. By now the orders and information he received directly from Fallon were redundant and served only to solidify his future actions.

"Am I to continue using Devil squadron then?" Merrill asked with the majority of his hope quelled below his monotone demeanor.

"They will continue to be at your disposal until either myself or the fleet admiral recalls them. In the mean time, you may use them in anyway you see fit."

Chapter Two

That was all he truly needed to hear. As long as the red striped fighters led his battle groups, the opposition would think twice before defying him.

The bulky flight officer Alder Kirkland sat at the back of the recreation room, enjoying his downtime with an alien ale. One of the perks of naval service: The Blackhawk's galley was full of exotic foods and beverages. As such, a position on either of Devil squadron's destroyers was the most sought after in the fleet, or in the entire navy for that matter. Years of loyal service and outstanding achievement were seldom enough. Both crews were mainly made up of heroes of many different battles. The best of the best.

Stroking his fine light brown beard, the six-month veteran of the squadron had seen his fair share of combat. He had fifteen confirmed kills and had a light cruiser capture to his credit. Though many of his fellow pilots contributed to the crippling of the ship, he had scored the final shot that disabled the old vessel. Lucky shots and latecomers to a fight were often credited with cruiser kills. It simply came down to timing.

The two pilots who had gathered in the cramped room all had abandoned their standard gray flight suits in favor of the lighter gray naval uniforms the rest of the room's six occupants wore. The other even went as far as to put on the dark blue flight jacket that was familiar to Devil squadron. Each had a red stripe running down the left sleeve and a demonic figure on the right breast pocket. It was not uncommon for a pilot to wear the jacket for which he worked so hard to attain.

Taking down the last large gulp of the red ale, Kirkland hardly noticed the arrival of Barger. He downed the thick fluid and shivered. The dense mixture was sometimes hard to swallow and even harder to keep down. It was more poison than nourishment, but the staggering side effects more than made up for the foul taste. Drunken stupors came much quicker, and in his line of work the faster a fight was put behind him the better. Especially one so pointless.

"I'll have one, too." Barger said as he sat down next to his friend.

Many a night cramming for flight academy finals were spent with a good ale by their sides. With nights off few and far between, the drinking done in student barracks was frequent and sometimes fatal. Information was crammed into a student's mind at a staggering rate, resulting in a few nervous breakdowns and the occasional over-drinking. It was tragic, but a fact of life. Though instructors did not appreciate drinking on campus, it did weed out the weak from the strong.

Both Barger and Kirkland had graduated from the academy at the same time, each with a final score that made them eligible for early entry into Varlet squadron. Varlet was the jumping off point for Devil and at times held up to twenty pilots. The need for a larger fighter group was simple. Anytime Devil lost a member to injury, retirement, or death a replacement would have to be found quickly and Varlet was the answer. The idea then was to show superb skills and be transferred to Varlet the moment an opening was available.

Three spots opened up three months after graduation. Barger took the first on recommendation from his flight instructors. Kirkland took the third after a competitor for the spot was killed in a minor air battle. As in the academy, the two were inseparable and watched each other's back intently. The ensuing cooperation led to fast advancement and even faster kill totals.

As happenstance would have it, Varlet was called into action just weeks after both pilots entered its service. Kirkland had three kills in the first minute of battle, and Barger had two with an additional assault shuttle kill. An immediate opening was found in Devil. Barger was given the transfer with Kirkland following four months later. By the time the two were reunited, Barger had already been promoted to number three and was in charge of two flight.

Now with forty kills and two star ships between the two, they occupied the number two and three spots on the squadron. The only pilots to attain such status faster were the current captain and the former commander. The squadron's current commander, Captain Vallejo, was well known throughout the fighter core for his fifty kills in three years of service. The former commander, Haggin Stead, did not quite have the kill ratio that his successor had. His reputation came instead from his extraordinary flying skills and ability to draw fire without a scratch. Paying no attention to his own kill totals he had saved many of his pilots' lives and allowed for many more to increase their own totals. He disappeared during an ambush by the Sutherlin Alliance and was presumed dead.

Kirkland turned his head towards his friend, swaying from the growing effects of the alcohol. He admired what he thought was the proud form of the squadron's first officer. He knew that if Captain Vallejo was either killed or promoted Barger would be the new commander. What he could not see was that he had slouched low in despair. His blurred vision prevented any identification of pain whatsoever.

"Nice day," he smiled.

"If you say so."

"You can have my next one," he slurred in reference to his drink.

Barger, all three of him, turned slightly to witness his less than professional or caring manner. "You ordered two?"

Kirkland swayed his head back to look at his empty glass, straining his eyes to focus. "I ordered three." He fell back against the headrest of the chair. He bellowed out a laugh. "To celebrate our victory over these pathetic, unarmed civilians!"

With that the alien form of alcohol hit his brain with a vengeance and he passed out.

"He was done with his first one before we got here," another pilot offered from a nearby table.

Barger cupped the back of his neck and sunk even further. He did not know what bothered him more. Kirkland had just blurted out a concern that should have been kept quiet. He did not care. He wanted everyone to know how he felt though he had not said the words. A true friend would have quieted the rambling of a drunken man

Chapter Two

and dragged him to his quarters for much needed sleep. Barger on the other hand let him mumble his distaste for the mission while he slept.

He quickly found that instead of shunning the belligerent second officer a majority of the surrounding crew were listening intently. For a fleeting moment Barger thought that they too were becoming weary of their current assignment. All of them knew that the next stop would be in a similar system to this one. That could only mean that they would be involved in another show of force. Hardly the duty for the pride of the empire.

Conversations stirred throughout the room from both the pilots and off duty crewmen. Some involved simple chitchat. The rest centered on their current mission and Captain Merrill. In every instant, there was something negative said about the captain, whether it was about the rumors or his choice in targets. In one case, the criticisms fell as far as Captain Vallejo in accepting the assignment. With his command he was also given the right to decline anything below offensive strike missions.

"Looks like the Lieutenant has racked himself up another cruiser kill."

The comment drew Barger's attention. He felt a bitter taste swell up within him and he wanted to stab out a harsh comment on the high pride in kills.

"It wasn't an official kill," the mildly amused voice of Captain Vallejo said.

The captain was born and raised on Sutherlin. He had applied for the naval academy a year before casual conversation about a rebellion against the Alcon Empire became a reality. Harsh training and life within the imperial system had given him a strong sense of loyalty towards the empire, which his own people hated so much. As such, he turned his back on his people and went so far as to fire upon them when he finally encountered the fledgling Sutherlin Alliance fleet.

He and the rest of the squadron walked through the main doors and spread out to occupy the remaining available seats. The well-built captain worked his way through the obstacle course of pilots and crewmen. His brawny shoulders barely cleared the heads of those he passed. It was a miracle that he could squeeze his body into his fighter at all. The cockpit was almost large enough to accommodate two people, but the access tube leading from the ship hardly fit one.

Vallejo clumsily dropped into a seat in front of Barger. "The ship had been abandoned for some time." He turned his neck to face the pilot who had made the comment. "But you can give him an ace for gunnery skills." His head whipped forward baring a devilish grin. "That was the best slap shot I've ever seen. If it had been a real engagement, you would have won the day for us."

Mumbling erupted from the surrounding tables. The lingering words were clearly understood. This wasn't a real engagement. Those weren't civilians that two flight massacred on the ground. The city must have been staged to test the squadron's flying abilities.

You're fools, Barger thought to himself. Why test the best pilots in the galaxy with an empty cruiser and no armed response? None of them could see the bigger picture here. This was a real engagement designed to strike fear into the populace.

The sight of Devil squadron with the distinctive red stripe running along each wing was feared among the known star systems. The fact that the local imperial government was not in operation and rebel forces had been here just six months ago meant that a show of force was needed and they were the most logical candidates.

Vallejo leaned in, giving him the same cocky, power crazed grin that had bugged Barger from day one. "You don't believe me," he said sarcastically.

Barger fed him silence.

"No matter." He leaned back, full of himself as usual. "I know you don't care for me personally, but it's your loyalty and respect in the cockpit that I need. I know you give it to me every time out. If that's as close as you care to get, I don't mind."

"Just tell me the truth, sir," he sneered. "You thought as I did that we would be encountering heavy resistance here. Captain Merrill played us for fools and used us in his own little game."

Vallejo nodded. "I'll admit I read the orders and thought as you do, but I hold no grudge for the captain. Admiral Fallon has his reasons for sending us along on his little terror tour of weak systems."

"Then you know of the rumors, too."

The Captain grinned again as he leaned forward. "Can I tell you a secret? They aren't rumors." He paused to let the bomb settle over his first officers before leaning back and continuing. "I served aboard the Valiant before transferring to Varlet squadron. It was on one of his fear strikes that we first encountered the Sutherlin Alliance. If it hadn't been for that battle I might never have made a name for myself."

Barger's eyes narrowed. "I heard about that battle. You scored eleven kills before the rebels retreated."

"You see," Vallejo announced with triumph. "From that day I was famous. The most kills in any single combat engagement."

This is where Barger had the edge. If anyone in the squadron could be considered a bookworm, it would be him. "I did some research on that day. I found out that most of those pilots were nothing more than kids who were training in what they thought to be a deserted system. Children, Vallejo."

Reaching across the table, Vallejo grabbed him by the collar and pulled him forward. "Better I vaped them before they grew up, got better, and became a serious threat." He let go, glancing to his sides to make sure no one was watching. "Besides, Devil squadron had a number of kills after they jumped in to assist us. Even your idol."

"I never said Commander Stead was my idol. I simply respected his concern for his squadron. As I understand it, he was drawing fire from one of your squadron when he was taken out. Quite honorable if you ask me."

Vallejo grabbed up Kirkland's third ale and drank down a third of it in one swig. "He was weak," he blurted. "Killed by a bunch of kids still in their training pants." He smiled, either from the powerful ale or by a thought that shot into his head. "Still,

Chapter Two

I can't say too many bad things about the guy." He raised the glass to his lips and spoke before taking down the rest. "He did save my life."

Back in his room, Barger had much to ponder over the past day's events. During debriefing, which Kirkland missed due to his forced illness, he could barely concentrate. The fighting had not lasted long and was entirely one sided. Debriefing was a necessity after heavy raids, where kill totals were high and damage or losses were reported. Debriefing for cakewalk missions was simply for record.

What's happening to me? He thought as he walked back to his quarters. His concentration was fixed. The terrible odor Kirkland gave off swayed him if only for a heartbeat. He remained in his trance as he limped his friend to the temporary quarters for pilots from Nightwing. Kirkland managed a gurgled thank you before passing out again on a slide out cot.

He left his room dark, backlit from the running lights outside his view port. He was one of the few to be given quarters on the exterior of the ship. The porthole peered through two-meter thick dura-glass encased in three layers of reinforced bulkhead armor. It gave off a tunnel view of the stars. He seldom looked out for fear of longing, but he appreciated the dim light the destroyer's running lights offered.

The Sutherlin Alliance was a hot topic within the fleet, especially the closer one got to the outer rim of the galaxy. Pirates and mercenaries were full of tales of rebels ambushing them and stealing their cargo. More often than not they were hiding the fact that they had stolen merchandise from someone else. As much as the Alliance had become a group to admire, on fearful worlds it had become the scapegoat of others.

For the Alcon Empire, the rebels were a stain against its shiny hull. While half the Imperial navy battled the remaining holdout realms for supreme power of the galaxy, a handful of decaying cruisers and reject pilots played hit and run with the third fleet – just as they had years before a single task force had been detached from the fleet to deal with the problem. Named the Badlands fleet like its predecessor, the force hunted through countless systems for the invisible mole.

How long would this last before one side faltered? Barger believed in his heart that he was part of the winning team even though he felt he was in the wrong. Even if the Alliance was able to defeat Admiral Fallon's task force, there were seven more waiting in the wings. Beyond that were the other fleets scattered across the four quadrants of the galaxy.

The whole thing gave him a head rush. The number of ships the Empire had sailed since its birth was staggering. There was one ship for every home world in the controlled galaxy that was of a destroyer class or greater. Every planet that flew an Alcon flag had a garrison of troops stationed there, with a full legion based in every sector. Another twenty transplantable garrisons were contained in every task force.

The Alcon Empire had the ability to fight a sustained ground war, then to pick up and move in a moment's notice. It was the basis for the Emperor's philosophy. A mobility and power he felt the previous galactic empires had lacked. He was determined to control the galaxy at any cost to both his own forces and the forces of others.

The power within the Empire, rather than the justice, was what confused Barger. When he looked behind him he saw the iron fist rising up from the galactic core. In front of him, he saw only open ground and a few souls determined to defy him.

"Screen," he said into the mild darkness.

On command a small viewing screen dropped into front of the porthole. Most of the time the thin device was used for data entry and receiving. During attacks it also acted as a deterrent from the blast shields that dropped on either side of the dura-glass.

"Level three clearance. All accessible information on the Sutherlin Alliance."

Barger remained glued to the screen until he fell asleep four hours later.

Chapter Three

    The Sutherlin Alliance was nothing more than a handful of outdated, converted Tualin Star liners, captured Imperial destroyers, and four mobile bases. Each of the four, 550-meter medium cruisers were modeled after the Kolbstar light cruiser without the ninety degree angles and with a single pier extending forward instead of two. The large recreation center that the Starliner once held for passengers was removed and replaced with a landing bay and barracks large enough to hold an entire garrison, two squadrons of twelve fighters each, landing craft, and four shuttles or transports.
    The cruiser had firepower comparable to the stable horse of the imperial navy, the Kolbstar heavy cruiser. It lacked in shielding and adequate communication and maneuvering abilities, giving it a serious disadvantage in point blank fighting. More so, each cruiser was unable to break through the highly advanced communication interference from the Kolbstar cruiser and could not send for assistance in a time of serious need. The alliance had lost three cruisers to this terrible flaw, prompting a need for lighter combat vessels and additional fighters.
    The alliance was only two years old and a majority of the rebellion's founders had been killed months after they organized the resistance, when an imperial cruiser surprised the fledgling fleet and nearly wiped them out. Not long after, the planet Sutherlin was destroyed by the Alcon Empire using an unknown technology. The surviving Sutherlin population numbered fewer than five thousand.
    Despite the loss of both their home world and their small fleet, sympathy began to flow beneath the feet of the empire. Lords and potentates remained stoned face before the audacious actions of Emperor Alcon, but sent support in the form of their youth. Disguised as runaways and accidental deaths, the royal youth and civilian volunteers slipped from Imperial notice and joined the growing resistance.
    Service in the Alliance was short, but not by choice. The average rebel was less than twenty standard years of age with no previous fighting experience. Very few in the alliance had formal military training and even less were comparable to the Alcon navy. Those that were had either attended imperial academies and were failed out or they defected outright. As a result these few were made officers and placed in posi-

tions where they could provide the most help to the cause. It seemed ironic that the Empire's deadliest enemies had once served as a part of it.

Pilots were the hardest to come by. In an age where few pilots survived to score their first kill, anyone skilled or lucky enough to complete two or more missions became an instant celebrity. Several such pilots stood on the flight deck of the mother ship Sutherlin. She was renamed after the destruction of the planet and placed at the head of the fleet. As such, the cruiser was never in the same place for more than a day and kept mainly on the outskirts of the empire. Any closer and the higher ups of the alliance might pay the ultimate price for defiance.

The three flight officers stood by a pair of Riordan star fighters. The Nova was a much simpler design then the bi-wing. They had a central body that formed into a rounded nose with two launch tubes embedded on either side. The communications array, shield emitters, and power converters sprung up behind the cockpit as small half spheres. Straight edged wings branched out along the sides, ending in a light laser cannon. Closer to the main body, two ion impulse engines sat over and under each wing. The combined four engines had far less power than the bi-wing reactor based engines, but they did have the ability to induce a starlight jump.

The fighters' shielding helped to lessen the bi-wing's edge in fights, and the range of duties the Nova had made it the obvious choice for the alliance. The missiles it carried, six to a launcher, had five times the range of light laser cannons. With proton warheads supplemented, each missile had the same effect as twenty cruiser laser blasts. This increased its available duties from strafing runs of larger targets to outright assaults.

Despite its abilities, the only true advantage a fighter had was the skill of the pilot. One such pilot was Flight Officer Narra Shadle. The lanky and strikingly beautiful young pilot had three kills since having her application rejected by the Alcon Naval Academy. All were pirate fighters, but they were kills nonetheless. After her first kill it was suggested that she shave the shape of the fighter she vaporized into the back of her short blond hair. She refused with a smile.

Across from her, leaning against the starboard laser cannon of his fighter was Flight Officer Nyssa of Sutherlin. He had been an intern to a diplomat when word spread of his planet's destruction. The official report was that the star had expanded and had consumed the surface before returning to its original size, but he knew differently. The diplomat he had worked with informed him just days earlier that the rebel Sutherlin fleet had been found and destroyed. Proof that a rebellion had started on Sutherlin automatically marked it for death.

The last of the three was flight officer Ogden Scio. He was mildly reptilian in appearance and in the way he spoke. The words that escaped his lipless mouth were slurred. If he had been human in appearance his friends would have labeled him a constant drunk. At times he could have proven them right. Tempest were synonymous with their drinking habits. It stemmed from a lack of moisture on their home world. Liquid was a treasure and alcohol was better than gold.

Chapter Three

There were no uniform standards for the alliance. You basically wore what you enlisted in. Soldiers were given light armor donated from three different militias, but they were painted the same dull blue. Pilots wore jumpsuits and jackets from whatever academy, fighter core, or piloting job they had. In most cases the jumpsuit still retained the advertisement for a cargo or other company. Crew fell at the bottom of organization. A majority was adorned in the civilian clothes they arrived in. Occasionally a few were rewarded with military jumpsuits when an Imperial supply freighter was assaulted. They were the exceptions.

All three of these pilots were fortunate. They were of consistent height and build, allowing Scio to supply them with the all gray jumpsuit he had worn while he was a pilot for his world's militia. His was one of the few planets in the Alcon Empire that had retained an airborne militia after occupation. It was stickily governed by the empire and fifty percent of its pilots were transplants from the naval academy, but still it flew.

As a show of unity all three had agreed to run a gold stripe down each pant leg and place a pair of black eyes on their backs. It did not add much to the drab outfit. It did show however that they were a team. Gradually other pilots had adopted the same pattern with the gold stripe supplemented with blue or gray depending on the training unit they were with.

The ship's intercom sparked to life and blared out the captain's voice. "All hands prepare for jump. Thirty seconds."

Nyssa glanced up to the chronometer that hung over double entry doors. In bold red numbers the current galactic standard time was displayed. Just below it was the countdown. "I never get used to this," he said. His voice, a mellow rasp marking an age his features did not represent, trailed off as he spoke.

"At least you aren't strapped into a cockpit," Shadle said. "Twelve hours in a confined space can be taxing."

"So you've already tested out the initiator."

"Simulator only," she said with a shake of her head. The advent of fighter-based star drive initiators marked a turning point in fighter warfare. It also meant that pilots had to endure long flights in the confines of a cockpit rather than enjoying the trip in a carrier or cruiser. The experience was less than desirable. "I smelled terrible afterwards."

Scio grinned, picturing her dirty and smelly. "I'm told that the engineers are modifying cockpit environmental controls to counteract that. They may even be installing stasis units to accommodate longer flights. Our companions would be in total control of us and the fighter during transit."

Nyssa shook his head. "I don't know if I like that. I still can't get my companion to acknowledge my existence. He simply does what he's told and nothing more."

"Have you tried bribing him?" Shadle asked. She reached to him and slapped his arm. "He needs more attention than a barked order. Why don't you try plugging him into your journal and let him get to know you?"

Scio moaned. "I wouldn't do that. He might find something he can use against you."

"Maybe for you," she snapped.

Nyssa's eyes narrowed. "Like what?"

"Whatever you keep in there," Scio answered. "Companions talk to each other, you know. If he feels neglected he could send parts of your journal over everyone's tactical screens. I don't know about you, but that could be a serious distraction during a combat simulation."

Starlight beyond the invisible protective shield, which preserved the landing bay's atmosphere, flashed outward and blended together in a harsh prism of colors. For a moment the deck plates vibrated and anything not locked down, including the conversing pilots, shifted aft as the ship jumped forward. Inertial dampeners embedded in the deck caught up with the cruiser's movements and increased in intensity. Quickly the atmosphere within the ship stabilized and adapted to the altered space outside.

"There's something to be said about bending space."

Nyssa glanced to an empty space where a fighter was supposed to be. To the left was another empty space normally used for a shuttle. "There's also something to be said about empty space." He looked back to his friends. "When are we expecting the captain's return?"

Scio shrugged. "Last thing he told me was that he was leaving for Horde Prime, and he didn't know when he was coming back."

"Aren't the Horde fanatical about their relationship with the empire?"

Again Scio shrugged. "Their freighters are just targets to me. If they love or hate Alcon I don't care."

Shadle's eyes narrowed. "That's a bit judgmental."

"Hey, as long as it has been defined as a target to me I don't care if my mother is behind the helm."

Nyssa cupped his mouth to contain a muffled laugh.

"What?" Shadle snapped. She felt like slugging him, though the impact of her fist against his tough skin would more than likely break her hand. She took a sidestep and jabbed her elbow into Nyssa's side. "He's got no conscience."

"Neither do the Horde."

Nyssa held his hand up in front of Shadle's mouth, predicting a harsh reaction. From the snide growl slipping from the corner of her mouth, he was correct in halting her. "No need to respond to that one." He stepped back, sneering at Scio. "And you can be a bit more sensitive and not such a racist."

"Now wait a minute. I don't believe in racism. I believe I can hate people on an individual basis. Besides, if anyone here should be racist it should be you."

"I am impartial to aliens. My friendship with you should be evident enough of that. My only hatred lies on Emperor Alcon for taking my planet and my family from me."

Chapter Three

Scio rotated his left shoulder, signaling his indifference. He turned and strayed off as he responded. "To each his own."

Again Nyssa stopped Shadle's impending comment. "Leave him be. Tempest are not known for their easy adjustments. He needs time."

"He needs a swift kick in the butt," Shadle bit back. "He's had a month to acquaint himself with the Alliance."

Nyssa frowned. "And you had it any easier."

Anger creasing across her face, she had to contain herself.

The scene through the large view port was that of wonder, like staring at the sun through a thin layer of mist. The Nightwing blasted its way beyond the reality of normal space. Starlight was nothing more than a blanket of white dotted by points of black and streaked with every color of the spectrum. Dark patches, representing a passing star system, came and went faster than the eye could transmit the image to the brain.

A hundred years of research on several worlds had produced this wonder of interstellar transport, changing the face of the galaxy forever. Shipping, which had been limited to short distances over months or even years suddenly opened up to systems that were only dots of light on the horizon. Worlds rich in one facet of life could now trade with those of another and for the first several decades the galaxy became a much smaller and more pleasant place.

It was only natural that armed star cruisers would follow. The first galactic empire came shortly after in a unified attempt to stabilize a galaxy not yet ready for hyperspace travel. The great experiment had begun. A new date was set with the birth of the first empire, as was a standard method of time and speech. Despite the problems faster than light travel had brought with it, none would say that it was a mistake. The benefits had far outweighed the difficulties.

"I wish I had studied more in astrophysics," Kirkland said to himself aloud. He turned around to face the wavy image of Barger, who was displayed in the center of the recreation room. A hundred years after the advent of star drive, a hyperspace communications system had been developed. The altered universe star flight occupied offered limited resistance, giving communications a sharp image and crystal clear voice modulations. With holographic imaging relaying full features it was as if the sender and receiver were in the same room. "Sorry, Alder. For once I'd like to stay in a system long enough to take a long look at the stars."

Barger was looking away from the imager that transmitted his image. From the angle he guessed that the lieutenant was also staring out a view port. "Some day my friend. A few more years of superb service and we can retire to the reserves and live out the rest of our lives in one location. On that day I'll buy you a home and you can buy me a drink."

"A pipe dream at best." He sat down in front of the holographic projector. "So what could have warranted a need to contact me like this?"

"Orders. Captain Merrill has finally informed Vallejo why we are staying with the group."

Kirkland folded his hands in his lap. The moment word came down that Devil squadron would be staying with the battle group, rumors began to spread. Under orders both destroyers were slaved to the Valiant, so that jump coordinates would not be transmitted over open channels. This just added to the speculation racing around the ship. By now both destroyer crews were well aware of Captain Merrill's reputation.

"Another threat attack on an unsuspecting peaceful system?"

Barger shook his head. "We're six hours out of the Gresham system."

Kirkland's eyes widened. "Gresham station?"

He nodded. "A freighter carrying fuel cells is due to dock there an hour after we arrive. Dormant probes within the system have reported increased transmissions from an unknown source in high orbit of the station. Intelligence believes that the freighter will be the alliance's next target."

"They would never attack a freighter docked with an Alcon station. The defensive systems have enough punch to take down a cruiser."

"Our orders have nothing to do with defending the station or the cruiser. Devil squadron is to deploy on the freighter's exit vector and tail her as she continues onto her next stop. When the alliance appears to hijack the freighter, we are to hold them until the rest of the battle group can jump in from the station and capture as many ships as possible."

"Capture?"

"I know," Barger said, agreeing with Kirkland's skepticism. "Merrill will probably just wipe out the entire assault force and claim there was no other way. I'm transmitting our orders to you now. Gather up your flight and brief them before we drop into the system. We are to stay on the outskirts of Gresham while the rest of the group docks on the dark side of the station."

"No kills?"

"No kills if possible. If any alliance ships try to jump we are to disable them."

Kirkland rubbed his chin. "I don't know, Wes. We're good pilots, but I don't know if we're that good. Dodging and vaping is one thing. Simply dodging is another. I'd prefer it if we take down the odds a bit before we play tag."

Barger held up his hands and shook his head. "Slow down, Alder. Let's see what we're up against before we decide on how to carry out our orders. I still don't think we'll be facing any sizable force."

"And that would be why?"

"My first reaction was the same as yours. If what I've read holds any water, the Alliance has neither the capabilities nor the desire to take such a risky target. Especially in the shadow of Gresham. I've gone over every incident involving security breaches of the station and none of them involved the area controlled by our troops. There have been a few cargo thefts and brawls, but all were contained to the outer ring and in areas patrolled by private security teams."

Chapter Three

Kirkland propped his eyebrows up and huffed out a breath. History and research had never been his strong point. "You've done your homework."

"I always do, Alder. I don't like to lose."

Six hours later the battle group dropped into the Gresham system and deposited twelve fighters behind a dead moon. Up ahead of the Valiant lay the Alcon Imperial way station Gresham.

Chapter Four

The way station was the only one on the main shipping route between Horde and Cadera Prime, and there was an average of six ships docked at all times. Three other minor shipping lanes utilized the station for stopovers, giving any intruder maximum coverage to sneak in. At least three different species were here at all times and the bars and rest areas had played host to more than thirty different species since it became operational.

With its location in the Badlands, Gresham station was the ideal post for both illegal traders and the Alcon navy. Both groups kept well away from each other, though they knew the other was there. The empire had their own direct access on the planet side of the station that led directly to the inner ring of the station. Traders and pirates had access to the rest. It was a healthy mix of every aspect of the galaxy.

Fights were frequent between members of opposing organizations. The only exception to the rule were the Horde. The tall race kept to themselves and had the uncanny knack of killing anyone who had the nerve to antagonize them. The Horde had their own recreational and storage bay dedicated to them along with two full docking arms for their larger than normal freighters. They were both respected and feared for their dedication to duty and loyalty to the Empire.

Breaking in was the easy part. Completing the contract was the hard part. Beyond the areas allowed to the freighter crews was a tight web of security. Security posts ringed the station with six guards patrolling their respective zones. In addition, a single, heavily armed guard stood posted at every door leading inward from the docking ports. With infrared nets backing up the guards, not a single path of access toward the heart of the station was left unwatched.

Under the cover of a Horde freighter engineer, he passed unwatched through the long docking arm and into the bright amber light of the outer corridor. Lest, as he called himself, stopped at the corridor and glanced to his right. Several Horde crewmembers passed in front of him, obscuring his view of the guard station momentarily. Once clear his bionic goggles, normally used to shield sensitive Horde eyes from the lights, zoomed in on the single-sided shielded glass and penetrated the black haze. He felt a mild sense of relief as he failed to detect his image on any of the ten monitors that were observing the arriving crews. As expected, station security was not interested in a lowly engineer.

Lest had fallen behind but not far. Extending his steps with the aid of two-foot stilts he quickly caught up with the other Horde. He towered over three human guards that stood at attention to a corridor that led inward into the station. Horde had similar body mass to that of their human hosts. The main feature that separated them from the humans was their longer legs used to traverse the rocky terrain of their home world. As on many other of the primary way stations, the corridors took the different sizes of the various species into consideration and were broad to compensate.

Following the twenty Horde crew, Lest walked to the inward corridor, stopping at the first access door to his left. He stayed with the others as they marched into an open room with a thick column in the center. Three servers stood within the serving station, attending to humans that sat around a thin bar ring. Not much of the servers could be seen behind an energy screen that showered the column openings in a light green haze. For their safety from the 'dregs of the galaxy', as they put them, the servers never exposed a single fraction of their bodies beyond the screens. Fights often ended in death and were not always contained to the freighter crews. Instead, the food and drink they provided slid out from secured openings around the bar.

Lest elected to leave his party and march towards the restroom facilities. Horde had no need for such facilities given that they recycled waste through their body until it completely evaporated from their moist skin. His only need for such a facility then became a challenge to his imagination. He knew that at any time there would be two to three monitors scanning past him and the station's security would be fully briefed on the practices of the species that visited.

With a simple flex of the muscles in his neck, Lest activated the translator that ran between his ears and a voice box that was wrapped around his scar covered neck. To himself he cleared his throat and heard that subtle hum of the Horde voice. He then gave himself a voice check and again the low Horde humming language rumbled from his mouth. Lest grinned to himself, ecstatic that the three thousand he had spent on the black market had borne fruit. Translators as complex as this one were seldom found outside the Empire or embassies.

Lest complained to his companions that his skin was dry from an overheating engine core. The other Horde shot back comments that the translator barely had time to keep up with. They agreed that it was in his best interest to moisten himself, since it took a minimum of an hour for the Horde digestive system to produce the needed waste to keep the skin moist and cool. The short conversation was all the cover he needed so he proceeded to the restrooms.

Designed mainly for humans and species that required them, the restrooms were cramped. Local realm regulations prohibited observation of the restroom facilities. Lest was still cautious. He bent down as he entered one of twenty stalls and he squeezed down onto a toilet seat. Carefully he reached down between his legs and

Chapter Four

he released a buckle that held his stilts in place. Both extensions slipped off his legs with a snap and a hiss. Slowly he lowered the extensions onto the floor, taking caution not to let them fall over. If he was being watched he wanted to leave the impression that he was staying put.

The rest of his Horde cover came off easily. As a standard the Horde wore light, absorbent clothing. Simple wraps were unwound in seconds and the translator that held tight to his skin unsnapped with ease. All that remained was a thin skin of armor that hugged tightly to his body and a light wrap that remained over his scarred face. In any cover that he retained, no one was ever allowed a view of his face. In the business he was in, such a view was fatal. It also was used to shield a wound that marked a point in his life he would rather forget.

From each stilt he removed opposite ends of a laser rifle. The two pieces snapped together and locked into place with a twist. Twin magnetic plates on the left hip of his armor clamped onto the side of the rifle with the force of a black hole. It would only budge if released by a switch built into the palm of his glove. Additional arms were carefully removed from the base of the stilts and locked into place along his chest plates and along his right hip.

The look was well known across this quadrant of the galaxy. Jared Guile was by far the most feared and respected warrior to be found. Some called him a bounty hunter, stalking species across countless star systems and returning their dead carcasses back to the source of the bounty. Others called him a mercenary, hired to strike targets with fatal results. Seldom were the innocent excused from the path of destruction that followed him. As for Guile he thought of himself as a simple hire. An entrepreneur of sorts. Someone not to be crossed under any circumstances. Someone never to be fully trusted.

Guile dropped to the tiled floor and slid under the thin dividing wall to the next stall. Still lying on his back he removed a small, black box from his right hip. With the flick of his thumb a blue flame shot two centimeters from the top. Swiftly he rolled over onto his stomach and pressed the flame against the back wall of the stall. In a heartbeat, he cut a square just big enough for himself and, he pushed the two-centimeter thick section into the wall.

Metal sliding across tile, Guile quietly pulled himself into the hollowed out one-meter wide wall. Snakelike in movement he rose to his feet. Foresight had allowed him to place the remote controlled magnetic plate within his boots. He activated one and then lifted the cut section and placed it in the opening. Utilizing his other boot he magnetized both the cut section and a portion of the wall. After removing his boot the cut section remained in place.

Guile began to side step through the wall. He closed the ten-meter span to a bulkhead in seconds. At the bulkhead was an opening leading upward and downward with a single access ladder running the vertical length. Guile selected upward from his memory of the station layout and, he began to climb rapidly towards the next deck.

His first obstacle came in the form of a laser net that covered the access chamber. Guile was still too far from his objective to risk triggering an alarm so he chose a different route. He repeated the same steps he had undertaken in the restroom and found himself standing in an empty corridor a minute later.

Hard footsteps marked the approach of a patrol. Guile looked around the immediate vicinity and identified a point of reference. He came across a wall control panel marking an entrance to fuel storage, which meant he was still a hundred meters to the nearest access corridor to the center of the station. His best bet was to hide out until the patrol passed.

The three-person patrol rounded a corner and walked past the thin burn marks in the base of the corridor wall, marching by unaware that Guile hung on the ladder on the other side. He waited long enough for the deck plates to stop vibrating, then he pushed the cut section out into the corridor once more. As before, he sealed the hole by magnetizing the section of wall before jogging away.

Guile evaded three more patrols on his long jog to the inner corridor ring. Beyond the double layer of bulkheads was a gap of space that spanned over thirty meters. Only one access corridor bridged this gap and it was on the far side of the station. Use of the corridor would have done him no good though. Guards were stationed at either end and there were no access tunnels leading inward.

The inner corridor ring ran around the octagonal station and was divided at sixteen points by bulkheads and blast doors. Schematics etched in his mind, Guile ran to one of the separating bulkheads and began to feel across the smooth surface of the inside wall. At about waist level he found the only discrepancy in the surface and he pressed in. With a subtle crack the hidden access door gave way and slid back into the wall.

Once he was inside, Guile allowed the door to slide back into place. He activated two small lights that nestled in the creases of his shoulder plates, giving him ample light to look around. From here there were no more access doors or easy ways of getting around. This time he had to break out the heavy equipment and start inflicting serious damage to the structures he came across.

He placed a thin concussion charge on the opposite wall as the access door, then he pressed the back of his armor against the charge. Guile counted down from five and slammed his body as hard as he could against the charge. The structural steel of the station moaned from a ripple of energy released from the small blast and a section the shape of his body shattered. The majority of the explosion was muffled in his armor. Both Guile and the shards of steel fell through the hole and into a two-meter opening between the double bulkheads.

Guile popped three centimeter thick packs from his chest and placed one in front of the chattered section of wall and the other two a few meters in either direction. As each was placed a screen of blue/green haze shot out and blocked the open areas. He placed a second concussion charge, three times as big as the one he just used against the thick, bulkhead.

Chapter Four

Double checking that his armor sealed off every part of his body tightly, Guile then removed a clear film from a pouch on his left leg, simultaneously unfolding the film while leaning against the charge. He counted down from ten this time, taking deep breaths at each count. At zero he slapped the film on his face. Instantly the film wrapped all around his head and sealed around the armor of his torso. At the same time he slammed his body against the charge.

In a flash the ripple blew out a two meter in diameter section of the bulkhead into space. Guile was thrown from the explosion. He never reached the opposite wall though. The sudden vacuum of air grabbed hold of him and pulled him into the darkness. The brief flame was extinguished without the oxygen to supply it, leaving only a human and shards of metal to billow from the hole. Station security undoubtedly detected the explosion and heard the blast, but without a sudden depressurization reading from any of the decks they would simply begin a foot search for the problem. With no visible intrusion into the bulkheads it would be hours before they found the hole left behind.

Guile had six full breaths of oxygen contained within the clear film. The sudden pull of the vacuum had given him enough momentum to reach the core of the way station, but he would be dead long before then. He took one breath of the limited supply with this in mind, then he removed another charge. As hard as he could he slapped the charge against his back. With a hard, stabbing crack the concussion increased his momentum enough to reach the core bulkhead in two more breaths.

A deep breath, then Guile activated the magnetic plates in his boots and braced himself. Boots first, he slammed into the hull of the station. The impact knocked the breath from him and he reeled back to take another one. His body wanted to repel back towards the outer ring, but the boots held firm. Despite an aching pull that wanted to tear his body apart, he was secure.

Wasting no time, Guile slapped the last of his charges against the hull and stepped firmly upon it. The brief ball of fire pressed him away from the hull, but again the boots held. Instead he began to fight the rush of air escaping the hull and he forced himself inside. His muscles ached with every tug at tattered steel. He took his last breath from the film, though he didn't need it. There was enough air slamming into him to last him weeks.

As his feet passed the opening, Guile pulled out his last shield emitter and he slapped it near the blown out section of bulkhead. The bluish green field sprung out and covered the opening, sealing in the escaping air. Almost on cue the gravity conduits embedded in the deck plates took over once more and the struggling mercenary fell to the floor with a resounding thud. It would not have been that bad, but the armor he wore provided little cushion.

Alarms sounded in his head. At first Guile thought the explosion had set off the stations internal alarms. He quickly realized that the ear piercing sound he heard was his own body crying out for air. With the rush of a stampeding beast he tore the film from his face and took in the deepest breath he could get. He inhaled so much that his chest hurt from expanding so fast.

Guile rolled to one side and sat up. He found himself exactly were he wanted to be. He sat between the outer and inner bulkheads, several meters from the nearest lateral support. The absence of a vibrating hull left him thinking that the internal alarms had not been sounding. As before that meant that security teams would begin a visual search of the effected areas instead of a thorough sensory probe. This gave him approximately five minutes to cut an opening into the core of the station and find a place to stash himself.

As it turned out he needed only three minutes. Using two handheld cutters he burned open a one-meter hole into the inner bulkhead, sealing it behind him. Once inside he worked his way to an access door and slipped into a ring corridor. From there it was a matter of a short search before he came upon a storage unit and a place to hide. He buried himself in cleaning supplies and relaxed for the first time since his mission started.

An hour had passed before the marching of security units had subsided to a normal level. He remained within earshot of the access door he had come out of so that he could monitor activity around the area. So far he detected no signs that the teams had entered the bulkhead rings through that door. This left him with two conclusions. Either the teams found no reason for investigating the bulkheads or they discovered a hull breach and were awaiting a space unit to seal the hole from the outside. In either case he was safe for an hour or two longer. It would take that long to find the portable shield.

Guile slowly opened one of a few manually controlled doors on the station and peered down one direction of the corridor. A brief shadow caught his eyes signaling the departure of a guard. Carefully he peeked around the door to look in the other direction. Again the path was clear of obstacles. One last look in the opposing direction found his gaze upon the access door. There was no sign of recent entry or char marks of sudden decompression. His abrupt entry had yet to be noticed.

Rifle in the lead, the cunning intruder crept along the corner without so much as a creak from his boots. Each step was cautiously observed as to avoid sensor traps placed in the corridor floors and walls. After ten minutes of not finding any, it did not mean that they were not there. If he let up for a moment it would be then that an alarm would sound. Throughout his life he lived by this policy.

Guile's journey carried him around the circumference of the station. The trip took unusually long given the number of times he had to duck down side corridors and climb into access hatches to avoid detection. He had to go so far as to bypass an entire section of the corridor to stay away from a random sensor net that appeared thanks to the station's computer system. Timing was everything in this mission, but when push came to shove, secrecy was more important.

One last course deviation landed Guile halfway along the airlock doors that connected the outer ring to the inner and the military cargo housing center. In a way he would have liked to test his abilities against the most secure section of corridor in the station. It was just as well that he stumbled closer to his destination. The less time he spent dodging patrols and sensor nets, the better off he would be.

Chapter Four

Glancing at his wrist chronometer Guile found the break he had hoped for since the entire mission had begun. His timing could not have been better. The mid day shift change had already begun, which left only three full time guards at the cargo bay end of the wide corridor. The majority of the sensor nets would also be down so that wiry guards would not set them off as they dragged themselves out.

Guile peeked his head out of the side corridor and shot a quick glance to his left. As suspected the three guards stood to either side of the massive cargo bay doors. Each carried heavy blaster rifles that had the capability of punching a hole the size of a Horde through the bulkheads. They also had the ability to widen the range of fire to take down multiple intruders. This left him with few options if he had to confront them in the open. His only other option was to take all three out from this distance and pray none of them could sound an immediate alarm. He was sure the loss of three guards would not go unnoticed for more than a few minutes, but a few minutes was all he needed.

Rifle still in hand, Guile removed his cutter from his body armor and ignited the flame. He locked the safety off with his thumb, freeing the laser cutter to remain active even without pressure from a gripping hand. The plan simply was to toss the cutter down the hall, allowing the beam to splash sparks into the air as it rolled end over end on the deck. It was his hope that the momentary confusion would draw the three guards closer together to give him clearer shots.

Guile closed his eyes and took in a deep breath. In his best underarm toss he threw the cutter in a mild arc. As the beam came within cutting distance of the floor he lunged into the corridor and drew a bead between the three guards. A shower of sparks erupted from the decking, drawing the attention of the guards, but only two responded as planned and they both stepped out on the same side. This left him with a five-meter gap between the first two and his third shots.

With few other options he targeted one of the two grouped up guards and fired a single shot. He quickly drew his second bead and fired as the first hit a guard between the chest plate and chin guard of his helmet. With the first guard propelled back against the cargo bay doors from the force of the bolt, the second shot slammed into the chest armor of the second. The heated beam of white light missed its target by less than a centimeter, launching the second guard back but not killing him.

As anticipated, the remaining guard widened his fire and laid a single arc at chest level. Guile dropped to his knees just under the plane of fire then rolled to his right. He could feel the superheated air above his head burn at the thin cloth that covered him. Sweat beads appeared all over the exposed portions of his face and were quickly evaporated.

Guile heard a snap from behind him. He recovered from his role with a kick that sent him in the opposite direction. A second snap behind him burst in a similar track as the first wave of fire, but it was more concentrated. The guard that had crept up behind him seemed more interested in a straight kill rather than the saturation of the corridor. As he barrel rolled to the opposite side of the hall, he began to wonder about the intelligence in using weapons at all.

Guile barely heard the snap of a third weapon as it armed above the deafening hiss of two discharging weapons. The snap came from the general area of the second guard he had downed. If he didn't rebound quickly, the addition of another weapon would cut off any avenues of escape and the guard that took a merciless shot to the chest would soon have his revenge.

The corridor wall came up quick and it stopped Guile's roll abruptly, though his head continued to spin. Pushing past his current state of thinking he dropped flat against the floor. A single pulse from behind him blasted halfway through the bulkhead at about the same level his head had been. Even before the edges stopped glowing white-hot, he pushed off to one knee then sprung through the hole.

The opposite side of the bulkhead was cramped and left much to be desired, but he was still alive and that was a start. He had scarcely enough time to combat his current dilemma before the guards realized what had happened and then flooded the air spaces between the bulkheads with neurological gasses. In his eyes that fate was worse than taking a pulse round through his chest plate.

Guile's salvation came from the halting of fire. The silence allowed the cutter to reveal itself down the corridor. Because of the fighting none of the guards had time to shut off the devise and halt the flow of gas pouring from the tip. The continuous hissing sound alluded to the device's blade being extinguished though. The eruption of a constant proton flow probably had taken away the oxygen needed to keep the plasma blade fluid.

Judging the steps of the guards carefully, Guile calculated the time it would take for the two guards closest to the cargo bay doors to reach the cutter. He gripped his weapon tightly as the time neared and he pictured the guard that had crept up behind him. He judged the first snap of his weapon armed and imagined where he might be relative to the blast that had punched the hole in the bulkhead.

One of the guards shouted something in Horde. Without the benefit of his translator Guile had no idea what the guard had said. One thing was for certain though. The guards could not have been very bright if they compared him to the taller species. This fact just reinforced what he was about to do.

Again taking a deep breath he clenched his teeth and propelled himself out of the hole. Blindly, Guile fired towards the lone guard catching sections of his torso and arm with each round. Each pushed him back and further disorientated him. He hit the ground slightly ahead of Guile and fell back, giving him a clear shot under the helmet. Ignoring the shouts of the other two guards he fired once and burned the inside of the downed guard's helmet.

Guile heard double snaps of two weapons discharging. Still facing the opposite direction he covered the exposed sections of his head and planted himself flat on the deck. The dual discharge erupted in a gas explosion ten meters behind him and pushed him across the deck towards the downed guard. Above and to either side he heard the tearing and moaning of walls as they buckled under the pressure.

The heat from the explosion subsided. Guile rolled onto his back and looked down the corridor. The cutter and both guards were gone, as was a three-meter sec-

Chapter Four

tion of decking. Apparently more fumes had escaped the cutter than he had envisioned. No matter. He simply picked himself up and pushed on. The destruction and death he passed was simply an obstacle in his mission parameters.

Guile reached the door. To the right was a square meter control panel with more unmarked buttons than he cared to count. Simple code buttons were never used to shield military installations, which this obviously was. He looked over the panel several times looking for anything that would suggest the panel was being used as a cover to scare robbers. Careful examination of the writing on the lower edge of the panel confirmed otherwise.

The butt of Guile's rifle smashed the panel into hundreds of dura-plastic pieces and a million sparks. The thin cover fell to the deck and shattered further. A slew of wiring sprung from neatly wound packaging within cabling conduits and spread out around the defaced panel. The solution to his problem suddenly presented an even greater problem. Every wire had the exact same color configuration.

Guile rolled his eyes then whirled around. Heavy footsteps began to rumble at the end of the corridor, quickly approaching his position. He glanced down at the first dead guard's weapon, pondering for a moment about using it against the door. Sanity returned and he realized that even at its maximum setting it would take hours to burn through the security door.

His left ear twitched as a warm breeze brushed against the side of his face. Guile turned back towards the control panel. He grinned as his luck continued on its unprecedented pace. The explosion had cracked open a hydraulic conduit behind the bulkhead. Guile's unwarranted destruction of the panel gave the pressure a path of escape and had given him a rare opportunity. If the density of the hydraulic pumps was high enough to burst a conduit under extreme stress, then a fluid explosion would be more than enough to crack the high tension track the security doors ran on.

Shielding his eyes away from the panel, Guile raised his rifle and fired into the opening the steam had escaped from. A brief spurt of fire erupted from the opening, engulfing the end of the rifle and forcing him to drop it. Just as quickly the small eruption pulled itself back behind the panel. Guile turned back slowly wondering if his plan had failed when every inch of deck plate began to rumble.

The guard at the end of the corridor barked orders as he ran towards him, but Guile ignored them. He waited patiently as the rumble grew stronger until the seams of the right security door cracked and began to spew a thick, black fluid. Fire chased the fluid shortly after. The rumble peaked out, leaving him with barely enough stability not to fall over. His eyes rebounded in all directions, distorting his vision and causing him almost to miss the right side of the security doors lifting off its track and falling back into the cargo bay. Weight carrying it away, a section of the length of the door tore from the backside of the bulkhead.

Guile knelt down once the rumbling had subsided and he picked up the dead guard's weapon. With a snap he armed the rifle and ran through the billowing steam into the cargo bay. To ensure that he had enough time to complete his mission, he pointed the weapon behind him as he ran and fired blindly down the corridor.

The cargo bay was dark from a loss of power. At least the section Guile was in. A few hundred yards in either direction the lighting system on the fifty-foot ceilings were still on. The rupture of the conduit must have also severed the power conduits. It mattered not though. For his mission to succeed he didn't need to see the cargo. His final objective was beyond the cargo bay bulkhead.

Guile set the guard rifle on overload and left it behind. The time it took him to span the sixty-meter deep bay gave the rifle ample time to overload and detonate. He barely had time to pass the cargo bay bulkhead doors before the shock wave slammed against them. For one brief moment as he laid against the closed doors he thought they would collapse in on him.

The steady rumble on the doors passed and Guile pushed off them. It was lighter in this corridor than in any other and the troubles of the outside didn't seem to matter here. The emergency lights were not lit and the alarms were not sounding. There were no heavy footsteps of approaching guards or snaps of armed weapons. The area was quiet and given the circumstances it was not a pleasant quiet.

Guile never came unprepared. From his boot he removed a small pistol with enough charge for six shots. If he kept his head it would be more than enough to pin down any more guards he might encounter. The military code panel he breached would mean that he would be running into more than just mere guards. The soldiers assigned to such areas would not be so easily taken down.

The primary control housing for the station's white fusion reactor was a hundred meters away. Guile glared down the thin corridor looking for light shadows from two adjoining corridors he had to pass. Seeing no recognizable shape, he hunched over slightly and snapped forward like a runner from the starting gate. Pistol firmly in his grasp and raised to waist level, he ran as hard as his body armor would let him.

The first corridor passed within twenty feet without incident. The second came up a bit faster, leaving a large distance to cover. That thought alone would have been enough to worry him if he had not seen the single figure standing out of the way as he sprinted past the second corridor. He could not stop and he was already running as fast as he could, so he could not turn to fire. He had to rely on his speed and remaining luck to see him through.

The first hit felt nothing more than the bite of a Tarelian ant in the square of his back. He twitched slightly but it was not enough to break his stride. The second hit slid off the side of his shoulder, knocking his arm in front of him. It was enough to break his stride. His balance was still too strong though and his momentum carried him on.

Ten meters from the single door, the third shot struck him. It hit square in his back again with the intensity of a sledgehammer. Guile could feel himself lift off the ground no more than thirty centimeters with the pulse carrying him along. He was no longer running. It felt more like he had been lifted from the deck with a hook that drove into his back. Though he could not feel the burning of a laser hole, he knew his armor had cracked open.

Chapter Four

The strike was high enough to force a forward tumble. Three meters from the door, the length of his body was parallel with the deck. The reality of things was that when he hit, he would hit the door head first at a speed that left much to be desired. The rate at which the end of the corridor approached confirmed this.

Guile had little time to react. In a last ditch effort to avoid a concussion, he threw his arms out to his sides and raised his head as far back as it could go. The bulky edge of his chest armor touched the metal decking first, forcing his body to back up a few centimeters. His legs touched down as his upper body rebounded up, and with a hard jerk he rolled his torso over. In one twist his butt flipped over and began to scrape across the deck. Slowing down only slightly he slammed against the wall in a partial sitting position.

The air had been knocked from Guile's lungs. He gasped in a desperate attempt to breathe before he reeled to his left from a stabbing pain in his back. He could feel the knot that had formed in his body armor from the impact. The second blast he took had weakened the metal enough for any high-pressure contact to do damage. He made a mental note to purchase stronger material the next time he took a job such as this.

Heated air burned at his right ear. A slight splash of burned metal hit the side of Guile's tattered covering. The door sizzled from a pinpoint burn hole that had been meant for his head. Only the pain of impact had saved him from a fatal hit. He decided to make a second mental note countermanding the first.

The person who had fired upon him was obviously a soldier and of officer caliber. The accuracy of the shots and the fact that he stayed behind cover made this clear to Guile. A station guard would have blindly run after him, sure that the second hit to his back was enough to down him. The military that installed the security panel at the cargo bay was more careful than that. The officer would keep him pinned down and await reinforcements instead of going for the kill. In his position Guile would have done the same thing.

Looking at his small pistol, Guile moaned. The small weapon had been with him since before he joined the military years ago. It had seen to his protection many times, having been concealed in tight places. Now it would save him one more time. The last of his luck today rested in overloading the small weapon and using the distraction to his benefit. In the end the mission was more important than the sentimental price of a pistol.

The throw was perfectly timed and aimed. The pistol rebounded off one wall and bounced into the open area at the cross section of both corridors. Guile heard a mild, unrecognizable cuss then the panicked scampering of the officer as he sprinted out of harms way. The pistol squealed in agony as the chamber overloaded and detonated, filling both corridors with a thick, choking smoke.

Guile rose to his feet, turned, then kicked open the manually operated door. At this point there was no need for candor. The door swung back and smashed into the inside wall. Guile stormed inside, thought for a moment about shutting the door behind him, then decided against it. At best he had three to five minutes to complete his task before the entire Imperial Gresham garrison would come down on him.

The primary control room for the station's power core felt more like a closet than a room. A single control desk sat in front of a two-meter window that overlooked the core. Guile pulled the desk's chair away and stood behind the controls. The sea of monitors, buttons, and levers was sickening. How anyone could remember which control masters what system was beyond him. It did not matter though. The only lever he needed was pinstriped in yellow and was directly in front of him. Smiling at the ease of this part of his mission, he pulled the lever as far back as it could go and smashed the console.

Guile waited a few minutes for alarms to sound throughout the room and down the corridor. He watched for which warning lights lit on the undamaged portions of the console, then he switched off the corresponding controls. The growing alarms cut off abruptly as did the intruder alert systems. The main lighting also began to dim which troubled him. Either the alarm controls also commanded the station's main systems, or he had less time to get out than he had originally thought. The latter gave him a cold shiver down his back.

Guile backtracked his path to the cargo bay and passed through the doors. The lights were still out inside the bay, but so were the lights of the main corridor on the far side. He ignored the minor inconvenience and activated his shoulder lights. One flared out as it turned on from damage during his fall. The remaining light provided ample illumination though, so he continued on his way back out.

Surprisingly enough, Guile encountered no resistance as he followed his original course back to the damaged bulkhead. He passed the guards he had downed, but no others. He took into consideration the brief sounding of the station's overload alarms and put it out of his mind. If in fact the guards and soldiers were attempting to evacuate the station, they would never make it. The nearest escape modules were along the docking ports, and they were a good five minutes of hard running away.

Guile worked his way to the demolished bulkhead and found himself staring out into space. The portable field emitter continued holding the vacuum of space behind its thin haze. In another minute though, it would fail as would every inch of space within several kilometers of the power core. From there the shock wave would crumble everything in its path for another hundred kilometers or so.

A shadow approached around the dark form of the outer ring. Guile removed a second slip of clear elastimat from his trousers and he slapped it over his face. In one motion he deactivated the field emitter then tightened his body. As if hit from behind by a speeding vehicle, he jutted from the safety of the station on a direct line for the approaching fighter. As if he had not taken enough of a beating for one day, his side slammed into the nose of the nova fighter craft and he rebounded off of it.

Flaying in the deep of space he managed to grab hold of the laser cannon on the port wing. He moaned, allowing an air pocket to form in the mask, then he began to work his way along the wing towards the cockpit. Once there he patted a small indentation under the cockpit canopy. It lifted in silence and slid back into a locking

Chapter Four

position. Carefully Guile lowered into the cockpit. As he strapped himself in, the canopy slid back into place and sealed.

Heat filtered over Guile's cold body and he could feel the rush of air over the clear mask. He quickly tore the elastimat from his face and took a deep breath of filtered air. After all the smoke he had inhaled, the pause was refreshing. A grateful set of lungs relieved themselves with a few short coughs.

"Backer," Guile said behind staggered wheezing. "Take me off silent running and get us to the jump point and outta here."

The fighter's small comlink located just above the throttle control beeped and whistled a response, then the ship rolled in two directions on an invisible axis. Guile kept an eye on his instruments as he pulled up a battered, blue and black helmet from under his console and slipped it over his head. The helmet felt better than the cloth he had worn for three days. After awhile it began to chafe. He wondered how the Horde could wear the same clothing for such a long period of time.

Guile jerked back in his seat for a heartbeat as the fighter leaped forward. The growl of the four engines reverberated through his seat and indicated the need for a tune up. Spending two months preparing this operation, a bold one to say the least, had drained his funds and supplies. A situation he would remedy shortly once he returned to his employer. The cost of this endeavor had secured his future for a good twenty years of comfortable living. Quite the vacation for someone who rarely took time off.

The nova cleared the station and leveled off along a designated route of travel. With the heavy traffic throughout the galaxy a complex series of traffic lanes had been established. Aided with interstellar gravity beacons designed to force a ship to normal running the system of hyper space freeways had the safest record of any transportation system both atmospheric and space worthy.

Guile's companion chirped through a speaker in his helmet. In response he flipped his navigational screen over to an aft view in time to see a billow of flame erupt from the heart of the elliptical station. Subsidiary explosions tore from the flat edge of the core of the station, lashing out at the outer ring and the structural supports that held the ring in place.

"I see it, Backer." Guile reached down to the left side of his body and gripped the throttle and the stick between his legs. "There's no time. Dump power to the thermal motivator and increase inertial dampeners." Backer spat out a complaint, frustrating him. "I know we're still in-system. I'll risk the fine over risking my life."

Backer acknowledged with a whistle. As his personal companion poured power into the impending jump and plotted a safe exit vector, Guile looked down at the last image replaying over and over again on the aft monitor. A single ball of white light engulfed the entire way station and three ships in a parking orbit; then the entire area shrank slowly into the distance, away from the fleeing fighter.

The image replayed two more times to his delight until Guile spotted something to his disliking. He paused the image just before the final blast and focused on a single ship on the far side of the station. A dark gray mass on the backdrop of space.

Sutherlin Alliance

The shape of the Alcon Imperial heavy cruiser was unmistakable. It quickly turned and four massive engines flared out blue rings of energy and rocketed off into the depths of space.

Guile terminated the image and sank into his seat. For the five years he had made his reputation as the unstoppable hire of anyone who could afford his price, he had survived by avoiding any Alcon entanglements. Now, under the watchful eyes of one of the Empire's hundreds of war ships he had committed the worst crime. One for which he would pay dearly if caught.

Chapter Five

Barger was the closest to Gresham station and was the only devil to see the Valiant forcibly breaking free of its moorings. His long-range sensors detected nothing that would warrant such an action from the cruiser.

Feeling he would not be breaking the mission parameters, he opened all channels. Sadler frantically searched through all fifty-six local communications channels for anything that might sound out of the order. Both he and his companion picked up the problem at the same time.

"...aliant this is control. We have a core breach in progress, please respond. I repeat, we have a core breach in progress, please res..."

The core of the way station erupted in a ball of fire as the Valiant pulled away and disappeared from the system. The raging fireball engulfed all three destroyers still moored to the dark side of the station as well as the Horde freighter on the light side. The wave of fire passed, leaving scarred hulls and raging fires. The central ring and core of the station was gone. The outer ring separated into eight, gutted sections, each listing towards the planet the station once orbited. All four ships and the surviving portions of the station began the long journey into the planet's atmosphere, burning up as they went.

Sadler chirped, drawing Barger's eyes to the tactical screen. For the first time his sensors picked up a neutral fighter, which until now had been canceled by the power reading of the station. The pilot of the fighter had to be the cause of the station's destruction. Besides the Valiant, he was the only survivor of the disaster.

The nova had a huge lead and was in a hurry. The fighter was on an escape vector that led away from both hyperspace navigational beacons and into an empty part of space. At best speed he would reach a safe jumping point in less than a minute with no way of tracking his movements there after.

"He's already a step ahead of us, Sadler." Barger angrily spouted. "Dump all power to the engines and get me to him."

Working much faster than a humanoid, the companion awakened the fighter from its powered down state and forced it to maximum speed ten seconds less than specs called for. The stress on the hull and the engines was evident in the moan that echoed throughout the cockpit. If any more power could be diverted to the engines, they would break clean of the fighter and race off on their own.

"Two to lead."

"I've got him, two," Captain Vallejo said. "You're the closest. Bring him down."

"Copy that, lead. He's mine."

How dare he, Barger thought to himself. What gave this outlaw the right to destroy an imperial station and three destroyers along with it? He'd vaporize the pilot in one pass and scatter his fragments throughout the galaxy.

Barger was gaining, but not as fast as he'd have liked. At the closer range the bi-wing's sensors were able to identify the fleeing fighter as a nova. The novas were not nearly as fast as his, but were shielded. The rebel pilot must have dumped power from his shields to the engines, giving him a bit more thrust. Barger still had the edge though, both in speed and in a long-range sensor cloak. The nova would not detect the bi-wing until he was within five clicks.

"Bring up power to the weapons. Link fire to one and two. Keep three and four drained to the engines."

Sadler barked out and opened a channel to the fighter. "Thanks, Sadler." Give him a chance to surrender. "Unidentified rebel fighter. This is Lieutenant Wes Barger with the Alcon Imperial fighter core, Devil squadron. You are ordered to power down or be destroyed."

No response and less than four clicks out.

"Rebel pilot. You are under suspicion for the destruction of an imperial way station and three destroyers. Power down or be destroyed."

Still no response.

Barger sighed. "You leave me no choice."

Proximity alarms sounded, shocking him from firing a warning shot. The tactical display splashed three red dots within two clicks of his position and closing fast to port. The novas came from nowhere. They could not have been powered down then suddenly powered up the way a bi-wing could, and no fighter with jump capabilities could have pinpointed an intercept like that. No, this had to be planned.

In anger Barger slapped off two linked shots after the fleeing fighter. The first dual laser blast missed far to the right. The second skipped off the port wing. With shields drained to the engines, the wing sheared away a meter inside the port laser cannon. The severed wing and body spun away from each other.

Six retaliatory blasts from the new targets struck the bi-wing's port wing and shattered the central panel. The entire wing broke apart at the pylon and sped off in all directions. Barger remained in control of the fighter, though he now had to deal with a power runoff from the port engine. The fighter wanted desperately to turn to port or give up all together.

A second wave of fire converged on his port engine, piercing the exhaust port and shattering the pylon. The entire strut split apart. Streaked with blast marks and en-

Chapter Five

cased in sparks of lightning, the engine fell away a few meters before exploding. If the engine had still been attached he would have joined the doomed engine.

The lead of the three attackers added an insult by firing a perfectly aimed shot in the small gap between the command pod and starboard engine. The thin beam sliced the pylon in half, stripping the engine away intact. The constant drag to port stopped immediately as did all forward momentum. Control thrusters embedded around the command pod saw to that. In an emergency the thrusters fired to slow movement that could cause a fatal collision.

The final insult came as the same channel Barger had used to order the surrender of the fleeing fighter sparked with the voice of the lead attacker. "Lieutenant Barger, this is Ghost two. Power down weapons and standby to be boarded."

For a moment Barger wanted to rotate the pod and unleash the last of his stored energy out at the lead Nova. Defiance was in his nature and the idea of being captured by rebels was less than desirable. The official report left behind would be less than glorious, and his once good name would be surrounded by rumor and shame. How could he have allowed this to happen?

The moment of anger passed as quickly as it came. He was still alive and that was all that counted. If he were at all as lucky as the destroyer of the station was, maybe the rest of Devil squadron would catch up and remove these three rebel attackers from existence.

"Powering down, Ghost two." He sank into his seat. "I'm all yours."

"Pull back, three!" Vallejo ordered.

Kirkland gritted his teeth. He could visibly see the disabled bi-wing surrounded by three novas and a transport. The novas had their weapons charged to full and missiles on a soft lock of his fighter. In another click, they would have a firm lock on him and he would be dead. That did not matter to him. All he saw was a helpless friend falling into the hands of the alliance.

"Pull back, three. You'll die long before you reach him."

"Back me up, lead. We've got to get him back."

"Six to three. You haven't a chance. I can read the missile lock from here."

Two members of the transport crew were now floating above the command pod of the bi-wing, escorting Barger into the forward hatch of the boxy craft. Another retrieved what appeared to be his friend's companion. Once inside, the hatch closed and the six engines flared up. Its three nova escorts stayed by its side as all three raced away from Kirkland. They disappeared in the distance.

Kirkland continued on his course. He passed by the disabled bi-wing at a blinding speed. He could still picture the transport in his mind, though it was gone. His companion chirped repeatedly, confirming the ship's jump out of the system.

Not you, Wes. You were the last one to go.

Chapter Six

Admiral Galt Fallon could hardly believe the damage caused by one man as he looked out from the bridge of the Vengeance. Granted, he had read Jared Guile's file cover to cover, but even such a skilled mercenary could not have pulled off such a feat. The way station had been the target of several attacks from pirate ships. Since the decision six months ago to have an Alcon ship in orbit at all times though, the attempts to raid the station of various types of cargo had decreased dramatically.

Yet the evidence was right in front of him. Half of the damaged portions of the station had already burned up in the atmosphere and crashed down on the surface. The rest had fallen into a low, decaying orbit. The breakup of the last destroyer worsened with every orbit, sending more and more Imperial technology to a fiery death. It was estimated that in another two or three days the last of the wreckage would fall to the planet.

The impact would be far reaching. Freighters and transports that required a stopover before leaving or entering the Badlands would have to add three additional days to their flights in order to divert to the nearest operable station. The incurring costs and increased risk of pirate raids in that time would place considerable strain on the shipping lanes and require that more of the Badlands task force be placed on patrol of the diversion paths.

The true plan of the Alliance had unfolded violently. Though this act could never be placed within the means of the rebels, Fallon knew this was the case. The official report from the Galactic would blame pirates for the destruction of the station. It was logical enough to assume so. Pirates would benefit most with the diversion of freighters, but only the Alliance benefited from the shrinking Imperial task force in this region of space.

Still, above all else the wiry Arlast male could not fathom what kind of person could have breached the station's tight internal and military security. The single fold of skin that wrapped around from one ear to the other behind his head twitched in disgust. He reached a webbed hand up to caress the active fold before looking away from the primary viewing screen. He could not bear to look upon the scattered wreckage with his pale blue eyes any longer.

The large deck Fallon stood on stretched six meters to the back of the bridge. A dual set of stairs branched off around opposite sides of the bridge command deck to the control deck below. The command deck featured two split rows of sit-down command consoles for officers of each division. Cluttered below were the sub-commanders who relayed orders and controls to the rest of the massive battle cruiser.

Fallon returned to one of three command chairs in the center of the command deck. The center chair with elaborate control consoles was reserved for visiting dignitaries and admirals like himself. The chair to the left of the center chair was the captain's and had a freestanding command console to its left. The first officer's chair on the other side mirrored that of the captain's chair.

The Admiral was not settled into his chair for more than a minute before the captain approached him with a data pad. Captain Forn S'Lendo was a good third of a meter shorter than the Admiral. His face scrunched together along his snub-nose and wide mouth. He resembled a boar in many aspects, but his body was built like that of a shorter human.

S'Lendo's voice grumbled and snorted, but was audible enough to avoid distraction. He had spent his entire schooling in standard academies, learning ways to pronounce his words clearly. A typical Kand was hard to understand without translators and seldom received military positions outside of basic engineers and gunners. S'Lendo had always considered himself fortunate, striving beyond his kind and becoming an officer.

"The initial report has come in from the Valiant, sir."

Fallon moaned then he took the data pad from his first officer. Without looking over the information, he dropped the data pad into a slot on his control console and let the information bleed into his files to be reviewed. "Just give me a recap, Captain," he said in his deep, rumbling voice. "I will review the entire report later."

"Visual recorded a Riordan Nova fleeing the area just before the power core detonated. Navigational data from a jump probe on the nova's escape vector confirmed this."

Then it was Guile.

"There is more, sir. One of our fighters from Devil squadron was able to catch the nova, but was ambushed by three more fighters. As a result we lost the pilot."

"Was there an attempt to rescue him?"

The captain shook his head. "None, sir. The novas that ambushed him had soft missile locks on the remaining devils. They were unable to approach without fear of being destroyed or captured themselves."

"Understood. Have all security codes within Devil squadron altered and contact Varlet squadron for an immediate replacement. Was the Valiant able to download any data from our computer core on the station before it went?"

"None, sir. They stayed until the last possible moment, but were unable to pick up any escapees or cargo. Apparently the intruder alarm systems were not sounding

Chapter Six

until after a firefight broke out between the intruder and station guards. Shortly after, a majority of the outer ring systems were disabled when an explosion tore open a bulkhead that housed power conduits. Our troops on the station didn't even know there was a problem until the first power regulator blew. By then it was only a matter of seconds before the core went critical."

An entire garrison, he thought to himself. Three destroyers and an entire garrison. Such devastation of manpower and resources was typical during times of battle, but not like this. One man had murdered over a thousand military personnel and hundreds of civilian personnel. Such an act automatically placed a death mark on the head of Guile with a hundred thousand credit bounty for the person or persons who would return the body for public display.

"Their analysis."

"Inadequate security measures in the central ring and a failure by station security to alert our people." S'Lendo relaxed onto one hip. "In my personal opinion the security measures implemented on these stations are more than adequate to handle single intruders. I would place total blame on a lack of communication between station guards and our troops. If we would have been notified about the intruder, he never would have made it to the cargo bay."

Fallon grinned. "You may relax, captain. I feel the same as you do. The idea that private contractors be allowed to supply security around military facilities is preposterous. Senator Ashland should never have agreed with this ridiculous proposal. It is not of our concern though. We will not have to worry about the political situation much longer."

"Have you heard something you aren't telling me?"

A speaker on his control panel buzzed to life and a deep males voice filtered through. "Con, Ops. The Valiant has entered the system."

"Nothing you need to know at the moment." Fallon reached to a series of buttons under the speaker and pressed the center one. "Comm, Con. Relay our departure to the Valiant."

"I already have Captain Merrill waiting for you, sir."

Without acknowledgment he stood and walked aft off the bridge. Three steps beyond the double doors he took a sharp right and passed through his personal chamber doors. Anticipating this, the chief communications officer had relayed Captain Merrill's image into the chamber. The Captain was waiting patiently with his hands folded behind his back and a nervous twitch in his right leg.

The communication from Merrill was a surprise. After such an obvious failure in all areas, Fallon had expected the ambitious man to wait for his transmission before facing an almost fatal confrontation with the admiral. His strength in being able to face his mistakes with as little visible fear was admirable and deserved some credit. Just how much was entirely at Fallon's discretion.

"Sir, I would like to explain what..."

Fallon raised his hand and stopped the worried captain. "Your apologies are not needed nor are they wanted. Though I would like to hold you responsible for the loss of a station and three ships you could not have foreseen such a turn of events. The mere fact that you were able to pull away and escape before the core of the station erupted tells me that you remained on guard even through the slow period before the rebels were predicted to attack."

"Thank you, sir."

The glare in Fallon's eyes narrowed and seemed to burn into the holograph of Merrill and right into his heart. "What does displease me with your actions is your inability to foresee the resourcefulness of the alliance. Though we do not openly employ the use of mercenaries and bounty hunters to handle small annoyances it is not out of the question. It is also not out of the question to say that we would not be the only power in the galaxy to use such a disreputable trade. Despite their lack of manners and form they do get the job done as you have seen for yourself."

"I think it's time that you take a closer look at just who you are dealing with. The Sutherlin Alliance is more than just a band of unhappy citizens of the empire. It is also a gathering of warriors from around the galaxy. A growing band, and they are not all fighters at heart. Some have been trained by the same academies that you and I moved through."

Fallon reached out of view of the projected captain and called up the file on the mercenary. "Take this Jared Guile for example. He graduated near the top of his class and excelled in both the art of espionage and hand-to-hand combat. He also has recorded nearly a thousand hours of combat piloting duty and was decorated twice by high-ranking captains. This is the type of person you should be considering as your enemy."

"If the alliance is not full of high caliber recruits they soon will be. With men like Jared Guile in their service they will be able to train their pilots and soldiers in not only imperial tactics but also mercenary tactics. This will give them both organization and improvisational skills. They will strike where you least expect it and with force and cunning."

"Consider yourself lucky, captain. If you had been just that much slower in your instincts you would be among the wreckage floating in orbit around Gresham."

Merrill's humble tone moaned above the hiss of the transmission. "Understood, sir."

"In the meantime you will be requiring reserve units to replace those that you have lost. I will be giving you two additional destroyers as well as a carrier as soon as I can get one from fleet command. The added fighter units should be more than adequate to deal with any resistance you may encounter. I suggest that you allow Captain Vallejo the freedom to conduct his strikes in the manner he sees fit. You can use your new units to protect your group."

"I will take your suggestion to heart, Admiral." Relief began to filter back into his voice. "Might I ask where you will be sending me?"

"The Horde system. You will begin your search for the resistance there. If I have understood Mister Guile's file correctly, he would have breached station security

Chapter Six

from the Horde freighter that you were to track. Whether he was hired there or somewhere else, Horde is the most logical location to begin the search."

"Do you have an idea of who may have hired him?"

"It matters not who I think employed this ex-officer. My only need is for you to trace the finances back to its source and cut the alliances' funds from where it flows. You will use whatever means to punish the royalty that feels it necessary to defy us."

Captain Merrill bowed respectfully before his three dimensional image wavered away. Fallon moaned, allowing his annoyance to echo through his chamber. Merrill was not a stupid man, but he was impetuous and non-observant at times. If it had not been for their long standing acquaintance he would have chose someone else to head up one of his three battle groups. As it was he was familiar with Merrill and felt he could trust the captain to follow his orders to the best of his abilities.

Behind the Admiral, Captain S'Lendo cleared his throat to gain his attention.

"You wonder if he can track down who is funding the alliance."

"I am, sir."

Fallon turned on his left heel. "If he succeeds or fails is irrelevant. With the reputation that proceeds him, he will undoubtedly apply pressure to everyone he comes across. Word will spread that he is punishing anyone and everyone affiliated with these rebels and those who are helping them. The fear factor alone will slow down the credit flow."

"I hope I am not being out of line when I say that I doubt it will have the effect you say it will."

"You are far from being out of line, but Captain Merrill will have an ally behind him." Fallon turned back around to an image of his battle cruiser hovering over a barren world. "One that should provide an effective edge to his fist. Should he turn up even the slightest clue I plan to be there to see our resolve through."

He turned back gleaming with self-induced pride. "I have come too far in the past year to see my efforts thwarted by this incident. Given the command of this task force was no small accomplishment and I intend to make this just another stepping stone and not the end of my career. I want out of the Badlands as soon as a window of opportunity presents itself. A second tour here is more than enough to suit my tastes."

"The fleet admiral might have something to say about that," S'Lendo warned.

"So what if he does?" Fallon folded his hands behind his back and stiffened. "He's not the only command admiral in this fleet."

Not for long if Fallon had anything to say about it.

Sitting amongst freighter crews, local riffraff, and other dregs of the galaxy, Guile wondered how many of them were mercenaries like himself, or even competitors for that matter. All but one of the deals he had made involved seedy bars like this one. Dark corners were abundant in the dank, smoky surroundings. In any given corner there could be a pirate ready to pounce on an opportunity and often times there were.

Several of the notches in the handle of his standard snub-rifle were pirates who had tried to take his bounties.

The bar had a low ceiling, as many did. It was barely high enough to compliment the taller species like the Horde. In size it was rather spacious with a central bar and three bartenders. Hanging on racks around the central bar were ales from around the galaxy. Vintage years were never younger then twenty years, except for Cadera Prime rum that was best if less than a month old. Any date after that and the substance caused serious illness.

Guile preferred the Cadera rum and had adapted his tastes to handle the stiff drink. One shot was enough to down the normal man. After years of drinking the foul smelling fluid, he had strengthened his system and could take a full glass before feeling the effects. Nevertheless, few other drinks could affect him the way they were supposed to, which aided in many victorious drinking contests. The only contest he ever lost was to a three hundred year old Cadera.

An elderly human with a thick head of gray hair moved through the main doors and stopped. Guile recognized the man as his contact. He was about to raise his hand to signal the man when two more people stepped up behind him. Each wore flight jumpsuits all in silver with black stripes running from the shoulders, crossing at the waist, and running down the sides of each leg. The pilots stood out among the crews who were dressed in rags and tattered flight suits.

Guile's eyes picked up on the heavy pistols the pilots wore at their sides. The jumpsuits alluded to private pilots, but the pistols were standard military issue. Even the helmets they wore, despite the similar color markings to the jumpsuits were standard military equipment. He found himself reaching for his snub-rifle. He had been betrayed on contracts in the past so he took no chances. If this was indeed one of those rare occasions, he would be ready.

The elderly man found Guile in the thin haze and guided his escorts through the crowd. Without asking or offering any introductions he took a seat opposite the mercenary. Casually he removed a thick, brown folder from his ruffled jacket and dropped it onto the table. Honor was a trait known throughout the underworld as an asset, so there would be no counting of the credits. Guile simply picked up the envelope and slipped it into his dark, black flight jacket.

"It's not all there," the elderly man said in a gravely voice. "The rest will be given to you after I watch your playback."

Guile grinned and leaned back. The rusty squeak of the old chair legs against the rough metal floor barely masked his amused snicker. "I would have appreciated you telling me this before now. You're mocking my honor. You gave me a task that no other would dare to attempt and promised a fee worthy of the undertaking. I expected my fee to be met with promptness, not with additional promises."

The old man held out his hand, palm up. "The data tape if you please."

Guile rolled his eyes as he reached into an outer pocket. He pulled out the thin disk and dropped it into his hand. "It wasn't part of the deal," he rolled his eyes. "But since you sounded so sincere on the transmission," he added with a sneer.

Chapter Six

"Much appreciated."

As the old man handed the disk to one of the pilots, Guile leaned forward. "I'll tell you right now that the Valiant was gone before the station blew."

Both pilots shot a glance to each other, but the old man simply chuckled calmly to himself.

Guile dropped his hand to the butt of his weapon. "Can you tell me why I went to all that trouble to destroy a Warship? You are aware that this will prompt an investigation by the Alcon and they will find out that it was me. I have to tell you, sir, that the idea of having Star Cruisers chasing me does not make me all too happy. If you would be so kind as to give me an explanation as to why you put me into such an unpleasant situation I would be grateful. I'd hate to waste a full charge on you and your friends here."

"You would do yourself justice not to threaten the Patron," the pilot to the right said behind an altered voice.

The Patron looked back to the pilot. "I have told you not to interfere." He smiled then turned back to his hire. He removed a second envelope and dropped it on the table. "You are a resourceful man. The destruction of one of the Alcon staging stations shows that." He let the comment draw a look of horror on Guile's face. "You are also an observant man if you identified the Valiant on what could not have been more than a split second of visual. Because of this you should be fully aware of what is going on in the Alcon Empire."

Guile shook off the thought of the trouble he was in for destroying a staging station. It was bad enough that he destroyed it at all. This simply complicated matters further. "I'm sorry mister Patron, but I leave Imperial matters to the Alcon. I dropped out of the scene years ago."

"Devil squadron did not follow your lead, Mister Guile."

How the hell did you know I was with Devil. Guile leaned back. The position didn't seem as comfortable this time. "You shouldn't speak of the dead. It's bad luck."

"Devil isn't dead, Guile," The pilot to the left said. "You found out firsthand that they are still in full operation."

The chair suddenly seemed even less comfortable. No one except his closest associates had spoken his name since his days with Devil squadron, and those that did seldom lived much longer. His confusion about his current situation kept him from drawing his weapon and burning down all three of them. He began to debate his whole philosophy about talking to his closest friends. Who else would have betrayed his name?

"My affiliation with Devil ended the day Lest joined the team."

"There never was a Lest on the squad," the pilot answered. "Lest is my father."

Guile's heart skipped a beat. He had not expected a correct response to his comment. "Bea?" He asked with childish curiosity.

61

The pilot removed her helmet, allowing a long braid of auburn hair to drop down over the shoulder. Crystal blue eyes, typical among Terelians, warmed his heart with a distance sense of belonging. The addition of her soft, flowing voice added to the once lost feeling. "Lieutenant Bea to you, scum wad, and you should never have left us."

The comment was harsh, but the pet name was his. No other in the galaxy knew him by that name and no other could say it and receive a bright smile in return. "What happened to Civil defense?"

Bea opened her mouth to respond before catching a glance from the Patron. "It didn't work out," she mumbled.

The Patron grabbed his attention by dropping his hands to the table with a slap. "You are a skilled hire, Mister Guile, and one that I would like to keep in my employment."

Guile picked up the envelope and slipped it into his jacket with the other one. "Sorry, but this fee is intended to keep me out of the game for awhile. No offense to you and whatever organization you run. I'm tired, hungry, and out of supplies. I've been shot at, had the crap beat outta me, and I have a severe case of elastimat burn to my lungs. If you don't mind I'd like to go home and pass out for a few days."

The Patron bowed slightly. "If you wish, Mister Guile. We will be in contact again."

"If you say so." Guile stood and backed away from the table. He made sure to keep the three to one side at all times. He had the nagging feeling to trust them after seeing Bea, but in his line of work he learned to trust no one; especially anyone who withheld funds for any reason. Those people always wanted more than they paid to get, and those were the people to avoid. Even though he wanted desperately to talk with Bea he could do no more than give her a glance back before walking out the doors.

The cold air and the night sky were a comfort to his dark life. He had more to think about now than he had before. The pilot that had actually caught up to him in the Gresham system was from Devil Squadron. He knew that for sure now and that meant that the Alcon's elite was still out there and would be after him once more.

The day he received his commission and target he had planned for a long and relaxing vacation. Completion of the station's destruction occupied his every thought, hoping that it would put an end to his need for personal vengeance against himself. He had the credits and several vacation spots in mind. He had everything planned out.

Then Guile completed his mission. He sighed in disbelief. This was supposed to be a great day.

The Patron watched Guile leave with a subtle grin on his face. Once the mercenary was gone he turned around and faced Bea. "Please return to the docking bay and wait for us."

Chapter Six

Bea looked to her counterpart who nodded. Frustrated that she would not be apart of the conversation she slipped on her helmet and walked away.

Captain Haggin Stead removed his helmet from his worn but youthful face and dropped it on the table. "She will not be a problem, Patron," he said.

"Your concern about her well-being is noted and unneeded. Bea has shown me no sign of discontent to this point. Mister Guile on the other hand could prove more than I can handle. His tenacity was formidable when he was with the Alcon Navy, and it has grown since his resignation. If he refuses to assist us, then he may have to be dealt with."

"That can be a cause for concern, sir. That task has been tried before on several occasions. Each time the outcome was discovered in the next days obituaries." Stead took a seat next to the elderly man. "No, sir, I believe he can be a valuable asset. If I had thought differently I would never have hired him."

"And you believe you can control him?"

"Quite frankly, Guile and I parted on not so enthusiastic terms. We have had a rivalry dating back to the academy. One that eventually forced him to retire and caused Devil squadron to publicly disband."

"Which is why you chose not to surprise him with your presence."

"The mere sight of me might have provoked my untimely death. No, Patron, I will let him be charmed back by the others before I make my presence known. After that I will make it my mission in life to keep him within sight. As I said before you ever decided to allow me to hire him. He is my responsibility and mine alone."

Chapter Seven

Barger awoke in an unfamiliar place with a headache beyond belief. His first thought was to the short battle that had downed his fighter. That led to the reminder that he was now in the custody of the Sutherlin Alliance. An embarrassment for any officer and practically an assurance that his career with Devil squadron was over.

The last thing he remembered was being dragged from his fighter and pulled aboard a transport. As soon as he was secure and the craft began to move off he found himself with an injection in his arm and his field of vision spinning. Heavy doses of drugs had knocked him out in seconds and had kept him out for as long as it took him to get here. Wherever here was.

A nurse, Barger assumed, walked into the spacious infirmary carrying a tray. The items of the tray were kept higher than his view. When he squirmed to look at the tray he found that both his wrists and ankles were tightly strapped to his bed. The straps were securely fastened underneath the bed, but were not uncomfortable. A thin layer of material had been ringed underneath the straps to keep his skin from being cut.

"You're finally up," the soft voiced nurse said.

Her drab, gray uniform looked as if it had come from a school rather than a hospital. Barger rolled his eyes. With his luck he was being attended to by a dropout and would die from a bad prognosis.

The nurse sat down on the end of the bed, giving him his first glance at the plate of food on the tray. "I'm afraid our rescue teams don't have the appropriate training yet. I'm just glad they didn't kill you with the dose they used."

Barger looked straight up and noticed his reflection in a body length mirror on the ceiling. His physical form looked fine under the light white gown that he wore. His face on the other hand was heavy under the eyes and pale. He could have been abandoned for weeks without food or water to look so bad.

The nurse looked up at the mirror and grimaced. "An unfortunate side affect of the drugs." She looked down at him. "You've been out for a week."

A what? Barger looked to the nurse in disbelief. The fight was just a day ago. He couldn't have been unconscious for more than twelve hours. "Where am I?"

"You're under my care and that's all you need to know right now. Someone will come for you the moment I say you're fit to answer questions." She set the tray down on his chest and released his right hand. "Rest easy, Lieutenant. We might be a strong little group, but we aren't that organized yet."

Barger searched his mind for a snappy Imperial retort, but could not come up with one. "Thank you," he said in reference to the food.

"Don't thank me yet, Lieutenant." Her voice trailed off out the door. "You've got a long way to go from here."

The food looked appetizing enough. Whether he trusted eating from an enemy's plate was another matter. Still, the hunger he felt was nagging him. So much so that he did not care if it was laced. He had already spent a week unconscious from a drug overdose and was in the hands of a lovely woman. How bad could the food be with such a wide range of treatment in such a short time span?

Barger decided that he needed two hands to enjoy food that appeared to be fresh and not processed. After months of recycled rations he wanted to enjoy a fresh meal for once. He carefully tensed his left arm, allowing the blood to build up around his biceps. He waited in that position, then released to flow of fluid and building adrenalin and pulled back, hard. The rapid expansion of his arm and forceful jerk snapped the strap.

He smiled as he settled in to enjoy his meal.

"What do you think?"

Captain Stead and Flight officer Shadle stood above Lieutenant Barger's bed, observing him through the two-way mirror mounted to the ceiling. Shadle had periodically stopped by to check on the Alcon pilot. This was Stead's first visit to the captured Devil. Neither seemed surprised at how easily he snapped the restraint, both having been affiliated with naval training and the diversity of its pilots.

"He's courteous, but has pent up frustrations. His file shows an arrogant yet highly resourceful pilot. His entire career has been spent in a hard climb to power. We might have a hard time convincing him to join us."

"I've spent some time watching him and following his career, sir, and I can respectfully say that he shares many of your ideals. From day one out of the academy he has sought out a position in Devil. You and I both know that Devil squadron is the most honorable if not the most skilled group of pilots in the Empire."

Stead grinned. "I don't know if I like that."

"He's a first rate pilot. I believe he will make the transition to the novas with ease."

"I have no doubt about that, Narra. My concern is with his past mission ratings. They may have been high, but some of them were against civilian targets."

Shadle grimaced. This wasn't the battle she wanted to fight. She thought that with the lack of experience the Alliance had that a pilot with Barger's skills would be welcomed with open arms. Even a little hesitation should have been quelled by now.

Chapter Seven

"Only two, sir," she finally said in his defense. "The first was on a hostile world and the attack site had been designated as unfriendly with severe prejudice."

"And the second was not," Stead finished for her. "He was directly in charge of the assault on the abandoned Alcon base that led to a hundred ninety civilian deaths."

"Might I remind you that we staged the area for their attack and the battle group commander was Merrill. We both know the kinds of assaults he conducts on a regular basis." Her voice had raised a pitch, further hurting her position. The desperation she had tried to hide shown clearly through with every word she spoke.

Stead stepped away from the mirror, shaking his head. "I don't know. We'd be taking an awful risk bringing in a Devil pilot like this."

Shadle kept right on his heels, defending Barger to the last. "You were a Devil once. I've read your files. You were shot down in a similar fashion."

"But I had been in contact with the Patron several times before the incident. I had already made up my mind to defect when I felt the appropriate time had come." He stopped before leaving the observation room and turned to face her. "This Lieutenant of yours is a different story. He has served the Empire diligently and has achieved his place in the squadron in record time. I don't believe a man with his background and honor will turn his back on Emperor Alcon so easily."

"But we staged the capture for this very reason. Why would you have gone to so much trouble if you did not expect to retain his services?"

"Barger wasn't the target. We were trying to nab someone else."

"But you kept him anyway. If he was the threat you say he is, then he should be in the detention block infirmary."

Stead stopped. Shadle had grasped at the right straw. "Give him a chance. Patron gave you one."

Stead's eyes narrowed, but there was no rebuttal for a comment like that. "Very well. As soon as the doctor clears him I want you to speak with him. If he can convince me that he's sympathetic to the alliance, I'll meet him on a one-to-one basis. Mind you though. I will be watching so no prompting. I want him on his merits and not yours."

Shadle let him leave before returning to the mirror. She knelt down by the glass and stared down at the captive and watched him eat. The only other time she had gotten close enough to see him was when she enrolled in the academy and he was on his way out. This was the closest she had ever come to her idol, and she was not going to let him get away.

Chapter Eight

It may have been a week and twenty lava baths after he returned home, but it did not make this one feel any more ordinary than the last. Guile sank into the bubbling water, heated by a mildly active volcano and let out a pleased growl. The nearest neighbors, some hundred kilometers away, called him crazy for building so close to an active lava chamber. What they lacked in personal knowledge was his gain. As payment for a job, an engineer had surveyed the volcano and determined the nearest point he could build, then designed a pair of flow chambers around his house. Guile had bought up all the land on one side of the mountain and lived in total seclusion from the rest of the citizens of Telestia.

From Guile's outdoor lava pool he could see Telestia's sister world, Terelia. The planet appeared no bigger than the moon that orbited his home world as it revolved around the sun at the same rate as Telestia. Some nights he would lay back, letting only his head rest above water, and wonder what it must have been like for Bea to have grown up there. Though they were only a few million kilometers apart, the two worlds were distinctly different.

Terelia was the older of the two societies by more then six thousand years. When their technology had advanced to space travel, colonists migrated to Telestia and began a new society: one that adapted well to the lush environment and healthier atmosphere. Choosing to separate themselves from their planet of origin, the new natives of the world added second names and altered their courses of development towards research as opposed to exploring. In the end Telestia had become the more technologically advanced of the two societies while the Terelians had spread themselves out among the thousands of inhabitable worlds in the galaxy.

Then came the formation of the Alcon Empire. Both worlds fell under the watchful eye of a single governor of the Empire and young men and women were heavily solicited into military service. Both worlds had become united for one cause: the unification of the galaxy. At first the idea was sound, but some had doubts. Those worlds were now unwilling members of the Empire and were treated as such.

Guile, as he smiled in his calm state, reflected on how gullible he once had been. He believed the propaganda from the day he could read and spent his entire young life preparing for the day he could become an Imperial Naval officer. The Alcon had been a strong influence for over fifty years to that point, longer than even his father could remember. It was the right thing to do.

Sure it was. Guile thought sarcastically to himself. He had seen firsthand just how the Realm was. As a member of Devil squadron, he was first in line whenever the Empire found itself in combat. The battles were glorious and so were the rewards, but sometimes activities slowed. Sometimes Devil was needed to put down any world determined to resist Alcon takeover. Sometimes those worlds were defenseless. It was then that he realized the true nature of the Realm. On one no-name world on the edge of the galaxy, where with a rifle in one hand and a flamer in the other, he was ordered to burn down innocent children and destroy simple hut villages.

Devil became a cursed word that day. That day and any other. From there he turned his anger at such an act towards anyone he was paid to steal from or kill. They became the victims of a misdirected rage. If he could not exact revenge on his former employer then his targets would feel his wrath. His only hope would be to rid himself of the guilt, but the reminder would always be there. Every time he saw himself the deep scars across the lower half of his face and along his neck were still there. And so his anger led to acts of piracy.

Guile allowed himself a smooth grin. This time though, the act may have cost him his freedom to move about as he wanted. He had been hired to destroy an Alcon staging station and he did so successfully. He only wished that the war-ship that was in orbit had been docked and could not get away: The very same ship that had led his attack on that no-name defenseless world so many light years away.

A small comlink resting on the side of the pool chirped. The distortion in the link left much to be desired. He could not recognize the person on the other end behind the haze of static. "Are you home, Guile?"

"Go away!" He shouted into the night air. The person to whom he owed a kick in the butt had no way of hearing him. His outburst was meant mainly for his own gratification. Guile simply gave in after another call for his attention. He wadded to the edge of the pool and activated the comlink. "Yes."

"It's Bea. Can I come in?"

Guile's eyes perked open and he released the front door lock by depressing a switch next to the comlink. His impulse may have cost him though as he felt the warm water brush over his entire body. Bashful at his current state and of meeting an old friend, he called out towards his home. "Can you grab a towel before you come out?!"

Bea, dressed in a light, informal jumpsuit walked through the back door and smiled. "And miss the best view in the galaxy? Are you kidding? I want to know if the scum wad I used to know is as bashful as he used to be."

Chapter Eight

Guile dismissed the playful compliment and pressed himself against the side of the pool. He scanned around the edges for the towel he had brought out with him. "I shouldn't have to say it, but you have impeccable timing, Bea."

"Why? What were you doing besides exposing yourself to my home world?"

"Oh nothing. Just contemplating my past. Every once in a while I like to lie back, give your home a little flash and wonder how things would have turned out if I had never joined the academy. " Guile clicked off the comlink and looked up towards her home world. "I can't tell you how relaxing it is to have a heart filled with doubt and remorse."

"I'm sure you could if you tried."

"Please tell me you're here for a better reason than to convince me to take Patron's job. If you are, then you're wasting your breath. There aren't enough credits in the galaxy to convince me to supply a resistance against the Empire."

Bea knelt down close to the edge of the pool. "That's one of the reasons. The other one is to ask you how you've been. I've missed you." She motioned towards the stars. "We've missed you."

"The only thing you guys have missed is a good simulated butt kicking. Anything beyond that was superficial at best."

"Devil was your life and we were your family," she growled at him defensively. "You shouldn't have left us over such a trivial incident."

"Trivial?" Guile responded with shock. He could not believe anyone would find the slaughter of millions of tribal people trivial. "Did you ever read my report on the incident?"

"I didn't have to. I was there."

"You didn't answer my question. Did you read the report?"

"I read the entire report and could find no reason for your resignation."

"That's why I left," he said as he stabbed a finger towards her. "It seemed at the time that I was the only person who had some humanity in the fleet. I guess now I was correct in having such a preposterous thought."

Bea dropped to the ground. "It's in the past." She slipped off her brand new boots and rolled up the legs of her loose jumpsuit. "A lot has changed. You'd be proud of our accomplishments since we left."

Why do you keep saying we? Guile momentarily looked away as she dropped her legs into the warm water. "Seeing as how your employer had me destroy a staging station I can assume you've begun to strike heavier targets." She nodded a yes. "Well that alone is an accomplishment. Anything beyond that is petty at this point."

"I would hardly call the defense of innocent worlds petty."

"That's all the alliance is, Bea, a defensive effort. The Alcon Navy has had the bulk of your forces on the run since day one. I'd be surprised if you had more than one light cruiser in any given place at one time."

Bea dropped her head and stared at the gentle waves of the water. "I'll concede that much, Jared, but there's more to it than just that. We've acquired two type one destroyers and a clipper from the old Salan Realm and have initiated hit and run attacks on some of the Empire's more distant bases."

"But you don't have the manpower to take control of the stations, nor do you have the firepower to defend them. Those old destroyers couldn't even hold their own against a frigate, let alone an entire task force. Face it, Bea. The alliance will be crushed the first time you encounter a sizeable force. Especially if your equipment is all over twenty years old."

Bea shot a cold stare at him. "Not all of it is old. Only the larger ships. Our ground weapons and fighters are all top of the line. Fresh from the Riordan factories."

Guile raised an eyebrow, impressed with her revelation. "So those three fighters that saved my butt at Gresham were yours."

"One was mine and the other two used to be acquaintances of yours. Unfortunately our pilots haven't had the training they need. The kill ratio has been two to one in the empire's favor."

Two to one was not nearly as high as he thought it would be. With untrained pilots flying advanced crafts he would have bet that the kill ratio would be at least five to one in the Empire's favor.

Guile grinned sinisterly. "You know, you're just confirming my point by telling me this. You also aren't helping your chances of getting me to join you."

"Why would I want you to join the Alliance?" Bea asked.

Good girl. Play it cool. "You tell me. Why would you need my help?" He rolled around, forgetting his lack of covering, and leaned against the edge of the pool. "The Alliance is low on funds, has heavy, outdated equipment, and a serious personnel deficiency to fill the equipment it does have. The Alcon Empire on the other hand has a vast supply of personnel and equipment coming from all over the galaxy and is featuring a star fighter that can fly rings around your latest piece of military hardware." He spun around and gave her his best boyish look. "And who better to bend the odds by poking holes in the Alcon hull but a skilled mercenary who has ways of breaking into even the tightest security?"

Bea huffed. "You flatter yourself, but unfortunately it's true. There's more to our request than just your hypothesis."

Guile dropped his elbows onto the poolside and rested his chin in his palms. "Oh? Spill the beans."

"My squadron and a few of the larger ship crews have the only experience among the Alliance. Families, who realize the Empire is more than it appears, have found out only too late for them to do anything. So they send us their young. They're just kids, Jared, and they're getting slaughtered up there. The Bi-wing may be a great fighter, but the Nova should be enough to at least match them in combat."

Guile's tone dropped a notch, losing its sarcastic edge. "But it's the inefficiency of the pilot that makes the difference."

"A fatal difference."

Chapter Eight

"I know I'm going to regret asking this, but what is the average age of your pilots?"

"The pilots are all around seventeen or eighteen standard years. That's averaging their respective aging to ours." Bea let him shake his head in disbelief before dumping the next load on him. "The transport and freighter crews are even younger. Many of them have a very limited education and are forced to take a crash course in their assigned fields. We lost one transport during a training run because a fourteen year old lost his cool when a regulator blew and he froze up. Since then we have been screening out kids who have not already had a harsh upbringing. The rest are placed into extended training and are stationed on three mobile bases in the outer systems."

Guile rubbed the sweat forming on his brow. He was leaning far enough away from the water that it had not formed from heat. The pressure was building within him. Bea was reading him like a book and he could see it in her face. Every time he flinched the slightest bit she pushed the issue. She would have made one hell of a politician. Her role had been clear since birth though. That very same intuition had saved her life and the lives in her squadron on many occasions.

You and I are more alike than you would ever admit. He smiled while cupping his face. "You aren't making this easy on me."

"I'm not here to ask you to come back. I'm here to pressure you into it. If this had been a social call, I would have come in a low cut dress and no underwear. No, Jared, I came because the rest of us were too afraid that you would turn your back on them again. I, on the other hand, know you well enough to say that you will at least hear me out before you blow a hole in my head."

Bea raised one leg up and dropped it on the other side of him. "The Alliance is the last line of defense against the Empire and we are it's champion, but how long will it take before we fall from fatigue or superior numbers? We need a stronger fleet to ensure our survival, and the survival of freedom. If the Alcon continue to control the galaxy with an iron fist, in just a few generations no one will be able to stand up against them."

Guile sank his hands into the water and moved them around until he found her legs. "You play your hand beautifully and you had me going there until you threw the galaxy into the mix. You should try to keep your pleas on a more personal level next time."

"That doesn't sound like a refusal."

"It wasn't." He gripped her ankles tightly. "But it wasn't an acceptance either. I can't change who I've become and I can't return to the past. I'll need to be hired for this and I won't come cheap."

Bea jerked her legs away from his grip and pulled them from the water. "Then shall I refer to you as merc?"

Guile reacquired his grip of her legs out of the water. "Let me finish." He tugged, but not hard. The ease at which he pulled her legs back into the water surprised him. "My fees will be limited to an instructor's pay. I'll also charge for any legwork I have to do, but it won't be much. As long as I don't have to take down a Star Cruiser the price will stay low."

Bea smirked out of the corner of her mouth. "Going soft?"

Without warning or struggle, Guile pulled back with his feet, pushing off of the edge of the pool and both he and Bea went under. He released her immediately upon impact with the water. His modesty returned quickly as he sprung back to the surface. With his towel a quarter of the way around the pool he scrambled along the edge and pulled it under. The thin cloth was firmly tied around his waist by the time Bea found her bearings and swam after him.

"You ass!" She snarled.

"I may be, but I'm not soft."

As much as the dunking was a surprise to Bea, her lunging against him and planting her lips against his was a shock to him. Guile jumped within himself, his heart lashing out in a flurry. The firm kiss was a surprise and he was not an easy one to be taken. By the time he calmed and was ready to give in though, she had backed away from him with a grin a hundred war-ships could not wipe off her face.

"You're a dear, Jared."

His eyes narrowed. "Now don't go getting your hopes up, Bea. I'm agreeing to come along as an observer. I won't say yes until I've seen your operation and agree that I can help. I'll also have to confirm your ability to pay. What if my last fee drained your resources?"

Bea flipped her wet hair back. "It doesn't matter. Just getting you to come back is a victory I'll cherish till my dying day." She turned on her heel and walked back towards the house. She let her hips sway back and forth in an obviously exaggerated motion.

"Don't let your words come back to haunt you," he blurted out.

Guile sank down to his chin into the water and let the warm waves brush against his cheeks. You sultry witch, he thought to himself. How can I refuse you?

An hour and a fresh change of clothes later Guile returned with Bea to a nearby star port. Backer was linked to a shuttle's navigational computer so that Guile could ride onboard with Bea. His friendship with her had been dead for many years. Could he trust her now? Could he let his guard down long enough to commit to a cause that he knew little about? Could he ever sit in the pilots seat again and fly formation with a squadron that he had abandoned? Every question raised within his troubled mind provided more and more distraction, so that even the beauty of his fading home world lost its luster.

Barger thought at first that the cool hand on his forehead was the lovely nurse returning to bask in his charm. When he opened his eyes and stared into the returned gaze of a lanky but no less beautiful pilot, he opted to keep his arrogance in check. This was an enemy ship and his attending nurse was one of them. Why would she find him so compelling that every time he awoke she would be there?

Chapter Eight

"Can I help you?" He asked nonchalantly.

Shadle stood to attention and saluted. "Flight Officer Narra Shadle, formally of the Imperial Naval academy and recent addition to the ranks of the Sutherlin Alliance."

Barger folded his lower lip under his top lip to contain his amusement. "Very good, Narra, but you didn't answer my question."

"No I didn't." She dropped her hands to her sides and sat down on the edge of the next bed. "The most you can do is just lay there and act arrogant."

Barger pushed himself up against the wall until he was in a sitting position. "It's not an act, I assure you. This is who I am. If I hadn't been ambushed I would be currently engaged in a heated conversation with two or three attractive service women on board the Blackhawk."

"I stand corrected."

"No, you sit corrected. Should you choose to stand though, I would be more than happy to admire your form some more."

Shadle did the exact opposite of what he had expected. She laughed at his egotistical joke. "Funny, Lieutenant. I wish I had the nerve you put forth given your situation. In your place I would be humoring anyone and everyone for the chance to leave in one piece."

"You have been captured by the Sutherlin Alliance. Your superiors have already altered all access codes that you possessed. They have already declared you dead and have placed a bounty for your extermination. As I see it we are your only chance to regain a life of your own."

"You were given a task and you just failed. You should never have stated my position before I gave you my views." Barger looked straight up to the mirror. "If you were sent to me instead of a commander or captain, then he or she is testing me to see if I would be an asset or a problem. Either way I could never leave of my own free will." He grinned and winked to the figure he knew was watching them.

Barger returned to capture Shadle's gaze. "You're right. By now every bounty hunter and mercenary on this side of the galaxy has my face among hundreds of others under the listing 'proof of kill required.' If you don't kill me, I'll be on my own and dead within the year. I guess then my question should have been, what can you do for me?"

Shadle looked up to the mirror with a terrible puzzled look on her face. She looked back to him. "You could join us and help in our fight against the Alcon Empire."

"Noble, but foolhardy. If the Empire were to get you all in one place you wouldn't stand a chance. Separated you could never take a large enough target to make a statement. It's a lose-lose situation at best."

"But worthwhile, Wes. If I know you half as well as I think I do, I know you can't stand the direction Devil squadron has taken. Serving under Captain Merrill could not have made things any better, either."

Barger folded his arms. This young lady had done her research and was prepared to tackle any issue he could put forth. Her answers may have been a bit off course, but the intention was there. "Devil is beside the point. What you need is a strong leadership basis, well-trained warriors, and a healthy flow of funds. I know you have the funds; otherwise Devil would not have been placed in the hands of Merrill. His sole purpose in life is to scare people into submission, and I'll wager my life that our last attack was a precursor to raids on nobility. Only the nobles could fund your little operation."

"As far as trained personnel, I know you cannot have what it takes to fight the Empire." Barger stopped her before she could respond. "Which is why you took me alive instead of blasting me out of the stars."

"You know a lot for a dead man," Shadle joked.

Barger grinned. "Like the fact that I'll be meeting with your commander before the day is out."

Shadle stepped into the darkened observation room. Standing above the body-length window were Captain Stead and Paltin, the Patron of the Sutherlin Alliance. She had met Paltin just once before, but knew much about him. He was the ambassador that Nyssa had worked for before the previous Patron was killed. It was Paltin who convinced Nyssa to join the alliance along with his entire staff.

"Well," Shadle said with mild hesitation.

"He's a rebellious sort," Paltin hummed. "He would fit in well with the rest of Ghost squadron. My only concern would be his loyalty."

"Loyalty is a hard thing to break," Stead interjected. "He would need to be watched closely. Should he try to betray us he would need to be eliminated."

At least they were considering him. That was some comfort and more than she expected after her last conversation with Stead. Any change in his position at this point could be considered good. "I would be more than happy to keep an eye on him."

Paltin folded his hands in front of him. "I worry that you may be too fond of this man to have an objective opinion, and Captain Stead has his own recruit to worry about. I think I will have to place the care for this man in the hands of your entire squadron."

Stead raised an eyebrow. "You would trust him enough to place him in my squad so soon?"

"You would do the same for Mister Guile, and he has shown far less loyalty than Lieutenant Barger." He slowly turned to the captain. "You forget what kind of reputation Jared has. Wes on the other hand has shown a strict sense of duty and a less than favorable opinion of how the Alcon deal with uprisings. If he were convinced of our purpose and the wrongs of the empire he could prove to be a valuable asset. Much like you are."

Chapter Eight

Stead shivered. He obviously did not like the comparison. "I will honor your wishes, Patron, but I will make my own judgments of the man. I need to see him in action before I can call him an ally."

"Then I suggest that you get him up as soon as possible. Utilize him in a training role and see how he performs with our rookie pilots. If he works to protect them above all else, then I think you should reconsider your position." Paltin turned to Shadle. "As for your feelings. I do not wish you to jeopardize your life or the lives of the Alliance for this man."

"We will arrive in the Luikart system in two days. I want him briefed on the Alliance and what his role will be until he can be trusted. He will go out on your next training flight and act as lead." He turned back to Stead. "The same goes for Mister Guile."

"I have no doubt that Bea will have him up to date on Alliance activity before he arrives. If we can get Jared and Wes to cooperate with us, I should be able to provide you with two additional fighter squadrons before Luikart base is ready to move."

"For all our sakes I hope you are correct, Haggin. The Empire is becoming more and more persistent in its dealings with us. If we cannot stay on the move and out of reach I fear the worst."

Chapter Nine

Barger was alone in a cramped, dark room with only the light of a terminal to see by. Just the place for someone that wanted to spend time by himself. This time he was reprogramming flight simulators for a slew of rookie pilots with little or no flight experience. As part of his new career he was required to design a series of flight tests to teach them with a gradual increase in difficulty. Not an easy task when he had to start from scratch. The existing simulator programs were taken from Alcon naval refresher files that were designed to keep already skilled pilots toned for difficult battle situations.

In the dark, damp heat he worked. Barger wedged himself behind the flight simulation room where he needed to dump the whole system, keeping only a few attributes, and rebuild the program with a wide range of skill levels. Most of it he could program from memory, but the rest had to be written from his imagination and personal experience. Granted, the computer adversaries would have a bit of his own personality designed into them, but he figured that a fair amount of unpredictability would allow the rookies a sense of reality.

This was an aspect of his life that he had never fully developed. Initially, he tested high in communications and intelligence work. Had he not failed a mental stability test he might have become part of Imperial Intelligence. He also scored high in piloting and planning skills, which made him a prime candidate for officer training in the fighter corps. The need for pilots and officers had always outweighed the Empire's desire for programmers, and so another of his talents was placed by the wayside -- until he became a forced volunteer of the Alliance. Shadle had made the offhanded comment that Barger scored high in communications so he was tested out on basic programming languages. Having no desire to play dumb he passed the basic tests and found himself here. He was told that with Guile busy it was up to him to take over as lead instructor. It was a duty he did not want, and would not undertake unless he was prepared to train the recruits to the best of his abilities. That meant spending hour after hour under simulators and in the cockpit.

"What am I doing here?" His words echoed in the metallic chamber. *I should be flying this, not designing 'em.*

He had only met the pilots he was helping in passing. They were young, too young to be risking their lives for a worthless cause. Even with his help the alliance would never assemble enough hardware to pose a serious threat to the Alcon. If they did they would face a very real manpower shortage. In a time where power ruled and fear dominated, the weak could never join together in the kind of strength it would take to topple the Empire.

Barger's sweaty grin glowed from the terminal light. It was amusing to hear himself think. For years he had ignored politics, leaving the galactic game of chess to faceless bureaucrats. Now in a matter of hours he had thrown himself into a deep political debate. It was tough to imagine how one slipup could affect him so much and so quickly. He did not know whether it was a good thing or a bad thing. It could go either way.

The long internal debate as to whether or not the Alliance was fighting a worthwhile battle remained unanswered. It would undoubtedly stay that way for some time. No single victory or defeat would change the outcome of the war or even the rebellion. The near destruction, then rebirth, of the Sutherlin fleet had proven that. Either side had a long way to go before this was over. Barger only hoped that he was on the right side.

Maybe the right side was not the correct word to use, he pondered. Maybe instead he was on the side of justice and honor. Barger grinned and shook his head. He was beginning to sound like Kirkland. In one of his many drunken ramblings he had spoken more like a councilman than a pilot. Barger often wondered if his friend could have made it in politics if he had not joined the fighter corps.

The terminal beeped at him signaling the completion of the first program. He looked at the chronometer in the lower left corner and could not help smiling. He had finished the hardest part in less than twelve hours. Quite an accomplishment for a fighter jock. He pictured his classmates' reactions if they had been here for this. The cadet who had failed systems programming once and barely passed it a second time had beaten some of the brightest minds in the galaxy.

If they had only known that he never chose to apply himself in a field that had nothing to do with piloting. For Barger the choice was a simple one. The fighter corps had won him by default so he felt no desire to keep up his studies in other courses. Only on his own, outside the academy did he resume his practices in the fine art of hacking and programming.

"System operational," a generated voice called out.

"Not yet, honey. I still have a base loop to set up before I let you take over."

"Ten seconds to simulation evaluation."

The program he had just written disappeared from the screen as it uploaded into the main computer. Barger slammed his fists to either side of the attached keyboard in anger. Without the base loop a single error in the system could overload all the

Chapter Nine

simulators. Someone was waiting for him to finish so that the program could be tested and he had a good idea who it was.

Barger pulled himself up a small hatch in the ceiling and found himself in a converted hangar. To either side of him were rows of simulators, each roughly the size of two cockpits smashed together. Down one end was Captain Stead standing behind a terminal. He was in a hurry and rightly so. They both knew what would happen if Barger found someone tampering with his program. Especially if it was the only person that openly resented his presence.

"Back away from the terminal, Haggin! Just because I admired you doesn't mean I won't shoot you!"

"I want to make sure you're not sabotaging the system. How do I know you aren't betraying our position to the Alcon?"

Barger pulled himself the rest of the way from the hatch. "From a program terminal? I don't even have access to the lights in this bay from down there. Why don't you pull your head out of your furry butt and leave me to my work."

"Not a chance, Wes. You are my responsibility and I intend to keep you honest."

"Honesty depends on the person who thinks up the lie, Haggin and you know it."

"Back off, Wes. I don't want to have to end this relationship prematurely."

Barger was at a loss. Stead openly resented his presence, and for reasons that escaped him. "What have I done to you? All I've ever been to you is a shadow. I followed your career closely and did my best to imitate it. Now you treat me as if I've betrayed the Alliance before I've even had a chance to join it."

"You'll never be a part of the Alliance."

Barger dropped his hand to his sidearm. He had the weapon out of his holster and aimed in less than the blink of and eye. With the slight squeeze of the trigger a thin pulse of light streaked across the bay and clipped the Captain on the back of his jumpsuit. Stead reacted by stumbling back away from the terminal and flaying about in a vein attempt to find a wound on his body. The shot had been perfectly placed between the thin inner layer and thick outer layer of the suit, leaving the white lining partially exposed.

"I told you to back away and let me finish, you impetuous turd. If you get me riled one more time I'm liable to program a fleet of star cruisers into the first mission." He lowered his weapon. "Now if you don't mind I'd like you to leave."

Stead stood up straight and growled. "You raise that weapon again and I'll have your head on the targeting screen of my cockpit. I'm still against you even having one."

"Save it for the simulators," The elderly voice of Patron said from behind Barger.

Stead froze in place, but Barger turned. "My apologies. I normally would not let someone like him get to me this easily, but this is a very unique circumstance."

Stead grumbled incoherently then spun around and walked out.

"I understand, Mr. Barger. We all have someone who is our rival in life. We do our best to either avoid this person or make sure he never harms us again. This is not always possible when this person sees it as his mission in life to make yours miserable."

"I wish I could promise that this won't happen again. I've always had commanders that resented me for one reason or another."

"Friendship is based more on your perspective of a given situation or series of events. To truly have a friendship with someone, you must look beyond that and see yourself as you would be if in the presence of this person for a great deal of time."

"You sound like you've done this already."

"Once, a long time ago." Patron slowly turned and walked away. "And it fared worse than your relationship with Captain Stead."

Barger watched the old man walk out of the hanger. He did not trust his last remark. It had something to do with the way he said it. It felt like he knew more than he would ever let on. Like his involvement in the Alliance was more personal than for the greater good. That was not necessarily wrong in his eyes. Many causes were spearheaded by rage. In the end the rage ended in victory. The question that eternally needed to be answered was who was the greater monster. The spark in the rage or the person who allowed such a primal emotion to govern his life.

The stolen, outdated Alcon shuttle burst back to normal space in a bright flash of amber light. Stars exploded across the growing darkness of space and a distant sun grew larger with every blink of the eye. The eight engines groaned back to life and gradually increased in power with an unsettling whine. If anyone had been able to sleep through the nauseating ride they were surely awake now. Even the most experienced space travelers had difficulty during the hectic trip.

Guile swallowed hard against the building army in his stomach. Gently he positioned himself so that the restraining belt failed to crimp his lower torso as tightly. His attempts proved futile as the shuttle slowed at an exaggerated rate. Inertial stabilizers fought the backwards pull against the hull, but as with any older model ship, the systems were just not capable of handling such a task. It was the price to pay for easily attainable hardware.

"You really get used to it after a while," Bea said from his right.

Guile rolled his head and stared at her across the aisle. If his looks could kill, he would have had another easy score. "You're not a very good liar."

She shrugged. "I had to say something. You looked like you were about to lose your lunch all over the cabin."

"I never ate." He rolled back and focused on the seat in front of him. "I usually have my Companion sedate me during Star Flight."

"That's typical though. That's one of the reasons companions were assigned to pilots of Star Flight capable fighters."

"I'm not just talking about flights over twelve hours. I have him sedate me for system jumps."

Bea's eyes widened and she faced forward. Hyper-space sickness was not an uncommon occurrence, even for veteran pilots. The degree of the sickness varied

Chapter Nine

depending on the traveler's mental state or physical condition. In most cases the nausea associated with hyperspace travel was based on nerves. Guile could never convince himself that this was the case, but from her reaction to his comment he had to second-guess his own behavior.

The shuttle slowed to maneuvering speeds as a planet passed in the blink of an eye. The normal subtle background drone replaced the sound of the engines. The blue haze that was visible out of the viewing ports faded away. A normally pleasant sight for passengers, Guile found it added to his woozy stomach. It was another reminder to him that he was traveling the way no one should travel.

Despite this feeling he would travel no other way. He could not imagine what cargo crews went through. The massive cargo ships that traveled from system to system seldom were equipped with Star Flight initiators because of the cost and the size required. Instead, they were propelled by detachable boosters that carried them just under the speed of light. A short jump that would take a freighter a few minutes took a cargo ship days.

Guile could not fathom such a trip. He could barely handle a Star Flight jump that took a day or two. How could anyone stay within cramped quarters for such a long time? At least on star cruisers, which could avoid ports for months, one had space to roam. Cargo ships had little more room to move about that the shuttle did. Perhaps an adventurous soul could maneuver along the access tubes, but even that would lose its appeal after a while.

The two were alone in the passenger compartment and Guile trusted Bea enough to leave his face uncovered. She had known about the scars on his face and that he chose to keep them hidden. The covers that he wore had just become a trademark, and he was not about to disappoint those that knew him by reputation alone. As the shuttle began its descent into the atmosphere of the target planet, he removed thin wraps from the bag under his seat.

Soft hands slipped the wraps from his hands. Guile looked back. Bea smiled, then straightened his head forward. Gently she tugged the leading edge of the strip of cloth into the breast of his undershirt. Taking in mind that the deep scars along his neck were at times sensitive, she slowly spun the wraps around several times. With his neck completely covered and his chin partially hidden, she let the other end fall over his shoulder.

"I'll let you finish the rest." Bea sat down next to him. "Does it still hurt?"

Guile lifted the end up and continued wrapping the cloth around his mouth. "Only when I sit still and have time to reflect." Using a thin clip he attached the end to a section of wrap on the back of his head. "The memory hurts more than the scars."

Bea rested a hand on his leg. "Something tells me there's more to the story than just the report."

"Everything was there," he sighed. "I guess it's just how you interpret it."

"Then maybe you should give me your interpretation." She rested her hands on his shoulders and gently squeezed. "I've spent a long time hating you for leaving us.

"For leaving me," she added softly. "I looked over your report and the official report hundreds of times, trying to find what drove you off."

"Who would you believe? I can tell you what I know, but I'm sure it is different than what Imperial Intelligence reported."

"I'll always believe you, Jared."

"Then prove it. Tell me why Patron is so interested in the Regent. Why is she more important to him than the Emperor? I know the history between those two, but not between him and the Regent."

"And you never will if he has anything to say about it. Not even Haggin knows his true motivations. We all like to believe that his rage is solely directed at the Emperor, but as you pointed out, he has more interest in the Regent than anyone else."

Guile reached up and gripped her hands. "I can't say that I blame him. I have my own interest in her, but I can't say why. I've never met her or have seen a picture of her yet I feel like she's watching everything I do."

Bea snickered. "Sounds like you have a complex or something. I doubt even the Emperor could find a way to watch you all the way from Perditia."

The compartment speaker snapped to life. "We're just about there."

Guile leaned towards the viewing port and looked down. Surprisingly, there was nothing below except for a densely rocky terrain. The planet the Alliance called home was a dead world, draped in a dull brown. There was no atmosphere to pass through, nor was there a base landing pad. All that rose up from below were dusty plains and rocky cliffs.

"Watch this."

He glanced back at her. "Watch what? Our fiery crash?"

She smiled. "Hardly."

The shuttle decreased its speed, although it was still traveling at better than five hundred when it reached the surface. Past moments of his life flashed through Guile's mind, and then he closed his eyes. His heart stopped as the shuttle rumbled, but there was no sudden stop or explosion. Instead the ship continued to slow and the flight smoothed out.

Death isn't that bad. Guile opened his eyes and was astounded. Instead of twisted metal strung out across the planet's surface he was gazing out over a vast underground complex with a large landing facility surrounded by dozens of various buildings. He could plainly see people inside the windows of the buildings and on the deck. Hundreds of people, though he could not make out species yet.

"It gets better." Bea stood and walked to the compartment speaker. She pushed a button next to it. "Rotate us to the right and give us a view of the hangars."

The shuttle jerked to the right a quarter turn and three large hangars came into view. The large doors on the center were open and the contents were clearly visible. Fighters filled the building from front to back. Fifteen in total. The blurry items towards the rear were not easily recognizable but the shapes to the front all but announced their identity.

Chapter Nine

There were easily two squadrons worth of Nova fighters and they were in pristine condition. Fresh from the factory with a shine that would be gone after their first flight. Even the shipping latches that kept moveable parts stationary were still in place. This was hardly the condition of fighters Guile had expected of a rebellion.

"We're in the process of improving the weapons package."

"How so?" Guile asked without breaking his gaze.

"We're adding an additional cannon to each wing and an interchangeable warhead loader. Our engineers are also replacing the secondary engine coolant panels with rechargeable power collectors to recharge the additional guns."

Impressive, he thought to himself. The standard nova was formidable in its own right. At first he had found it difficult to adjust to the less agile and slower Nova after years of piloting a bi-wing. He soon found that the less popular fighter's shielding and internal warhead launchers made it an acceptable and more cost-efficient switch. Although the bi-wings came off the assembly line at a much reduced cost, in the long run the novas where easier to maintain and the their spare parts were half the cost.

The shuttle touched down with a mild rumble. Guile quickly unbuckled his safety belt and stood up. He was about to leave his bag behind when his boot snagged on the strap. Stumbling around he picked up the bag and slung it over his shoulder. Bea walked towards the landing ramp ahead of him and was halfway down before he was able to clear the aisle. He struggled down the ramp to catch up with her.

"Attention!" A stern voice shouted, drowning out the dying engines of the shuttle.

Guile stopped at the bottom of the ramp and dropped his bag. In front of him were several pilots in uniforms that matched Ghost squadron's new configuration. In one row Black stripped silver jumpsuits were well organized and impressive. Each held their black helmets under their left arms and rested their right hands flat against their side arms. They stood in perfect attention, which reminded him of his days with the Imperial Navy.

Bea took up a position next to Flight Officer Nyssa and straightened to full attention. "Mister Guile, this is Ghost squadron both full time and temporary. The pride of the alliance and angel of death to Alcon pilots. You give us a task and we'll kick some ass."

Guile frowned and reached down to pick up his bag. The focus of his disappointment rested solely in seeing how young the seven pilots were. "Pleasure to meet all of you. If you don't mind I'd like to get situated before any formal introductions."

The disappointment on more than one of the recruits' faces was evident, yet ignored. He had expected youth, but not this young. If anything he had hoped for early to mid-twenties. Two of the pilots could not have been over sixteen. The revelation was more than he could take, further adding to the fatigue he felt from the flight.

Bea broke ranks and approached him. "Let me show you to your room. It's not situated within the military barracks, but it is right next to the command center."

"That's fine."

Both hopped into an eight person pilot shuttle with Bea maneuvering the vehicle. The ride, which carried them across the landing pad to a circle of four buildings, was long enough to prompt a question from Guile. He rustled uneasily around in his seat, looking for a spot that might ease what he needed to ask. He found one closer to Bea, but it wasn't exactly what he was looking for. He knew she could not fully answer his question.

"Why are they so young?"

Bea gave him a sideways glance before letting out a sigh. "Necessity, but they aren't all totally inexperienced. One of them used to pilot in a local militia and another was an applicant to the academy."

"You still haven't answered my question."

Bea took in a deep breath. The question hurt in more ways than one. "Patron wanted pilots and we had no time to recruit the more experienced. It was either these kids or retired Alcon pilots that were too frail to grip their controls. I would like to have introduced some of our more experienced pilots, but they were reassigned to our other cells. What you've seen is their replacements. Patron hopes that you can weed out the less than perfect and bring Ghost back up to operational status."

"He's a fool."

Bea turned down an opening between the buildings and pulled into a small courtyard. "He is maybe, but he's still the assigned leader of our cell."

"Cell? You keep using that word. You mean there are more bases like this?"

"More bases, but not like this. We have two ground bases in the outer systems and one more mobile base that's constantly jumping from one system to the next. This is the largest of them all and houses a majority of the command staff."

"It's not wise to keep everyone together."

"Not everyone," she corrected herself. "Just a majority. Our top staff is elsewhere."

Guile grabbed his bag and hopped out of the pilot shuttle as it came to a stop. Bea stepped out and directed him towards the tallest of the buildings. He followed her through the double doors and passed the reception desk, which also acted as a guard post. The interior of the building was supported by visible columns inside metal framework. The walls that were covered had a simple carpet-like material that was held in place with corner clips. By all appearances the entire building was modular in design and could be erected in a day. For obvious reasons these people were not planning to stay in one place for long.

Down a hall to the left, Bea stopped at an estate room with Guile's name on it. Whether or not he planned to stay, it was obvious they knew he would come. The room itself gave even more evidence to the fact. The spacious room had a thin bed like his back home and next to the restrooms was a portable six-foot pool with an industrial heater attached. Careful planning had been done to make sure he felt at home.

Guile dropped his back inside the door. "It sure is quaint."

Chapter Nine

"I hope it's more than quaint, Jared. We went to a lot of trouble to make you comfortable so you'll stay."

"You should know that comfort has no effect over my decision making. If I'm going to stay, then I need to see what kind of help you need and what kind of support I can supply."

"The help we need is simple. We're short on supplies and we're short on training. What you can provide has yet to be seen. Patron says you have more connections than the Noblemen, but I don't believe him. I think you just scrape by on what people pay you and that you shop for scrap parts."

Guile bellowed out a laugh. He turned on one heel and walked to his bed where he promptly spun around and fell on his back. "I love it." He propped himself up on his elbows. "I assure you, Bea, that I don't just scrape by and the equipment I use is hardly scrap parts. If you would like you can inspect my Nova and tell me how many parts on her are scrap."

"Good. Then you have connections that can get us nova parts."

Guile nodded. "Everything but new stabilizers. Everything else is compatible with the Nova. I can even hook you up with someone who can supply you with a thousand warhead launchers. I'd have to go somewhere else to get the warheads, but that's even easier."

"Great. Then you can arrange a meeting for first thing next week."

Guile pushed himself up. "Now what a minute," he said, his tone dropping quickly. "This isn't something I can just jump into. The people I deal with aren't going to jump when I holler. I'll need to meet with middle men first so that prices can be agreed upon."

"Fine. Patron will want to know as soon as possible what will be required of our finances. As you can imagine our funds are not drawn from an inexhaustible well. We need good equipment, but we also need it at an incredible price."

"That's asking quite a bit. I suppose if I skip the middlemen and deal with manufacturers and can get supplies at whole sale." It was not a smart thing to do, though. It had taken him his entire mercenary career to establish several working aliases. If he were to deal directly, he would have to use each of them up with every dealer he made a contact with.

"Can I have some assurances that the trouble this is going to cause me with be worth it? I mean, will your Patron help establish a new set of credentials should this little venture of mine ruin my future as a pirate?"

Bea leaned her knees against the edge of the bed. "You can be sure that whatever happens to the name you have made for yourself it will be for the best."

"Vague, but I'll expect that as a no."

"Patron will be expecting you for dinner tonight. I will be by around five, so I suggest you wear something nice and be ready. He doesn't like to be kept waiting." She turned and walked down the hall.

Guile dropped back onto the bed. What a change in attitude. Bea had always been one for abrupt emotional turns, but this was unusual. Either the pressure of fighting as a resistance was getting to her or she was truly becoming the pirate the Empire was making them out to be. This is going to be more difficult than I had anticipated, he thought to himself.

Chapter Ten

Fallon's smile seemed genuine enough. He had won many unspoken rivalries with his warm smile. Superiors and peers alike had fallen to his Arlast charm before they had a chance to see him as a threat to their respective commands. They found out only too late that beneath his demure exterior he had an ambition that eventually pulled in a star cruiser command. He had become the youngest Admiral in the Alcon Navy and the deadliest.

The dual suns were setting behind the capital walls with rays of light piercing the decorative openings along the ridge of steel. Fallon stood in the center of an open courtyard, his back to the sleek form of his personal shuttle. The shuttle was dwarfed by the surrounding towers, which seemed to stretch up to space. What it lacked in majesty though, it more than made up for in form.

The shuttle was twelve meters in overall length and divided into two sections. The bulkier, passenger compartment rested almost on the ground and was box-like in appearance. The command portion of the craft angled up from the back and extended forward until it sloped down ahead of the passenger compartment. A large viewing window filled the front of the command section. A pair of fins raised up and away from the body from the joint between the two compartments and angled outward slightly. Along either side there was a pair of atmospheric stabilizers with four engines to each wing. Each stabilizer spanned out a meter where mechanical joints separated the rest of the wings. In their current position the stabilizers were locked upward so that the craft could land. During flight the wings lowered and locked so that they extended further away from the hull another two meters before angling fifteen degrees and six meters downward.

Both parked and in flight the shuttle was impressive and, to those that knew it to be Alcon, it was frightening. Fallon often used the ominous form as his backdrop as he greeted dignitaries and fellow officers. It was a standard tactic picked up from academy days, but one that he had perfected. With the right amount of steam pumped from the hydraulic passenger ramps he could create an almost eerie form out of himself.

The Caderan he was to meet with was the chief advisor to the Prime Dictate of Cadera Prime. To many he was considered the brains of the government. He had personally orchestrated the treaty between Cadera Prime and The Alcon Empire, further solidifying the Empire's control over the galaxy and strengthening Cadera's hold on trade lanes. Cadera Prime became the dictator of every trade agreement and thus assigned its own freighters to trading groups to further increase their profits. Horde gained from the agreement as they were contracted by the Caderans to supply a majority of the ships and crews.

Though Fallon supported the Caderan hold over legal shipping he denounced it privately. It was his personal belief that the serious price fixing the deal had produced was putting too much strain on small time traders, and that smuggler operations would continue to rise. This led to a diverting of military resources to contain the smugglers and a weakening of battle group integrity. He had proof of this as the fifth fleet had been stripped of all but two battle groups in order to track down smuggler and pirate organizations.

This man is the focus of my rage. Fallon watched the blotted, stubby man emerge from the capital building and wobble down the stone steps. *If only you knew what was in store for you.* Every chance he had, Fallon laid into Minister Gesh for any problems that arose within the trading circuit. Even if the problem lay outside the circuit he would still get his chance to interrogate the man. It was a simple pleasure, but one that he looked forward to.

Even in the worst of circumstances he held his demeanor and acted up to his rank. The simple bow held true to most civilizations and was the standard greeting. It showed political respect and, should the bow be followed by a local custom, sometimes held a deeper feeling of honor. For the Caderan the honor would be if the greeter offered his hands palm up, showing him to be a trusted friend.

Fallon took a modest bow as Gesh approached him, but nothing more. "Minister," he said clearly and emotionless.

Gesh's voice gurgled as he spoke from the masses of fat that had built up around his throat. "What are you doing back so soon?" He demanded. "You were just here three days ago. I thought we had resolved the station's destruction."

"This does have to do with the stations' destruction, but more about the individual who caused it. With the permission of the Prime Dictate I'm here to escort you to Horde so that you can aid my search for this man and his hires."

Fallon could see the heavier man fumble about in his little brain. He was hurrying himself to come up with an excuse. The hesitation was enough to cause Fallon some delight. Gesh despised leaving his home world. Traveling under the banner of the Alcon simply added a burning insult to the task.

"I know who did it," Gesh said with some hope that he would not have to go. "I know his name and I can give you my file on him."

"I have your files," he said in a cold wave. "I have studied this man for a week now and I know his patterns. I know the type of weapons he prefers to use, I know that he is highly unpredictable, and I know that he has connections that can supply

Chapter Ten

him with enough equipment to arm a planet. I also know that he goes by the name Guile. What I don't know is where he is based and who his connections are."

"How can I help? If you know what I know then you shouldn't need me."

Fallon took a step towards him. His boots stomped heavily against the ground, forcing a tremble out of the much shorter man. "You are my greatest connection to the trading circuit and you can provide me with access to areas that local controllers would not normally allow. With your assistance I will hunt down this elusive mercenary and tear him apart connection by connection until he is nothing more than a worthless pirate with a bounty."

"You believe Guile will lead you to other operations?"

As if you didn't know. "I'm sure that any smuggling or pirate organization we happen across on our search for this man will only add to the Empire's collection of shattered upstarts." Fallon turned on one heel and marched towards his shuttle. He left the chubby man to follow him up the single ramp into the passenger compartment. The first row of seats inside was reserved for the guards that were hidden around the outside of the shuttle. As he took a seat in the second row, he watched as Gesh jumped at the sight of six soldiers dressed in black on black taking up position behind him.

The main ramp started up with a hiss from the twenty release valves along the lifting arms. One of the two pilots shot back a liftoff announcement. The shuttle began to shake from side to side as the anti-gravity pods fought to equalize amongst themselves. After the brief moment of discomfort the ride smoothed out and Fallon watched out a viewing port at the capital city as it shrank in size.

The hull on either side moaned. The stabilizers locked into place, freeing up additional viewing space for the admiral. He could clearly see the surrounding city now, a metropolis of sorts. No building rose above three stories so that the capital city would stand out like a pillar to be seen for kilometers. The idea was sound, but not original. The Alcon Imperial palace on Perditia stood over a hundred meters above the tallest building on the planet.

Fallon's comlink chirped to life and Captain S'Lendo's voice perforated the speaker. "Admiral Fallon."

He depressed the side of the comlink. "Yes."

"The last of the scout ships have returned from their patrols along Guile's last known trajectory. Scout eight reports that a repair facility in the Bromos system repaired a damaged initiator on a Nova. The name of the registry did not match any of Guile's known aliases, but the fighter matches the visual image taken from the Valiant."

Fallon sank into the cushioned seat. "Very good. Recall scouts and patrols then lay in a course for Bromos. It isn't much of a lead. It's a week old at best, but it's a start."

"Understood, sir."

"Then we aren't traveling to Horde," Gesh hoped.

"I am not," he grumbled.

Gesh took the hint and kept to himself.

Fallon clicked off the comlink and stared out the window. Cadera Prime had an outer beauty that rivaled the grand houses of the powerful. The deep purple that filtered up through the atmosphere brought out the bright specks of light that made up the planet's backdrop. The twin suns of the systems provided the surface with constant light, giving the shell a glow all its own. The breathtaking scenery did not fall on cold eyes for Fallon, who had been to countless worlds in hundreds of star systems. He could appreciate the beauty of a world -- even one that was covered in a detestable race of greedy beings.

Reality burst back in one bright flash, then starlight illuminated Shadle's view once more. Ahead of her, three other novas had already dropped from Star Flight and were grouping up in an open diamond pattern. Shadle was the last to fill in the formation, coming up behind the lead fighter but staying in back of the wing fighters. Her targeting computer came up green as she dropped into place and all four fighters registered friendly.

"Lead to group," Barger said through her helmet speaker. "Solid jump. Alcon pros could not have dropped from Star Flight in better formation, and they have the benefit of at least a transport cabin to relax in. All right, let's begin. Check in."

"Two standing by," Flight officer Nyssa said.

"Three standing by," Flight officer Scio said.

"Four standing by," Shadle said.

"This is your first run against a heavy target so be prepared for the worst."

Shadle could tell by his voice that he was not at all happy about leading a simulated attack. He had protested, saying that pilots learned more from real mistakes than computer generated ones. Patron had countered by saying that the alliance could not afford to lose any more pilots during training missions. Both had valid cases, but it was Patron who had the authority. Barger backed down, stating that eventually they would have to attack a live target before he could clear the younger pilots for combat.

Though Shadle did not have the confidence to assault the Alcon in live combat, she was forced to agree with him. From experience in her few days with the academy she had seen how live flights were different from simulations. Computers, though programmed to act as pilots would, had no real emotion. In an actual fight or even a staged battle it was the emotions and irrational behavior of a humanoid that added a dangerous edge to a fighter battle.

The temporary trainee pilots of ghost squadron had experienced heavy loses in the first few simulated runs, prompting Barger to join the missions that he had programmed. This was the fifth in fewer than twenty hours and the first in which he was to participate. The idea was to add confidence by alleviating some of the pressure offered up by the simulated Alcon fighters. Neither he nor the pilots involved had any idea if it would work.

Chapter Ten

On the edge of the nova's short-range sensors two blue targets appeared. They registered at over fifty clicks, but at top speed that distance would vanish quickly. The novas had yet to force power into the cannons and shields, allowing the full flow to pump into the engines. With engines at one hundred percent the speed was equivalent to that of the bi-wing.

"Check your targeting screens. You should see our objective: one cargo freighter and a cutter. Now you know the cutter has limited star fighter defenses, but what it lacks in defenses it more than makes up for in maneuverability. If you're not careful, you could end up between two firing arcs if the ship comes around on you and brings two sides to bare."

The mission briefing included exterior schematics of an Imperial escort cutter. The lightly armored vessel was designed to outrun the fastest attack ship and even enter the outer atmosphere of a planet. The ship was smaller in length than a destroyer and was armed with two dual defense cannons mounted on either side of the hull.

"Let's go get 'em. Increase speed full throttle and target your first salvo on the cutter. I want her shields down on the first pass."

Shadle did as ordered, pushing her throttle to max. She toggled her weapons control to the thermal missiles. She eased her fighter just under Barger's and lined up her holographic targeting reticule with the port side of the slim cutter. The rectangle burned red almost instantly as a target signal bounced off a navigational probe near the ship. Her eyes popped open wide at the sudden change in tactics with Barger in the lead. She had never seen someone use a foreign probe to target ships before.

"At ten clicks you are cleared to release."

The flight grouped passed twenty-five clicks and the mission began to look like a cakewalk. The aggressor squadron that was lurking out there was nowhere in sight and the cutter had yet to begin evasive maneuvers. That may have something to do with their current distance. Normally fighters have to be within three clicks to acquire a target lock. Whoever was in charge of the ship's operations did not take into account Barger's unorthodox methods.

"Threat!" He blurted out.

There it was. At fifteen clicks two groups of three Bi-wings appeared from around the far side of the cutter. They had been waiting in stasis until the novas were close enough to have full warhead capabilities.

"Three and four, break right and continue your attack. Two, you're with me. Spoil the rod and spare the child, two."

Shadle pulled up and out to the right with three staying close to her right wing. Both rolled out on their right wings, keeping the remaining fighters under their bellies. Shadle kept the roll out another three clicks before pulling back to the left and flattening out. She was still eight clicks out, but both pilots needed only two more before they could release. They may not have kept up adequate thrust, but with safeties off, the warheads would still impact the ship.

"Three, kill safeties on your first salvo and release on my mark. Five. . .four. . .three. . .two. . .one. . .mark."

The two novas released a pair of gold trails simultaneously. Ahead of the fiery tail was a small warhead, hidden beneath the wave of phased energy. The tails extended away ten meters as the energy-dispersing field the warhead produced gradually broke down. The gold glow shrank in the distance then disappeared abruptly behind a pair of dark images. As luck had it, both Bi-wings passed the missiles without any attempt to down them.

The Bi-wings closed quickly and gradually made their form visible.

"Three, switch to cannons and break hard right. Continue your run."

Shadle broke left just as a missile lock on threat flashed on her targeting screen. Her quick decision had spared a missile launch and probably her wingman as well. Bi-wings had no shielding, but occasionally came equipped with disposable missile pods. Shields or no shields the Nova was more than a match if the combination was backed by a competent pilot. Doing everything right she began to dodge random fire from one of the Bi-wings. Arcs of amber flashed across her canopy prompting an automatic dimming of her flight mask.

"Four, I have solid tone."

"Snap shot two and break off to engage."

"Copy, four."

Shadle pulled her Nova into a tight backward loop that brought a view of the fight above her canopy. She was now parallel with the cutter, which received the first volley of four missiles without much damage to the shields. A click away, three was dodging a dual wave of fire from both Bi-wings. As Nyssa ran back and forth over the two Alcon fighter firing arcs, he took a few splashes across his aft shields.

Throwing the fighter to the left, Shadle rolled the Nova into a tight roll. She slightly adjusted her rudder pedals to fight an uncontrolled barrel roll before pulling the stick into her chest. The maneuverability was close to that of the trainers she had piloted years ago, so her violent moves were not beyond the fighter's capabilities. Overall speed lacked though. In the time it took to swoop in behind the two Bi-wings, Nyssa had already lost most of his shields.

Shadle grabbed a weak lock on one of the Alcon fighters and snapped off a pair of missiles. She flipped her weapons over to guns and lined up behind the second. The first broke off from his impending death, allowing both missiles to fly off into space. The second did not have the luxury. The Bi-wing hull, lacking its shields, splashed away in sparks from a combined quad burst to the wing panels. The pilot jerked out to right at first then pulled back hard to the left on its left wing. A second quad burst caught the tail of the craft enough to knock it off its intended course.

The damaged Bi-wing punched up to full throttle and with its superior speed began to gain ground back towards the cutter. Shadle maxed out her engines and managed to keep the distance the Bi-wing was gaining to a minimum. The fighter was already out of positive gun lock, but not out of missile lock. She switched back over to warheads and quickly re-acquired a positive tone. Just as quickly, a distant pair of

Chapter Ten

gold darts turned in sharply and struck the Bi-wing. In a shower of glowing hot metal the fighter exploded with it's right wing spinning madly out into space.

Both missiles she had previously launched were still searching for a target and were close enough to receive data from her targeting system. The advanced tracking systems were not easily attainable by the Alliance. The only reason Barger even added them to the mission profile came on the reassurance that the Alliance would be receiving a shipment before too long. Whatever the reason, Shadle mentally thanked him for the addition.

"Watch it, four."

Shadle bumped forward, rolling a half turn on her right wing. Her shields registered a five percent loss to the aft quarter.

"Hard to port, now."

Following the younger pilot's lead Bea pressed in on the left rudder and pulled back on the stick. The Nova banked up and to the left sharply, avoiding a single line of gold rocketing past. A dual blast of amber followed the missiles, but they were not from the Bi-wing. The second volley had struck the Alcon fighter's aft and was visible in a sparked rain as it passed. Nyssa passed shortly after, unloading all that he had into the Bi-wing's failing hull.

"Keep on him, three. Let me know if you run into trouble."

"Copy, four. Lay into 'em."

Shadle leveled out her course with the cutter. Her targeting system chirped out and turned red at five clicks. A single streak of cyan burst from the belly of the beast and arced away. The Nova's threat indicator sounded missile warning. It spat out a distance and time to impact. Shadle judged her time to positive missile fire and decided to take the chance. She need only wait out another two clicks and she could fire.

"Lead to four. Status."

"All clear, lead," Shadle responded. "Starting final run on the cutter."

"She's all yours, four. We've kinda got our hands full."

The targeting screen buzzed a positive fire and she released two missiles. She remained on course even as a second missile rocketed out from the belly of the cutter. Her warhead system buzzed again and she fired another volley, her last. Both volleys flew straight on course and would easily knock down the ship's shields at this distance.

The first of the two missiles launched from the target ship struck the shields below her left wing and threw her into an uncontrolled roll. Inertial dampeners failed, as did the control thrusters so her spiral led her on a direct course with the hull of the cutter. At this point the larger ship was within heavy weapons range and the dual starboard guns began to track her movement. Without the ability to evade she made for an easy target.

The second missile struck the aft quarter, killing the shields, and sending the fighter into a forward somersault. Control thrusters regained power halfway along the second tumble. Shadle dumped weapons power into the shields and pushed forward to level the fighter. The Nova leveled out one click from the cutter giving both the ship and the fighter clear shots at each other. Considering the condition of her shields though, she elected to pitch and run.

Between hard turns Shadle checked the status of the cutter and was not surprised to see its shield rating at zero and minor hull damage to the aft quarter. "Four to group. Shields are down. Finish her off."

"Copy, four." Nyssa said. "Commencing attack."

Good boy. Finished off the bi in little time. Two quick bursts across her aft shields reduced the Nova's field strength to nothing once more. Shadle pulled out of an elongated loop and brought her nose along a line with the cargo ship. She dumped the last of her weapons power into the shields and redirected recharge rate to engines. Her speed jumped five percent, enough to force the cutter's gunners to adjust how far they led her.

The belly of the cargo ship passed overhead, bringing an end to the cutter's fire. Shadle slowed to match the ship's speed before rolling the Nova end over end. Momentum continued to carry the fighter along with the freighter. Checking her damage board she found no serious problems. Shields were finally peaking out of red so she redirected recharge power to weapons and armed her laser cannons.

Shadle had the nagging urge to look over her tactical screen. Both target craft were steady on the display. Three threats remained, all of them in the immediate vicinity of Lead and two. Three was all by himself several clicks out from the cutter. Yellow threats appeared ahead of the attacking Nova on a direct line for the cutter. So far the mission was running smoothly considering the trouble everyone had faced to this point.

"I'm under heavy fire!" Nyssa shouted out.

On impulse alone Shadle kicked up engine power to maximum and eased the Nova from under the cargo freighter. The situation was apparent as three came into view under a combined crossfire from two sides of the cutter. The bright pulses of energy ripped by the edges of the dodging fighter, tearing off the edges of the shields with each near miss. A missile streaked out from the belly of the ship on an intercept course with the young pilot.

"Three, break right and pull back towards the cutter."

At full throttle Bea was under the cutter in seconds. The missile launcher was clearly visible in the center of the hull. It glowed red from an eminent launch, encouraging an opportunity. The nova's targeting system locked onto the signature given off by the next launch and zeroed in. At less than two fighter lengths, she released a pair of quad bursts around the launch tube opening and pulled out of her approach. The subsequent explosion combined with the remainder of the first quad burst tore open the end of the tube and scattered hull fragments into space.

Shadle rolled over, keeping her belly to the cutter. The second quad burst tore into the damaged hull and ripped apart the missile system within. Multiple tertiary explosions erupted from the hull as the warhead storage gave into the fireball. A series of mild shock waves rocked the nova into a quarter roll. Shadle recovered

Chapter Ten

easily and pulled up and away from the cutter. For a brief moment the ship's gunners were stunned from the blast, but they too recovered with ease.

"Three, pull out and regroup."

Nyssa did not respond. Shadle rolled over and pulled up parallel with the cutter. Directly in front of her she saw a spinning hulk. Electrical pulses raced around the gutted Nova. A pair of wings spun wildly out of control away from the vaporized fighter.

"Four to lead. We've lost three."

"Continue attack, four. I've got my hands full here."

"Watch it, four. Aggressor has broken off and is heading your way."

"Copy, two."

Shadle turned in towards the cutter, avoiding an amber line cutting across her previous course. The gun turret on the starboard side was visible and firing. She switched fire control to dual burst and released two snap shots at the forward gun turret. The four shots blasted up metal around the turret, throwing the gunner into a moment of panic. Shadle turned aft and lined up with the extreme starboard engine. She shook off two direct hits to her forward shields, which took them down to ten percent. Quickly she switched back to quad burst and released two volleys before banking out. Both bursts struck dead on target, tearing the engine housing apart.

The cutter's hull integrity displayed at thirty percent and was dropping with every hit, but the shields were beginning to come back on line. Bea's missile threat sounded out and a target appeared at five clicks. If she timed it right she could utilize both problems. Bea cut in close to the hull, lighting up as much of the surface as possible. Solo cannon bursts bent up twisted, heated metal at each point of impact. She even managed a hit on the damaged gun turret, killing the gunner and knocking it offline.

Missile impact sounded and Bea pulled sharply away from the hull. Both missiles from the aggressor Bi-wing slammed into the hull before they could adjust course and track the Nova. The cutter's hull integrity dropped to three percent. Safety rather than duty took over and the cutter began evasive maneuvers off course. The ship accelerated to its maximum speed on a perpendicular line of flight away from the cargo freighter.

"The cutter's getting away, lead."

"Let it go and get the cargo freighter before it reaches it's jump point."

"Copy, lead."

The Bi-wing was still five clicks out, giving Shadle two passes on the freighter before she would have to engage the fighter. She leveled out with the engines of the cargo freighter and opened up with single bursts. Lasers crossed on the center of three main engines, splashing across the ship's minimal shielding and causing minor collateral damage to the engine. She passed under the hull, scoring a few more hits as she passed.

Shadle dropped power to propulsion and rolled the nose back. She increased to full throttle slamming the fighter to a stop before accelerating back towards the cargo ship. The nova poured on the laser bursts across the forward shields. She hit the freighter as hard as she could during the pass drawing the entire shield integrity down to ten percent. As she passed over the top her job was done. She need only assist in finishing off the Bi-wings.

Missile warning sounded. Bea ran a brief systems check. Shields were at maximum, cannons at full charge, propulsion at maximum. She decided that she could take a direct hit and kept a level flight on a head to head encounter. What she did not realize was that the bi-wing had fired a pair of missiles and a second salvo was already on the way.

Forward shields dropped to thirty percent then failed after the second missile grazed off her right wing. Bea pulled out and away from the level plane. She glanced out the side of her canopy and was shocked to find both cannons and a majority of the right wing gone. In its place she trailed a crackling blue stream of particles and frayed control cables. In her immediate danger with failed shields and a weakened craft, she had no clue that the other two missiles had tracked behind her.

Shadle could no longer see. She no longer shook from violent maneuvers. She was at peace with her surroundings, but not with herself. The last confrontation had already begun to replay itself over and over in her mind. She should never have taken her situation so lightly. When faced with a fighter with dual missile pods, she should have always assumed that there were two threats and not just one.

Light cracked in around the edges of the canopy then it automatically lifted up. Bright overhead lights filtered in from the ceiling of the simulator room. Three technicians reached in to help Shadle up and she graciously accepted. She did not feel like moving, given her feelings about her performance, but she would not pass up someone offering her help. Unlike actual fighters, one had to climb up to get out instead of climbing down.

Nyssa was sitting against the edge of his simulator, shaking his head. The simulation room had two rows of cockpit simulators, with eight units on either side. All but three were silent. Canopies were open and pilots sat along the edges, each with the same expression. None of them could believe what had happened. In less than three minutes all but three of them had been killed, both by the computer and by each other.

Shadle pushed off her simulator and walked towards Captain Stead. "So who's leading the aggressors?"

Stead grinned as he leaned against his simulator then turned to watch the last three active simulators pitch and roll on their supports. "Don't know. I was already in-flight when the aggressor team arrived."

"Who else survived?"

"Ogden, so far. He kept close to Barger's wing and followed his lead. He played it smart and it's paying off. Barger grabbed the lead aggressor's attention after you were killed, freeing up Ogden to finish off the cargo freighter. He put three missiles into the hull and one more into an emergency shuttle as it tried to escape."

Chapter Ten

"But I thought the objective was to pacify the cutter then let an assault team capture the ship."

"Originally it was but your last pass turned up the trap. There were two fighters sitting inside the cargo bay waiting for your numbers to dwindle. We were about to jump Barger and Ogden when he passed and blew us out of the fight." He lit up his charming smile, forcing his embarrassment to subside. "I never had a chance."

"How did my last pass uncover the trap?"

"Your weapons lock interrogated the freighter's operations computer. Acting on impulse I guess, Ogden slaved your target lock for his warheads. He shouted out something about a trap, then broke Barger's wing to go in for the kill. I tell you, Narra, this kid is one hell of a pilot. I don't know what kind of militia his home world had, but it gave him incredible instincts."

At the far end of the simulator room were the mission status screens. There was one screen for every simulator showing views from the cockpits and an additional screen displayed a tactical view of the battle. Three targets remained on the screen, one red and two green. The rookie pilot was keeping close to Barger's wing, working as his opposite. Every move that the lead aggressor made was reacted to in two directions from the remainder of the assault team.

The fight continued for another three minutes before the screen fell blank and all three simulators settled back into the resting positions. The canopies cracked on all three mock fighters and the exhausted pilots were helped out.

"So who won?" A rookie pilot shouted out from the back of the room.

Patron, who had been sitting close to the monitors stood up and walked to a small platform. From there he addressed the gathering crowd of pilots and crew. "The attacking squadron completed its mission by discovering the trap and destroying the freighter."

"No, who won the dog fight?"

Barger stepped away from his simulator and turned to the young woman. "No one did. We called a draw after it became apparent that neither side was going to get the final kill. Missiles had been spent and the fighters were at maximum power. A fight such as this could last hours, and unfortunately we do not have that kind of time."

"Not if I could have had you one on one, Wes." Guile walked up to him covered in perspiration. He allowed a few gasps at his sight to pass. "Next time I'll polish off your rookies so I can have you all to myself."

"Rookies!" Shadle snapped.

Bea, who had piloted another of the aggressor bi-wings stepped up behind her and gripped her shoulder.

Barger smirked. "It's nice to see the man I replaced has a sense of humor. Too bad you have to be paid to have one."

Guile turned to Bea. "You never told me this would be a gathering of Devil's alumni." He caught Stead's gaze for the first time and frowned.

Bea shrugged. "I thought you'd be the last. I didn't know about Barger."

"Then you should have at least told me about Haggin. He's reason enough for me to dump this contract." Guile grumbled and pushed his way through the group.

Stead gave Bea a look of disgust. She in turn spun on her heel and chased after him.

"What's going on here?" Shadle blurted out.

"A reunion," Barger said. "Of Devil's elite. A combination of two generations of the best pilots the Empire turned out." He closed on Stead. "Why was I not told that Jared Guile and Bea were a part of this ragtag team?"

"The same reason he was not told about you and I. We needed to get you here. We were prepared to deal with the consequences afterwards."

Barger looked past him and caught a glimpse of Guile and Bea as they walked out. "Well you certainly do have consequences." He grinned as he pushed past him. "At least you can be reassured that I have no where else to go. Jared may be another story."

Shadle leaned against her toes with a need to chase after Barger the way Bea had with Guile. She stopped herself, earning a glare from him as he passed. She instead watched him walk out of the bay with a sulk to his step. "What happened?" She finally asked.

"You were witness to two of the greatest assets we have," Stead answered from behind her. "Aside from me."

Shadle turned on a toe and came face to face with him. "And you brought them here under false pretenses?"

"Not at all. They were both told exactly what their role would be with us. I simply left out a few details."

Nyssa came up behind him and patted him on the back. "A pretty important detail, sir. I wouldn't consider them as assets if they hate each other."

"Trust me," Stead said to him while looking at Shadle. "They hate me far more than they hate each other."

Shadle shook her head in disgust.

Chapter Eleven

Captain Gulf Merrill sat impatiently in the private briefing room of Admiral Fallon. He, Captain S'Lendo, and the brawny ground forces commander, Colonel Bauman Wells, awaited the Admiral's return from his ready room. At the moment he was on a long-range briefing with the fleet admiral. Such an impersonal briefing usually meant one of two things. Either the admiral was receiving specific orders regarding deployment or urgent news about the Empire.

With a growing resistance to the Alcon within the galactic council, news about the Empire was never good. On the other hand, a sudden need for fleet redeployment usually meant serious trouble. It was plain to see that neither situation was desirable. Given the current situation of the Badlands task force, any further stain to the fleet could be catastrophic.

Fallon walked through the doors at the back of the room and rounded his desk. He sat down, shielding any emotion with a calm aura about him. "Gentlemen."

"Sir," Captain Merrill said. "I trust the admiral is well."

"The admiral is fine. What I need to know now is what your mission turned up, if anything at all."

"Nothing," Merrill said bluntly. "I paid a visit to three royal houses and each of them was able to produce adequate records of all their financial transactions. I was also able to visually account for all their sons and daughters. That does not mean they are not involved with the Alliance and further investigation would be prudent." Merrill grinned. He had given the textbook answer. Now he waited for the response he usually received from Fallon.

"And you applied the appropriate pressure?"

He nodded. "Adequate would be a better word. I restocked my ship with their finest ales and Devil disabled any orbital defenses they had. Before I left I deposited units in each capitol city on the promise that there would be more troops on the way if intelligence turned up anything. I also made sure to download new information about garrisons being reassigned to their sector before I left. All and all I would say that my visit left a memorable impression."

"How contained of you," Fallon said.

"They are the ruling families after all, Admiral." Merrill grinned. "I would hate to upset them."

"Very good. Monitor your units regularly and send more if you have to." He looked directly at S'Lendo. "Captain, have our scouts reported in yet?"

"They have found nothing," S'Lendo responded. "But they admit that their efforts have been hampered by local governments. We have to wait for clearance from the provincial council before we can enter two of the systems."

Colonel Wells rolled his eyes. "We bust our guts to claim these systems then politicians go and place independent governors to run them. Then what happens? The governors set up independent states with full approval of the senate. How can the Emperor allow the galactic council to take away what they gave us?"

"That will no longer be a problem for us."

"What are you saying?" Captain S'Lendo asked.

"By a slim margin the galactic congress has disbanded the council and martial law has been implemented. The Emperor has assigned his Regents to each quadrant and local governors will assume total control over their sectors. As of now our navy is in direct control of all system enforcement. Vice Admiral Ishat has given all cruiser captains and group admirals the authority to remove any and all resistance when we enter a system. We no longer need to worry about public opinion of our activities."

The eyes of the three officers brightened. "How long before all the star systems are informed of this?" Merrill asked.

"If they aren't now they will be when we arrive. The admiral informed me that the badland systems would be the last to be informed that we have full access to their worlds. If we want to catch a fresh trail on Guile and the Alliance then we have to move now. If all goes well he won't know we are after them until we sweep out the rug."

"Orders, sir?" S'Lendo asked.

"Captain Merrill, I want you to take the Valiant and search the asteroid fields outside the Bromos cluster."

"But you were just in the Bromos system."

"The system, yes, but not the asteroid field. At the time it seemed pointless because he would have had no place to run if we had pinned him in there. What I'm looking for this time is if he made contact with anyone as he passed the field. It has been known that many pirate groups operate out of dense fields."

"I am well versed in pirate tactics, sir," he growled.

"Good, then you won't be caught off guard if you are jumped."

"A pirate group wouldn't be so bold to jump a star cruiser," Colonel Wells said.

"It's not the pirates I'm worried about. It's the Alliance. It would be a foolhardy attempt to undermine the Empire by attacking such a large target, but lately they've grown a backbone, and I'm not taking any chances with the only two battle groups I have."

Chapter Eleven

"Understood, sir. Am I excused?"

Fallon nodded. "Depart as soon as you are ready. For the time being I am reassigning Devil squadron to my ship. I do not wish to endanger them should a trap arise. As soon as you have completed your task I am sending them back to you."

Merrill stood and gave him a short bow before leaving. Outside the briefing room awaited his senior staff. He raised a hand to halt the onslaught of questions they must have had. He wanted no part of it. At least until he could reach the safety of his own ship and escape the eyes and ears of the Admiral.

Wells waited for him to leave before commenting. "He rushes into things too easily. It could get him into trouble."

"I know, but I like his tenacity. It might come in handy if he keeps fighting even after he knows he's beat. It's a trait many other captains lack."

"You should give me his ship."

Fallon surprised him with a bellow of a laugh. "Hardly a chance of that happening, Colonel. You'll make a superb ground forces general, but you wouldn't last a month in naval command. We are an entirely different beast."

"Is that why you choose to let me decide troop movements?"

"Colonel, I wouldn't have it any other way. What I will decide though is where to use your men. At the moment they are to remain idle, but I will need them ready shortly. I'm short handed as it is so you will be bearing the brunt of security needs when any shuttle leaves this ship."

"Understood sir."

"Dismissed."

The Colonel stood and saluted. He received a stiff, sideways salute in return then he turned on one heel and marched out of the room.

"Where did you find him?" S'Lendo asked.

"On Ramsey's ship. That fool had him running ships security. He had no idea what kind of officer was serving under him."

"And you did?"

"Damn right. Bauman had been a corporal when I was on the Blackhawk. He showed enough promise that he was promoted twice while I was there."

"My next question is why bring him here. Shouldn't he be with the second fleet? They've seen more ground action than we will in a life time."

"Eventually they'll dig in somewhere and we'll have to drag them out. Wells is perfect for the task." Fallon shrugged. "Call it intuition. Something tells me that the Sutherlins are not going to simply roll over and play dead when we track them down. By all rights this rebellion should have died during our first encounter, but it grew stronger. I'd hate to think what would happen if this trend continued."

"Do you think with the council disbanded the Alliance will gain more open support?"

"Not if we quell it before the last of the government breaks down." Fallon folded his hands in his lap and sighed. "Or at least contain their activities to the Badlands.

Not many people seem to care what goes on out here. No, Captain, if anything the liquidation of the council just puts more pressure on them. If the council had gained interest in the Sutherlin's activities and had grown a conscience, they could have publicly protested and gained the Alliance a flood of support. The emperor must have foreseen such a problem and inserted supporters into the congress. I see no other way for a vote in favor of disbanding." I would have done the same thing.

S'Lendo moaned, alluding to the overwhelming amount of information Fallon had deposited upon him. "Are there any specific orders for me, sir?"

"None that I can think of now, captain. I just need a hundred percent out of you if we are to be successful. There's no room for almost on this mission. Admiral Ishat stressed the importance of this one above any other order we've received. He says the pressure is coming directly from the Emperor."

"Any reason why?"

"In his own paranoid way he told me that at this point I know more than he does, which is as much a load of Calaf beast dung as I've heard in some time. The day I know more than he does I'll be grand admiral and he'll serve me."

It was a remark that drew a chuckle from both of them; only for Fallon, he meant it.

Guile leisurely crossed the tarmac to his waiting fighter. He held his companion close to his chest, letting it chirp to him its anger at their early departure. Even the miniature sentient beings desired the time to rest and soak in new data. Overheated circuit panels and neural pathways deserved time off as much as their humanoid user did.

"Keep it down, backer," he scolded the device.

"He has a point, you know!"

Guile stopped and turned. Bea had shadowed him for a good twenty paces before saying something. The look of dismay over his leaving was apparent and unwarranted. He could find no reason for her to be upset. "Leave me alone."

Bea caught up to him in three steps. She stopped, panting heavily. "Why didn't you come to dinner last night?"

"Why should I? It was made perfectly clear that I am a contract hire and not a physical part of the Alliance. That dinner last night was for pilots of Ghost and their crews." He waved his hand at the lone Nova in the center of the tarmac. "I don't see silver stripes, do you?"

"Ghost hasn't been officially assembled, Jared. Only a few of us have the silver stripes. That's the reason Wes is here and one of the reasons you are here."

He shook his head. He did not want to debate Barger's presence or the fact that he had not been given even an honorary rank. He had overheard a few grounds crew calling Barger by his Imperial rank of Lieutenant. "It doesn't matter," he eventually conceded. "I have a job to do and not much time to do it in."

"Your job is here. Why can't you make the connections and send someone else to pick up the supplies?"

Chapter Eleven

Guile closed his eyes. "That's impossible, Bea. My contacts would eat your people alive. Besides, I've spent years building these contacts and I'm not about to ruin my reputation because you don't want me to leave."

Bea took a step back. "Who said I didn't want you to leave? None of us want you too. You're an important part of the Alliance now."

"I'm the gopher," he snapped "You pay me to supply and feed your armies. If I were a true part of the Alliance I would be dusting Bi-wings and not kissing up to scum traders. I would also be flying for the good of the galaxy and not being paid to help."

"Then why don't you volunteer? Why don't you abandon your self- absorbing lifestyle and fight for the common good."

"I'm not a volunteer. I'm not even a go to guy. I'm the guy you fall back on when you have nowhere else to go. If you need someone killed or a few thousand warheads you call me. If you need to assault a cruiser you send me home." He felt a bit hypocritical after complaining about not being a part of the action. The confused look she returned confirmed his mistake.

"You were a volunteer at one time," Bea insisted.

"Don't remind me." Guile turned on his left heel and stormed off towards his fighter. "That was the first and last mistake I'll ever make."

"You must be perfect, Jared," she called out behind him. "Because I seem to keep making the same mistake with you."

Guile stopped. He gripped the first rung of the extended ladder to the nova. That hurt more than he thought it would.

"I see you still consider my opinion to be important."

More than you'll know. He squinted hard then continued up the ladder.

"Don't go away mad, Jared. At least give me a smile or something."

Guile swung one leg into the cockpit and dropped his companion into the seat. He folded his arms at his waist. "I'm not mad, Bea. At best I'm upset that you couldn't tell me the truth. You should have told me that this was a gathering of Imperial rejects. I could have stomached a cruiser full of Imperial gunners, but even the majority of combat command is Alcon."

"You wouldn't have come if I did." She took a few steps so that she was under him. "It was more important to get you here than it was to tell you everything you wanted to know. Besides, you only see their past. What you fail to notice are the kids that need you here."

"So, that sweet smile that I fell in love with years ago has been replaced with a look of deception."

Bea gave him a cold stare that paled to the frost of her words. "Much like yours."

"I have a reason to be bitter. Everything I believed in died with Devil squadron. I trusted the Empire and what it was doing. I made an oath to the Emperor saying that I would be his protector and his rage. He promised me that his purpose was for the good of the galaxy and I believed him."

"We all took the oath and we all believed his words. Now we know the truth and we are fighting to correct our mistakes. What more do you want me to say?" Bea threw up her arms and looked around the vast underground base. "Everything we're doing here is to right those wrongs. Everything we stand for holds true to the oath we took in the academy. Only now we have just leaders and a better cause."

Guile pointed an accusing finger at her. "Your Patron has more up his cloak than what's good for the galaxy. I hope your Sovereign knows that."

"We all know that. He cannot hide his feelings from any of us. His anger runs deeper than anyone in the Alliance because he was working with the emperor when Sutherlin was destroyed. On trust alone he stood before the galactic council with countless other worlds and was lied to about how the Alcon Empire was the champion of the council and the rights of everyone in the galaxy. He was the perfect politician and he is an even better dictator."

"How would you react if someone told you he was your friend right before he shot you in the chest?"

"About how I feel now," Guile solemnly answered.

Bea placed her hands on each hip. "That was uncalled for. I don't think I deserved that. I don't think even Haggin deserves that. He's risked a lot allowing you to come here. It was on his honor alone that Patron agreed to it and on his head that the Sovereign approved the use of a mercenary. She neither wanted nor cared to fight the kind of fight you were hired for. It was against her better judgment that she trusted him. He knew the consequences should you turn on us and he will pay the price."

"I would never have turned on you. Haggin is just an annoyance. What I want to know is if you trust me enough to believe that I'll be back."

"That's open ended. You have to trust me, too."

"That goes without saying."

"I don't think it should," she snapped. "Just for once I'd like you to say that you trust me with your life. I know we took an oath to protect each other, but that was an open oath made for the benefit of the entire fighter corps. This is now," she said with a stabbing finger towards the ground. "You owe me more than and open ended profession of trust. You owe me your life, your love, and an explanation for deserting us."

Guile folded his arms. "So that's what this is about. You want to know why I left. The real reason and not just the published one. You wouldn't believe it if it came from me."

"Try me."

"I don't have time for this."

"Dammit, Jared!" She growled in her harshest voice. "I haven't seen you in a long time and now I'm faced with the possibility that I'll never see you again once you fulfilled your obligation to the Alliance. You can at least tell me why."

"No."

"Then tell me you trust me."

Chapter Eleven

"No, and this conversation is over. Unless you want me to miss my contact." Without another word he slipped into the cockpit and sealed the canopy.

Bea backed away with her arms folded around her in a self-comforting squeeze. Then at least tell me you love me.

Chapter Twelve

Admiral Fallon laughed out loud, drawing the attention of the command level's occupants. He was reading a report from the Valiant on their patrol of an outlying Alcon sector. Their navigation computer had faltered on an approach vector to an asteroid field and the ship had suffered heavy impact damage. It always amused him when incidents like this happened. He had decided long ago that when man relied too heavily on computers, disaster was bound to follow --which was why he had his officers verify all coordinates and computer commands before executing them. It cost valuable time in the long run, but it saved lives and hardware.

"Admiral?" S'Lendo asked.

Fallon closed the report and relaxed. "Nothing Captain. Just taking in the day's reports from our groups. It appears Captain Merrill forgot a few details before his last jump. One of these days Gulf is liable to run his ship into a moon."

"You say it as if it were amusing."

"It's very amusing, Forn. You should take note that computers can be in error as well, but if we work in conjunction with them then all miscalculations should be ruled out."

"I'll remember that."

"Con, Comms. Message for you from Minister Gesh."

Fallon reached over and activated the speaker. "Minister," he said in his most chipper voice. "What can I do for you?"

"You can get me off this horrible planet for starters, Admiral." Shouting in the background caused a brief moment of static then Gesh returned. "I don't know why you found it necessary to leave me here with your detachment."

"But Minister, you said you could convince your traders to help us if you were there in person."

"I did convince them. Now I would like to return to the ship. I've spent over a week hopping from place to awful place and haven't had a decent drink in that time. If I don't get out of here soon I'll go insane."

"Now we wouldn't want that, now would we," he beamed. "If you transmit what you have, I will go over it immediately then I will send a ship to have you picked up."

"Why don't you send the ship now?" sniveled Gesh. "I can present my findings to you in person?"

"Oh come now, Minister. You wouldn't want to come all this way only to have me send you back if you've missed something. I don't want to waste your time like that."

Gesh huffed something in Caderan before returning to the speaker. "No, Admiral, I wouldn't want that at all. I will transmit right now."

"Stay online, Minister."

"Of course," he snapped.

Fallon gave his first officer a sideways glance, signaling him to go below. S'Lendo nodded, then slid across the bridge. The captain knew of his simple torturing pleasures and chose plausible deniability should Fallon ever be called upon for the way he treated dignitaries.

"Con, Comms. Captain Merrill has a follow up on his last report."

"Hold on, Minister." Fallon switched lines. "Captain."

"My apologies, sir, but I have good news from my apparent misfortune."

Fallon bit his lip before he lashed out at his officer. Despite his amusement with Merrill's lack of plotting ability he was not about to let the slip up go by. "What good news can come from damage to your ship?"

"During repairs I stayed within proximity of the asteroid field. Per standard procedure I released three patrols, one of which focused on sensor sweeps of the field. Apparently there was an Alliance field outpost within the asteroid field. They panicked after the patrol scanned a larger asteroid and they made a run for a jump point."

Though he gave no real reason why he sent Merrill into the system, Fallon had an idea what he was looking for. This pleased him immensely that one of Gesh's more untrustworthy sources was accurate. "How did you handle them?"

"We managed to destroy three of the five transports attempting to flee."

"You destroyed them? You didn't make a capture?"

"I'm sorry, sir, but we were well out of range of the Valiant's photon guns. The best we could do was attempt to halt their escape."

Fallon shut his eyes. He wanted an interrogation of an Alliance officer so bad that he could taste the blood on his lips. No species, save one, had a resistance to the tortures that he was capable of. He had to concede the minor defeat though and accept what little could be gained from the discovery alone. "Very well. Have you begun a search of the abandoned outpost?"

"It has been completed. We downloaded all information that was not drained before the Alliance ships could escape. As usual, all data concerning the whereabouts of the scattered Sutherlin fleet were erased, but we did acquire plans that de-

Chapter Twelve

tailed the purchase of six new fighters from Riordan. We also recovered highly encrypted files, but it will be some time before we break the codes."

Too simple. Riordan would never openly sell fighters to the Alliance. "Transmit all the data you captured and rejoin me as soon as you complete repairs."

"Yes, sir."

S'Lendo walked up behind the Admiral's chair and dropped a data tape into his console. Fallon called up Gesh's report as he switched lines back to the Minister. As expected, the Caderan was panting from the high temperatures on the planet he was at. Caderans were not known for their ability to handle extreme temperatures, which was one of the reasons he had sent the hefty man there. A little suffering to command attention.

The majority of the report read as he had anticipated. No one had seen Guile in years and those that did had no clue as to where he was. Traders had reported that a limited amount of Nova parts had been delivered and picked up on the planet by unnamed parties, so Fallon knew the pirate had been there. He was in no position to find out when though. No smuggler in his or her right mind would supply Alcon officers with that kind of information.

One part of the transmission did confirm an earlier report on Guile. The Nova that he possessed had been acquired as trade for the assassination of an ex-Riordan executive who had threatened to sell secrets to a competitor. This ruled out possible Alcon service during his youth or even current service. Though it would make finding him that much easier, Fallon had no desire to learn of such treason from an active or ex-officer.

"Are you still there, Minister?"

"Where else would I be, Admiral?"

"Is there anything you might be leaving out from this report? Maybe Guile worked as a legitimate trader for a while."

"If he did work as a trader it was not legitimate. I have run this man's name through every crew file I have on record, and the closest I've found is a man by the name of Lest Guile who worked briefly on a Horde ship, but he died on the way station."

Fallon shot a rushed look to his first officer who quickly turned to his console. "How long did this Lest work on the freighter?"

"A few months."

You're blind, Gesh. He had a lead right in front of him and could not see it. "You're coming back. I'll have a ship there in two days."

"Thank you, Admiral. That's all I wanted to hear. You really should try…"

Fallon cut him off and opened the bridge line. His voice echoed over both decks. "Comm, Con. Request Horde for crew manifest for all the freighters that was docked at the way station." He terminated the announcement and focused in on S'Lendo. "As soon as it comes in begin a search on Lest Guile as far back as it goes. I would wager my command that his past is only as long as his service on that ship."

"Con, Comms. Message coming in from the Palace. The Quadrant Regent wishes to speak with you personally."

An un-ordinary day at best. First, Minister Gesh stumbles across a possibly sound lead, one that he misses as being important. Now the Regent wishes to speak with him away from normal channels. Neither had any real appeal except for curiosity, though Fallon would hardly pass up on a chance to speak with the quadrant's overlord. Only regional Noblemen and higher-ranking admirals were allowed such an honor.

Fallon stood and turned towards the back of the bridge. He heard S'Lendo order communications to forward the transmission to his ready room. The large double doors parted ahead of him, revealing a long corridor. To either side of him were two sets of doors. Each door opened to the ship's personnel lifts. Each lift could carry someone from one end of the ship to the other in seconds, a feat matched only by the speed of a passing fighter.

Beyond the lifts to the right, Fallon came across his ready room. Inside the short but wide room were several smaller tables and a single desk encircling a large viewing screen. The screen displayed an image of space so clear that it felt as though he were looking out an actual viewing port. In reality though, his ready room rested behind three bulkheads that could repel the strongest blast from a war ship.

Fallon walked around his desk and dropped into the massive, black chair. He spun around so that he could face the viewing screen, then he sat up at attention. Though on his end the image was two-dimensional, his projection would be in three. For the Regent he chose his best posture. "Open," he said in a clear voice.

The view of space crackled then collapsed in on itself, replaced with a head view of a clocked figure. The Regent sat motionless in front of a massive window that overlooked the capital city. Fallon could make out a flash of lighting in the background, which only added to the Regent's awesome presence. He had never actually spoken with her or the Emperor himself and he had only been within eyesight once when he graduated from the Navy academy.

Maybe there is something to speaking with the Regent after all. "Madam Regent. It is an honor that I speak with you."

The Regent's words rolled from under her cloaked face like a fog. The temperature she required to remain comfortable was just above freezing to most species. "Your actions have drawn my attention on more than one occasion. This is no exception."

"You honor me with the compliment, madam Regent. How my I serve you?"

"You may bring me the core of the alliance so that I may have the pleasure of terminating its leader personally."

Fallon's eyes narrowed. "Pardon my saying so, but it was my understanding that my current mission was to find the mercenary Jared Guile. The Sutherlin Alliance was to be a bonus should I come across them."

"Jared Guile will lead you to your ultimate goal before your mission is complete. This mercenary can serve you better as a tool than as an enemy. You will continue

Chapter Twelve

your search for him. In the meantime you will take every advantage you receive to press our resolve in the outer systems. You will have all the resources required to complete this task. Once completed you will no longer need to find ways to complete your missions. They will present themselves as gifts to you. Do not underestimate your abilities."

"Might I inquire as to how you have followed me so closely these past few weeks? We are well over a week's travel from the capital."

"You are a servant of the Empire as I am a servant of the Emperor. As a servant your actions do not go unnoticed by my eyes or by his. Complete your task at hand and bring the Empire closer to its true destiny. You will find the rewards far outweigh the problems you encounter along the way."

"If I may, Madam Regent. I am not a first line officer and I don't have the pull my colleagues have within the chain of command. Just recently one of my ships encountered a small pocket of rebels and did not have the capability to contain them as they escaped. My men were forced to destroy the Alliance cell rather than capture and interrogate them."

"Transmit your requirements and they will be met in good time. Success Admiral Fallon. Do not fail me."

Fallon shot a salute at the screen as the image of the Regent dissolved into the outside image. "Bridge," he said openly. "Captain Merrill."

The screen blinked out and reappeared with an image of Merrill. "Yes, Captain."

"Have you received word from Horde?"

"We have the manifest for the Horde freighter and access to crew files."

"Excellent. Set a course for Riordan corporate facilities and dispatch a transport to pick up Minister Gesh."

"Riordan, sir? Doesn't that sound like a false lead?"

"Yes it does, captain, but it's one I am prompted to follow up. If we cannot find what we need there, we will create something we need."

"As ordered."

The screen faded back to the outside view. Fallon relaxed into the comfortable seat and moaned. I have become the fist of the Regent for a reason that escapes me. What could be of so much value in Guile that it would draw her attention? What is it that she's not telling me?

Minister Gesh could not have imagined a hotter planet anywhere in the galaxy. The average temperature on any given day was around sixty-six degrees Celsius. Nighttime temperatures dropped to thirty-two and during the hottest days of the year the surface reached ninety-three degrees. It was no wonder either. The closer of the two suns in this binary star system filled the sky like a giant comforter. Nowhere else had he been where the nearest star was so large in the sky. If not for vast overhangs spanning the width of the streets more of the populace would die from overexposure and sunstroke.

The general mood of the citizens of Volana Three did not help the heated feeling of the air. The system was on the edge of the Badlands and trading here between Alcon worlds and independent worlds was heavy with no less than six cargo freighters in orbit at any given time. The star ports were always filled with landing barges and smaller transports and more species than Gesh could identify. He could not fathom the problems the local security force had maintaining order. At every corner he could identify at least one pirate looking for his next target of opportunity. To keep himself safe he made sure to have his issued pistol within everyone's sight at all times.

Along the old and decaying streets, Minister Gesh was to meet with another Caderan. A former associate of his, Administrator Newby now ran the trader center on Volana Three. The profits taken in by Cadera Prime had made him a rich and powerful man. Rumor had it that he even had strong connections with the planet's extensive black market. The fact that he was able to run such an operation without threats from the local pirate and smuggler factions suggested the rumors were true.

He stood alone in a city where it was not wise to do so. Unless you had the firepower to fend off a roving gang or the agility to escape one you were considered insane to stand on a street corner. Gesh felt this with every heartbeat. His other option was even worse. If he were seen with his Alcon escort he would be dead before he reached the star port. On top of that, Administrator Newby would never have agreed to meet with him.

Gesh was assured by the administrator that he would be safe while he waited. So far he had reason to believe Newby. Anyone that appeared as if they could be trouble simply walked by without so much as a glance in his direction. Normally this would surprise him seeing as how he was Caderan and his people were the richest species in the galaxy. In the past some of the more prominent Caderans had been kidnapped from places such as this for hefty ransoms.

The citizens in the street began to part as a stubby bald man and six taller Horde approached down the center. Administrator Newby, like other Caderans, looked similar to Gesh in height and general shape. He was half as wide as he was tall, and the thin, flowing clothes he wore made him seem even heavier. His companions were a sharp contrast though. Each was twice as tall and wore a thick layer of the moisture-soaked clothes that the race had to wear outside their natural environment.

The Horde fanned out with their rifles raised to their waists as Newby opened the conversation with a light smile. "Welcome to my little world, Minister Gesh. You honor my business with your presence."

"It's nice to be appreciated after spending so much time on an Alcon ship. I never realized how much of a hassle they can be until I've had the pleasure of spending time with Admiral Fallon. He is a much more persuasive man when seen in person."

"I understand, my friend. You are not the only one fortunate enough to have dealt with the Admiral. He called upon my services not long ago." Newby put his stubby arm over Gesh's shoulder and offered the way back towards his office. "Walk with

Chapter Twelve

me, Minister. I find the heat of this world more bearable when spent with trusted allies."

Gesh stayed with the friendly man as the two and their Horde guards walked down the street. "How has business been as of late?"

Newby shrugged. "I can't complain, but it has slowed down a bit. Profits are down five percent from last year at this time, but they're still higher than many of my associates. I'm even managing to make a better profit than my smuggling competitors."

It's no wonder since you take kickbacks from them. "That's good to hear. I'd hate to have to take any special interest in your operation. I prefer to let my Administrators handle their own affairs."

"Your support is appreciated. I'll admit that it took me a few years to establish myself here after you removed my predecessor, but I've done my best to secure my position."

"You do not have to worry about your position, administrator." If I pulled you out because of your illegal operations it would mean my political death.

Newby turned Gesh towards a large, elaborate building that stood out among its decaying surroundings. The mostly transparent structure had no doors, only a pair of lightly armored guards at the wide opening. Inside, the slightly tinted walls allowed a gray shade to befall its occupants. Surprisingly, the slight shade provided the building with much cooler air than the outside. Gesh could not find any air vents that would pump out enough cold air to keep the temperature as low as it was.

He was answered without verbally posing the question. "The glass that my administration building is made out of is from the Hass cluster and is organic. The material's natural surroundings are so hot that no plant life could survive, so this transparent mutation of natural plants has developed. It thrives off heat, drawing in all that radiates off it. What is left is cool air that flows through microscopic porous openings in the surface. The engineer who designed the building left out the main entrance doors so that some heat could filter in. Otherwise, the entire building would be an ice box."

"Ingenious."

"Luck," Newby said. "If I hadn't called for the inspection of a suspicious transport I never would have learned of this stuff. The installation of the panels is saving me a fortune in cooling costs each year."

Gesh followed Newby into an elevator. "Can you answer me one question? How do you keep the locals in line with no security doors and only two guards?"

"The locals are manageable and the area's trouble tends to be, well, containable for the most part."

The elevator stopped on the top floor. "How do you mean?"

Newby took a step out then stopped. He turned back with seriousness in his eyes. "There are sixteen major smuggling and pirate groups that have bases of operations on this planet. At last count there were over fifty small time operations that frequent this city. There is enough firepower poised on the streets that a civil war here would level the surface of this world. Out of all that possible chaos, the few of us that can barter with all sides and reason with those that have a mind to reason with are in a unique advantage in that we know enough about everyone that no one dares to tackle us."

Us? "I will accept that as an answer. Your accomplishments here will overshadow any undertakings that may be needed to ensure healthy trade."

Newby grinned. "My office is down the hall."

The administrator's office was surrounded by the same organic glass that the large lobby had. In two places there were holes in the material to allow a healthy amount of heat in. There were positioned as such so that during the day the temperature remained the same. Newby's desk and the three chairs that were in front of it were also placed in a way that the sun never illuminated them directly. Gesh found his surroundings comfortable and also intriguing. Although Newby had all the comfort he wanted he was not close enough to the window to overlook the city; a view that most administrators cherished.

Newby walked around his desk and dropped into his chair. "So, what is it that brings you to my operation? It can't be to ask me about my building or the underground. You can find out more about that just by reading the reports from my subordinates."

Gesh sat down in the center chair and sank into the thick padding. The seat eased his tired body and felt much better than the hard chairs on the Valiant. "I'm sorry to say that I have no other reason for being here than to ask you about a man that you may know through your dealings. Someone who could not survive without visiting this planet more than once in a while."

"And you couldn't ask me over a com channel?"

"I was afraid that my inquiries would fall on ears that they were not meant for. I also thought that you might respond better if I asked you in person rather than behind an Alcon header. I know that loathing for Imperial operations is not contained to myself."

"You guessed correctly." He tapped a button and a small monitor rose from the left corner or the desk. "So tell me who this man is and I will tell you all you wish to know."

"He's a mercenary that goes by the name Guile."

Newby froze before typing in the information. "Jared Guile?"

"You know him."

"Only by reputation." He began to type. "Rumor has it that the man single-handedly destroyed an Alcon staging station."

"Sometimes rumors tell more of the truth than one would care to believe."

Newby stopped typing and his screen began to scroll. "So this is about the station and not about any illegal trading."

"Our stiffest punishment for illegal trading could not possibly match what the Empire wants to do with him."

Chapter Twelve

The screen stopped scrolling. Newby looked over the displayed information and shook his head. "I have nothing on him, legal or illegal. Either he hasn't been here or he's kept his nose clean while dealing." His eyes narrowed as he looked back to Gesh. "How did you track him here? A man with a price would not be easy to find."

"A month ago we came across the name Lest Guile on the crew manifest of a Horde freighter that was docked at the time the station was destroyed. I used several connections on Horde and discovered that there was no one by the name up until a few months before the explosion. My sources reported that an unidentified system hacked into the Horde registry and created a person by that name a day before the freighter began its assigned runs."

"Last week Alcon code crackers broke the download code from the unknown system and identified it as a Companion."

"Companions are pilot computers."

"Not just any fighter computer, but a Companion with a Nova configuration. A Nova was recorded fleeing the station before it was destroyed. The markings matched that as those used by Jared Guile."

Newby shrugged. "So you pieced together that Guile broke onto the station using a Horde identification. That still doesn't answer my question. How did you trace him here?"

"The Horde freighter's only stop before its scheduled stop at the station was here. Thirty units of particle charges were delivered as well as an unidentified container and one crewmember. I believe Guile, under the name Lest Guile boarded the freighter from one of your star ports. I also believe that the unknown container, which was roughly the size of an Riordan Nova class fighter, was used to transport his craft."

Newby sighed then began to input a new request. Information immediately scrolled up. "You're right, Minister Gesh. Lest Guile did board that freighter from star port nine, docking bay three. The container that went with him was reported to be a new power core for the freighter and the captain did confirm the contents upon delivery."

"I have no doubt of that, but this does mean that Guile was here."

"Under an assumed identity and appearance."

"Agreed, but you should have a file on Guile's arrival. If not then you should have something on a Nova that arrived with markings used by Guile. Either way the answer I need is here."

Newby folded his arms across his wide belly. "I see you've become quite the investigator. Not at all the same man I knew years ago."

"You'd be surprised what an Admiral's insistence will do to you. All I want to do is find this man, give him to the Alcon, then return home."

A buzzer sounded next to the monitor and a sultry voice spoke. "There is a gentleman here to see you. He says he has an appointment."

Newby looked to a chronometer that was mounted above the door. He cursed to himself. "Tell him I will see him in just a moment. He can wait in the security lounge."

"You have business today?" Gesh asked.

"I'm sorry, Minister. I had forgotten. I made this appointment a week ago. If you would like I can set you up with my port controller and he can assist you further."

"I would." Gesh slowly eased his spacious body up. "He will have manifests for all incoming and outgoing flights?"

Newby nodded. "His office is two floors down, directly below mine."

"Then I take my leave of you. I will be back to meet with you when I have concluded my search."

Newby waited for Gesh to clear the room and for the door to shut before buzzing his assistant. "Wait until he's on his way down, then send in my appointment."

Through the thin door he could hear Gesh's heavy footsteps fade down the hall. The thick doors of the elevator parted, then closed shortly after. A second set of footsteps started up. They were harder rather than heavier, alluding to a thinner, more determined man.

The office door opened and the slightly covered face of Jared Guile appeared from the hall. Although his mouth and lower face was hidden he had a noticeable smile. From the one sided glass of the security office he had seen Gesh walk by and had a good idea why he was there. "Fortune always seems to surround me," he said.

"Sorry, Jared. I forgot about our appointment. Otherwise I would have had him come tomorrow."

Guile dropped off his feet and into the center chair. "That's not a problem, Newby. I'm used to close calls."

"Well, your close calls are getting even closer. The Empire has tracked your Horde identity back here. Hold on one second." Newby reached for his intercom. "Get me the port controller."

"One moment."

"He's looking for my arrival."

Newby nodded. "And he might find it if he knows where to look."

"Port controller."

Newby livened his voice as best he could. "It's Newby. Minister Gesh is coming down to see you and he's going to ask for some very touchy information. Give him the usual then let him take what he wants. Let me know everything after he leaves."

"The usual?"

Newby frowned. "He's the trade minister you idiot. Don't hide anything. Just don't offer anything and pray he isn't the bright man everyone says he is."

"Yes, sir."

He turned off the speaker. "I can't do anything more."

Chapter Twelve

"Understood, Newby, and I wouldn't ask for more. I'll be out of here in a hour or so anyway."

"Then you've completed you business?"

"In record time. I found everything I needed in one stop." He leaned back. "You'll get your usual ten percent and I'll even throw in a favor for having to deal with the minister."

"No need. The only thing I'm doing with him is keeping my mouth shut. It would take more than a favor from you to cover up your tracks."

Guile grinned. "They are a bit wide, aren't they?"

"You do more business with more people than anyone else that passes through those doors. You know more factions here than I do."

"And I'd be happy to update your field records if you ask."

Newby closed his eyes and shook his head. "No need. It's probably better that I don't know everything that goes on around here. I'm just interested in what can gain me profits."

"I've always been there for you, sir, and if things go the way I hope, you will continue to make money off of me for a long time."

Newby's eyes lightened up. "You've signed a new contract."

"More than just a contract, my friend. With the way this galaxy works I may be in business for years."

Newby saw the images of credits floating in front of him. "That's great to hear, Jared. I only hope that the Empire doesn't catch up with you first. They seem to be hot on tracking you down and I think it has more to do than with your little act of sabotage."

Guile shrugged. "What can I say? I was contracted to destroy a way station to draw Alcon attention away from a particular system. I had no way of knowing it was a staging base until after I was already committed to the task."

"But you completed the contract and drew their forces away from the system?"

"I believe so. Now they're after me."

"Don't worry about it. You fulfilled the contract and signed a new one. No one will dare turn you in if you keep business up."

"Even you?"

"Hey now. You were and still are one of my best associates. I wouldn't be where I am now without your services and purchases. If I turned you in now I'd find my head on a pike before I could draw my next breath." Newby turned slightly so that the city's horizon rose up behind his head. "When can I expect you to pick up your supplies?"

"Several transports with Terelian call signs and forged Caderan passes will arrive tomorrow morning and be gone within two hours. The transfer of funds will happen as soon as the transports make the jump safely out of the system. I've already arranged it with my new boss to filter an added ten percent your direction during the transaction."

Sutherlin Alliance

"May I ask who your new employer is?" Newby asked, tilting his head to one side. "I know it's a breach of ethics, but I'm curious as to who has the funds to keep you in business for more than a few months."

Guile stood and stretched his legs. "Believe me, Newby, I'd love to tell you. You could never guess who wanted the hardware I've ordered and what's in store, but unfortunately that's information that could jeopardize my contract and the future of an old friend."

"Understood." Newby stood. "I wouldn't dream of breaking your trust with your clients. I'm ashamed of myself for even asking."

"No you aren't," Guile teased. "You're a Caderan. How could you not be curious about other people's finances?"

Newby let the nudge slide. "Will you be back here for the pick-up or do I have to say goodbye now?"

Guile shook his head. "It's never goodbye, but the answer is no. I'm off to my next contact then I'll be going home for a while. I've been at it almost non-stop for the past seven months with very few breaks and I'm getting fairly tired."

"Well, enjoy the rest my friend."

"You can bet I will. Somehow I doubt I'll be getting any once my mini vacation is over. All I see are stars." He grinned, hinting to the credits his contract was to produce. "Big shiny bright ones."

Two and a half hours later a nova class star fighter lifted off from star port eight. At the same time an Imperial transport rose above star port nine, following the same exit vector as the fighter. Once out of the atmosphere both ships traveled less than fifteen clicks away from each other as they approached the exit jump point for the Volana star system. Both pilots knew of each other's presence, but neither knew of the occupants.

The nova commenced its jump to star flight just ahead of the transport, en route to a smuggler headquarters on the edge of the galaxy. The transport jumped seconds later on its long journey back to the Vengeance. For both parties, their days were at an end but the road ahead continued to stretch out further than the eye could see.

Chapter Thirteen

The canopy of the fighter simulator hissed open. A steamy glove grabbed for the side of the mock cockpit followed by a fatigued pilot. Thirteen hours of the most intense and complex combat had been fought across two star systems. In total, twenty star cruisers and a hundred fighters were involved from both the Alcon Empire and Sutherlin Alliance. Lives were lost by the hundreds and debris rained down on three inhabited worlds.

If this had been real it would have been devastating.

Working off a theory, Barger had programmed two full squadrons of drone fighters that acted off his direction. Each fought independently of human control in one-to-one combat, but worked together for an overall goal. The lack of creativity the drones possessed gave the randomly operated bi-wings a harsh edge. To compensate, the drones were instructed to suicide against the nearest Imperial cruiser should their chances of survivability drop below twenty-five percent.

The outcome was the same as it had been in each of the four times he had run the mission. The Alliance lost all the drones and had taken substantial loses before being forced to withdraw. On the other side of the battle line, the Empire had lost two cruisers and half its fighters in a painful victory. In reality it would have been a victory they would have accepted given the destruction to the Alliance.

Barger slipped off his sweat soaked helmet and dropped it into the cockpit. He was far from disappointed with his own performance, taking out twelve fighters, two transports, and a clipper before absorbing multiple cruiser hits in the end. The fight had been over for ten minutes yet he continued to inflict as much damage as he could. It finally came down to himself versus two cruisers with a predictable finish.

A look of dismay countered what should have been exhaustion. He had spent the better part of a day reprogramming the simulator to what he thought would give the Alliance an edge: one that the trainee pilots had yet to provide. After all was said and done, the Empire was still too strong. Even against lighter targets, if the battle lasted more than thirty minutes, reinforcements would arrive. From there, more ships would appear in forty-five minute increments. The calculations were based on the known fleet deployment.

Barger shook his head in utter disbelief. Even if his knowledge of fleet deployment were one hundred percent incorrect, the calculations would not matter very much. The Alcon simply had too many cruisers and attack craft spread throughout the galaxy. For the Alliance to engage any sizable force they would have to be fast and overpowering. Two traits that they currently lacked in entirety.

"You look exhausted," Shadle said as she climbed the ladder to the simulator. She flipped a face cloth from her shoulder and handed it to him.

Barger accepted then soaked up the perspiration from his face with it. "I am. The mission took a new twist this time."

"I saw," she said with a nod towards the status board. "The Alliance commander pulled back to the staging system for a quick regroup. I believe that's the first time I've ever witnessed a simulator conduct a mission in multiple systems."

"Call it bad programming on my part. I gave it too much of a brain."

"Don't kill yourself over it. A lot of lives could be saved from the realism. Give our kids a scare and they may learn something."

"You're never to old or experienced to learn," said Barger as he cleared away the last of the moisture. He gave into his body's demands and leaned against the closing canopy. "I've learned more than I bargained for this week."

"And that would be?" she prodded.

"That you don't stand a chance in a straight fight. Every option I could come up with was met head on and crushed. Until you can get some sizeable numbers and experienced crews you're better off playing hit and run."

"That brings me to a point, Wes. You are still referring to the Alliance as if you weren't a part of it, and I think spending all your free time in the simms is the problem. I don't even think you know who you're fighting with."

"I know enough to get me by. What I am more troubled with is who I'm fighting against and I know them extremely well. Why do you think I busted by butt reprogramming the simms? Why do you think I'm in here every free moment instead of getting to know the others?"

"I have no doubt about that, but you have to see things from my point of view. The Alliance is more than just a rebellion. It's a way of life. The Sutherlins wanted a return to better times and we're the result."

"And they're dead and you will be too unless I can convince you otherwise."

She parted her lips to argue the point when his comment struck the nerve it was suppose to. She paused, pondering her next response. He wanted it to be about the two of them, but it reverted to her first thought. "And keep me from the fighting? Keep me from making a mistake in defying the Empire?"

"No, no. You missed the point. I know you're a great pilot, but you aren't good enough to take on a squadron all by yourself."

"I would never do something so foolish."

Chapter Thirteen

"You may not want to, but you will. Whether by the sheer numbers the Empire will throw at you or by the inadequacies of your pilots."

"There you go again," she insisted. The frustration mounted across her face in tired streaks. "You have to stop excluding yourself from what's going on here. Yes you're our teacher, but your duties to the Alliance don't stop there. When it comes time to face the insurmountable force you predict we will have to face, I expect you to be leading the charge. I've seen your numbers even when you're by yourself. I don't think even Haggin could mount a better attack."

"It's his show," said a reserved Barger. "Patron would never give me a command. Even if he did I doubt Haggin would stand by and let me keep it. He hates me as much as he hates that mercenary."

"Believe me," she snickered. "You are low on that list of people he could do without. I even think he might be warming up to you."

"Not if I can help it. I idolized him at one time until I met him. He may be a different person in the cockpit but he's a real pain in person."

"Give him time. He's Patron's pet and go to guy."

"That worries me more than his attitude. If he is the designated leader of Ghost, then he should be down here during every run and participating. Instead he's been spending all his hours with Patron in the command center."

"That's because Haggin is our fighter corps commander, not just Ghost's. His place is with the command structure."

"His place is with his pilots!" Barked Barger. He closed his eyes and let the snap of his voice echo down the bay. He never meant for his temper to rise out of control. "I'm sorry," he said, opening his eyes. "I've just become so used to squadron commanders not having the sense to lead correctly that I'm starting to doubt the validity of a squadron at all."

"Then what if I were to push to have Bea placed in full command and given Ghost?"

Barger glowed. "Then I'd say you're delusional, but thinking correctly. She at least knows how the pilots have been trained and can use them to her advantage. Haggin might stage a fight based solely on his own skills and get everyone killed."

"I'll talk to Bea then and see if she likes the idea. Now," she said. "Shall we talk a bit or are you going to spend another day crammed into that cockpit?"

Barger pursed his lips. The idea of getting to know the pilots he was helping to train bothered him beyond words. He had trouble enough opening himself up to the rest of Devil squadron and they were more likely to return from a mission. These kids were a higher risk. He was unsure as to how he would react if he were to befriend them then lose them.

"Come on," she insisted. "If you lose them in combat or even in training you can take it out on me."

"I don't know about this." He hesitated then gave into the frown she produced. "Very well," he moaned. "Just don't expect that cute look of yours to work every time."

"Why not?" Shadle fluttered her eyebrows. "It seems to be working so far."

Once down the ladder she took up his arm in hers and held it close. She was wearing the standard white undershirt so her warm skin was closer than it had been before. His last close encounter with another woman had been with Devil squadron's crew chief, Loma Cole. That had gone as far as a night spent in each other's arms wearing the same type of underclothes as he was now.

This felt different. Cole was a good friend and knew what he needed. That particular evening he needed someone to spend time with him, but nothing more. He may have wanted to push things further along. He still wished that he had, but her advanced age had given her insight that he lacked. To this day he wondered what a hundred year half-life would be like. He would have to live and die at least twice to witness what she had.

Shadle brought something new to his life. He watched her from the day he met her, wanting desperately to learn what her driving force was. One minute she was the caring individual that walked by his side now. The next she could turn on him and bury him into the ground. He had lived through terrible times before the academy straightened him out, but she never had the same chance he had. Whatever had scared her as a child, the rejection offered up by the academy simply deepened them.

Had they met in his youth they could very well have been together today, somewhere on the rim of the galaxy, stealing what they needed. Living the smuggler's life if they could have raised the capital to buy a ship. He might have turned out more like Guile in that case. Hardened by bruises left by the Empire.

On the other hand, he could have restarted his life as she had. Taken in by the Alliance and given the chance that the Empire had given him. If he actually stopped and thought about it, he might have gone nuts.

No, this was the best way for things to turn out. Right here and right now. He would have to revel in meeting her at this turning point in his life, after years of thinking one way then suddenly being given a wider view of the galaxy. One that encompassed not only the controlled aspects of the Empire but of the terror that was brought with it.

Barger would be in for an even greater shock.

Shadle brought him to an empty storage bin where two other pilots sat. They were quiet with his entry and not altogether glad to see him. This was their getaway from the rigors of everyday life. Projected on one wall was an image of Sutherlin, which Nyssa turned back to observe. He knew of the young man's past and could only imagine his pain in his loss. Scio on the other hand found no apparent solace in the view other than that he seemed to enjoy the company he kept.

"Why did you bring him here?" Nyssa asked.

"I thought it was time."

Nyssa turned around, letting the heels of his boots prop him up off the floor. "Sorry, sir," He told Barger. "It's just that this is where we get away."

Chapter Thirteen

"I understand fully." He took Shadle's lead and sat down close to the slightly parted entrance. "I used to hide out in the storage hold of the Blackhawk when I first transferred there. Somehow the rec room just didn't offer the privacy I needed."

Barger gritted his teeth and looked to Shadle for direction. When she offered none he took his own initiative and leaned a tad towards Scio. "So. I read your file. It must have been tough flying alongside Imperial pilots in your own militia."

Scio perked up. Many of the young pilots had refused to delve into his past service given that it gave him an edge over them. "It took some getting used to. When I first joined it was an all-local team under Imperial governorship. Gradually they replaced half of us with Alcon pilots. As I understand it the entire militia was transferred to ground duty after I left."

"If you don't mind my saying this, the experience had prepared me for working with a captured Imperial pilot such as yourself."

"Reformed," Barger corrected him. "But it is all right to say so."

Scio reached over and patted Nyssa on the shoulder. "For my friend here it seems to be a bit harder."

"Because of Sutherlin," Barger assumed.

Nyssa grimaced. "Because I did not know if you were the typical Imperial officer or just another pawn." He turned on his knee. "Sutherlin was the result of pawns acting out strict orders passed down from the Emperor. Though I loathe the pawns for carrying out the orders, it is the officer giving them their directive that I wish to tear apart with my bare hands."

Barger dropped back off his knees and leaned against the side of the container. "Sutherlin meant that much to you?"

"Wouldn't you feel the same way if they took away your home?"

"I couldn't say one way or the other. I was taken from my home and left to fend for myself at an early age."

Nyssa was stumped. He was not expecting that answer. He shook it off with a blink of his eyes. "Yes, Sutherlin meant a lot to me, but that was no longer my home. Had the situation not changed as it did I would still be living on Perditia and working for Realm representatives and planetary senators. The Emperor took that away too. My only other choice would be to serve the quadrant Regent."

"Then you knew about the collapse of the galactic council that long ago."

"Patron saw the breakdown years ago. Even before Sutherlin was destroyed, he knew the council and the entire congress would fall. It had already been over forty years since the council handed the Galactic Defense Fleet over to the Emperor in order to keep the peace that they could no longer manage. The Emperor had jurisdiction over fifteen former Realms when Sutherlin made the decision to mount a secret rebellion. As is the case in most rebellions though, the fleet was betrayed by a handful of its own. The traitors were rewarded with positions in the Imperial government and armed forces, and Sutherlin was marked for destruction. Publicly, Emperor Alcon grieved for the loss of Senator Paltin's home world while privately he reveled in it."

"Alcon and his grandfather used to be friends, or so Patron told me. Alcon could very well have been using him to gain power in the senate. When Patron assumed his grandfather's seat in the Senate, Alcon had the support of three Realms, giving him the clout he needed to take a place in the ruling council. He merged the Realms into one under his name and began construction on what would be the second and third fleets of his empire."

"Believe it or not the Sutherlin Alliance was not the first organized rebellion against the obvious rise in power of the senator. Alcon used the small uprising to his advantage and blew it out of proportion with altered reports. The council panicked at what they thought to be a growing discontent with their method of rule so they authorized Alcon to consolidate four more Realms and form the Fifth Galactic Empire. With the two that had been built in secrecy he now had three full fleets at his disposal."

"That's not the way academy history texts have it. Galactic records doesn't even come close to that."

"You don't have to believe me or even Patron to trust my words. Just ask the three senators and one councilwoman who were killed a year ago when they refused Imperial occupation of their Realm. Two task forces were sent within an hour. That Realm is now part of the Alcon Empire. Only three holdouts remain and we expect one of them to fall within the month."

"That's about the only thing that coincides with the last report I read. The emperor has mounted a sizable force to deal with what he calls a serious threat to the security of the galaxy."

"Don't mock him," said Nyssa in reference to his harsh tone of voice. "He truly believes what he says and does and if his methods leaned more towards the ways of the third empire he would be considered a great ruler and not a monster. As it is, his people fear him and are punished for saying otherwise."

"I don't know though," Barger said in haste. "Not everyone within the Empire feels the same as he does. Most of us joined and served for the benefit of the galaxy. I would wager that only the occupational troops have seen what you've talked about. A few of the pilots, like myself, are exceptions, but most fleet personnel live charmed lives. I guess what I'm trying to say is that I am not fully prepared to climb into a fighter and battle alongside you. The chance of flaming an old friend might be too high."

"Such is the price of war."

Barger glanced down and smirked. Nyssa's face was as smooth as a fresh recruit and his voice was high and pert. Yet every word that escaped his lips was years beyond his age. "I must say," he finally admitted. "You have a way with words that mark a much older man."

"That's an easy one to answer. I may be twenty standard years of age, but in my race I am already at middle age. Emotionally I am already your elder."

Shadle leaned towards Barger and nudged him jokingly. "He's always trying to rub that it our faces."

Chapter Thirteen

Barger paid her no mind. "But I thought you were Sutherlin."

"In heart and spirit, but only partially in blood. My grandmother was Sutherlin."

"Yet you retain your single name."

He nodded. "In honor of my dead heritage, I do. I dropped my surname when I learned of Sutherlin's destruction."

Folding his arms, Barger pursed his lips and let out a slow sigh. "This is a lot to take and I'm sure we haven't even hit the tip of the iceberg."

"Everyone on this base has a story to tell," said Shadle. "Not all of them are as interesting as Nyssa's, but most are worth listening to. Give us a chance to prove that the possibility of fighting an old friend is justified enough for you to fly along side us."

Barger shook his head. The depth of life the younger pilots presented him with eluded his passing glances of them. "Give me time."

"As you have so fondly expressed we do not have the luxury of time," Shadle pressed. "We appreciate the time you have spent preparing us, but I think a strong connection with us would benefit just as much."

A subtle rap at the makeshift door drew everyone's attention as Barger finished. "I'll consider it." He stood up and peeked his head outside. To his surprise Stead stood before him with his hands folded behind his back. "What is it?"

"A word?" He requested then he turned around.

Barger looked back into the compartment and shrugged. "Maybe later." The three accepted with a nod and he stepped out. Stead had not moved, allowing their conversation to be heard by the other pilots. "Trouble?" he asked.

"Yes and no. I couldn't tell you." He dropped his arms to his side and faced him. "We received a delayed transmission from an outpost operated by another Alliance cell. It was an emergency beacon signaling that they had been discovered."

"Could that lead the Empire here?"

"Doubtful," he said with confidence. "The beacon merely states that they were discovered. What now has to happen is a team will have to board the outpost and retrieve the commander's final log."

Stead's somber facial expression betrayed more than he was saying. Whether it was their proximity to the three pilots in the storage compartment or a need-to-know only type of message, he did not care. At this point anything involving him was need to know. "Go on," he insisted.

Stead hesitated, looking over his shoulder at the three pairs of ears that were undoubtedly listening before giving in. "There was a blurb hidden within the beacon that was heavily distorted. We were only able to make out the words Sutherlin and weapon. The rest of the transmission had broken into fragments."

"That leaves us with two possible answers. Either the force that found the post now knows the location of at least one of the cells and is preparing to destroy it or..."

"Or they stumbled across how Sutherlin was destroyed," Barger finished for him.

"In either case we are in danger and we need answers."

"Why tell me? Why not go to Jared?"

"Patron and I discussed that already and we both think you might have a better idea."

His insinuation slapped Barger in the back of the head. "You think I can get into the Imperial database." He snapped his head back. "Hardly," he bellowed out before looking back at him. "My codes would have been erased the moment I was captured. On top of that I would need to have access to a pilot terminal and the only way to get close to one means breaking onto a star ship and accessing the Imperial database from a secured terminal."

"That's what I said, but I went with the idea anyway. Being that you have such a shady background you might have another way of doing it."

Barger smirked. They had done some research on him. It explained why he was not as trusted as he would have liked. Back to what Stead said, he thought about the possibilities for a moment. There were several ways to break into the Alcon information directory, but none of them were linked to the fleet database. Only command headquarters and star ships had direct links. Even the system back doors were located in hard to get to places.

There was one way. "I'd have to get aboard the Blackhawk."

At first it looked as if Stead was going to have a heart attack. The appearance of absolute terror seemed genuine enough until a smirk then a brief chuckle followed. "You've got to be crazy. You want to sneak aboard the ship where you were stationed the day we abducted you."

Barger's eyes narrowed in disgust. "First of all it was pure luck that I was the one that tried to shoot down Jared. You could very well have captured someone else. Secondly, that ship would be the last place anyone would expect to find me."

"I have a good friend who happens to have a third level security access who probably has my old quarters. If he does, then that means he has my old data entry pad which is linked into the ship's secondary memory path. As your luck would have it, I had a fixation with Imperial history and the only way I could reach the Galactic library was to break a fourth level code and use the ship's starlight comm relay to access files."

"If the path I wrote into the security protocols still exists, then a backdoor to the fleet registry will exist. If I were to take Guile with me then I'm sure he could come up with his own access code to gain entry into the registry. Once inside, you'd have updated locations and capabilities, including class diagrams of every ship in the fleet."

Stead appeared taken aback by the amount of information he had poured onto him. "Well," he murmured. "I guess you do have another way of doing it."

"Damn right," Barger said with a snap of his wrist. "What works better than sneaking in through the front door?"

"Maybe asking first."

"That'll be up to Jared. I'll give him a way to steal the information. He has to come up with a way to get us there, then to get back."

Chapter Thirteen

"Then I think we need to go see our friend, Mister Guile, and see if we can't arrange this. I'll prep a shuttle. Meet me in an hour."

Barger nodded. "With bells on."

A tug at his jacket followed Stead's departure. He spun around on his right heel and looked down at Shadle, who was on her knees. "Snoop."

"Very funny," she said as she stood to meet him eye to eye. "It's not hard to overhear a couple of airheads while they bellow out a stupid idea. I thought you were going to get to know us."

Barger glanced over his shoulder at the departing Stead. "You think I don't know what a risk this is." He looked back to her, concerned with her opinion of him. It was not a feeling he had expected of himself. "It's like I said before. I'm not sure if I can fire on an old friend and the pilot I spoke of was who I was talking about. I need to look him in the eye one more time and convince myself I belong here. Somehow, doing this any other way just wouldn't feel right."

"Think of this as a selfish act on my part. An alternate reason for getting Patron the information he needs. Besides, Jared will be there. He's lived through a lot more than I have. I may not care too much for the man, but I will trust him with my life."

"Why?" She asked with an innocent crick in her neck. "Why him and not us?"

"Trust has never been something I judge based on a person's appeal of experience, but mainly on character. His life is a testament that no matter how bad things have become, he still chooses to live. Even if it means living in the mud. Learn to live in the mud and survive beneath the valor of others, and I will place my life in your hands."

"You mean cheat."

"In every aspect of your life. Just remember that there is a thin line drawn out there. If you ever have to make a choice that you doubt in any way, make sure it comes from the heart." He gave her a lopsided grin. He briefly ran the backside of his hand down her cheek and turned to walk away.

He knew a hard choice of his own was coming and it involved her. Everything he said meant something to him. Barger had no way of knowing if Shadle had found similar meaning to his words. It was barren ground and there was still a long way to go.

Chapter Fourteen

Guile returned to the lava pools of his home just a month from the time he had left. It wasn't long in the greater scheme of things, but a lifetime as far as he was concerned. In the four years he had owned this house he had spent a total of five months here. Each visit was just that, a visit. After some contracts he returned home to piles of built up dust and unfamiliar surroundings. On those days he hated his profession.

There were no stars on this night. Instead, the sky was filled with a light gray haze. A storm was brewing beyond the mountain range that contained his volcano, large enough to cause everyone to take notice. In a strong way it reminded him of his current situation. The duties he had assumed would ensure an escalation in fighting and an increase in the loss of life. Though Guile had no great affection for the Empire he didn't want to see young men and women sent to their deaths against them. In his mind the coming conflict would be a waste of life and nothing more.

And he would profit from it.

Guile sank further into the water until he was neck deep. He suddenly felt his stomach turn much worse than it did during Star Flight. The realization that he was contributing to the deaths of hundreds of underage warriors was sickening. He tried to justify it by thinking that he was a hired gun and nothing more, but the faces of the pilots he was training refused to fade. They were good pilots, but none of them had actual flight experience, and the pilots they would be facing were far from green.

Devil squadron may have been the elite of the Alcon navy, but the standard pilots could hold their own in any situation. The Alcon Empire had expanded dramatically to eighty percent of the galaxy, though Guile wondered if the training of the pilots and crews had been shortened in order to rush them into the field. If this was the case then his overall strategy would have to change. The more experienced pilots would use complicated moves, but the greener pilots would engage in simpler maneuvers.

Guile shook his head, splashing water over his face. I've got to let it go. He thought to himself. The more he thought about his contract the more confused and disoriented he became. He had to stick to his guns and remember that he was hired to train and supply and nothing more. Where he was taking his duties was more along the lines of a tactician or unit commander. He preferred not to have a commission and he surely did not want to get involved with strike planning. That was left up to Stead and the Patron.

The comlink sitting at the edge of the pool chirped to life and squeals and whistles filtered through. Guile waded slowly towards the edge and slapped on the speaker. "What is it, Backer?" His Companion chirped back. "No. Go ahead and let them pass. Just keep an eye out for any of their buddies."

Guile had ignored flight laws and had landed in front of his home instead of at the star port. He did this for laziness as much as he did it for protection. Although the presence of a star fighter at the front door with the weapons systems on standby worked well as a deterrent to anyone who might want to break in, his motivation was purely for rest. The trip from the star port would have added four hours to his arrival time and he did not want to wait that long.

"Some mercenary," a smug voice said from behind him.

Guile put his arms up on the edge of the pool and smiled. "Some captain," he called back to Stead. "What brings you this far out?"

"We didn't have far to go."

True, he thought to himself. Terlelia was not that far from the Luikart system when you looked at the galaxy as a whole. A day's travel, even in a slow ship.

He could feel Stead and his shadow stop close to the waters edge. "Have you come to bring me back or just harass me?"

"Neither," Wes Barger's voice snapped.

Guile turned and looked up at the last two men he cared to see. "It's bad enough you came," he chastised Stead. "But to bring him with you just adds insult to injury." He never meant it, but he knew the rise he would get out of his visitors. In truth his hatred of Stead and distrust of Barger were subsiding below greater concerns.

"He had to come. It was his idea." Guile rolled his eyes, prompting Stead to kneel down. "He needs your help."

Guile glared up at Barger. "More than he knows."

Barger smiled, satirically before turning and striding back to the house.

Stead gave the departing Barger a sideways glance before closing on Guile. "As much as I hate to say this, he has a good plan."

"Better than the one that got him captured."

Stead's eyes narrowed. "Cute. No, this one isn't based on impulse. He put a lot of thought into it and I agree with him."

"There's a shock."

"Are you going to listen or did I waste a trip?"

Guile shrugged. He wanted to confirm the wasted trip, but curiosity got the better of him. "Shoot."

"Wes wants to get aboard the Blackhawk and download all her files on the third fleet."

Chapter Fourteen

Guile's eyes widened and he was ready to explode with laughter. "He's crazy. And you're crazy for agreeing."

"You got aboard the station, didn't you?"

Folding his arms, Guile prepared himself to give his former superior a verbal lesson. "That was a heavily trafficked way station with a private security force as its primary means of defense. You're asking me to get you on an Alcon destroyer whose primary occupant is the lead flight of Devil squadron. The Emperor himself barely has more security than that ship."

"All three of us served aboard that ship at one time and we know its corridors back and forth."

"Yes, but she has four levels of access codes, only three of which we held. I will stake my reputation and my life on the fact that those codes have long since been changed."

"The codes, yes, but not the control paths. It should be a snap for you to break them."

Guile sank to his neck into the water. "Again I have to remind you that we had three code levels and not the fourth. I need that one in order to download fleet information."

Stead looked back to the house where Barger stood. "Wes says that he can take care of that part. He just needs to get aboard."

"I don't trust him."

Stead shot a harsh glance back to him. "And I don't trust you, but I also brought Patron to you and I'm here now. Don't you dare bring up the issue of trust."

"Fine then. I won't bring up trust again. What I do want is your assurance that Barger won't turn traitor and hand us over to the Empire."

"I can't promise anything relating to Wes. I can tell you though that we received a delayed distress call and a fragmented message from an outpost stating that the Empire has a new weapon that may be responsible for the mass destruction of Sutherlin. We need direct access to an Alcon database to confirm this."

Curious. The Alcon would not have been foolish enough to transmit technical data across open frequencies and typical outposts would not have the capabilities to break highly sensitive encoded messages. There had to be more to the message than what Stead knew.

"If the message you received was genuine," he said in response, "I'd have to check out the outpost for myself."

"That's acceptable. When can you go?"

"It will take some time to set up." He paused to run a brief scenario through his head. "Right after I get you the two transports you requested. Have Ghost ready to fly when I return."

"Ghost is ready to fly right now," Barger announced from the house.

Guile's eyes narrowed. "What does he mean by that?"

"He means that the pilots he had spent extra time with are ready for a live training run. All but one have passed the delta trench run."

133

His narrow eyes widened. "You've got to be kidding me."

The delta trench was a five thousand kilometer rift on a dead planet close to the core of the galaxy. The planet had been the sight of the deadliest space and ground battle in the history of the galaxy. The twenty-day fight had ended when two squadrons of the era's more advanced fighters entered the treacherous trench at speeds that were the highest ever recorded at the time. Only one fighter reached its objective, destroying the heart of the planet's defenses before it turned skyward.

For centuries the delta trench had been a required simulation in the academy and for many pilots it took years to complete. The sharp turns, powerful defensive guns, and lack of escape made the run far more than ordinary. Three quarters of the trench, leading up to the target reactor, was buried beneath fifty meters of solid rock. Once a fighter past beyond the leading edge of the canopy it was do or die, and many died.

"How many?"

"Three of them. You probably know which ones. What makes it more incredible is that we ran down the trench in formation, not alone."

Guile shook his head. Formation in the trench meant that each trailing fighter had to remain within eyesight of the fighter in front of them. With turns in excess of ninety degrees that task proved most difficult. Had the years of simulations been real, the trench, which had been named a monument, would have been jammed with the wreckage of hundreds of fighters.

"Are you satisfied enough to bring them along?"

"More than enough." Guile looked to Barger. "You can come too."

Barger bowed with a mock smile.

"I like him," Guile said. He reached up and gripped Stead's arm. "But don't tell anyone. I don't want my reputation tarnished."

Bea often found herself looking out at the stars from the only viewing window in the rock. The resistance base rested beneath three kilometers of solid rock. Hours of concentrated fire from star cruisers could not break through. There were only two ways in and out, and one of them was impossible to find without knowing where to go. The massive shield generator and a holographic imaging system provided the wide opening in the rock face with an undetectable mask -- an illusion that one could neither see nor penetrate.

The second entrance was just large enough for two people to walk through at any given time and was twenty kilometers from the main opening. This small, rock-shaped bunker was nestled at the base of a mountain and was surrounded by a series of booby traps and camouflaged gun emplacements. From here the restless few could sit outside of the confines of the base and look out at the peaceful sky; a view that never changed in a system whose sun had burned out centuries ago.

She belonged out there, snug in the confines of a fighter, racing around her enemies. She lived for the dogfight and the chance to prove herself against overwhelming odds. The rush of a quad burst of laser fire filled her body with energy. The pull of a pair of thermal missiles rocketing from their pods excited her every pore. The

Chapter Fourteen

eruption of a fuel pod and ultimate destruction of an enemy fighter gave her a strong sense of accomplishment.

The first year of Ghost's service to the resistance had been relatively quiet. Engagements were few and far between. While with the Empire Bea had racked up more kills in one month than she had in her new home, the rush had long since passed and was more of a wish and a dream than a reality.

The return of Jared Guile had changed all of that. Once again she could feel the thrilling sensation racing up her back, even in simulated combat. He represented new life in the squadron. A challenge. He felt that their training had lacked, so twice now he had split up the group for head-to-head combat. The additional intensity Wes Barger provided to the training increased the thrill. It was a welcome break from the monotony.

Normally Bea was alone, sitting inside the bunker, looking out the one-sided ceiling. On this occasion, she was joined by Narra Shadle. She could no more answer why she sat with her than say why she came up here. There was no real reason except to dream of better days. It was rather childish in some respects, but no more so than the need to fly. Everyone had his or her love in life. Just because hers was confined spaces and stressful situations did not make her any less of a person.

Shadle on the other hand had no great desire for combat. Her true love was the political arena: a one-on-one confrontation with an equal or superior opponent in the mental forum. If she had her way, a mission would involve espionage. It was a sharp contrast to Bea, who liked the thrill of a massive battle; the thought that at any minute she could be faced with a three-on-one competition is what attracted her to the heavier missions.

Bea knew the heavy missions were out there waiting for them. Until now, Ghost squadron had been subjected to escort missions against lightly defended bases on the rim of the galaxy; outposts that were the dumping stations for the Alcon underachievers. Kills came easy on those missions and most of the time the pilots surrendered at the mere sight of them. They were easy, quick, and extremely dull.

The true test of these seasoned warriors lay in the form of giant spears, lancing their way through space. The empire's battle cruisers and battle groups were considered unstoppable, even against ships or groups of equal size. The sheer firepower each of the warships held could level a planet's surface in hours. The last Realm to fall to the Alcon was defeated by just three massive battle cruisers, and two of them returned home with only minor damage.

The real danger though lay in the tactics of the Empire. When they attacked they did it in tight ship formation with a wedge of fighters and bombers leading the way. Whatever did break the fighter line was left badly damaged and open to the heavy laser cannon assault. Death came in many forms when confronted with such odds. What did not get you in the opening stages of conflict would catch up with you in the closing stages.

It was the danger that gave Bea her desires. She and the other members of Ghost looked forward to the day they could prove themselves. She knew they could not do

Sutherlin Alliance

it alone. The plan had always been to tear down the fighter defense then press forward with a full attack force of heavy transports. In the end though she would have the final shot. In her mind she pictured the last missile exploding out of the launch tube and detonating through the bridge of a battle cruiser.

The problem still lingered with the skills of the younger pilots. Bea knew far too well that for Ghost to be able to attack harder targets that the rookies would have to be able to defend the rest of the resistance cell. It was a task that did not come without extraordinary responsibility. If for any reason the cell had to pick up and move, the escort squadron would have to defend the withdrawing ships at any cost. That meant dealing with four or five-to-one odds.

Bea remembered such an encounter before the cell had moved here. Ghost was the only squadron available to defend twelve transports that were departing from their last base. A Battle Cruiser dropped from star flight and released its entire compliment of twelve squadrons. Thirteen fighters against sixty. They lost half their numbers that day but all but one transport made it out safely. She doubted that the younger pilots could have pulled off such an accomplishment.

"Dreaming of glorious battles?" Flight Officer Nyssa asked as he exited the bunker's lift. "Or glorious deaths?"

"I'm just trying to relax," Shadle answered.

Bea shifted in her folding chair so that she could look at him. "Neither. I'm thinking about the future."

Shadle grumbled. "Our future rests in the hands of a mercenary."

"One that hasn't done that bad for us so far." Nyssa knelt down next to her. "We just received another supply of thermal warheads. We have enough now to take out a wing of fighters with more on the way."

"Goody for us," Shadle moaned.

"How does Patron feel about this?"

"He thinks we're ahead of schedule. He believes that once the green pilots can prove they can handle themselves then we'll be ready to hit the big time."

"What we need is rest," Shadle snapped.

Bea leaned closer to Nyssa and whispered. "What she needs is a bolt in the head."

"I heard that."

"Your point being?" Nyssa asked her. Shadle did not respond so she ignored him. "Patron released Jared's mission schedule. He has us assigned to scraps."

Shadle's eyes opened. "Scrapes." "Scrapes" was the name given a fighter that was made up of more than fifty percent spare parts

"According to the mission scope he wants everyone to become accustomed to slower, less maneuverable craft during space flights so that we will have an added edge when fighting in the newer novas."

"A waste if you ask me," Shadle grumbled.

"It sounds like a sound idea, but why not save that part of the training for the simms. Far less risky."

Chapter Fourteen

"I spoke with him before he left," answered Bea. "He doesn't think Riordan is going to release the number of fighters he had hoped to get. He said he'd be lucky if he could come up with enough parts to add ten more novas to the group."

"Then he wants the rookies to be ready to fly our newer novas if that's all they'll be able to fly."

Nyssa shook his head. "He hinted towards Ghost using nothing but scrapes."

Shadle shot a glance to Bea, but she did not stir. "Why us?"

"Why not? We have the experience and the know how to fly rings around Alcon pilots in those things." He shrugged. "I don't know. I guess I'm just speculating. We'll have to wait and see until after the upcoming missions."

"What does Wes have to say about this?" Shadle asked

"Nothing. He looked over the orders and set them back down without a word. Haggin did the same thing."

"Funny," Bea said. "For three guys who apparently hate each other they sure do agree on a lot of things."

"You don't have to like someone to trust them," Nyssa corrected. "From what I hear, you two have not grasped that concept yet."

Shadle raised her hands. "I..."

Bea cut her off. "No, we haven't. I'm from the old school that thinks both should go hand in hand."

"Old school!" Shadle exclaimed. She leaned closer to her. "This has nothing to do with the way we feel about them."

Nyssa cut short the response he had planned, falling back on the obvious uncomfortable moan.

"Way to let the cat slip out of the bag."

"What's a cat?" Nyssa asked. "And what does it have to do with you."

Bea was almost too amused for words. Not only had Shadle stated the obvious, but she had also clarified what had likely been a rumor floating around the base.

"I'm sure glad I'm not my sister. Females have such a complicated way of looking at things. If you two were males you would have taken Wes and Jared and made them your own by now."

"Maybe so for you, Nyssa, but our races find attraction to be a precursor to the chase and not the conclusion."

Shadle finally threw up her hands to stop both of them. "Now look. I don't know how or why the conversation suddenly took this turn, but I want it stopped. I have, am not, and never will chase Wes around like some lovesick beast until he admits that he feels the same about me."

Nyssa shrugged, but it was Bea he backed her down. "You don't have to worry about the conversations turning towards you two. Rumor alone from today will be enough to keep the base talking."

"What rumor?"

Bea patted her on the back. "Never mind, Narra. If you don't know then it's best I don't tell you."

Shadle looked to Nyssa who was doing his best to contain a laugh.

You're lazy, Jared, and this is the wrong business to be that way.

His eyes wide, Guile swirled around in the water looking for whoever spoke those words. In all directions he saw shadows, but no figures. He stopped turning and leaned against the edge of the pool. Stead and Barger had left hours ago. If there was no one there then he must have thought the comment. How could that be, though. It was one thing to say something and not realize it. It was something totally different to think it.

Don't panic. You have a gifted friend.

"Vigdis." Guile spun around and looked towards the house.

Standing in the doorway was a slender woman with long, lanky arms and hair that was double braided down to her knees. Vigdis Stornoway was a Tolan and like those of her species had a special knack for interrupting ones thoughts with open conversation. Her slopping cranium, which ran from her forehead back down her neck and over the back of her shoulders, held a mind that could do wonders. Her mental capabilities allowed her to function without the need for verbal conversation. Her strong mental control over her body also allowed her to go for days without a breath of air simply by shutting down her system and working solely by thought.

"You look well, mercenary," she said openly. "I had pictured you scarred beyond recognition by now."

Guile grinned. "I'm a hard man to touch, Vigdis." He spotted distant movement behind his old friend and reacted accordingly. "Who's your friend?"

"An associate of mine. He keeps me from the dangers that I used to engage in regularly. Call him a bodyguard if you will. I prefer shadow."

Stornoway had been Guile's assigned wingman for the last six months of his service to the Empire and was by far the one person he trusted to keep him safe. No matter the risk, she watched his back and assured him a safe return home. For that reason alone she was the first to know his reasons for leaving the Alcon. Out of the entire Devil squadron she was the only one who truly understood his position and could admit the same.

"You are a hard man to keep up with. I have attempted to follow your post military career for years with limited success. Business always seems slow when you appear in a system."

"So you're private." She gave a limited nod. "I'm sorry if I've stolen contracts from you. Nothing was ever meant by it."

"You have never stolen a contract. Your reputation for success has given you an edge most of us can only aspire to. It takes a crew and six days to accomplish the same task you complete by yourself in hours."

"I have a special knack."

"A knack that lands you profitable contracts, but dangerous ones." Stornoway bent inward and her legs arched back to form her own place to rest. "You have signed a contact with the Sutherlin Alliance, yes?"

Chapter Fourteen

Guile's eyes narrowed. "I signed an arms contract." He looked past her again at the figure standing in the doorway.

He is trustworthy. He would find it hard to breathe if divulged information I prized as secret and he is fully aware of it.

Guile eased up a bit, but was still hesitant. A woman who could read thoughts reappears after several years and speaks of a contract he had told no one of. Though he had used to trust her, his mental alarms sounded louder than memory.

"You aren't just dealing with a just cause, but with a political strongman. Your contractor used to be an influential man within the galactic congress and he has ties that rival yours. If he has alternate plans for you, then you will find it hard to survive in any system. Your current situation with the Alcon is nothing compared to dangers you will face from Alliance sympathizers."

"You had the original supply contract with Patron's resistance cell," he said in a flash of realization.

Stornoway nodded. "I did, but anger about losing such a profitable deal is not what brings me here. In another year I would not have been able to keep up with their demand and both Patron and I realized this. He began to ask questions about my suppliers and about their suppliers. He wanted to know how to influence Caderan administrators and what shipping companies would run weapons outside normal lanes of traffic."

"He wanted to know how we do business?"

"He wanted to know how to turn the Alliance into a pirate group," she said in correction. "His motives are far from honorable, which brings me to dangerous conclusions. If he finds out what he needs to know and where he needs to go, he will no longer need your services. You will have to die so that you cannot spread the word of his betrayal. To do so would mean that even if he did know how to trade with the underground no one would deal with him or the Alliance."

She had a valid point, but he had not lived this long without taking precautions. "Don't worry about me. I've taken care not to go directly to my sources. Every jump I make is preceded by three or four random jumps that never last longer than sixty seconds. If Patron is sending spies to follow me they won't catch me."

"Can you be sure?"

"Haggin Stead is the fighter commander. You know as well as anyone that the rivalry we had allowed us to study each other. After meeting with him I came to the conclusion that he hasn't changed since the old days and I have."

"Just watch your back, Jared. His mind is an open book as is Patron's. What they want does not fall within the vested interest of the Alliance leaders or its followers."

Guile pushed away from the edge and floated out towards the middle. "And what do you want? You couldn't have come all this way just to warn me about Patron. Does the lure of all the money I'm making from him seem too good to pass up?"

"I am already rich enough to last myself and my associates the rest of our lives in peace. It is my conscience that brings me back. It is my memories that bring me to

Sutherlin Alliance

you. I have followed you from the academy to Devil to smuggling and contracting. I thought it my duty to follow you the rest of the way."

"And where might that be?"

"I am not sure, but I know the next stage of your life is building to climax. I can see it in your eyes and hear in your thoughts. Like the storm that builds overhead, the tension is building in the galaxy and you are in the middle of it all. Maybe it's the thrill that seems to follow you around. Maybe it's the reputation that has become your past. Maybe it's just you, Jared. Whatever it is it has drawn me along in your shadow and once again it has changed the direction I take."

Stornoway rose up and straightened her lanky form. "I am at your service. You need only call. There will be no need for contracts or formalities. Simply request what you need and it will be at your disposal. Any financial compensation that is needed can be decided at a later date. I have a deep trust in you, so this will not be mentioned again until you are ready."

She turned to leave. Your true friends are your true allies, Jared. Choose them well. She and her associate disappeared into his dark house.

Guile allowed himself to relax and his body floated to the surface. His eyes gazed up into the darkening clouds. Backer chirped through his comlink, announcing the departure of his visitors and he shook. Her words had stung him. This was not a new feeling after dealing with her. She had been the strength he turned to during trying times. The twist though was that he turned to her even when he did not know he needed to. She had always just been there for him.

'Your true friends are your allies, Jared.' She spoke the truth. He trusted no one, except himself. Now he was faced with the return of members from his old squadron. People he had been to hell and back with. People he had no other choice but to trust during battle. Even his rival, Stead had been a valuable ally in the heat of combat.

It was simple irony that she arrived after Stead had left. 'Choose them well.' Guile could do no more than reflect.

Chapter Fifteen

The remote sun peaked over the horizon of Terelia and blanketed Telestia in a warm, morning light. Distant rumblings from the volcano bubbled under the home of Jared Guile, a well-known symbol that the dawn of a new day was at hand. Throughout the history of the planet the surface volcanoes had acted as the wakeup call for the day and the harbinger of nightfall.

While the rest of the citizens awoke and indulged themselves in the preparation for a new day, one resident was completing his. Backer fired up the nova's primary systems as Guile threw a few of his things in a bag. They were not important items as far as necessity was concerned. They were more sentimental than anything else. All that he owned that was not of great need came from his time in the service of the Alcon navy. Medals, holo-photos, even his original flight suit in the traditional gold and gray. All of it represented a time in his life that was regrettable, but at the same time memorable.

The last of the items he dropped into the oversized bag was a framed photo. Taken on the flight deck of the Blackhawk it was a picture of the original Devil squadron against the backdrop of a bluish green planet. He remembered the day the photo was taken as if it were yesterday. It was a happy time before the Badlands campaigns had begun. Before they were ordered to kill innocent women and children in the name of peace.

'We're the best', was the quote under the picture. The quote had been decided upon after the debate over whether they were better friends or pilots. Now, after many years, Guile convinced himself that their piloting skills were the better of the two.

He frowned then dropped the photo into his bag. Outside he heard the quadruple whine of four engines powering up. Backer was becoming impatient so he slung the bag over his shoulder and walked out the front door. He tossed the bag into a hatch behind and below the cockpit, then sealed the door shut. He then climbed up the retractable ladder.

He rested on the edge of the cockpit and looked over his home. Guile let a mild grin crease the corners of his mouth. He had always loved his home, but now it appeared more beautiful than it had before. The last two days he had enjoyed its warm surroundings and pleasant atmosphere like he never had before. For the first time he knew he was going to be truly homesick.

Backer chirped from the cockpit speaker. Guile obliged the impatient computer and dropped into the seat. His onboard systems were already reading normal and an exit trajectory from the atmosphere had been plotted. Backer was an exceptional assistant, but Guile did not care for his attitude sometimes. He always felt he was being rushed whenever Backer was told of flight arrangements ahead of time.

The nova picked up off the ground with ease. Guile pulled the nose up perpendicular with the surface and kicked in full power. For a brief second he felt the force of the powerful engines against the gravity of the planet before the inertial field around the fighter corrected the pull. At times he had wanted to deactivate the field so that he could feel how powerful his fighter really was, but the idea of unprotected star flight always held him back.

The darkness of space filled the cockpit in less than two minutes. Guile glanced back out of the canopy to give his home world one last look. Telestia looked so small from ten million kilometers out. Once again he said goodbye to his home with his heart and mind. Every time it was like saying goodbye for the last time. An uneasy weight settled on his heart. One that he never felt before. Despite his past and his ability to overcome astounding odds, this time he really meant it.

The mood on the two bridge decks of the Vengeance was somber despite the circumstances. It was a good sign of the experience the bridge officers had. Each was seasoned, having spent at least five years on other, smaller ships. Many had served with Captain Fallon on the Blackhawk during the Badlands campaigns against one of the smaller Realms. Every day brought a new challenge and a new victory. Such tours of duty built experience, but even more importantly, the battles gave the officers confidence in their abilities.

In front of Fallon, displayed across several of the massive viewing windows, was a dull blue planet. Long since abandoned by the inhabitants after the first appearance by Alcon cruisers ten years ago, it had been a well-known stopover for pirates and mercenaries. On this day though, the surface of the world was not of interest. The battered, outdated defense platform in orbit was the target. On a tip Minister Gesh received, Fallon had come here personally to investigate.

Word had come from an informant that Jared Guile had been instrumental in the acquiring of the old platform by a small time pirate group. The group was using it as a base for smuggler operations and pirate raids of some of the lesser-traveled shipping lanes. The infringement on legal trade wasn't what brought the Empire's Badlands group flagship to the system. It was the prospect of a solid Jared Guile lead that had sparked Fallon's interest.

Chapter Fifteen

On a series of holographic imaging screens around the large viewing windows, computer generated tactical information was displayed for all to see. Bright gold triangles represented the Realm attack force of fifty fighters, ten bombers, and three heavy attack transports. Their opponents, shown as red dots numbered at ten fighters, one light patrol craft, and an outdated defense platform. The size of force Fallon had arranged to take the platform was more than enough to destroy a force three times its size, but he was taking no chances. The nearest carrier ship that could refresh lost craft was a month away. In the Badlands a month was too long even for the most powerful ship in the Alcon fleet.

"One minute to contact," S'Lendo said from his first officer's seat. "Missile locks have been acquired from both sides. According to our wing commander the type of warhead system the raiders are using is an old style freighter design. Even if they can get off their shots before our missiles hit they might not be able to reacquire for over a minute."

"Excellent. This should be brief. Inform Captain Merrill that his services will not be needed on this endeavor."

"As ordered," said communications.

A dozen gold targets erupted from the lead Alcon fighters, indicating missile launch. Six missiles were returned from the pirate fighters, but barely cleared the defending group before the bi-wing missiles struck their targets. Five of the outdated pirate fighters disappeared from the screen. The remaining fighters and patrol craft broke off and ran at the sudden appearance of an additional thirty missiles fired from the bi-wings.

Fallon grinned then activated his speaker. "Colonel Wells. You may dispatch your boarding party."

The assault force closed the gap on the platform. Two missile targets rocketed out after the fighters, but were taken from the battle by carefully aimed laser fire. In retribution, the lead fighters released a salvo of missiles and the bombers fired two heavy torpedoes each. The attacking group was still out of laser range of the platform when the warheads slammed into its weak shields and tore apart sections of the hull.

"Con, Comm. The Platform commander is declaring his surrender."

"Accept his surrender and order the fleeing pirate fighters to stand down or they will be destroyed."

"Con, weapons. I've got a fix on two shuttles exiting the platform. They are on an escape vector to the planet."

Fallon's eyes narrowed. "Release pursuit and landing party."

"They can't get far," S'Lendo said.

"They aren't trying to escape. They're trying to draw us onto the surface and into whatever traps they've set up. Helm, Con. Once the platform is secure move us into parking orbit." Fallon clicked off his speaker and swiveled his chair towards his first officer. "I want you and Minister Gesh to accompany the landing party down to the surface. You have yet to have field experience and I want all my officers to have a first hand account of what decisions up here turn into down there."

"I also want a short leash on Gesh when he deals with these pirates."

"Yes, sir." S'Lendo stood and walked aft.

"And, Captain. Keep your head down."

Fallon had adjourned to his ready room after the boarding party had secured the platform. After the shuttles had left, only a skeleton crew remained behind. They were all tired and worn down from the constant moves pirates had to endure. The platform had only been in place for two days and the rest of the pirate group had yet to arrive to solidify its position. The people Fallon was left to deal with were engineers and grunt workers. Hardly a force worth the effort he put into the assault. No Imperial lives were lost and the mission could be considered a victory so he had some solace.

The patrol craft that was guarding the platform had been killed by the second volley of missiles. The five surviving fighters were a bit more fortunate. Each had been retrofitted with star flight initiators and engine upgrades. It was a visibly sloppy patchwork job but it was enough to save the pilots. All five jumped ahead of the pursuing bi-wings to an unknown location. Undoubtedly to join the rest of the pirate group and update them on the situation.

Fallon had an updated report on the size of the pirate group and saw no threat of open retaliation. Two light attack craft were no match for a battle cruiser. He instead focused his concern on the possibility of guerilla tactics used by the pirates on the surface. Though he was more than equipped to handle a small, well-entrenched group, he did not have the time it would take to complete the task. With every day that past, Jared Guile moved further away.

The latest report from the ground units stated that they had found the two shuttles buried in the thick forest canopy. From there scouts were sent out in all directions, but there was no sign of the passengers. On foot they could hide anywhere and not be found for weeks, or even months. Fallon's only other option was a full bombardment of the surface for a hundred kilometers in every direction.

"Admiral, there is an incoming transmission from Captain Merrill."

Finally. Who would have thought it would take so long to complete repairs? "Send it through and secure the channel." He heard two distinctive clicks. One of the communications officers muted her end, then switched to the long range channel. "Captain Merrill. I take it you are at full running again."

"We are, sir, and we have resumed our search of the outlying systems. Minister Gesh's leads have proven useful in undermining some of the pirate raids. We have successfully removed two minor operations from the trade routes in the past forty-eight hours."

Fallon closed his eyes. "That is commendable, Captain Merrill, but I need to know if you have turned up any more leads on Jared Guile. Though I am pleased

Chapter Fifteen

that we have proven successful against pirates these minor victories gain us no ground on our more prominent foe."

"No leads, sir. The only significant lead I have come across has come from the Alliance outpost. We dumped its computer core into our database and have been working on the encrypted files for several weeks. There wasn't much left of the files, but we did find a galactic map that had all Alcon military installation locations from five years ago."

"That doesn't help us in either area, but it is something to look into. Either they had scouts place all the bases or an inside source, and I doubt they had the resources five years ago to scout out all our bases." Fallon licked the underside of his upper lip. "Just for the record. How accurate are the maps?"

"Very, sir. I personally compared them with ours and can say with confidence that they are a one hundred percent match."

Fallon rubbed his thumbs together. The maps were five years old. Too old to make any difference. All but a few bases had been moved a year ago and those that remained were of no strategic value.

"Shall I follow up?"

"No," Fallon said bluntly. If anyone would find use of the maps it would be Imperial Intelligence. "Increase your efforts finding the rather cold trail of this mercenary. Transmit all you have uncovered about the outpost to me and I will decided how to proceed in that direction."

There was a long pause from Merrill, but not an unexpected one. The captain was an ambitious man and he knew an opportunity when he saw one. If a traitor within the Empire could be uncovered it would mean advancement in his career. On the other hand, it was well known that the Alliance was full of Imperial turncoats who could easily have supplied them with older maps.

"Is there anything else you have to report, captain?"

"No, sir."

"Then carry on." Fallon leaned back and grinned. He was not about to let the ambition of one of his commanders surpass his own

"Admiral, Colonel Wells for you."

"Open channel," Fallon said. The same double click sounded then the rustling of a strong wind blowing through the trees was clearly audible. "Yes, Colonel. I hope this means you have good news."

The raspy voice of Colonel Bauman Wells filtered back. "Good news, bad news, and even worse news, Admiral. The good news is that the scouts have found the pirate bunker and were able to secure the area themselves. The bad news is that everyone in the bunker was dead on arrival. They all appear to have taken some sort of suicide drug."

"And the worse news, colonel?"

"You're not going to like this, sir, but a majority of the dead were Alliance."

Fallon sat up, his eyes wide. "Are you sure?"

"Very. I identified two of the individuals personally. Both were senate assistants before the provincial government was disbanded. One worked for the congressman from my home world and the other was a friend of my family. About six months ago I received word from my home that both had joined the Alliance when rumor of the disbanding of the provincial government began to spread."

"And the rest?"

"As soon as I identified the two I compared the others against our records. All held positions within the galactic council and had defected to the Alliance."

The emperor was right in his assumption that Sutherlin sympathizers were ramped throughout the council and congress. His move to disband the council had now been justified.

"Was there any indication that the Alliance representatives and the pirate group were negotiating a trade?"

"None. It looked more like the Alliance was helping the pirates set up operation here. I would like to bring the shuttles back to the ship and download their files to confirm."

"Then you're ordered to do so. Strip the bunker clean of anything that might be useful then return to the ship."

"Admiral," S'Lendo interrupted. "I would have to concur with Colonel Wells assessment of the situation. Most of the equipment on the platform is the type used by the Alliance."

What are you doing on the platform? "Have you been able to recover anything from the computer core?"

"The majority of the core has been dumped. All that's left is the registry and telemetry. If this is correct the platform is one of our scraped outposts and it has been in transit here for three weeks from the Haron salvage yards."

"Military surplus is supposed to be scrapped in secured yards. Is there any indication as to how a small time pirate group could remove the platform from such a facility?"

"None, sir. It must have been purchased or stolen by an outside group. The station's commander reluctantly blamed his suppliers for not providing him with the defensive capabilities he needed. He alluded to the fact that the organization to which he is a member had nothing to do with the theft of the station, leaving a well-equipped supplier to blame."

"Like the Alliance," Colonel Wells said.

Or Jared Guile. "Strip the platform, captain, then place charges. I want you back aboard as soon as possible."

"We aren't going to call for a lifter?"

"There isn't time to wait for a lifter to take it back to the scrap yards. This is a hot lead and requires our immediate attention. Return to the ship as soon as possible. Out." Fallon disconnected the line and reopened one to the bridge. "Helm, lay in a course for the Haron system and engage the moment our away teams have returned. Comm, order Captain Merrill to drop what he is doing and proceed there at once."

Chapter Fifteen

Opportunities seldom fell into his lap, so he was not going to waste time when it happened. Fallon was sure that this was a connection to Jared and even if it wasn't it was the first definite link between the pirate organizations and the resistance. No one cared about the Badlands. Maybe if the rest of the Empire would wake up and see a tide that could change the face of the galaxy was brewing out in the depths of space, he would receive the support he needed to finish off the Sutherlin Alliance once and for all.

Chapter Sixteen

It was a long jump. Thirteen hours at maximum speed. Guile would have preferred to ride in the comforts of a light carrier rather than being placed into stasis in the cramped quarters of a cockpit, but constraints on the Alliance prohibited that. Over the past month, he had spent the seemingly endless supply of funds on six massive shipments of weapons and supplies. Though Patron had strong connections to receive more credits, the supply would be limited for a while. This provided the incentive to raid Alcon locations and to address their immediate needs. It was not an act Guile enjoyed doing, but one he found opportunity in. He had orchestrated the purchase of a fifty-year-old defense platform from private hires that happened to work in the Haron salvage yards. The removal of the platform by four contracted heavy lifters was easier than expected and prompted the yards as a prime target for a training run.
    The plan had been simple enough. Guile's sources informed him that two ten-year-old attack transports had recently been signed over to the scrap yards for demolition and recycling. For a small fee the private hires moved the transports to the edge of the yards and deactivated the marking beacons that allowed yard controllers to keep track of inventory. In approximately one minute the sensor net around that particular area of yard would drop for twenty minutes for any rescheduled maintenance, at which time a small insurgence team of ten novas and two transports would enter the area, assume control of the targets, and leave.
    Starlight burst out around his canopy and fell into place. The high, almost peaceful hum of the engines shouted to life with a harsh rumble that slowly weakened in intensity. Numbers reduced just as fast on the speed indicator, dropping to one fifty and holding. The tactical screen sparked to life and displayed eleven friendly targets to either side and behind him. In front, all he detected was a white ribbon across the screen. As expected, the sensor net was blocking any probe into the yard.
    "Lead to group. Decrease to half throttle and assume approach formation."

The two transports broke to his right and took up position a hundred meters off his right wing. Four fighters arced overhead, rolling over and spreading out around both vessels in a tight diamond formation. The remaining five fighters fanned out around Guile in a star formation. The two groups stayed within that one hundred meter gap, ready to form up at a moment's notice if threatened.

"You have your assignments. We've run the simms, but prepare for uncertainty. If we do get jumped, stick close to five, two, and myself and keep an eye out. You'll be our wing men and our backs."

Seven of the pilots were rookies with no actual mission flight time. The task Guile had chosen was an easy one, but he did not want to take chances. To secure the run as both a good training exercise but a safe one he had brought Barger in two and Bea in five. To add even more security he assigned the brightest of the younger pilots to guard the transports. Nyssa in seven, and Ogden Scio, who had acted as Guile's wingman during earlier simulator runs were in charge of that part of the operation.

The white ribbon disappeared from the tactical screen. Dozens of target beacons suddenly popped up as dark brown targets. Out of the fray two single, blue targets emerged, still so far out that Guile could not get an identification of the targets; but he already knew what they were. In the past he had had his contacts set up encoded beacon emitters that looked like asteroids on tactical screens. This allowed his acquisitions to remain anonymous.

"Lead to group. Lock those two blue targets into memory. Those are our objectives. Four, five break left and cover our flank. Two, take three and scout the area. Six, you're with me."

The fighters broke up into their two ship teams and spread out. In the meantime, the two transports and four escorts accelerated towards the salvage yards.

Guile's com channel cracked to life. "Unidentified fighter group, this is salvage yard three control. Please state the nature of your visit."

"Now what?" Barger grumbled over the squad channel.

"Escort flight to salvage control. We are depositing two freight transports for demolition and recycling. We request a good location to drop off our junk."

The two brown targets brightened.

"Much obliged salvage control. We will be out of your hair in five minutes. Escort flight out."

"Why didn't you tell us about this?" Barger snapped.

Guile grinned. "There's a lot of things I won't tell you, two. I stay alive longer if I know things others don't."

"One minute to target," the deep voice of one of the transport pilots said.

"Copy that. You're on patrol, group. Keep it tight but stay loose."

The two fighters led by Barger continued into the spread-out hulks that had once been fully functioning ships. Guile and his wingman broke off to the right and rolled away from the salvage yard. The transports slowed on approach with the awaiting

Chapter Sixteen

transports, each lining up carefully so that docking ports would match up. Their escorts slowed in conjunction, always keeping within ten meters.

So far so good. After three minutes, the acquisition teams on the two transports had powered up the craft and were in the process of preparing them for star flight. The sensor net was still fifteen minutes from reactivation and there was no sign that someone other than his contacts had discovered them. In this far from normal star flight lane, a call for help so late into the mission would not get an armed response until long after they were gone.

"Target one is captured."

Guile rolled over and looked into the yard from a thousand yards out. The captured and acquisition transports were slowly picking up speed and approaching him. "Nine, ten escort them out and home."

Two of the stationary fighters powered up and matched the transports' speed. The four craft crept out and accelerated away from the yards. After a minute they had reached the exit jump sight and were gone in a flash.

"One down."

No sooner had Guile said the words than a red target appeared on the edge of his tactical screen. He rolled a quarter turn to the right and pulled back so that his nose came up on a direct line with the ominous figure of an Imperial cruiser. It was not something he had wished to see on a simple mission.

"Seven, eight power up and begin a tight loop around the transports. Two, three you are on close support. Four, five form up."

Guile had not finished barking orders when six threats registered on tactical and began closing the distance to the Alliance fighters quickly. Just by speed alone he could tell they were bi-wings and at least one of them would break the forward line of four novas to engage the others. With the sudden appearance of six more fighters from a second bay he began to get a deep sinking feeling in his gut.

"We're going to get buried really quick here. Get those transports out of here, now."

"It's got a lock on me," the young pilot in four cried out.

"Kick shields full forward and take the hit," Bea calmly told him.

Good girl. Guile looked out the right side of his canopy and could see him shaking in his cockpit. Sorry, kid. He wasn't meant to face such strong opposition on his first live mission. If he survived the encounter though, this would be more of a proving ground than he had ever expected.

Guile's threat indicator flashed from a positive missile lock. He quickly switched weapons control to warheads and armed his thermal missiles. A target acquire came up on the lead bi-wing, then turned red as it locked. He fired two missiles and switched back to lasers. Blindly, he thumbed his target select a few times until it lit up with the incoming missiles. His targeting screen flashed green and released several quad burst from the laser cannons on his wings.

Ahead, the two missiles from the bi-wing erupted momentarily then flared out. Behind the brief explosion he witnessed both of his missiles strike their target and

151

shear off the left wing at the jut. The fighter rolled to starboard as a fuel cell erupted from the gap in the hull. For a moment it looked as if the pilot was going to be able to eject. That moment passed in three quick explosions, one of which tore through the cockpit and nose of the craft.

Out of the corner of his eye Guile saw four's shields flare up from a direct missile hit. He panicked and rolled out to the right. A move that otherwise could have been considered foolhardy saved his life as a second missile streaked through his previous course. Satisfied that the young pilot would survive a little while longer, he throttled up and pushed closer to the impending dogfight.

Three of the bi-wings rolled to the right to engage Guile's wingman and Bea. The remaining two pulled up on an obvious attempt to avoid him and chase down the transports. Guile killed forward momentum and rolled end over end and reversed his course. He released power back into the engines. While fighting the push against his seat, he switched back to missiles and pulled the nose of the nova up to cut off the two Alcon fighters.

Bea rolled up on her left wing. She cut power to the port engines and dove in an almost flat spin. Balancing out power halfway through the rotation the nova leveled out facing the opposite direction it was flying. She slowed as she switched her laser cannons to dual fire and released two salvos blindly towards the two pursuing Bi-wings. Both fighters broke off, allowing only minor splashes of laser fire across their wing panels.

"Break left," her wingman said. "I've got the one to the right."

Bea pulled the nova to the left as her wingman shot across her horizon after one of the Bi-wings. The young pilot had his laser set to single fire and was firing madly after the Alcon fighter. With any luck the massive amount of fire would confuse the experienced pilot, who was undoubtedly used to more straightforward tactics.

Rattling the canopy and forcing her deep into the seat, Bea pulled the nova into a tight port turn that brought the nose up ahead of the arcing Bi-wing. She quickly switched to single bursts and lit up the fighter's path with an array of light. Anticipating his next move, she pulled back to the right in time to again cut off the Bi-wing's attempt at dodging. Continued fire splashed up sparks of damaged regeneration panels away from the wings.

"Shields are gone!" Guile's wingman announced in a flustered voice.

Bea had wanted to save her missiles for the next wave of fighters, but the lives of the rookies were more important. It was a waste and she knew it, but she switched to missiles and fired a single warhead wildly ahead of the Bi-wing. The pilot jerked back to the left and up just slightly behind the turn of the nova. She switched to quad burst and pumped two full salvos into its starboard wing. The right engine flared up and went dim, severely cutting down on the fighter's ability to maneuver.

The holographic targeting screen flashed green and Bea fired one last quad burst. The bi-wing's right wing was almost gone and the hull was already damaged. The addition of four full-power laser blasts easily tore into the engine housing and

Chapter Sixteen

erupted the power core. The back half of the fighter split from the rest of the craft and exploded in a single fireball. The right wing disintegrated in the blast while the left engine and wing spun off away from the hull. The canopy blew off as the pilot attempted to eject, but all that followed the clear shielding was a fireball as the forward fuel cells exploded.

"Scratch two," Bea said. Now, where are you, kid?

Guile acquired a lock on the lead bi-wing, but lost it when it broke off. He switched targets to the remaining and released two missiles before he too could break off. The pilot would be able to survive one hit and shake off the other, but it would take some dodging to do it. This freed up Guile to focus on the first fighter. He switched back to guns and reduced fire to single bursts, edging closer as the pilot rolled several times to shake a missile lock that was not there.

The first salvo of laser fire missed over the right wing and the second barely scratched the jut. Guile jerked slightly to the left to get a cleaner shot. He fired a third salvo that cleared to the left after the Bi-wing rolled out. The Alcon pilot was not going to make the kill an easy one. He would become another painted symbol on the side of the Nova though. A careful fake roll to one side would see to that.

An unorthodox move in combat, Guile rolled the craft on a straight-line axis. In conjunction, the bi-wing pulled out to the left, exposing the top of the craft to the nova's guns. Guile continued the roll to the right until his canopy was facing the bi-wing. The Alcon pilot banked up and pulled right to come up along its previous course. When he got there he was greeted by the splash of laser fire across the right wing. The panels evaporated.

Guile switched back to quad burst and set the conversion distance out ahead of the Bi-wing. He fired and as he had expected the pilot pulled up. Right into the upper cannon blasts. The spread out lasers clipped both juts and sent the fighter into an end-over-end, uncontrollable tumble. With the grin of death on his face he pulled the conversion distance back to normal and finished off the bi-wing. Two salvos later, the hull split down the middle and exploded.

"Lead, this is team two. Transport is secure."

"Seven, eight stick close and make sure they get out. Everyone else, fall back to five hundred meters for perimeter protection."

Out of the corner of his eye, Guile caught a regeneration panel rippling out from the wing of the other Bi-wing. He banked to the left to intercept. He brought his nova along a perpendicular course with the fighter. As he closed to laser range a second missile cut off the Bi-wing's path and split the left wing in half. Both the wing and fighter curved into each other. The engine in the center of the jut smashed into the cockpit and erupted. The fighter died in a bright flash that left nothing more than hurtling debris.

"Scratch three and four."

"That's five," Bea's wingman said.

Sutherlin Alliance

Bea kept on the Bi-wing's tail, but the pilot was just too good. He continued to stay one step ahead of her and two steps ahead of the rookie nova pilot. Each pass the Alcon fighter made weakened its shields and further damaged the engines. She knew it was only a matter of time before he had a clear shot and the rookie was dead.

The moment came. The rookie lost maneuvering control and the Bi-wing lined up to finish him off. Bea had just seconds to score a direct hit so she switched to her thermal missiles and armed for dual fire. She didn't have time to wait for a solid lock, so she took the shot at yellow and switched back to guns. Both missiles pierced the right engine core of the Bi-wing. The core exploded and engulfed the fighter in one explosion and several secondary blasts.

"Scratch six."

As she flew through the explosion she expected to find Guile's wing man alive but beaten up. Instead, she caught the final image of a quad burst sinking into the aft quarter of the nova. She could do nothing but close her eyes and accelerate towards the rest of the group.

"I've had it!" The rookie pilot shouted out.

Static burst threw Guile's helmet and was cut off. "Seven, how long before you jump?"

"Thirty seconds."

The nova's tactical screen registered twenty fighters closing on him. Four and five were ten meters off his left wing and the rest of the Alliance fighters were right where he had told them to be. If they did not jump now they would never make it out.

"Forget the nav-probe. Jump now or we're dead."

Threat warnings sounded. Guile checked the tactical screen again and his jaw dropped. The twenty fighters had launched a combined forty missiles that were less than thirty seconds out. As ordered, the two transports sped up then disappeared fifty meters from the probe. Its escorts followed a split second later on the same course. The remaining novas did not have the option of following. Each jumped into the darkness on whatever heading they currently held. Only luck would see them safely out of the system to a point where they could change course and return home.

Guile pressed into his seat slightly ahead of the first missile targeted to him. His visual spectrum blurred momentarily as his eyes adjusted to the sudden change in brightness. The brief loss of sight did not bother him. He knew that, though he was silent throughout the fight, Backer was watching over him. If anyone could see him safely along it would be his artificial companion.

Backer picked up the first navigation probe he came across and used it to drop the fighter back into real space. Guile looked out of the canopy expecting to see blank space or a distant space platform. Instead, he saw the opposite end of the salvage yard. He laughed at the irony of the situation.

"Unidentified fighter. State the nature of your visit."

Chapter Sixteen

For a moment of impulse he almost opened the channel and said course correction. He stopped himself, realizing the mistake that would have been. If he had announced his intention the yard controllers would, by regulation, track his exit vector.

"Backer, plot our exit vector home then store it."

Backer whistled a positive. With that Guile fired an unaided quad burst that caught the edge of the probe and tore it apart. With the salvage yard controllers screaming in his ear he reactivated the star flight initiator and jumped from the system.

With the nova under Backer's complete control he relaxed. This has been more than an interesting day. Someone has sold me out. No one sells out Jared Guile.

Bea dropped from star flight in a system not far from Haron. Her tactical screen displayed five other novas and the two transports. The group was spread out over the entire system, but each had detected the two navigation probes that were designed to prevent ships from flying into the star. There wasn't time to regroup, so each craft was already realigning to make a proper jump home.

"Five to two. Where's lead?"

"I don't know. He was ten degrees off everyone's exit vectors went he went to star flight. He could be light years away by now."

Or face to face with another war ship. "Do you think this was a set up?"

"Not a chance. If it were, the cruiser would have appeared before the first transports jumped. No, this was just coincidence. See you back at the base."

Several of the fighters and the transport reached the nav-probes and disappeared past light speed. Bea turned sharply to align herself with the nearest probe then released control to her Companion. She neither felt like piloting or calculating a jump rate. There were too many uncertainties surrounding the mission. Too many coincidences. She only hoped that Guile would make it back to find out what went wrong.

Merrill frowned at the casualty count coming in from the wing commander. The last of the alert fighters disappeared under the ship and first patrol flight took its place. In total he had lost all six of his rapid response fighters against one kill. Not a good ratio considering the group his fighters went up against was comprised mainly of rookie pilots. Or so monitored communications led him to believe.

"The sensor data is coming back now," the first officer said.

Fallon heard his junior officer but was not listening. Instead he was focused on what had just happened and what had just gone wrong. The Valiant had made an unannounced stop on the far side of the system wide salvage yards, even though the main control station was on the other side. In a flash of sensor alerts the short range probes picked up star fighters and two powered up transports, one of which still held an Alcon registry. He had obviously dropped into the middle of a theft not prepared for what was to come.

He outgunned the small force astronomically, but he failed to take them. Merrill could not help but feel a limited amount of anger and an even larger amount of embarrassment. If word got out that his rapid response fighters had been destroyed by a half squadron of rookie pilots flying old model novas, he would never receive the respect he desired so dearly. His only comfort came with the fact that any further theft the resistance may have had planned had been cut short.

"Sir?"

Merrill shook off his shame and turned to face his first officer. "Sensor data."

"Yes, sir. Unfortunately the Alliance ships jumped without the aid of the nav-probe. Their exit vectors were all erratic and a search along their courses would be sketchy at best. The only contact we could have followed up on appeared on the other side of the yards. The controllers report though that it destroyed that nav-probe before it jumped so there is no way of tracking it."

"There would be no use. The various ships would have completed at least three side jumps by now. What else can you tell me?"

The commander grinned. "Just that the fighter that appeared on the main yard screens was Guile's."

Merrill's heart stopped. "Can you be sure?"

"The yard sensors scanned the ship twice before it escaped and the registry matched that of the fighter that left Volana Three at the same time as Minister Gesh's shuttle."

Merrill slammed his fist down on his control panel. Twice now he had been close to Guile. The first he learned of on the trip here after data teams reviewed shuttle sensor logs before they erased them. Gesh's shuttle had been so close to Guile's nova that the sensors were able to scan the man himself. His profile checked out with that of the man who had destroyed the way station and committed multiple acts of piracy.

Now he was within sight of Guile. His own eyes had seen the speck of light that was the mercenary's nova. The frustration of the situation was more than he could bear. In his dismay, Merrill stood and walked off the bridge. He entered his ready room and sat down with care. He was not fatigued nor was he disappointed in his own actions enough to drop to the seat with the full force of his body. Instead he took his place where he belonged.

Any other captain would have abandoned his fighters and chased the transports on their last course. Merrill may have been an overly ambitious officer but he was not an impatient man. Experience had taught him to be aware of his opponent's tactics and to take opportunities as they arose. He had to smile. His ability to see those opportunities had brought him here. Had taken him from a dead end or lost lead. He brought him to within eyesight of his objective.

"Record."

"Ready," a computerized voice responded.

"My lord. I have new information that could be of use to you. Acting on your order I have unexpectedly interrupted an Alliance raid on the Haron salvage yards. Jared Guile was leading the assault. Though nothing was missing from yard records I can account for one stolen transport. The small group of fighters also managed to

Chapter Sixteen

kill six of my fighters. It is my belief that he is training Alliance pilots in Imperial tactics and also in pirate tactics."

"I am requesting that the light carrier and additional fighters I was promised to aid in star fighter attacks be expedited." Merrill stopped. He leaned back, hit with a realization. "I am also requesting that the sealed files of Devil squadron be reopened and transmitted to me."

"Stop."

"Message ended," the automated recorder said.

It all began to make sense. Jared Guile is hired by the Alliance to destroy an Alcon staging base. After the job is done he is informed that Devil squadron exists as a new squadron in the Alliance. Out of loyalty he rejoins the squadron.

Jared Guile was from Devil. Irony sank in even further. Merrill had commanded the Nightwing during the Badlands campaigns. The same ship that had housed two flight from Devil during the two years of constant combat. The same ship that was home to the man he now pursued to the ends of the galaxy.

Fallon grinned out of the corner of his mouth. The revelation made his mission all that much more inviting. Not only was the man a rebel against the Empire but he was also a traitor. An act looked down as the lowest crime against The Emperor and a direct insult to himself and to Admiral Fallon, who was once the commander of the Blackhawk.

"Comms, this is the captain. Encrypt my message and send it to Admiral Fallon."

"Are you ok, captain?" the first officer asked.

"I'm fine, commander. Recall all flights and move us to the other end of the yards. Make a request of Yard control and pull all personnel files. Correlate that with current pirate and mercenary profiles."

"You think they had inside assistance in the raid."

"They must have. The sensor screen was down during the theft. If you do find a correlation arrest those involved and hold them for the Admiral." Merrill leaned back to silence all communications to his office when he paused. "Oh, and commander. I should be receiving a personal response from the Admiral once he arrives. Send it directly to my ready room then seal the file."

"Yes, sir."

Merrill placed his office on a do not disturb status before relaxing. You have made a mistake, my friend. You should never have worked with the Alliance.

Chapter Seventeen

Fallon stepped from the interrogation room with a heavy step and looked both ways down the long corridor. He could not help but sigh. Eight straight hours of torturous interrogation was more then he could bear. It was not so much the punishment he had inflicted on the two pirates who were working at the salvage yards, but the time it had taken to do it. Both were extremely resistant to the long series of mind probes, a product of a harsh environment.

In the end long needles stabbing deep into the brain had extracted the desired information. The process eventually led to death as the wounds inflicted were not repairable. Those that did survive were clinically brain dead and of no use to society. The rest were cataloged and launched into space in disposable tubes. Doomed to drift until they burned up in some distant atmosphere or star. A fitting end to an enemy of the Empire.

MU-12 robotic maintenance units rolled past as he walked away from the room. Having no emotions they simply picked up the bodies, logged them, then disposed of them in an orderly manner. They were nothing more than heartless pallbearers. To the rest of the ship's crew they were a valuable asset as they were left with all the jobs no one cared to have. The ship remained spotless and in prime condition do to the diligence of these short, black-domed units.

Fallon stopped next to a sectional control panel mounted flush with the corridor. Slowly he leaned himself against the wall and depressed the communications button. "This is the Admiral. Get me the bridge."

Interrogations were not as enjoyable as they had once been. With the Alcon Imperial fleet now having autonomous control of star systems, interrogations were now considered a duty and not a pleasure. Something about running outside galactic law in extracting information from prisoners gave the chore a perk.

A moment passed and a female answered. "Bridge control."
"I need to speak with the captain."
"One moment."
"Yes," S'Lendo answered promptly.

"We have all we're going to get from them. Our initial assessment was correct. Guile was the principle involved in the acquisition of the platform. The deal was to steal the platform for the Alliance. From there, it would have been given to the smuggling group in exchange for trading rights and sanctuary. In addition to the two transports, Guile was also in contact with these two for six light freighters and twelve fighter warhead launchers."

"He wanted to arm the freighters."

"Or his fighters. Either way we now have proof he is trading for arms and not just supplies. This will dictate our next move."

"Which is?"

"Contact Administrator Newby and have him send us his current listing of known arms dealers. We have a partial list to compare so we will know if he is holding something back. Explain this to him so that he complies the first time around. Once we have the list I want scout teams to investigate the dealers."

"Very good, sir. I would like to add something though."

"That is?"

"An hour ago you received an eyes only message from Admiral Ishat. It was marked at your earliest convenience so I thought it unnecessary to disturb you."

Fallon closed his eyes. "Understood, captain. Have it displayed in my ready room and I will read it when I get there."

He pressed the communications button again and pushed off the wall. Fallon added a spring to his step to help him along his way. He may not have wanted to receive a transmission from the admiral, but he was surely not going to waste any more time not reading it.

Guile rolled the Nova over and accelerated through the asteroid field. It had been days since his harsh encounter with the Valiant and he was still upset. All arrows pointed to the people he traded with. Each would have had a reason for giving him away and exposing his link to the resistance. One name stuck out from the rest though. One man who had influence from all sides and could easily give in at the sight of a laser bolt.

Administrator Newby was not known for his ability to hold information back when threatened. He did have ways for avoiding the key questions, but that seldom was the case when dealing with the Empire. They were a thorough bunch of soldiers who never left out a question and always pushed their point across with a fair amount of force. They were the perfect investigators and he was the fox on the hunt.

In a way Guile could not blame Newby for giving him away. If he had been in the same position under similar circumstances he would have given in as well. He just would not have made it so visible. Only an idiot would miss the red carpet leading back to the portly Caperan. And only an idiot would not call him on it.

First things first, though. While on his quest for vengeance he had to make a stopover at the destroyed Alliance outposts in the Bromos system. Backer chirped warily, drawing Guile's attention off the starboard wing. A glimpse of light from a

Chapter Seventeen

piece of metal glittered in his eyes and he dropped power to the main engines. Working strictly with the control thrusters he rolled the fighter to the right and hit the forward lights. Right there, under the heavy lights he saw the tail fin from a Nova. Blasted from its hull and burned from the inside out.

Guile rolled the fighter back to the left and caught the sight of more wreckage as the powerful forward lights illuminated everything they passed. He pushed the fighter forward, keeping a close eye out for any of the metal pieces to be crossing his path at a high rate of speed. He was really more concerned with asteroids slamming into him, but that seemed irrelevant at the moment. The outpost fighters had been torn apart in an attack, leaving little to the imagination on what could have happened to the crew of the station itself.

Buried in one of the larger rocks was the control tower and landing bay for the resistance outpost. Guile eased in and landed. He had been expecting a few of the fighters to still be here in pieces, but by the looks of things they all made it out before the attack commenced. Even the escape modules and transports were gone. Still, with no word from the crew he had to assume they were all dead or captured.

Backer shut down all but the main power systems of the fighter in the distant chance that they had to make a hasty retreat. In the meantime, Guile climbed down from the safety of the cockpit and proceeded on foot inside the asteroid base. He led with his rifle, but it was his gut that had him turn down certain corridors. His keen intuition had not failed him this far into his life.

His search led him to the control tower and communications room of the small, but spread out outpost. What it lacked in rooms it more than made up for in long corridors and tall access ladders. Ideally the design was meant to slow down the heavily armored Imperial troops. In reality it did nothing more than aggravate the rotating crews.

The small combination control tower and communications room was empty. There were no signs of struggle and little or no evidence that the Alcon had been here. The only indication that they had boarded was the slight indentations from the armored boots in the decking. Given the speed with which outposts were constructed, cheaper and lighter decking was used. The flimsy metal gave way easily under the weight of armor.

Guile sat down at one of the terminals. He typed in the access code given to him by Patron and pulled up the memory core system information. The last legal entry into the system had been made a while back and the first of several illegal entries was made shortly there after. The majority of the core had been dumped somewhere in between there.

What Guile looked for was the last entry made by the outpost commander. He was sure that it would not be included in the dump, since being invisible to the Imperial troops, it would have been buried in one of the non-essential systems. What gave him trouble was in the choices of where to look. There were over thirty non-essential systems spread out over the station and each was at the end of a long series of program loops.

161

Sutherlin Alliance

It was going to cost Patron extra, but six hours later Guile found the entry. Located in the toiletry maintenance program the entry was encoded using three separate encryption types. Luckily for Guile all of them were familiar to him so the code-cracking portion of this little side mission took less than ten minutes. The result was worth the effort. As the entry opened a command code within the log activated the outposts primary systems and unlocked all the buried files.

"Congratulations, my Alliance friend. You must be very cunning, as you've just succeeded where even I would have failed. You either must be a pirate or a friend of one to have found my log and cracked the codes."

Guile grinned. If only you knew.

"You probably already know who I am, so I will skip to the details of this message. Under any other circumstances this would primarily be a release command for the outpost, but because the Empire has yet to discover us I am given the opportunity to give a detailed report."

"An hour ago a star cruiser dropped from star flight and collided with the outer edge of the asteroid field. It sustained heavy damage to the forward sections, but not enough for us to attack her with any success. Our best chance is to initiate a full evacuation and leave as soon as we are spotted. It should not be much longer now. Scout ships continue to sweep scanning screens closer and closer to our position."

"As the files you unlocked will show, we have made some very good connections within the smuggling community. We were also able to find more information on that mercenary Patron was asking about. It appears that Jared Guile has already received a major contract and will be unable to assist us. I only hope that the information we provided earlier did not go to waste."

I'm living proof that it didn't.

"A matter that could use looking into should an acceptable smuggler be hired would be a new ship that the Empire has been testing out. A probe in a system in the outer edge of the galaxy picked up on a single, unknown ship, then a strong energy surge that fried the transmission. It could be a prototype of a long-range weapon, but that's merely speculation. It would take an inside source to find out more."

"I would like to add that there is one person you should avoid if you decide to trade with the smugglers. There is a Caperan administrator that has a disliking for the Alliance. I believe that he may have sold us out to the Horde. We tracked the star cruiser's entry vector and believe that it came from that general area. This is all speculation of course, but I still wouldn't trust him."

"They spotted us," a voice in the background said.

"If any of us manage to escape once they find us, the survivors will make for a small, uncharted system on the edge of the galaxy. With any luck we'll make it back to the cell."

The log entry ended. Guile continued to stare at the control panel for a moment longer as his mind began to cycle through the information he had just learned and what he already knew. From what he could tell, the outpost had been hit by a star cruiser entering the Horon system, but since it only stopped because of a mishap, the

Chapter Seventeen

Alliance outpost was not the intended destination. No, the ship was after him. He came to the assumption given the short gap of his stop over and the arrival of the star cruiser.

Guile had only met with three people on Horon and all were trusted smugglers. None of them would need a payoff for information or fear Alcon torture. All were well off in their line of work and could make an escape just as quickly as he could. No, someone else had to have sold him out. Someone that had enough ties to the underground to have found out he had been there.

"Backer, fire up the systems," Guile said with the comm channel to his fighter open. We'll be visiting Newby sooner than I had expected."

Barger sat in the cockpit of his fighter with Sadler whining profusely at him. His companion disliked the fact that it had not been informed of a mission ahead of time. Barger attempted to tell him that he had not known either. There was simply no reasoning with it. Sadler had not served its master this long without picking up some of Barger's less than honest traits.

"Shut up!" Barger snapped as he plugged the personal computer into the fighter consol. "You can stop chastising me now."

"He doesn't trust us?" Shadle called up from below.

Barger leaned over the edge and looked down into her warm eyes. The mild attraction that he felt for her had grown in the past few days, having spent more time with her. He decided that the unannounced mission Patron had given him would allow him the opportunity to reevaluate the situation.

"I'm not sure if I agree with him anymore."

"Why the change of heart?"

"Not a change. I'm just going to take this as a break and nothing more. You told me yourself that I need to stop over evaluating things."

"Good," she beamed. "It's nice to know that you feel safe with us."

"I'm not going to go that far. I'm still confused as to why Patron chose now to have me visit another alliance cell with the last simulated training run coming up tomorrow."

"Maybe he agrees with you that it's time to have Bea lead a mission as she was intended to. Ghost will more than likely be hers one of these days."

"I hope that's the reason."

Shadle slapped the nova's ladder. "Let it go. The Alliance isn't that complicated. You sound more like Imperial intelligence than a fighter jock."

Barger smirked. He did not want to let her see his amusement. "If you say so."

Get going, stud." She stepped back from the ladder. "I'll be waiting for you."

"I'll remember that."

Barger let the canopy close then seal. He kept his eyes fixated on her as she backed away from the Nova. He noted that she would not take her eyes off of his, and then realized he was doing the same.

"Puppy love," he whispered. Sadler barked at him, drawing his attention and a quirky look of dismay to his face. "Don't worry, buddy. I'm not blind." He returned his gaze to hers. "I'm just beginning to see."

Chapter Eighteen

The Rookie pilots of the Alliance dropped into the heavily padded chairs of the briefing room relieved that they were finished with yet another arduous simulator session. This time the run had been a bit more intense then any other the twenty-five young pilots had experienced before. Either they were being rewarded for their improved piloting skills or they were being punished for failed objectives. Either way, the mission was taxing and much too long.

The reptilian looking Ogden Scio and the only Sutherlin represented among the pilots, Nyssa, sat in the front row as they always had. Their abilities had not earned them their place in the room. Rather they were told to sit in the front for reasons beyond them. They did not know whether Captain Stead thought they needed to pay extra close attention to instructions or he just wanted them close. In any case it gave each of them a more personal feeling towards their superiors, being as close as they were.

After a few minutes of being allowed to cool down, Stead and Bea walked in from the right side of the room. Neither held any emotion on their faces. That could mean anything considering the outcome of the simulated mission. Their target had been a heavily defended Alcon station. Half the squadron had been killed inside two minutes. The rest exhausted their resources, succeeding only to knock down the station's shields and weaken the fighter defense to six. It took an additional wave of fighters to completely destroy all fighter defenses and to weaken the station enough for a boarding party to raid it.

As expected, the entire mission had taken over six hours. What was not expected was the rapid turnaround between being shot down and fleeing before they were thrust back into battle. The brief flight briefing had informed them that even if they had gotten killed they would rejoin the mission under a new identification number. It was unusual, but no one questioned their orders.

Bea leaned against the facing wall while Stead stopped behind a central podium. "Welcome back from your last official simulated run."

Murmuring erupted around the room, but was silenced by Stead. "You can celebrate later. After you are informed of your new role in the Alliance."

"As of now you are no longer considered rookies or green pilots. Your flight status is being upgraded to field service and ranks will be given according to your flight performance."

"The situation as it stands now is that Ghost will be losing two of its own to assist on a mission. Because of this, three of you will not be joining Blue and Gray squadrons as you have anticipated. The choice was a difficult one and required a final test of your growing skills. That is one of the reasons you were given the difficult task of attacking an Imperial space station."

"I would like to start off by saying that the mission you undertook was by far the most difficult in our simulator database. Though we downsized its defenses and removed the warships that are a normal part of station protection, this was still a task that is next to impossible to complete. Especially with the size force sent up against it."

The lights dimmed and a wall screen illuminated with a tactical readout from the mission. "Your initial losses were expected. To tell you the truth, I personally thought you would have lost more after your first pass. The skills of the defending fighters were higher than you're used to and you were going in without the aid of more experienced wing men."

"The second attack wave was designed to test your ability to jump into a battle after it had already begun. Much to my surprise you all preformed flawlessly and picked up right where the first wave had left off. The time it took you to finish off the station's defenders and pound it down to a respectable level was far above my expectations. If this had been an actual attack, the raiding party would have had more than enough time to secure the station and prepare for a counterattack from war ships."

"The only aspect of the mission that troubled me was the heavy losses you sustained during the second wave. You should have lost two, maybe three fighters during the attack. Instead more than half were either destroyed or forced to return to base for heavy repairs. For that reason alone, none of you made squadron commander of the newly formed Gray squadron. Instead I am pulling the first officer from Blue and placing him in command."

"I would like to add though that a few of you came close to getting that command. Therein lies my problem. Those pilots are going to receive the enormous responsibility of joining the permanent formation of Ghost." Stead stepped back from the podium and gave way to Bea.

"Flight officers Nyssa and Scio are hereby ordered to report to Ghost briefing tomorrow morning."

Nyssa was plainly overjoyed by the promotion, but Scio seemed reserved. He sat back and took in a deep breath, letting his companion know he was not at all pleased. Nyssa leaned towards him to ask him what was wrong. He shook his head before the

Chapter Eighteen

words could come out. If he was upset he was not about to express his feelings verbally in front of his superiors. He was above that type of rookie display.

"As for the rest of you, your new assignments have already been posted in the barracks. Should you have any questions or problems with your new positions please see myself or Captain Stead. We will be in or around the flight area the rest of the day."

The door at the back of the briefing room quietly shut, but it did not escape Stead's attention. He saw the pilot enter and saw his upset face. This was neither the time nor the place for the confrontation he knew was coming so he quickly wrapped up the briefing. "I wish you all the best of luck in your new assignments. I know the Alliance is going to prosper with pilots such as yourselves defending it."

"Dismissed," Bea casually said. She too saw Barger enter the room.

While the rest of the pilots stood and walked out, the two Ghost recruits stopped in front of the two officers. They each shook their hands in turn, then gave a group salute. Nyssa promptly left the room, but Scio stayed. He had caught a glimpse of Barger and drew a curious look to his face. His mercenary teacher was not supposed to be back for another week from his long excursion, leaving his Imperial defector teacher to take full charge of the training. Needless to say, he had taken the job quite seriously and it showed with every mission.

"Mister Barger," he said as he approached him.

Bea reached out to stop him.

Scio reached the back of the room and what he had to say the others could easily hear. "Thank you, sir." He raised his hand to shake Barger's.

He accepted. "No need to thank me, Ogden. Militia pilots are known for their skills. You were a prime candidate from the beginning."

The curious look that held strong to his face thickened. "You don't approve of something. Is it my assignment to Ghost?"

Barger shook his head. "I recommended you for the position, as did Jared. I'm here to speak with your superiors."

Scio looked back and caught the stunned expression on both Stead and Bea's faces. He faced forward. "Do you know something we don't, sir?"

Barger pushed his way passed him. "It's none of your concern at the moment and don't call me sir."

"You can leave now, mister Scio," Bea said.

The doors barely shut behind the scurrying Scio when Barger reached Stead with a strong shove. The brawny Captain rebounded off the wall behind him and ended up in his strong grasping hands. Barger shook him once then released him back against the wall.

Bea held her hand in front of Barger to stop another attack. "Calm down," she insisted. "Whatever brought you back early doesn't have to end in a death."

Barger grabbed Bea's hand and swung her around once so that she lost her bearings, then he pushed forward and slammed his shoulder into Stead's gut. In the only response his body would allow, Stead collapsed to the floor in pain. Bea stole enough balance to grip both of Barger's shoulders and pull him back. It was all she could do to keep him from killing the Captain.

"Get up, Stead!" Barger demanded of him. "Get up and take the punishment you're giving these kids."

Stead rolled up. He was still on the ground, but in a sitting position. He had his hands firmly wrapped around his stomach to put pressure on the growing bruise. "I was ordered. It wasn't my decision, Wes. I may want you gone, but I don't want my pilots killed."

"What orders?" Bea asked.

"You could have disobeyed them."

"I couldn't disobey a direct order from the Patron."

"What orders?"

Barger shook Bea loose and turned to face her. "Those rookies that just walked out of here are being sent to intercept a destroyer convoy. You and I both know that those convoys consist of three destroyers and twelve freighter haulers. The crossfire alone will kill half of them in the first minute of battle."

Bea's eyes widened. She stepped out from behind Barger to see Stead. Her left boot moved close enough to kick him in the ribs. "Is this true?"

He nodded. "But I don't know how he found out. The attack group was supposed to be gone a day before he got back."

Barger whirled around. "I found out from Patron, though he didn't know he was telling me. I requested that I be given a small assault team to assist on a raid I was to undertake. One that Jared had set up before he left. Patron told me yesterday while I was leaving for a little intelligence work that the team most qualified to help had been assigned to the convoy raid so he was going to give me a few Ghost pilots. That meant that the only fighters available to cover the assault team would have to come from Blue squadron."

Stead grinned. "He's too smart for his own good. I thought with Jared gone that the brains had left with him. I see our other hire has a mind as well."

Bea anticipated a move and grabbed Barger's shoulder as he began to lunge. "Save it for the sims, Wes. We need him alive."

Barger shook her off and gave her a cold stare. "You need him alive."

"You can blame me all you want, but it's out of my hands. The rookies were only mine until they completed their training. From there they receive their new assignments, then they're out of my control. I wish I could pull them all into Ghost, but that isn't possible."

Stead eased himself up still holding his gut. "I may not like you. I may not like your methods. I may not approve of the course your life has taken. What I can say is that I've come to admire your abilities and can appreciate your concerns, but they fall on deaf ears when it comes to Patron. He had his mind set on this course of action from day one when he accepted you and Jared. The whole point of having additional squadrons was to broaden the reaches of the Alliance."

"You don't share his views?" Bea asked.

Chapter Eighteen

"Oh I do, but not on this. These pilots are still too inexperienced to be taking on such a task, which is why I need you to go with them."

Bea grinned. "Patron won't like this."

"He doesn't have a choice," Barger said. "If he disapproves of Stead's idea then he's going to find himself short on supplies in the coming months. I may not have any say as to the way the Alliance is run, but we all know a very touchy mercenary who can put some serious pressure where it's needed." He pointed a finger at Stead. "And you can quote me on that to him."

"I will. Now if you'll excuse me I have to change my shorts and take a pain killer." Stead gave Barger a sarcastic smirk as he walked passed. Any anger he may have felt towards Barger's assault was well hidden. He left out the door in the back of the room.

Bea opened her mouth but found it difficult to speak with Barger's hand covering it. "You can come in now, Ogden."

The door all the pilots exited from slowly opened and Scio walked in. Behind him came Nyssa.

"Welcome back, gentlemen," Bea said. "How did you know?" She asked in a whisper.

"It wasn't hard."

Scio and his companion stopped in front of Barger and Bea. "Sorry, sir."

"Don't call me sir. I'm not an officer and I'm not your superior. I'm your teacher and nothing more."

"That's not true. You are my mentor. After our little talk the other day, I studied your tactics and I know your moves. You were the best fighter pilot the Empire ever had."

Barger grinned, but not from appreciation. He accepted the compliment, but not for the reason he had intended. He neither considered himself the best pilot or a mentor. If anything, he felt like a hired tutor. In his mind a traitor had no place teaching kids how to fly. He should have been milking his role in the Alliance for everything it was worth, going on to abandon them with nothing. The eyes of the young men he looked into told him differently though.

Bea noticed the vague expression on his face and stepped in. "I'm sure Wes appreciates the compliment, but he's never been very open." She looked to him for reassurance. "Or so I've been told."

Barger's glazed look melted away. "Thank you, Ogden, but as I'm sure you heard, you aren't out of the woods yet. You have the distinct honor of attacking a near impossible target for lightly armed young pilots. You will have little to no veteran support and you will not be allowed to return to base unless the mission is a success or you're all dead."

He was in the process of walking away when Bea grabbed his arm. "I think you can be a bit more optimistic than that."

Barger sighed. "If it makes you feel any better, the two of you and Narra have the best chance of living the longest. I suggest that you preprogram an escape route before you leave so that when the last boarding party is destroyed you can make a run for it." He shook loose and started for the door at the back of the room.

Nyssa turned. "We'll be victorious, Wes. We'll make you and Jared proud."

Barger stopped at the door and squeezed his eyes shut. A lump formed in his throat as it sank in that no matter what he said, no matter what he did, these kids were going to look up to him and respect him as both a pilot and a teacher. No amount of credits could buy away his growing feelings for his students.

"I think you hit a sour note with that one," Scio said.

Just a sore one. Barger threw the doors open and as he walked down the hall he heard Bea tell the two that they would be fine. A noble gesture but one that he could not ensure. Not even if he went along, a limited assault would never be successful without a strong backup and a healthy mix of experienced pilots.

What was worse? How could one compare attacking a defenseless city to allowing the defenseless to walk straight into the arms of death? The citizens died at his hands because of orders from a higher power. Now kids would die because of similar orders.

Barger opened his door to a brightly lit room. Sitting across the living area was Shadle. She was not in her usual flight suit. Instead she wore a soft, white dress that hung loose around her shoulders and waist. Given the circumstances he felt nothing towards her alluring look. If he wanted, he could think back to her soft touch in the infirmary from weeks past.

"You're back early," she softly said.

"You expected it." Barger let the door shut behind him, but he did not walk further into the room. "Why are you here?"

"I knew you'd confront Stead before you did anything else. I thought you might want to talk."

"You thought wrong." Barger turned into his room. He lost sight of her as he dropped onto his bed.

"He stopped by here after you attacked him. He knew I'd be here and he wanted to warn me that you weren't exactly in your right mind. He also said that you don't approve of the convoy raid."

"As I understand it, not many people do."

Shadle appeared in the doorway. "To counter your disapproval I don't approve of your current plans."

Barger raised his head enough to look at her. "I thought we went over this."

"Why haven't you told your team the real reason for this mission?"

Barger sat up. "Because that aspect of the mission has nothing to do with the rest of my team. When our primary objective is complete, I'm sending the rest of them back and continuing on myself."

"Stead won't allow you to do this alone."

"What say does he have in this?"

"Because he's going with you."

Chapter Eighteen

"Like hell he is," Barger growled. "He agreed that it would be myself and Jared conducting the break in."

"It's not up to you on who you take. Stead gets to pick the team."

"You know what will happen, Narra. Within the first five minutes there'll be a power struggle between the three of us. It's bad enough that I have to spend two days in the same cabin with Jared. I already have mental scares from the trip I took with Haggin."

Shadle shook her head. "It won't be like that. Stead knows that this is your deal and he has accepted that, but as soon as he finds out you plan to stay on that ship he'll want to come with you to keep you from making that mistake. There's a lot at stake here and he wants to make sure that the job gets done. Even if that means he has to risk his life to make sure you come back."

"And what about the convoy run?"

Shadle took a step back. The question caught her completely off guard. "What about it?"

"It'll be a slaughter. You and the others will die and you'll be going down with a flight load of kids. Pilots that would still be in their first year of the naval academy. Not even ground crews are placed into active duty so soon."

"You're growing a conscience on me, Wes, and I don't like it. You're suppose to be this hard-backed Imperial pilot with a taste for blood, not a simple-minded politician."

Barger dropped back to the bed. "Tell me about it. I had built up a stomach for killing people in cold blood. Now I find myself caring for kids that until now were a faceless enemy to me."

"And now they have faces."

Barger grabbed a pillow and put it over his face. His voice was muffled by the thick filling. "Faces, minds, hearts, and a strength I only wish I could get back." He threw the pillow to the floor. "I lost their innocence years ago and with it I lost my ability to see the positive in every challenge. Now I only see the impending dangers and try to come up with ways around them."

"Yet you still chose to take on the task of destroying Devil squadron single handedly."

"What other choice did I have? You know that eventually you'll bump into them and not be able to run. If I at least remove the best then maybe the fight will level out. I only hope that seeing Alder will make it all easier," he added under his breath.

"Then you find out that Patron replaced one danger with another." Shadle leaned against the door jam. "He has the best interests of the Alliance in his mind."

"Does he?" Barger pushed himself into a sitting position. "I don't know, Narra. I don't know what I'm going to do anymore. I've destroyed my livelihood by taking your side and possibly the lives of those around me. Before, I was a man who loved nothing and had nothing to lose. No one could stop me because I feared no one. I was a man to be feared and people respected me. I was to make Captain in another month."

He stared deep into her eyes. "I've taken those kids into my heart like a teacher and his students. I do my best to prepare them for the worst, but it will never be enough. I'm going to lose them and in the process, I'm going to lose the last bit of humanity inside of me. And the worst part is that I took your advice and now I'm beginning to see them as friends."

"Is that what you fear most, Wes?" Shadle asked. "Do you fear crossing the ledge to pure evil more than the loss of your edge? Do you truly fear becoming what you have fled?"

"I stand on the cliff overlooking the abyss that is the Emperor and his rule. I've fought it by defying his laws and committing crimes against his territory. What better am I though? That thin line between defiance and power is almost unrecognizable to the naked eye. I only see it when I look into the eyes of someone I'm about to kill or in the eyes of a pilot I have trained. It's there that the battle is fought."

His eyes narrowed. "The true battle for the galaxy isn't with fighters or with star cruisers, it's within ourselves. If for some stroke of incredible luck the Alliance is victorious in taking down the Empire, then where do we go? The ruling house is assumed by someone like the Patron and the cycle starts anew. Who's even to say that the galactic council that the Emperor replaced was any better than his? It's all about where that power leads and who's leading it."

"I am a prime example of that. I have the abilities to kill with the simple twitch of my finger. Would I run the organization better or just bloodier? These are the questions that have run through my mind of late."

Shadle stepped towards the bed and sat down next to him. "You've had a lot on your mind."

"So much so that it hurts when I sleep. I have dreams about the needless assault that changed my attitude about my career and about the cruiser that we ran into at the salvage yards. The faces of those young pilots and of my friends flash before my eyes on a daily basis. The worst part is that the more I speak with old associates I've found within the Alliance the more I begin to wonder if I shouldn't drop everything and disappear as I had planned. I may have no credits at the moment and nowhere to go, but that has never stopped me in the past. I never settled into one position until I enrolled in the academy."

"But you won't go." She rested a hand on his leg.

"No, I've just acquired a mean streak and a talent of scarring the hell out of people."

"And yourself."

He grinned. "Especially myself."

"That's not always a bad thing." Shadle stood and patted him on the shoulder. "Just don't forget that just because you are the acquired help here that you are not alone."

Barger watched her walk out of the room. He wanted to say something to her. To tell her that he appreciated speaking with her. Somehow the words never materialized. Shadle knew how he felt but he still felt the need to tell her so. Since his

Chapter Eighteen

acquisition into the Alliance she had been there by his side. He never really understood why, just that he appreciated it.

Life. What an ironic word in this day and age. He had just poured his heart out to a new and close friend yet the looming threat still remained. He did not care about his own mission, knowing that he would do his best and that the pressure lay entirely on his shoulders. The convoy mission was more of a concern to him. He had done his best to prepare them for the worst, but he knew it was not enough. He had to do more.

Administrator Newby walked through the opening to his trade administration building with the exuberance of a new day. Profits were up, trade was high, and the locals seemed to be more content then they usually were. Even the guards, who leaned against the edges of the entrance, were more relaxed then they normally were. It was strange for a Horde to be so relaxed, but it was shaping up to be a pleasantly strange day.

Newby stopped at the reception desk and leaned over towards the strikingly beautiful Caperan woman on the other side. Caperan women were not short and overweight like the males. In sharp contrast they were tall and proportioned like Telestian women. The only feature that connected the males and females to the same race was the face, but to a Caperan the compacted features were far more attractive than the slender shapes of other women faces.

"Good morning, my love."

The female sat motionless with a blank expression on her face.

Newby's eyes narrowed. "Pres?"

Pres' lifeless body fell forward onto the desk as if responding to his plea for a response. Her head smashed onto the metallic desk. Her back was exposed for him to see and it was a sight he truly wished he could have avoided. A three centimeter wide by ten centimeter long cut had been made along her spine and her cracked backbone was exposed. The wound was cauterized marking the impact of a light blade so he could see straight through to a burned out heart.

Newby stumbled backwards in utter shock. He had seen people murdered before, but not here. Not within the hallowed halls of the administration building. Not his own staff. Now, as he looked over Pres' dead body, he realized that even the great Newby could not curtail the problems affecting the rest of the city.

A cold thought washed over him. Newby looked back to his Horde guards. He stumbled again at the sight of blade wounds to their chests. The cuts were precise and fatal. The cauterized slices stretched from under the right arm to the right hip. The exact location of the Horde heart. The cut was so precise that the two guards could not have been openly attacked. They would have to have been attacked from behind and killed quickly enough so as to not disturb the other.

Newby scrambled towards the guards. Carefully so as not to disturb the lifeless bodies, he slipped the rifles from both the Horde. Both weapons were still set on standby, confirming his theory that the kills for subtle and quick.

Newby knew he had been the target, which meant that there would be more dead bodies on the upper levels. The sight of two dead men in the elevator confirmed this. The addition of his personal secretary on his office level added even more tension to his face. The worst was yet to come though. If the person or persons who broke in had intended to kill him, then they would have had to pass the guard station down the hall from his office. There were always four guards stationed inside, each with training in riot control and hand-to-hand combat.

He could not believe his eyes. All four lay dead on the floor of the security office. Each had a single blade cut to the chest. There was no sign of struggle, no damaged walls from rifle fire. Their weapons were still in their holsters. Rifles were still locked in the clear weapons locker. Light blades were still in their boot clips. Even the calm expression burned onto the guards' unflinching faces left a disturbing feeling within his bones.

Newby feared for his life. He counted ten bodies on his way to his office, six of which were intimidating guards. How could he defend himself against a group with such vicious swiftness and accuracy? He pondered this thought while he took the safeties off both rifles and raised them to hip level. They may have sat unusually against his wide hips but they could still blow holes a foot wide through the thick walls.

A few steps from his office a deep voice filtered out. One that he knew well and one that he would normally welcome.

"Welcome in on this fine morning, Administrator Newby."

Newby lowered both rifles and walked through the door with his face fading red. "What are you doing here, Jared?"

Guile sat in Newby's warped chair with his heavy boots firmly planted on the desk. The light blade used to kill the morning shift was buried a centimeter deep into the desk, still stained red from it's victims. The thin covering over his face was hanging slightly so that the top of his smiling mouth was exposed. The deep scars on his face curled up above his lip and twitched as he spoke.

"You seem to be having a personnel problem today."

Newby raised the rifles and squeezed the triggers but nothing happened.

"You can drop the weapons. I removed the power chambers."

His eyes narrowing, Newby dropped the rifles on the floor. "Why not just level the building? I know you have the ability."

"I wouldn't get my point across. More importantly I would not have been able to speak with you."

"Why not just come in an ask me what you need? Why did you have to kill my staff?"

"I didn't want you to die alone."

The anger on Newby's face paled away and his eyes hung open. "Then you still plan on killing me."

Chapter Eighteen

"If you don't answer my questions correctly." Jared dropped his feet to the floor and leaned forward. "And remember, fat man. I have better connections than you do. I will know if you aren't telling me the truth."

Newby waddled to the center seat and lowered himself down. "Ask me what you need to know, Jared. I won't lie to you. I have too much to lose."

"Good. Then you can start by telling me why a platform that I purchased for the Froment Raiders was intercepted and destroyed by the Empire."

"You don't know what you are asking of me. If they find out that I gave you the answers you seek then I'm as good as dead."

"You're as good as dead anyway if you don't tell me. Because of that intercept the Empire was led straight to a pickup I had previously arranged. The Empire was also made aware of two hires I had working in the Haron salvage yards. They are good hires, but they aren't good enough to withstand an interrogation session with the captain of the ship that jumped me."

"Then Captain Merrill has been given the task of finding you."

Guile glanced over his shoulder at the city below. "He has and he is chasing me with Admiral Fallon close behind." He looked back. "I was lucky the first time and escaped. The next time he jumps me I'm as good as dead."

Newby placed his hands palm up on the edge of the desk. "I don't want that. You've got to believe me. You are the best source of revenue I have and the last thing I want is a profit drop off so early in my career."

"You mean so late," Jared growled. "I believe that you want to keep me alive, but you're risking my business future by divulging sales to your superiors. If I catch you doing it again I won't wait for the chance to discuss it with you. This building and all you own, including your miserable life will be a memory."

"Then you will let me live?"

"For now. Look Newby, I still have business to conduct and I need you alive to ensure that my trades aren't interrupted by legal restrictions. You just need to keep your drooling mouth shut. I don't want to have to do it myself."

"But I can't lie to Minister Gesh. If he asks if you have made trades then I need to inform him of them. If I do otherwise then I risk far more than death by your hands. I will end up without skin, hanging in Captain Merrill's ready room."

"I'm not asking you to lie for me, Newby. If you need to give your boss targets then you will have them to give. I just need to be able to trust you to keep my major moves a secret."

"How can I do this?"

"Easily. From here on out every trade or purchase I make will be accompanied by a false one. When asked you will be able to, in good conscious, inform Gesh of the false trade while keeping the real move to yourself."

"And if the Minister finds out what I am doing."

Guile's eyes narrowed and his lips thinned out. "Then I will use my imagination and come up with a fate more horrifying than your scrambled brain could possibly produce in your worst nightmare." He straightened himself and stood. "Are we on the same level?"

Newby looked away from his cold eyes. "Clearly." He reached up and grabbed onto his shirt, stopping him from leaving. "Jared, this visit was not necessary. I would have listened if you would come here peaceably."

Jared removed the stubby hand from his clothes and started to walk out. "I know you too well, Newby." His voice began to trail out down the hallway. "We've been friends too long. I needed you to remember the nightmare you first met."

Unlike their previous meeting, he heard no heavy boots down the hall. Guile blended into the background noises, silent and deadly. He truly appeared as he had when they first met. A man of intense anger and incredible skills. A man whose friends were rich and whose enemies seldom lived long.

As Guile climbed into the cockpit of his Nova, Backer was busily chirping at him. He settled in and called up the waiting message. He frowned at the header, not wanting to read something written by Barger. His frown creased even further behind his thin facial wraps as he read the disturbing contents.

Chapter Nineteen

The Valiant first appeared in the sky above Raleigh as a bright star in the daytime sky. Ordinary citizens traveling about the dusty city paid the anomaly no mind as they went about their daily activities. Only the local government had any idea what the star truly was. The Alcon had returned to this long since abandoned center of trade for little reason. Not since the days after the fifth empire was born had an imperial star cruiser entered the system.

Little more could be said about their intent then a bright flash from the already visible ship. A beam of energy as wide as a low level building pierced the serenity of the afternoon and shattered the tranquility that had befallen the inhabitants of the planet. With the center of trade moving to Cadera Prime all the crime and added activity had left, leaving the natural population to the peace they could only have dreamt about.

The first of what would be many pulses of destruction centered on the modest, one story capitol building. The roof all but burned away from heat alone. The energy beam struck solid and expanded outward along the interior of the once active center of commerce, tearing away exterior walls and throwing them into nearby buildings. The streak of cannon fire ended, leaving not a splinter of flammable material behind. The first punch from the orbiting cruiser struck true and the capitol building was gone.

The gunners of the cruiser waited long enough for the citizens in the city to realize what had happened before they let loose a full barrage. Blast after blast of cannon fire rained down on the city in a never-ending stream of fire and terror. Screams erupted only to be cut short. Heated steel and large fragments of formocrete hurled up from points of impact, bringing a new danger to men and women who were fortunate enough to escape the targeted buildings.

Twenty minutes of sheer horror ended as abruptly as it had begun. The wail of multiple laser fire was gone. All that remained was a city filled with gutted structures and a lucky few who avoided both the fire and the debris of an unprovoked assault by the Alcon Empire. The survivors knew not why their people were singled out in such a way. As they struggled out from under rubble they did not care. They were alive and that was all that mattered.

Captain Merrill leaned forward, straining a tired pair of eyes to view the sensor data that scrolled across any number of screens. Enhanced visual sensors showed a few hundred of the city's recorded two hundred thousand inhabitants slowly moving about. He let a smirk crease the corners of his mouth at the sight.

"There was a time when that city had enough firepower to bring down this ship."

"Excuse me, sir?" said the Valiant's first officer.

"Raleigh, Commander. Do you not remember your trade history?" The commander shook his head. "It doesn't matter. The pirate element that once held this world the way it holds Volana Three is long since gone. Only the sons of those that made a fortune from trade remain. My only wish is that they were present to witness the destruction of their new trade. I find arms dealers lower than pirates and mercenaries."

"I've seen enough," Merrill submitted. "Conclude your scans then send down a detachment to secure the weapons hold. If intelligence is correct then it should be located below the remains of the capitol."

"Sir," said the communications officer. "I have an incoming transmission from the Vengeance."

Merrill moaned. Once again Admiral Fallon was hounding him for progress reports. "On my screen."

"No, sir. It's a status-keeping message. We're being ordered to continue our present course of action and await the Admiral's return."

Return? Merrill thought to himself. Where is he off to? "Very good. Send my usual response then attach a status report. Inform the Admiral that we have quelled two arms dealers and are en route to a third."

I don't like this, Admiral. Merrill relaxed as best he could. Though the absence of his group commander would mean he could catch up on much needed rest, the lack of an explanation for his departure was troublesome and would give him several evenings of grief.

The nova dropped from star flight and immediately sensors sounded proximity alarms just as the fighter appeared inside the target system. Casually checking his tactical screen Guile confirmed the presence of thirty fighters on patrol, a bulky destroyer in orbit around the second planet from the local star, and phantom mines scattered throughout the system. As a precaution he had already set his navigational probe to transmit his fighter's transponder signal and he had programmed the mine frequency into his targeting computer.

Guile had been here before. He had experienced the heavy security only twice, but it was enough to be cautious. This particular pirate organization was well known for its ability to keep the unwanted away. Before moving here two years ago it was reported that the tight defenses had even turned away two Realm destroyers during a surprise raid.

Chapter Nineteen

Backer whistled into Guile's ear. He looked out of the right side of his cockpit in response. Clearly in view he could see two older model fighters. Not much different in design from his nova, the scraps had two engines and a single cannon on each wing tip. They were far from the maneuverability of the Nova and had limited firepower, but the shear number of flights would be more than a match for any unwanted visitor.

"Hold course, mister Guile. You are cleared for approach."

Guile looked to his left and caught a glance at four more fighters pulling along side to escort him. "Understood, patrol. Thanks for not shooting me down."

The nova and ten scraps kept on a straight-line approach to the gray planet. Backer, being the paranoid artificial life form that is was, barked at Guile in upsetting popping noises. He dismissed his companion by muting the channel. He knew the risks of coming to this particular organization, but he also knew the rewards. Such ventures have proven successful in the past.

Guile glided through the thin atmosphere. The nova stabilized its descent at a kilometer and the fighter began to slow. A thin layer of ice coated the canopy in a breath as he completed entry and the heat dissipated. Defrosters automatically activated and the ice melted away. There was not much to the view without the ice though. A thick, toxic cloud layer pressed against the surface of the planet, making visual descents impossible.

The nova slowed dramatically as an invisible hand gripped the fighter. The energy ribbon wrapped around the hull and prevented its propulsion from performing effectively. Guile sat back and smiled. He was glad he had muted his companion. Backer was probably shouting up a storm. He never enjoyed being held in a tractor beam.

The thick clouds never parted. The nova simply set down in the deep gray and the systems powered down by themselves. The tractor beam used was obviously of high value to be capable of the things it had done. The old system he was honored to be held by was a bit harsher. Not only did it slam his fighter onto the ground hard enough to crack a majority of the hydraulic lines to the landing gear, but it had also damaged his star flight motivator. This system was kind enough to extend his ladder and open his canopy for him.

Guile finally opened the channel to Backer and received an immediate earful from the built in computer. "I know. I'm sorry, buddy. Next time we'll fly in on our own."

Backer more than likely knew he was lying, but it was the gesture that counted. Anything less and he would find his cockpit twenty degrees cooler the next time he hopped in. He sometimes wondered if purchasing a self-improving program from the nova was such a good idea. Although it aided him in battle in more ways than he could possibly count, the rest of the time he could be a real pain in the neck.

"Mercenary Guile," A light voice called out of the haze. The words seemed to hiss from the speaker's mouth.

Guile slipped his helmet off his head, but left the mask over his face. He dropped his helmet onto the seat, then flipped himself out of the cockpit. Wasting no time he gripped the edges of the ladder and slid down. He stopped with a hard thump from his boots. He was doing nothing more than showing off that he was a fighter jock. It seldom worked, but he enjoyed it. It wasn't often that he allowed himself such trivial pleasures.

"You surprise me," the same hissing voice said.

Guile stepped closer to the voice, knowing full well who it was. The sight of the lizard-like being was both expected and unwanted. Kaylar Altass, a Phalnx male, was someone he had problems with in the past and someone he had not expected to see. He had thick, gray skin that appeared as scales, though it was just coarse to the touch. He would completely blend in with the heavy cloud cover if not for the dark blue jumpsuit that he wore. It was cut high up to thick shoulder plates. From personal experience he knew that the armor-like pads were as tough as they looked.

"Your transponder code was not expected, mercenary Guile. This should have been your last stop after offending the Empire in such a way."

Guile took a short, sharp bow. "I live to offend." He started to walk past the tall Phalnx, but was stopped with a strong grip. He backed away and looked at him in disgust. "We have no business, Kaylar. I'm here to speak with your sister."

"She does not wish it, mercenary Guile."

The way he termed Guile was of great offence in Phalnx. To be first addressed by title then by last name was considered the lowest of class in their society. The typical way of addressing a person was by the last name alone, and friends were spoken to by their first name as in most societies. Knowing the Phalnx, Guile took the offense to heart and returned it with narrowing eyes and a harsh twist to his words.

"I want to hear it from her, lowlife Altass."

Altass let out what sounded like a deep hiss mixed with a rumbling growl. It was apparent that he would rather tear Jared's head from his body than let him by, but something held him back. He had had his best opportunity while the nova was under the tractor beam's control.

"Look, Kaylar. I'm not here to steal business and I'm not here to fight. I have a deal for your sister and I need a favor in return."

"Your deals are as worthless as your life, and the only favor you'll receive will be to end your miserable life."

"Let Malane decide that for herself."

Altass opened his mouth as if to slap back with another round of harsh words. His head twitched and he grew a smile on his tight face. "You profess your love for another?"

"I don't profess my love for anyone and your sister would be the last person in this galaxy I would sleep with. I wish you'd just believe me and leave it at that. Besides, a night with her would probably kill me."

Altass's eyes narrowed. "Do not insult her."

Guile held his hands up. "I wouldn't dream of it."

Chapter Nineteen

"Good." His eyes narrowed even further until his pupils were hidden. "This way."

Guile let the taller man turn before he rolled his eyes. He had run into Altass in more places than here and this happened every time. At first it appeared as if he were about to lose his life. Then, after a few minutes of a rehearsed speech he calmed down enough to where Guile could continue on. It was a routine he was growing tired of.

The building Guile entered could have been a palace or an elaborate bunker for all he knew. He had not even seen the entrance until he was already inside. The regulator his mask was hooked up to detected breathable air and shut off. The dry air he sucked from the mask told him to take it off and inhale un-recycled air for the first time in days. It was refreshing as exiting his fighter usually was. The taste of processed air never easily went away.

The inside of the complex was decorated much like the imperial palace on Perditia, though the symbols represented an entirely different society. This planet had once been the center of an earlier empire. One that was modest and lasted a mere two hundred years. It died in a flash when the system's sun went nova. The radical variation in temperature and gravitational pull had first stripped the majority of the atmosphere from the planet, then took all the life. All that remained were the barren cities and elaborate sculptures.

Altass hurried him through the large entrance hall and down a long corridor. He stopped at the end in front of golden double doors and straightened to attention. "She will see you at her will."

The double doors parted with a rumble and a slithered voice echoed out of the throne room. "It is my will."

Guile grinned as he passed Altass. The insulting gesture was ignored. He simply received a snort and a growl as he walked passed. The insults would stop there. Whatever their personal grievances with each other they were set aside in the presence of Altass' sister. Not only would she find their little feud a waste of time, but also an insult if it arose in her presence. Neither wanted anything less than to keep her happy.

The throne room was spacious in ceiling height, but it lacked in overall floor space. There was hardly enough room for the throne pedestal that once held the monarch and matriarch's ruling chairs. Instead, the pedestal held a single, swiveling chair encircled by small viewing screens and a variety of controls. Jared took it for granted that in a clutch she could run her organization by herself successfully from this room.

The chair with which the pirate group was controlled faced away from him, but only for the moment. At the sound of his boots coming to a stop at the base of the meter high pedestal the chair whirled around and came to a stop facing him. Sitting within the confining comfort was a Phalnx often referred to as the most successful and feared pirate in the galaxy. Malane Altaff, was one of a select few females from her race that had achieved as much as she had and that alone made her a respected member of her species. The fact that she had the power to back up that respect just added fire to her reputation.

"This is an unexpected visit, Jared, but not an unwelcome one." She rested her dark head against the high backed chair. "Tell me what brings you to my part of the galaxy."

"A proposition and a favor."

Her eyes perked up. "A favor? What could ever bring a mercenary to ask for a favor from a pirate?"

"A price on my head that only the Empire could cover. I also have friends that are in trouble."

"It's a price you deserve. The destruction of an Alcon station is a serious offence. You drove the price up even further when you stole their property and killed their pilots."

"I've stolen from them before. It's the station that disturbed the bees. The hell of it is I didn't know I was hired to blow Imperial property. I thought my contract was part of a pirate feud."

"You didn't do a background check."

"I didn't care. I was two contracts away from permanent retirement and I wanted the credits. I know it's a stupid excuse, but it's still the truth."

"The truth can kill in your line of work. The price on your head is proof of that. Some of my associates would find me a fool for talking to you right know instead of cashing in. I find your little dilemma too inspiring for that, though. You intrigue me and you always have. That may be why I did not have you killed when you left me."

"Tell me, Jared. This price for your capture would normally drive you into hiding. Why would you choose to hold your current contract, or come to me for that matter? I would think you a smarter man than that."

"I guess I'm just an idiot. I thought that with a price after me that you would jump at the opportunity to make a profit at my expense."

Altaff thinned an eye. "How is that?"

"I have recently discovered that some of my more trusted associates have been selling information on the open market. Mainly to Alcon agents. Because of this I am forced to initiate false purchases in order to cover my tracks. This is not only inconvenient, but also expensive and I have to cover contract losses with personal credit. What I offer you is a golden opportunity for some serious profits."

"Go on."

"I'm offering you the entirety of my three current trade contracts with a twenty percent markup. That should be more than enough to cover the acquisition costs and the credits you would lose for not turning me in. The only catch deals with an Imperial convoy."

Altaff sat up and leaned to one side. "You will supply me with these contracts at your earliest convenience?" He nodded. "Convoys aren't a concern. Just give me the details."

Chapter Nineteen

"I have a copy of the contracts with me. I also have a third of the total payment reserved for immediate transfer if you approve of my proposition." Jared walked up half of the ten steps to the top of the pedestal. "If the time I spent with you has taught me anything, it's that you never turn down a chance to turn triple the profit you normally would make on a contract."

"Six months of service to my organization is hardly enough time to gain a lifetime of experience from me."

"It was enough to get me started in my new career."

"As your reputation has shown." She settled back into her chair. "I will agree to your offer. Whatever you need you will have."

Guile removed a data pad from his jacket and tossed it onto one of the status panels. "The time frame on shipments is non-negotiable, but payment dates can be bumped up to ensure that."

"I do have one thing I need to know before I look over your contracts. What is this favor you need of me?"

"It's a big one, but one that I know you can handle. Your background with the Empire is as strong as mine and I know you still have ties."

"My ties were severed the day I retired from active duty twelve years ago," she said. Altaff's voice had dropped an octave and her skin had begun to lighten. "I have not seen nor spoke with my friends and commanders since then. I have not even climbed into a cockpit in that time. My memories were and still are not happy ones about my service. What I have now are informants among Imperial shippers and spies within trade routes."

"The only military link I had was you when you first left the navy and joined me. The only reason I elected to take you on had to do with your service to Devil. Out of all the areas of the Empire, I know from personal experience that Devil pilots are the sharpest thinkers. More importantly, they know the true nature of the Alcon from the sorties they're forced to fly."

"It's for them that I ask this favor of you. Devil lives within the resistance and because of my involvement they may be heading down a path that will see their destruction."

Guile knelt down on the top step and put all his weight on one leg. "These are young pilots. I could see the innocence in their eyes, but I could also see the experience. These are kids that could one day reign as the champions we had always dreamed of becoming, but without the watchful eyes of the Emperor over their shoulders."

"They will never live long enough to see the Alcon die. I doubt it ever will."

Guile was grasping at straws and she knew it. Altaff had never been one for sympathy. "Whatever your doubts they deserve a chance. I need to return that chance to them. I need to know everything you know about the man who is chasing me."

The light returned to Altaff's eyes. "You want to take care of him yourself."

Guile nodded. "All I know of this man is that he is tenacious and not the typical drone captain the Empire assigns to command battle groups. If I can remove him then I know it will set back their search long enough for me to complete my contract with the Alliance and quietly disappear."

"You're thinking again, but foolishly. You will never get close enough to remove him from the equation. This captain does not live by the same reckless abandon that the other captains do. He should have shown you nothing less in his pursuit of you."

"Then you won't grant me some insight into the man that calls my life his mission to take?"

"It would do you no good."

Guile closed his eyes. He was afraid she would say this. If anything he was at least glad she accepted his contract proposal and he could get away from Administrator Newby. "Thank you for hearing me out."

"I owe you that much for bringing me such a high profit margin."

Guile stood and walked down the pedestal steps. There was nothing more that needed to be said. He had presented her with a deal, she had accepted. Final arrangements did not have to be made in person. Everything she needed to know about requested supplies and the price paid for services rendered was on the data pad he had given her. Supply times and locations would be returned to him at a later date.

Altass was not waiting for him at the throne room entrance. Instead he was clear to walk straight out of the building and to his fighter. He proceeded out into the large entrance hall and strapped his breathing mask to his face. Outside the doors he ran into the same cold, thick air that had weighted him down before. He found that the climb to the cockpit was much harder than the drop to the deck.

Backer chirped a welcome back as Jared shut the canopy. He was not in the mood to return the gleeful gesture. He left his companion to activate the nova's systems while he strapped himself in and slipped on his helmet. Somehow his attitude had turned drastically worse since his arrival, knowing deep down that Altaff would not help as he had hoped she would.

The nova lifted off with the aid of the anti-gravity pods and control thrusters. Backer pointed the nose skyward and poured all the power he could muster into the main engines. Guile felt the impact of a thousand fists against his torso from the sudden increase in g's, only to have the weight alleviated once the inertial dampening field caught up with the forward momentum. He hardly noticed the initial pain of the high rate of accent. The rejection of his personal request weighed heaviest on his heart.

Altaff had been the first commander of the squadron that eventually became Devil when it was officially formed at the birth of the Empire. She was young as far as the Phalnx were concerned and for over thirty years she reigned supreme as the best pilot and most skilled fighter tactician. Then, along with Guile, she was ordered to murder the survivors of a star cruiser bombardment. Consisting of children and their assigned caretakers they were in all ways, defenseless. Altaff obeyed her orders and

Chapter Nineteen

had Devil carry them out. A week later she submitted her retirement and walked away.

As Guile had, she turned her attention to the only release she deemed worthy or her rage. Twelve years later she owned and operated the only pirate and smuggling operation to span over half the galaxy. A territory larger than most Realms of the past. To this day she regretted the acts she committed and the victories she gave the Empire. A tragedy she would never fall victim to again.

For that reason, Guile thought Altaff would help him. He thought wrong. Once again he laid trust in a hunch and it slapped him in the face. He had to remind himself that a mercenary hardly ever had the luxury or trusting people of hunches.

Backer barked in his ear as the fighter pierced the cloud cover and rose into the starlight. Guile ignored his pleas for attention long enough to select a destination. "Ok, ok. What is it, my friend?"

A message scrolled across the tactical screen. A private message in his native tongue. What the translator that was planted in every child's ear at birth could not decipher, he could easily read. The message plainly told him that he would shortly receive a transmission written entirely in Telestian and a communications system seldom translated in the written word.

"Backer," he said in a puzzled tone. "Secure the channel you received this on and don't try to trace it's origin."

As soon as the Companion had carried out it's orders the message was received and it began to scroll across the screen. Guile read it slowly so that he would not mistranslate a single word. "You are a stupid man to ask me for something that could bring about the destruction of my operation. If I were to expose my informants within the Empire to any suspicion it would certainly lead back to me. I am already walking a very thin line between being a simple annoyance to the Regent and a major threat."

"Now that I have expressed my business concerns regarding your request I can give you my personal concerns. If I were to give you what you need to know you would certainly kill yourself and anyone close to you. I know that given your skills you will reach Captain Merrill and you may even dispose of him, but you will never make it back alive. Hide your tracks well and make sure that no one is drawn into it with you. Especially me. Even in death I can still curse your name."

"The man you seek is Gulf Merrill but the man you should fear is Admiral Galt Fallon of Arlast. I'm sure you know this to be the task force commander directing Merrill but I know you will not recognize the race or the dangers he presents to you. That is because it was discovered by the Realm on the edge of the galaxy ten years ago and it is their best kept secret. These people are very bright with an intelligence that could easily match that of the Tolan. This man seems to exceed even that. He is the only Arlast to achieve the position he has and for one very good reason. He is the best and he has a loyalty the rest of his species has yet to develop."

"Fallon directly commands the Vengeance, but he also has an entire command battle group at his disposal. This includes the Blackhawk and Nightwing. You may remember these ships from your days with Devil squadron. Alone these two ships don't stand much chance of finding you or the Alliance in an area as vast as the Badlands, but as you have discovered this hardly renders Fallon incapable of tracking you."

"He has one weakness. He is ambitious in a way I have never seen before. If left unchecked he will make Vice Admiral and have an entire fleet at his disposal in under a year. You seem to be the key to this. My sources tell me that if he takes you, then the galaxy will be his oyster and he will have the Regent to back him."

"I don't know how much of this will help you. If any of it does just remember, this is all the work of a crafty mercenary and not a worried pirate. Good luck, Jared, and I hope we will meet again."

Chapter Twenty

The stars always seemed brighter in this section of the galaxy. Perditia was the center of the galaxy as far as the Alcon Empire was concerned. The planet that held the governmental center for the Empire sat amongst the starry backdrop, shining bright green from a nearby sun. It was a vision of beauty. The color sparked warm shivers up Fallon's back. From this distance it was impossible to see the steel and concrete. There were no trees within a thousand kilometers of the capital city. From here the green simply reflected what the imagination produced. A lush green forest surrounding a glorious palace of gold.

Fallon had been here before and knew the truth. The city around the palace expanded with the Empire. Crews worked day and night building expansions in every direction. A kilometer of city was added every month. Engineers estimated that within the next twenty years there would be no natural vegetation left on the planet. A cruel reminder of the Emperor's desires gobbling up world after world.

The Vengeance came to a rest a thousand kilometers out of standard orbit. No ship larger than a medium freighter was allowed to come any closer. From here Fallon could see the planet's defenses. Like a ring, twenty station platforms were in synchronous orbit. Stationed on each platform were two squadrons of star fighters and a battery of weapons that could rival that of the smaller star cruisers. The Perditia battle group, consisting of three of the smaller Interceptor class star cruisers, was also in orbit.

Fallon's ship pulled along side one of these ships, giving him a good look at the sleeker design. The six-month-old war ship was similar in design to its larger predecessors, but slightly elongated. The longer design gave the ship an edge when fighting in areas of increased gravity or in breaking tractor beams.

"The admiral has come aboard," S'Lendo said.

Fallon shifted uneasily in his normally comfortable chair. He never cared to meet with his superiors unless it was to receive an accommodation or promotion. He was still a ways from catching Guile so he knew he would not receive either. No, this had something to do with his requests to add to his command. Power struggles within the Alcon navy were not uncommon. He may have taken his requests as a push for more power. Given Fallon's reputation he would be right in assuming so.

"It must be like the first time I met you."

Fallon turned to his first officer. "The difference is that I know this man. He has been the officer I have answered to during my entire career."

S'Lendo grinned, exposing the sharp fangs in the corners of his mouth. "He is well aware of you too, sir. That alone is enough to give him the shakes."

Fallon fought the urge to grin. "I doubt he will ever fear me beyond any treachery he thinks I am capable of."

"Admiral on the bridge," a guard at the back of the bridge announced in a strong, clear voice.

Fallon stood and whirled around on one heel. Standing at the back of the bridge with guards on either side was Vice Admiral Solis Ishat. He wore the same standard uniform that the other officers wore with one addition. As was customary for fleet admirals and higher, he had a cape attached to either shoulder that ran the length of his back to his knees. The sight of an officer walking with the cape flipping up behind was intended to add a sense of power. Watching him approach proved that the idea worked effectively.

The admiral stopped in front of S'Lendo and Fallon. The three exchanged salutes before the Beefy Telestian spoke in his deep voice. "I appreciate your promptness, Admiral Fallon. I realize that a return home from the Badlands will set you back a month or more."

"It is time that Captain Merrill will make up."

"It is Captain Merrill that prompted my request that you see me. Rather it is events surrounding the captain."

"I do not understand."

"You shouldn't. For him to be successful you would not know of his plans until the last minute." Admiral Ishat stepped past the two and sat in the central chair. "I have had eyes within your command group since the day you received command."

As if this was news to me. Fallon sat down. "What have your eyes seen?"

"I do not wish to offend your sense of duty, Admiral, but I did not trust you at first. Your ambition and actions to fulfill that ambition are well known amongst your colleagues. I myself have had some reservations about giving you added power, but the Regent insisted on you being given a command battle group. To satisfy my fears I placed operatives within eyesight of you to make sure you do not make an unwelcome grab for additional power."

"I would expect nothing less, Admiral." *Little do you know that I've done the same, you old fossil.* "If you'd be so kind though as to tell me what your eyes have seen. I hope it is nothing offensive about my actions."

"On the contrary. You have performed above my expectations. Your handling of your subordinates has been anything short of suburb. No, you are here because of Captain Merrill's actions. For two months now he has increased communication

Chapter Twenty

traffic with an unknown party in the Badlands and he has made plans to move on your command."

Fallon had not expected such an accusation about Merrill. The captain had been given every opportunity by Fallon and would not be where he was now without his support. Merrill went from a desk job that was to be his future if Fallon had not requested that he be given the captain's position on the Nightwing. With Fallon's promotion to group commander Merrill was given a star cruiser.

"How can you be sure of this?"

"My sources are reliable. They have had the captain under a close eye for some time now and assure me that this is so."

This couldn't be true. Fallon had eyes on that ship also and he had heard nothing of this. Unless his sources were working with Merrill, but that was next to impossible. There was no way that Captain Merrill could pay more than he was. His salary was far less. A majority of the funds he had were locked up in naval trading bonds. Even if he did have the funds, he could not touch them.

"I beg the admiral's pardon," Fallon conceded. "But why bring me here to tell me that my cruiser captain is a traitor? Why did you not just let the treachery run its course? Or if you truly do care about my command then why not simply encrypt a message to me?"

"If I had wanted your command taken away you would not be alive to hear me speak. What I chose to do and chose not to do is not of your concern. Right now you are the closest any of us have been to tracking down the Alliance. If you succeed in finding them then you will be given all the support available to destroy them. In the mean time you are to be protected from treachery from within."

That was refreshing to hear. Since the day he had graduated and became an officer he continuously looked over his shoulder. "Your concern is taken to heart. I will deal with the captain when I return to the Badlands."

"Not just yet, captain. You will indulge fleet command and myself by staying a day. You are to brief us personally on your progress and receive direct orders on deployment of ground units. From there I would like you to join me for dinner. We've brought a master cook from one of the rim worlds and he makes the best shell dish I have ever tasted. I think you will enjoy it."

"I am honored, sir."

"You should be worried. An invitation like this usually sparks concern."

"It does, sir. I simply choose to accept this invitation in good faith rather than take it as a threat."

Admiral Ishat stood up and stared down into the Admiral's eyes. "You scare me sometimes. I have seen your kind come and go. Your smooth speech hiding ambition beyond your years. Your harsh features striking fear into your enemies. Your deadly persistence and gaining what you desire." His cape flipped up as he turned and walked towards the back of the bridge. "You will be expected in two hours. Have your briefing prepared by then."

The bridge door slid shut, leaving Fallon to exhale the choked breath he had been holding. "I hate admirals." He turned to the ships captain. "I want transmission logs from every ship in the group dating back at least one month. Even if you cannot open them, I still need to know origin and destination. Send me your findings as soon as you have something."

"You think Captain Merrill may be after your command."

"Possibly, but not to the degree Admiral Ishat believes. Just confirm my thoughts and put my mind to ease."

"Anything else, sir?"

"Dock the ship and take on supplies, then give me a summary on recent activities. Fortunately I've already prepared a briefing leading up till a month ago."

S'Lendo grinned. "You know. You scare me sometimes, too."

"I wouldn't have it any other way."

The briefing went much as Fallon had expected. He spent the first three hours displaying tactical positions and reviewing his actions on the past six months. It was impressive as far as how much he had accomplished in thwarting smaller resistance uprisings, but it was apparent that the six admirals attending would rather have heard more success in the hunt for Jared Guile and the Alliance. He could find no other reason why they would want the mercenary found other than the fact that the Regent made the search a priority.

What did spark their interest was the connection between Guile and the Alliance raid of the Haron salvage yards. Till now, Fallon's reports were directed solely to the Regent. They were not made aware that the resistance had hired him. The admirals were also in the dark about Guile's extensive connections to the illegal trade groups. This gave Fallon the motive for his protection. He was the only source of information concerning the task the Regent had laid down.

The remaining hour was spent listening to the admirals discus their options and plan out movements that Fallon would not follow anyway. He would follow their orders, but only the goal of those orders. When it came to execution he would make up his own mind and handle the situation accordingly. His new position finally gave him the levity to act this way and so far it had paid off. His only worry was whether or not he would become one of these fossils once his ambition had achieved their ranks.

The end of the briefing eventually came. The admirals left according to rank with the grand admiral leaving first. One by one they walked out, satisfied that they had provided Fallon with the guidance he needed to complete his mission. Little did they know that the minute they all walked out the door he would clear his data pad of helpful hints then write his own.

In the midst of his brainstorm a flood of updates scrolled across the pad. Most were standard requirements of Imperial protocol and did not concern him. A minor maintenance mishap in the forward laundry hold and a power outage on the number

Chapter Twenty

twelve port gun turret were included. Fallon hastily ran past what S'Lendo had marked as standard. His captain knew him well enough to act as such.

Two points of interest came up at the end of the report. One related to a rebellion on a fringe Badlands world that Captain Ramsey took upon himself to quell. The other was in regards to Captain Merrill's current mission of intimidation. As expected, Imperial intelligence had been correct in identifying illegal arms dealers. What was out of the ordinary appeared on one of the last of Merrill's target worlds. The impetuous captain had inadvertently uncovered a second dealer working out of an abandoned command bunker under a capital building. The cache of weapons was marked for private use and were in enough quantity to warrant further investigation.

As expected, Merrill sent all captives to the fleet interrogators and claimed the weapons for his own use. It was not out of the ordinary for him to do so. There were no protocols regarding such an occurrence. Fallon could care less either way. He was more interested in determining whom the weapons were for and who was to supply them.

Having no direct control from his current location his only response was limited. He sent back the order to pursue the lead, though he knew it would be long outdated by the time it reached Merrill. He judged the date of his find at over thirteen hours old already, making his response time at over a day and a half.

He gave the order never the less.

Later that day Fallon found himself in the private quarters of Vice Admiral Ishat. He had had no idea that the invitation to dinner would lead him here. He had expected to have the informal meeting in the palace or at one of the finer establishments in the capital city. This far exceeded his expectations. To have a meal in the home of a fleet admiral was a high honor for a group commander. That alone prompted his uneasiness.

A captain joined them for dinner. He arrived just before they sat down to eat. Fallon did not recognize the man, nor was he given any introductions. Ishat simply referred to him as captain and offered a seat at the end of the table. No doubt he was the admiral's cruiser captain and ate with him often. Either that or the man was in a similar situation as himself. In any case the presence of a Tolan captain could not have made his dinner any easier. The idea of having a mind reader around was disturbing.

Towards the end of the meal Fallon could tell that Ishat was building up his confidence to speak with him. The reason for such preparation eluded him. A man in his position had little to fear from a junior officer. Treachery was rewarded by death and ambition seldom posed any risk to an officer's position. Even Fallon's ambition would not knock an admiral from his rank. He would simply pass him by.

"I would like to thank you on a personal level for being straightforward with myself and the others." Ishat shifted. The chairs were heavily padded and were most comfortable so it was the situation that bothered him. "Loyalty is essential. Your cooperation will benefit you in the long run, I assure you."

Fallon's eyes narrowed. "This has nothing to do with the nature of my report, does it? You need me to be in your corner. Why?"

Ishat glanced to the captain then back to him. "You have no idea the political upheaval that is shaking the palace. The galactic council has been disbanded and the congress suspended, perhaps permanently. All trade with non-allied worlds has stopped. The second and sixth fleets have been reassigned to aid in the takeover of the last holdout Realms. Even the regional governments have been replaced. The Regent has ordered the installment of platforms in orbit around all major ports and is in the process of selecting Alcon officials to govern allied systems."

Fallon could not believe what he was hearing. He was troubled by Ishat's quivering voice as he updated the admiral more so than the news itself. In his mind what the Emperor was doing was justified by the vast amount of territory the Empire controlled. Ninety percent of the galaxy was either allied or under pressure by the Empire and the last ten percent was soon to fall. The addition of two more fleets would simply speed up the process.

"You're worried about control," Fallon assumed. When he received a nod he continued. "Two more fleets pulled from active patrol means that the current patrols will have to be thinned. The addition of some seventy platforms will mean an added radius to the existing patrol routes. Pirate raids could pose more of a problem then they already are."

"Or new routes all together," Ishat added. "The rest of the Alcon navy will be as thin as your battle group. At best each group will contain two cruisers within twenty light years of each other. The worst case scenario has cruisers spread out over a hundred light years."

"Pirate groups can inflict heavy damage before help arrives at that distance."

Ishat agreed with a moan. "The added assaults by Alliance cells only complicates matters. They seem to be becoming more daring with each raid. If some of the cells were to organize their efforts, I'm afraid we could be looking at a seriously underrated situation in the near future. I fear our understanding of the situation is weak at best."

The unnamed captain growled in a deep, penetrating voice. "You are near to the largest of these cells."

Fallon skipped a heartbeat. The voice was beyond terror. It bored deep into his soul and gripped at his heart. He battled his own emotions, straining against the aching in his head. The Tolan had learned to use his mental abilities to amplify his voice inside others. The effect was genuine and left the receiver trembling inside. The strength left it there and denied him a physical reaction.

Ishat rolled his eyes. "What my friend here is saying is that you have the best chance out of all the group commanders in the Badlands at finding the primary cell."

Fallon was taken aback. It had been his understanding that he was the sole task force commander in the region. This was the last revelation he had expected and it was certainly not taken lightly.

Chapter Twenty

"We strongly believe that, although it does not contain their leader, it does bear the hopes of the rest of the Sutherlin Alliance. Your report clearly states that this Guile person the Regent is so bent on finding is supplying them with weapons and training."

"You're saying that we should concentrate our efforts on stopping this cell?" Fallon asked. "That's a bit focused for a group that has limited itself to hit and fade operations."

"They have shown us an increasingly aggressive tendency and I don't just want to stop it, Admiral. We mean to eliminate it entirely. I want nothing more than a black stain to remain on the planet they call home. A reminder to the rest of the growing resistance that even their best cannot stop us."

"Noble, but what does this have to do with me? I know you have six more ships still assigned to the original Badlands fleet on perimeter patrol." If they aren't already in the Badlands. "Why not simply redirect the rest of the fleet to finding the cell?"

Again Ishat trembled behind his voice. "I have my orders to leave you alone and allow you to continue your search for Jared Guile. The Regent will not permit the thorough search of that region of space that we require."

"Did she give a reason why?"

"None," the Tolan captain grumbled. " We can only assume that she has plans of her own that may have something to do with the current campaign against the remaining realms."

Who are you? He groaned. He did not like the idea that the Tolan would know more about Fallon then he did of him.

"May I?" The captain asked of Ishat.

He shrugged. "He'll find out on his own eventually."

The Tolan raised his long arms onto the table and folded them. "I am Captain Karros Detrose of the devastator class star cruiser Nullify."

"There is no devastator class," Fallon said smugly.

"There is," Ishat corrected. "And she has enough fire power to incinerate the crust of a planet six kilometers below the surface and halt all thermal activity within the core in one shot."

Fallon could not believe his ears. It would take three fleets of star cruisers to destroy a planet at that magnitude. Even then it would take days, even weeks to punch all the way to the core. No one ship could possibly inflict so much damage in one blast. It would have to have the power of a star behind it.

"It does," Captain Detrose said. "Or rather it utilizes the energy of an entire solar system to complete the task. The ship simply extracts the energy from its surrounding planets and the nearest star and redirects it in one, directed blast. The energy released reacts with the makeup of a planet and turns it's own forces against itself. The very crust that it forced to the surface by the core is thrust back down and destroys the core inside two minutes."

"Impossible," Fallon objected. "Even if such a ship were possible why hasn't it been utilized? I can think of several non allied worlds that would give themselves to the Empire if such a ship were parked within their sight."

"It has already been utilized on several occasions. The most notable of which was the planet Sutherlin. The timing must be right for a more public demonstration," Ishat added. "If the Alliance were to find out about the cruiser they would surely find a way to exploit or destroy it. We want to save its debut for the day you discover the main cell. On that glorious day one cruiser will end the Alliance and strike fear into all that oppose us."

"All for the greater good of the Regent and the Emperor," Fallon added with a bit of an insinuated tone. "She does know of this plan?"

In her own mind.

Fallon shook his head, then glared at the Tolan. I know you can hear me. If you ever invade my mind again you will find yourself hanging lifeless at the back of my bridge. He stood up from the table. "I beg your pardon, Admiral, but I have a ship to attend to."

Ishat stood. "I will walk you out."

Fallon turned, but not before giving Detrose one last look of anger. Not many people were able to stand down a Tolan and survive the mental response. He relied heavily on his position and past dealings with the race to see him beyond one bad seed.

Ishat opened the front door for him and put his hand on Fallon's shoulder. "I won't ask you to get along with your fellow captains. What I will ask you is to trust your superiors. We are in the dark as much as you as to the direction the Regent is taking us, but she is the Emperor's hand. We live to serve and nothing more."

"And nothing less," Fallon added. "You know my ambition and you know what lengths I will go to secure my position in the Empire. What you should also be aware of is my loyalty, to you, to the Regent and to the Emperor. I will keep you informed of my progress and let you know the moment I have a solid lead. Until then I can do no more than I am currently allowed. I will continue my search for Guile and rely heavily on following him to the Alliance. He is the link in all of this as you have so plainly suggested."

"Excellent, Admiral. I wish you nothing but success."

"Good evening, sir." Fallon saluted. He broke his stance once Ishat returned the salute.

For reasons he could not fathom, Fallon walked away from the spacious home and turned towards the palace, the opposite direction from the star port that held his shuttle. The day had already been longer than expected or wanted yet he could not fight the urge to approach the home of the regent. He could think of nothing more than seeing her. Meeting with the lord of the Realm and bowing to her presence. An absurd thought considering how tired he was.

The palace rose up ahead of him. A shining example of ancient engineering the central tower reached a kilometer into the sky above the already tall city structures.

Chapter Twenty

A ring of shorter towers encircled the central spike, forming what looked like a giant rocket with massive boosters at it's sides. A third ring of much shorter towers finished off the palace base. The entire structure was surrounded by a wall the height of the city. A city that had more layers that would never see daylight than could be imagined.

Built during the time of the third galactic empire, the palace had survived several changes of power over its 550 years of existence. With the rise of the Alcon Empire it was only natural for the Emperor to choose the palace as the capital for his reign. As a result the young ruler became the center of attention in his quest to take over the galaxy. As the past occupants of the palace had ruled with justice it was expected that he would do the same. Within fifty years, fleets of Star Cruisers had proven the then-powerful galactic congress wrong.

While some might have found the Emperor's methods for ruling wrong and impetuous, Fallon was one of the loyal few who would have ruled in the same fashion. Military tactics were nothing without the power of fear behind them. To win a battle and take a planet were accomplishments fitting the skilled officer. To keep that same planet in line through intimidation and power took a ruler with enough strength and resolve to take on the strongest of opposition.

Fallon walked past the guard post leading beyond the palace walls without being stopped. Orders had been given to let him enter unchecked. Those orders also included that he be directed inside the extensive lower level of the building to a single, heavily guarded lift. The feeling that drew him on gave him little incentive to look around the massive room that stretched out across the diameter of the palace.

Soft curves and ancient carvings gave a hint as to the nature of the first empire. Figures with powerful forms and deep eyes gazed down upon the guests and soldiers that filled the palace. They were images of the six emperors that ruled during the time of the greatest empire. Each wore gentle robes and beautiful crowns that the carvings played up. The displays were meant to present the rulers as powerful, but forgiving leaders of a great society.

Fallon grimaced. The empire may have lasted five hundred years, but it had failed in less than six months. He saw through writings from the time the same thing that rising powers had seen a thousand years ago. The empire was weak and the last emperor had chosen to trust the loyalty of his subjects rather than keep them in line with the power he had. In the end he was repaid for his kindness with a galactic-wide revolution and a knife in the back.

A door built into the woodcarvings slid back into a wall, revealing the private lift. For no reason beyond sheer will, Fallon walked across the palace hall and entered the lift alone. Darkness gripped him in a cold blanket during the long ride to the top of the central tower, a two-kilometer journey straight upward; an eight-minute ride underneath dim lights and surrounded by a dull hum of guide rails against magnetic lift plates. After a few minutes he could not imagine what it would have been like to start at ground level.

Sutherlin Alliance

    The lift came to an abrupt stop two and a half kilometers above the once green surface of Perditia. The double doors parted and gave way to similar darkness. A distance away, Fallon could look out a large window that was open to a thick layer of clouds. He was told that on a clear day one could see to the horizon, ahead of the advancing city. In another three or four months though, the Regent would see only steel and concrete.

    A crack of lightning lit up the room momentarily, giving Fallon a decent grasp of the size of the royal court. It was as he had expected. Spacious with a robe covered steel throne. To either side were chairs that looked uncomfortable. Undoubtedly they were home to the Emperor's personal guard. The heavily armored soldiers had no need for comfort. The suits of armor plating they wore had no feeling beyond the cushioned insides. They held their own limited comfort.

    "Enter," the Regent's voice said, echoing in the empty chamber.

    Fallon stepped from the lift and took two steps inward. He stopped, not knowing where to turn and address the Emperor's overlord. He wanted nothing more than to make a good impression. It was one thing to come across respectable on a communication screen. It was another to come face to face with his ruler and remain calm.

    "Approach my stunning view."

    Fallon crossed the smooth floor and stopped in front of the slightly outward angled window. In every direction he saw only dark clouds and a thin layer of water washing against the glass. There was no view beyond the rain soaked window.

    "Forgive me, my lord. I see no view."

    "You must look beyond the clouds and see the empire, Admiral. It is there. I see it whenever I close my eyes. I see it whenever I look upon the layer of clouds. And I see it when I look upon you."

    Fallon turned, but saw only darkness. "You honor me. Might I ask why I am given such a compliment?"

    "You do yourself justice in speaking with your commanders. You do yourself even more justice speaking with them in private. They are worried and fear my methods, but they must understand that the galaxy cannot be run by the military. Even with the strongest fist there will be resistance. We must remain strong, but competent at the same time."

    A cloaked figure emerged from the shadows and was illuminated by the dim, outside light. "As you know the past empires failed because of a lack of strength or a weak leadership. One or the other can be and have been dangerous traits. One must command both with wisdom and strength. The Empire can neither appear weak of mind nor weak of power."

    Fallon mentally patted himself on the back. "I have felt the same. I devoted a large portion of my naval training to studying the mistakes of the past."

    "I know. I have followed your career, Admiral, and you have impressed the Emperor and me. Though you might think that patrolling the Badlands for pirates was a waste of your time and talent, I found that you were a valuable asset there. Sometimes the need arises to have a capable officer in an area that would otherwise seem without troubles. I chose wisely in having you assigned to the Badlands. Now it has paid off and I have one of my best in command of a grand venture."

"Risks sometimes do pay off as you have proven to yourself and to others. Your peers may have found the duty of housing Devil squadron during the original Badlands campaigns as gofer duty. Not you, though. You stepped up and volunteered to spearhead their assaults. In doing so your command decision led to the discovery that not all the pilots of Devil held the Empire as their highest priority."

"Not all, but most."

The hood that covered the Regent's face shifted as she nodded. "Granted that only three of the original fifteen remained with the navy. That is not the issue. The issue is that by subjecting them to what our soldiers are committed to, you drew out their true nature. We found out early what could have been discovered in the heat of battle. And since then the twelve traitors have split up and are no longer the danger they represented as a team."

"At least until Jared Guile rejoined two of his comrades in the Alliance," Fallon added.

"He is more of a danger now than he ever was before. As a pilot he could be contained to the combat arena. As a mercenary and pirate he brings with him the criminal element that has penetrated deep into our control. If allowed to continue his current contract with the Alliance, he may be able to prepare them for what lies ahead."

She's still hiding something. But what is it that she refuses to tell me?

"I brought you to me for a reason, Admiral Fallon. Your insight has brought you to within sight of this man and it will again. What I want from you is not to kill Jared Guile, but to make an example out of him. His fame will be the destruction of him and those like him. The Guiles of this galaxy believe themselves unstoppable. You will prove them wrong."

"I will make it my mission in life," Fallon proudly said.

"Your mission has many observers, one who plans to use your success to further his own career in the Imperial navy. He thinks he can hide his intentions from me, but he is sadly mistaken. He is even more of a fool to let you in on his little plan."

You know about the devastator? What else do you know about?

"He is also unwise to inform you about traitors within your own ranks. His reliance on his own spies is sorely overrated. You know more about your own men than he ever will. You know more about his men then he ever will."

"And you know more about all of us," Fallon said. He had hoped that the comment would spark a pleased response. He was wrong.

"I am a lord of the strongest empire the galaxy has ever seen. In two month's time the Empire's last powerful opposition will fall to a stronger force, as the emperor will combine four fleets to conquer it. At that time, every resource I have will be to subvert any and all uprisings that may arise within the galaxy. Admiral Ishat's creation of the devastator class star cruiser will ensure this. His plan to crush the largest of the Alliance cells will proceed, but not at his whim. He will obey me and we will be triumphant."

Fallon had the urge to take a step back. The force in her voice pushed against his chest and gripped at his mind. There was more to her than a lord of an empire. Her form under the cape was not that of a Tolan, nor was she as aggressive as a Caperan. No, she had to be of another race. No one he had met had the persuasive powers she had. Even at a great distance she was able to draw him to her.

A flash of lightning exposed the lower portion of her face for a heartbeat. In that one glance Fallon learned more about the Regent then all the reports he had read. Ten years as planetary governor. Fifteen years in the galactic congress. Fifty years as a Regent of the Realm. It was all there, but hidden behind the soft skin of a twenty year old. She was younger than he was, yet years beyond.

No species he had encountered could age a hundred years and still look this young. The oldest species he was aware of were the Horde, who could live in excess of five hundred years, but no Horde female even closely resembled the features of the more prominent races in the galaxy. Even Fallon considered himself among the humans, which was a wildly general term for similar species.

Another flash of lightning exposed the grin the Regent held. Again Fallon wanted to take a step away. He came to the shocking realization that she could read his thoughts, or at the least was aware of them. What else could she do with that mind of hers? What could the person who had helped build an empire in a third the time it took for the first galactic empire accomplish with a thought?

Fallon grimaced. And why would a simple group commander question such a person? What must you think of me?

"There is one more thing, Admiral. The faces you see before you are hidden behind many masks of deceit. You see one worn by me so I know you are not without distrust. Hold that feeling close to you and never give yourself freely to those that would use you. It would also do you justice not to take what you hear at face value. Those that you trust could betray you as easily as those you do not. It is also the same with those that you are without trust."

"The masks that people wear are convincing. The one that you present before me is just as convincing. Use your own ability to sway others from your true intent to aid you in uncovering hidden agendas. Your life could easily depend on it."

The regent turned away to face the darkness. "Now leave me, Fallon. You have a duty to attend to and far too little time to complete it."

Though she could not see it, he bowed to her then walked towards the lift. His name ringed in his ears as if he had never heard it spoken before. He turned around within the lift and stared into the darkness, hoping to see her silhouette in front of the window. She spoke his name, which was unheard of in most cases. Something was both exhilarating and eerie about the circumstances surrounding the way she dealt with him.

The lift dropped five levels. Fallon's communicator beeped, announcing that he had passed below the artificial interference that was used to shield the Emperor's court. He tapped the communicator and spoke freely. "Galt."

"Sorry to trouble you, sir," S'Lendo said. "The ship is ready for departure."

Chapter Twenty

"Lay in a course for the Badlands, then send word to the Valiant that we will be returning in the next few days. I'll leave it up to you on where we will rendezvous."

"I don't mean to insinuate anything, sir. Have you misplaced your chronometer?"

Fallon leaned against the side of the lift. "I know I missed my rendezvous with the shuttle, Captain. I was side tracked."

"Anything I should know about?"

S'Lendo was his first officer and his most valuable advisor. He was hand selected for the strenuous task of serving him. If anyone could be trusted it was him.

No, commander. Everything is fine."

Chapter Twenty-One

Three weeks had passed with no sign of her, and now there she was. The Vengeance dropped into the system and came to a rest along side the Valiant. A shuttle launched from the smallest of the bays on the smaller of the two star cruisers. It more than likely held the captain of the Valiant. After weeks of no contact it was standard naval procedure for the captains to give their reports in person.

A little under a month had passed though. Just enough time to make a trip to Perditia. If the assumption that Admiral Fallon had returned to the Imperial capital was correct, then it could mean only trouble for the Alliance and Guile. Plans made in person were plans too important to risk interception.

Guile leaned back in the cockpit of his nova and sighed. "Backer, run a passive scan from the probe we dropped near that nav-probe. Run a telemetry check and tell me where that cruiser came from."

Backer went to work, but Guile already knew the answer. It did not matter anyhow. By the time his Companion could retrace the cruiser's path both ships parted company and jumped to star flight. The confirmation came a minute later. Stopping three times at various way stations, the Vengeance had come directly from Perditia and the heart of the Alcon Empire.

"I know enough, Backer. Lay in a course for Volana Three and execute."

Bea leaned against the nose landing gear of her fighter. She looked out across the tarmac to the line of twenty novas. In the center of the line were two empty spots. One represented the pilot who died during the training mission to the salvage yards. The other had been designated for the man who had long since left to seek revenge for the young pilot's death. Just the absence of the two novas hurt in more ways than one. Each represented a part of the Alliance she cared not to admit existed.

Stead stepped in front of her line of sight and stopped. He looked towards her and radiated a warm smile. Both of the former Devil pilots that were still alive and had stayed with the squadron were there for different reasons. Stead remained because he was given the opportunity to lead. Bea stayed because she truly believed in the cause the Alliance fought for. Six others had died in the line of duty.

There was no real love present between the two except for a feeling of belonging and deep friendship. Bea was a superb pilot in her own right and Stead was not far from the best, but both had been teamed up during the most heated of their Badlands missions. She became an invaluable asset as his wingman and she soon felt a need to remain by his side. 'A wing man never leaves his lead's side', Guile had once said and Bea took those words to heart.

Even now, light years from the nearest combat she was there to watch over him. Stead approached her with worried intent in his eyes. She suddenly needed to walk away and lock herself in her room, but she had to face him. He would find out sooner or later that she was worried and now was as good a time as any to tell him why.

"We'll be back soon enough, Bea." Stead stopped an arms length away. "He's always been impetuous when it comes to personal maters. He'll resolve what needs to be resolved and come back."

"I don't know if what we're doing is right anymore, Haggin. In the beginning we had Ghost and a few light transports. We hit minor military targets and ran for cover until the coast was clear. Now we've become the center of attention in many influential circles, one of them being the pirate trade. Neutral worlds send us their young to fight and smuggler groups provide us with the supplies. The more it escalates the more we become vulnerable to our kids getting killed by the same suppliers. We become targets for sellouts so the rich become richer and the innocent become dead. It bothers me more than it should."

"It was bound to happen sooner or later, Bea, but the mission was not a total loss. Jared and Wes' training is paying off and our rookies are starting to excel where they lacked before. You said it yourself. The rookie who was your wing man scored his first kill without assistance."

"It was luck."

"It was persistence speared on by a modest level of confidence in the abilities he had," Stead insisted. "The same confidence you have in your own flying." He shifted onto one hip and smiled. "Now, do you want to tell me what is really bothering you?"

"No. I thought my minor problem would suffice."

"Not a chance. I want the whole scoop or I won't stop bugging you. This is the last chance I'll have for awhile."

"We all want the whole scoop," Barger said as he rounded the nose gear. The latest Devil defector stopped in front of the two with Patron at his side. "What troubles the person who brought us Jared Guile?"

Patron reached up and gripped his shoulder. "Enough, Mister Barger. Mister Guile has provided us with an invaluable service. He has done for us what would have taken years without him. The other resistance cells are now as strong as we are and can finally fend for themselves in the Badlands."

Chapter Twenty-One

"What are you saying, Patron?" Stead asked.

"I think it's time we consolidate our forces and strike at a larger target."

That's an awful lot of power. "And how did you come about this decision?"

"After careful review of the training mission to the Haron salvage yards I have determined that Mister Barger and Mister Guile's training has enabled some of our younger pilots to combat Alcon pilots on their own. I have therefore authorized the forming of a second tactical assault squadron to aid in raids so that Ghost may be allowed to assume its role as an aggressor squadron."

Bea shook her head. "I can't agree with that decision, Patron. Half of the pilots involved in the mission were either seasoned veterans or above average rookies. I might also like to add that two of the inexperienced pilots escorted the first transports out before the real fighting began."

"Which is why the new tactical squadron will stick mainly to escort runs. Please do not get me wrong, Lieutenant. Mister Guile will continue to train the younger pilots as he has, but without the aid of Ghost. Once Mister Guile, Stead, and Barger complete their next assignment the three of you and the rest of your unit will be leaving immediately along with a strike force of five transports and one attack craft." Patron promptly turned around and walked back towards the command building. "It is my wish and my command," he said with his voice trailing off as he distanced himself.

Stead grinned. "Looks like we get to do what we were trained to do."

"I don't like this, Haggin," Bea said. "It's bad enough Patron wants us to attack a destroyer convoy."

"You don't have to like it." He turned and jogged after Patron.

"Sometimes he can be a fool," Barger snapped.

"Just since Jared returned." She turned to him and put both hands on his shoulders. "Pray Patron doesn't make any mistakes anytime soon. I don't think the Sovereign realizes what is happening here. If she did she never would have approved the use of a mercenary nor would she have let the Alliance's best squadron go off and leave the cell in the hands of rookies."

"I intend to change his opinion of our strength."

Bea dropped her hands to her sides. "Your mission."

"You've heard?"

"Only that you plan to sneak aboard the Blackhawk and break into her fleet's mission parameters."

"Then you know everything."

"You really think you're going to find something big, don't you?"

Barger leaned a shoulder against the nova. "Until the last task that got me captured, Devil had been assigned to the fourth fleet. We were heavily engaged in spreading the Empire into one of the last few holdout realms. Then suddenly we were placed into the third fleet and under the command of Admiral Fallon and Captain Merrill. In addition, three cruisers were transferred along with us, with one of those going directly to the Admiral. Now, tell me that the Emperor isn't planning something big for this quadrant."

"I won't argue the fact. When do you leave?"

"Shortly. Only a handful of people have been aware of the mission since it's conception. Haggin and I are due to meet up with Jared on Volana Three. From there it's in the hands of our mercenary."

Again Bea placed her hands on his shoulders. "Just promise me one thing." He nodded. "Don't do anything that will place Jared in danger. I want him back."

Barger snapped a smirk to the corner of his mouth. "I won't go turncoat, Bea. Despite my feelings for him and Haggin I hold my ideals far above any prejudices I might have for them. If I have any say in it, they will return in one piece."

"Then is there anything I can do for you to make those words have meaning to me?"

Barger looked to the next fighter in line. Painted in a small patch under the canopy was the Imperial Academy symbol, which consisted of two concentric circles with a sun flare through both. "Look after Narra while I'm gone." A gloss rushed over his eyes.

Bea smiled and reached to her heart. His words suddenly meant more to her than any she had heard in weeks.

It wasn't like the times he had left home for a tour of duty aboard the Blackhawk. This was much colder and impersonal. Barger picked up his bags at the front door and turned around to look at his room. Unlike his personal home, his new quarters would have a new occupant before he could relax on the shuttle. Much like that stabbing feeling pierced his heart during star flight, this too was unpleasant. His home was not a family in any sense of the word, but at least he had something waiting for him when he returned to his home world.

Barger walked out of the thin walled building and dropped his two bags onto a personnel lift. He sat down on the rear bench. Out of the corner of his eye, he caught three people approaching him from the pilot barracks. Curiosity drew his gaze towards them. Maybe he should have trusted his deeper instincts. Though he knew Stead was coming along he still could not believe it. The urge to regurgitate his morning meal was more than just a coincidence.

Stead and two pilots he had never met stopped at the rear of the lift and dropped their bags into the open hold. The grin was there and his intentions were obvious. Ignoring the growls, Stead sat down next to Barger. An arms length away, but it was still too close. Anywhere within eyesight was too close as far as Barger was concerned.

Stead gave him a sideways glance. "I understand Narra informed you ahead of time." He joined the angry pilot in looking straight ahead. "A pity. I had wanted to surprise you myself."

Chapter Twenty-One

Barger choked down the need to lash out at him. "She probably saw the impending danger of that. The last thing this mission needs is for two of us to be at each other's throats before it even gets started, let alone three"

"Quite right. Besides…" Stead paused long enough for the vehicle to start up. "There's plenty of time for that on the shuttle."

Barger could not help the grin that materialized on his face. What he could do was force it to the side of his mouth opposite Stead. "Watch what you say," he said in a low tone.

"Or what?" Stead asked in an equally low tone. "You'll kill me?"

"Maybe. Or maybe I'll just leave you in the hands of the Empire. Maybe I'll hand you over to Captain Vallejo in exchange for my freedom."

"Hardly a notable move for Lieutenant Wes Barger. The best of the best. The untouchable. The…"

"Knock it off," Barger growled. "My Devil reputation is only a front."

"For intimidation." He nodded. "It's effective in any line of work. Even ours."

"Yet the Alliance lacks that intimidation."

"Don't put us down."

"I wasn't. I was simply stating a fact."

The lift raced across the tarmac towards a boxy looking shuttle. At the base of a thin ramp stood two disreputable looking persons with heavy rifles slung over their backs. The one on the left, a short man with a thick black beard and a worn, gray jumpsuit, appeared to be a boorish looking Kand, but appearances could easily be deceiving. With the thick layers of dirt and hair on his body his true form was hidden. The other was a thin female with a strong upper body. Neither looked sociable.

The lift stopped at the shuttle, staying just long enough for the passengers and baggage to be offloaded before speeding off. It was apparent that the young driver wanted nothing to do with the pair of pirates. Barger didn't blame him. When Guile had sent these two to pick them up he wanted nothing to do with them either.

"We're running late," The woman said in a raspy snarl. "Not a good start."

"Sorry about that," he responded. Barger approached the two and dropped his bags at their feet. "I've had to work out a few things."

"Like?" The man asked.

Barger glanced back to the three pilots and shook his head. "Inside."

"Are you going to introduce us?" Stead snapped.

"Single names only," The male said.

"Is this necessary?" The female asked of Barger. "I have no desire to know these people."

Barger grinned. "This lovely creature is Vipryn and she has a very short temper and no manners." He turned to face the Alliance pilots. "And the gentleman who is neither gentle or a man is Aeon. Jared sent me full profiles on them. He says he can trust them but that wasn't saying much. When I first joined Varlet I had a run in with them."

Aeon slapped him square in the middle of his back. "Let's not go there, shall we."

Stead moaned. The concern on his face was clear. "The light haired pilot to my left is Halash. He was acquired from the Empire a year ago after he was left for dead. The tall, well-built person to his left is Savash. He had been with the Alliance for four years and oddly enough is Halash's brother, though neither had ever met before."

"And you are Haggin Stead," Vipryn pointed out. "No introductions with you are necessary."

Stead's eyes narrowed. "I assume Jared has told you all about me."

"Enough to warn us to watch his back against you."

Barger rolled his eyes. He could already see the coming arguments. "Alright, alright. Can we get this wagon on the move? We have a lot of ground to cover and less time to do it in."

The small bank of pilots and smugglers boarded the shuttle with the less civilized of the bunch leading the way. Inside they found that Aeon and Vipryn's surroundings closely resembled themselves. Barger could afford a mild smirk as he looked around the once luxurious shuttle passenger area. At times he had spent days on end in ships similar to this.

It was not as if pirates, mercenaries, and smugglers particularly liked living in this manor. Every piece of filth had a purpose. What the foul stench and greasy walls provided was an atmosphere undesirable to boarding parties. The piles upon piles of tattered wardrobe and scrap metal also made handy places to hide smaller items that could get the holder in serious trouble for having.

Barger dropped down onto what looked like a command chair from a larger ship. Stead stopped in front of him and stared at his choice with astonishment. Barger replied with a sheepish grin that gave away his delight and dropped his rival to a lower level of existing. Barger's smug expression boosted the insult to a higher level.

"Have a seat, gentlemen," Aeon said as he and Vipryn stepped through a small hatch and into the cockpit.

After looking around the small compartment Halash remarked to Stead, "and what seat would that be?"

"Anything under a pile of clothes is a seat. Anything under scrap metal is either merchandise or a dead body."

All three stopped and gave him a puzzled and worried look.

"Just kidding," Barger laughed. He straightened up and dropped a tone. "The bodies would be in storage."

Nothing was said about his last comment.

Barger pointed to a bench a few feet from him. Stead cleared it off with a quick wipe with his boot and dropped onto the end. He and the two pilots buckled themselves just ahead of the rumbling of the shuttle's engines. Neither of the two younger pilots appeared comfortable on the hard, metallic benches. Stead on the other hand seemed rather relaxed. All that time spent on star cruiser briefing room benches must have worn down his need for comfort as much as it had for Barger.

Chapter Twenty-One

"We'll jump in ten seconds," Aeon said over a speaker.

"He's jumping in the system!" Halash exclaimed.

Barger rolled his eyes. "Calm down. These are pirates, not law abiding citizens. They do what they want."

"What about use of the star flight lanes?" Stead asked. "They still have to avoid the navigational probes."

"They still use the lanes. They just enter them from different points. It's not that uncommon even for Alcon ships."

"Or Alliance fighters," Vipryn said from the cockpit hatch. She walked into the compartment and sat close to Barger. We've seen a few fighter squadrons jump from inside a system."

"Not our cell," Stead said in his own defense.

Vipryn grinned. "That's why your younger pilots get killed so easily. You need to start rejecting standard rules of flight and engagement."

He folded his arms in disgust. "You mean become more like you."

"No, not like us. You need to be more aggressive." She rested a hand on Barger's shoulder. "So you need to be more like Jared."

"Fat chance of that," Stead laughed. "He's the last person I want to be more like."

"Don't laugh. Where we're going you'll need every advantage you can get." She leaned towards Barger. "We're still going there, right?"

He nodded. "But not for the same reason as before."

"What were we going there for?" Halash asked.

"Wait a minute! Where the hell are we going?" Stead demanded.

"Volana Three," Vipryn answered. "We were originally going there to obtain our new cover and pick up Jared."

"And we aren't now?"

Barger shook his head. "Because of a recent revelation Jared chose to close up a loose end. Our mission won't be safe until he does so and any cover we pick up will be vulnerable."

The shuttle shook violently and the passengers were drawn towards the rear of the compartment. The dim lights flickered off several times from the diversion of power to the engines only to come back brighter than before. Aeon emerged from the cockpit shortly after the shaking stopped and the flight leveled off.

"We're on our way," he said as he took a seat next to Vipryn. "We should be on Volana Three in seven hours."

"Ahead of schedule. Good, we'll need the extra hour."

Stead moaned. "Ok, we're settled in and you have everyone's attention. Can you please tell us what the new mission parameters are?"

Barger crossed one leg over the other and leaned back on the stiff seat. "As you know we were originally going out to gain information on the task force that has been searching the Badlands for your Alliance cell. In the process we were going to set up a series of informants and gain access to Alcon construction plants. Jared though has informed me that we will be proceeding with a second task once we have completed our mission on the Blackhawk. If I understood his position we are to board the Vengeance for reasons he has yet to include me in."

Stead was speechless. "How are we to do that?"

"We're abandoning the freighter crew cover for a smuggling crew. After we leave the Blackhawk we'll link up with a legitimate smuggling group and run cargo for them to Horde."

"Horde?" Vipryn blurted out. "You never said anything about going to Horde. I have a death mark there."

"I know about the mark, but you and Aeon won't be setting foot on the surface. All we're doing there is delivering the cargo and picking up another shipment. The contact we're meeting with is someone Jared knows well and he'll be sending us where we want to go."

"And that would be?" Stead asked.

"I don't know yet. I'm flying blind here and am in it for the ride with the rest of you."

Stead rolled his eyes. "Great."

"Sir, please," Halash pleaded with him. "We're already committed in this. Complaining will only complicate matters."

With a cold stare Stead backed him down before lashing out at Barger. "You should have let me know about this before we left. I never would have agreed to place my pilots' lives in your untrustworthy hands. I should never have agreed to give you assistance."

"It's up to you," Aeon said. "When we reach Volana Three you can catch a shuttle back to your base and we'll do this ourselves."

It was a stretch, but he was right. If Jared worked everything correctly he could hire one or two more smugglers and pull off the mission with mild success. He really did not need unknowns though, and these three were at least trusted as far as completing the mission was concerned. Aeon also knew this so his comment was thrown out just to slap Stead in the face. With what Jared had said about the Captain, Aeon was aware of Stead's short fuse.

"That won't be necessary, but I will have one demand. You're not involving myself or my pilots in any part of this mission without consulting me first. I want to be a part of the planning process in every stage."

"Fine," Vipryn said. "As long as you realize that a smuggler's life is hardly ever planned. Spontaneity and serious risk-taking is a part of every day life."

Barger folded his arms. "Look. If anyone is aware of the danger involved in changing our plans this late in the game it's me. I hate jumping into a situation without having a firm background and a multitude of ways out if something were to go wrong. Jared and I have spent weeks planning this whole thing out only to have the objective change at the last minute. Of all of us, I'm the most concerned and least likely to jump into the unknown with my eyes shut."

"I do have plans, though they are sketchy. They involve a lot of trust in contacts Jared has not spoken with in over a year. They also rely heavily upon matters going

Chapter Twenty-One

our way on the first few legs. This is a major danger, I know, but what other choice do we have? If we wait and plan this out then we risk the Empire gaining a serious advantage on us. If we rush in then we risk becoming pinned with no way out. We have to slip somewhere in between there without getting killed or having our cover compromised."

Stead pursed his lips. "Valid points. As long as you understand my position I am fine with this arrangement."

"Good, then I'm sure you'll be fine with what comes next." Barger pointed to a door at the back of the compartment. "You will need to change out of your jumpsuit and get into something a little by more grungy."

"You mean like them?" Halash asked.

Barger nodded. "You have to look like you just climbed out of a garbage compactor."

Both of the younger pilots opened their mouths to ask questions. Stead stood and grabbed both of their shoulders. The urging was enough for them to calm down and follow him aft. They both gave Barger a glance back as they moved from the compartment. The look was not of disgust at having to dress down, but one of concern. A look that told him they were realizing what kind of places they would be visiting.

"Noble speech," Vipryn said.

Barger slowly stood. "I meant it."

"For them or for all of us?"

He looked down at her. "I was serious, Vipryn. I'm facing barren walls here. I haven't been this much in the dark since before I joined the academy."

Aeon shuffled his way towards the cockpit.

"I hope your direction is open?"

Vipryn gripped a leg of his jumpsuit. "It's open as long as you don't drag us down the same path. Remember that we're getting paid to supply you with a ship, our contacts, and our abilities. Nowhere on our contract does it say that you own our lives. If either of us believes that the deal has gone sour we're dropping you."

"Understood," he responded with a nod. "Just don't let your judgment cloud your trust. I've never let someone hang."

"I'm holding you to that, Wes." She used her grip of him to help herself up. "Don't let your over protectiveness ruin the mission, though. If we decide to take a risk then it's our risk. Jared's contract is far more important than the one you have with us."

Barger jerked back as she let go and walk towards the cockpit. He grinned. He had several options on who to allow Guile to hire, but only one choice, and it was already turning out to be a good one. He was feeling better and better every second.

Chapter Twenty-Two

Bright, unrelenting light flooded the passenger compartment, blinding the occupants momentarily. Heat unlike anything Barger had experienced before washed over him in an unrelenting wave of dryness. Every pore on his body closed up tight. His covered lips shriveled within seconds and the corners of his eyes dried up. A pain rose up from the back of his head, rolled over his ears and forehead, and attacked his entire head with the mother of all headaches.

Summer on Volana Three.

"I hate this place," Aeon said as he staggered passed the group and down the landing ramp. "It feels like hell itself."

"I couldn't agree more," Barger said.

Once, long ago he had spent three days in an escape pod simulation where a third of the trip brought him to within the outer reaches of a star. Heat unlike anything he ever felt before gripped him tightly in the small space he was confined to. For twenty-two hours he lived in forty-nine degree conditions, drinking twice his body weight in liquids. It was an experience he never cared to relive and thought could never be equaled.

He was proven wrong.

Led by Aeon, the six raggedly dressed and dirty smugglers walked away from the shuttle. The landing ramp automatically rose back into place and all systems shut down. Thick, black vines made up the shuttle's surroundings. A dark surface paint added to the camouflage, hiding it from above and the ground. Anyone five meters away would have had to take a long, concentrated look to catch the metallic edges behind the vines.

As promised Guile was there waiting with a small hover car buried in dead vines less than seven meters from the landing site. He grabbed on the edge of the intertwined vegetation and pulled it from the boxy little lift. To the group's mild dismay, it had no top and limited passenger space. The heavy weapons the smugglers had brought would have to stay behind. As would the two younger pilots. So much the better.

"Pleasure to see you again," Guile said with a devilish smirk. "I'm glad my hires didn't scare you off."

Barger pushed passed him and hoped into the back seat. "Hardly."

The rest joined him with Guile driving. Halash and Savash were left behind to guard the shuttle. The remaining five sped away towards the capital city. This was an unusual approach for Guile. It was not unlike him to slip into the city under an assumed identity and undercover. Having to come in from beyond city limits was the stretch. Administrator Newby had always protected him from customs and security checks. Newby could not protect him now.

Newby was the target.

The small band slipped through the towering city walls just before what passed for dusk on the planet. Their dirt-covered faces and ratty clothes displayed them as peasant workers. A few brief words in the local language to the gate guards deepened their cover. Guile was fluent in the language and easily compensated for unexpected questions.

Guile pulled the vehicle into a back alley and hopped out. "I'll be back in a moment."

"Couldn't you have taken care of business before we arrived?"

"There wasn't time," he said, then he rolled away into the shadows. In mid tumble he pulled his hand blaster from its holster under his shirt and brought it up to his ear. He pressed himself against the wall and slowly slid up to a standing position. The cool, slick moisture on the wall soaked threw his thin shirt and mixed with the applied grease on his back. Oddly enough, he had to smile at the sensation. It had been a while since he was able to indulge in such a dirty task.

The luxurious apartment of Newby was six floors above him with only one way up that was undetectable. Removing a grappling line from a pouch in his pants he attached one end to the tip of his blaster and the other to his belt. He aimed skyward, with a slight lean towards the building. With a thin thump the blaster propelled the solid end of the grappling line upward and at a minor arc. At the edge of the roof the momentum died and the line embedded itself into a bulky ledge.

With speed and grace Guile pulled himself up the line hand over hand. He let his legs dangle below him as he resisted the urge to use them to assist his ascent. All it would take would be too much pressure placed against the wall and a tremor alarm would sound; a commonly used security devise for the rich. It was sensitive enough to detect the slightest amount of force against the exterior, yet smart enough to determine if the cause was artificial or natural.

The climb took Guile three minutes, although personally he felt it to be much longer than that. By the time he had his hands firmly gripping the penthouse roof, his arms were quivering and lifeless. The addition of a held blaster worsened the fatigue to the point that he could not hold up the barrel. Wisely he decided to find a shadow and rest for a bit.

"Here to kill me, Jared?"

Pain aside, Guile had the blaster raised and aimed at Newby in a flash.

Chapter Twenty-Two

"You could have come through the front door. I would have let you in."

A bead of sweat rolled down his cheek and evaporated on his chin. "I didn't want to be seen."

"Everyone here knows who you are and wouldn't talk even if tortured. You'd do yourself justice if you'd honor your reputation."

"You knew I'd be coming."

"Eventually I knew you'd be back. The nature of the visit is in question though. Is this a personal visit or a contract visit?"

Slowly Guile lowered his weapon to his side. "It could be either at this point."

"I hope the cover I set up for you will make this a contract visit."

Newby knew he was in trouble and was doing his best to save his own life. "Give me the details and I'll decide."

Guile eased himself up onto his feet and followed Newby inside the building. As he had imagined it, the inside of the penthouse was spacious and filled with little trinkets that only a Caperan would appreciate. A wide variety of items from all corners of the galaxy that could easily be classified as junk. Smugglers did not care. To them they were gold as it cost the Caperan collectors a bundle to bring them such merchandise outside legal shipping routes.

Newby sat down on one of six fur-covered couches. He sank into the over padded cushions with his lower body all but disappearing. "You are an arms trader looking for your first major score. I have you making three stops before you switch identities and become a naval officer. The switch will be made at a supply depot that is used by both the Alcon and traders. From there you will be assigned to a long-range communications freighter. You will have a code eight commercial clearance so you should be able to get what ever information you need."

"Do you have me anywhere near the Vengeance or the Blackhawk?"

Newby clearly shook his head. "As you asked I'm keeping you as far from them as possible. Any contact will be purely coincidental."

"Excellent."

"Since you're a few days earlier than I had expected your first contact won't be ready."

"That won't be a problem. I do have one question though. Will you be expecting updates from my contacts or are they on a fixed schedule?"

"Fixed schedule. Why?"

Guile brought the blaster up and fired a single pulse into the chubby man's chest. Newby bounced off the back of the couch then rolled onto one side before falling to the floor.

"Because I have no intention of meeting with your contacts." He reached into his back pocket and pulled out his communicator. "Vipryn."

"Any problems?" Vipryn asked.

"None. I may even have a better way of getting onto the Blackhawk thanks to Newby. He may have been worth something after all."

"Got anything yet?"

Shadle looked over the nova's fighter control display and frowned. "Nothing yet. The interlink might be fried. You'll need to replace it."

"Damn!" Bea cursed from behind the pilots seat. "I'm coming out."

Shadle swung her legs out of the cockpit and onto the ladder. With a hard push Bea slid the seat forward, giving her a tight gap to climb out of the storage compartment. With sweat streaming down her face and grease covering her hands, she eased out and sat down on the edge of the cockpit. A cut ran the length of her index finger. It was not deep, but it did emphasize her contempt for her assigned fighter.

"Scraps," she hissed. "I want my nova back."

"Take Wes'. I'm sure he won't mind."

She grimaced at the thought. "Easy for you to say with him not here. Besides, his little companion has been keeping a twenty-four hour watch on it. He left the little guy plugged in and running."

"Security?"

With a soiled rag Bea managed little more than to smear the grease on her hand and aggravate the cut. She moaned at the sight. "Maintenance. He feels the same about these hunks of junk as we do."

She dropped the rag into the seat and leaned against the open canopy. "I agree that we need to spec these hunks of junk, but this isn't the best time. Experience doesn't mean much in a decaying box like this. I swear half the circuitry must be pre-Imperial."

"You want me to get a crew over here?"

"Aren't they working on yours right now?"

Shadle nodded. "It's only a once over though."

"Forget it," Bea objected. "Let 'em finish. I'll replace the part myself." She eased herself onto the ladder and chased her friend down. "Wes seems like a nice guy," she said on the way to the supply bunker.

"I wouldn't know. I haven't had luck cracking his shell."

"Give it time. Something about the way he talks about you is encouraging."

"He talks about me?"

Bea grimaced. "Perhaps I should have phrased that better. Let me just say that his reactions when your name is brought up is encouraging."

"How encouraging?"

"I'm still working on Jared aren't I?" Said Bea with a frown.

Shadle slowed a bit and diverted more concentration to the conversation. "What is it between you two?"

Bea opened her mouth without an answer. She gritted her teeth. "I'm not sure there was anything there in the beginning and I don't know about now. I have had little or no time with him to tell one way or another."

"Give it time," Shadle said, amused with herself.

Bea sniffed a laugh. "I will. I mean I am. We were just starting to get close the way good friends do when he left Devil." She looked up to the rocky ceiling high above. "It's like I'm starting over again." She shook her head picturing Stead and Guile in a fistfight. "My chaperone doesn't like the idea of us together." With a nudge to her side Bea picked Shadle's pass up. "Haggin has been a big brother to me, which only complicates things."

"When did that start?"

"Since the day we met. All the recruits were given a day off to see visiting families and friends. I had neither." She paused to catch her up. "It would be another year before I met Jared. While I stood at a window and watched cadets meet with their visitors Haggin passed by. He stopped. He later told me it was because I looked lonely." She blushed just enough to have a hint of pink show. "I still think it was because I was wearing a jumpsuit that was enough to reveal more than a sensible person would dare to at a military academy."

That drew an innocent grin from Shadle. "You tramp."

"Don't start. I've seen what you wear on your off hours." Bea snapped herself back to her story. "Anyway. He said his friend could wait so we talked for a while. I told him that my family had all died in a construction accident on Perditia and I was left alone with my caretaker on my home world. From that day he took me in as family. In fact," she laughed. "He's the one who introduced me to Jared."

"Touching," Shadle said with sincerity. "I wish I had a story like that."

"You will. Just don't let Wes turn you off when he doesn't seem interested. Stay persistent with him and he'll come around, if he hasn't already."

"What do you mean?"

"I've seen the way he looks at you. I've also seen the way he calms when you confront him. There's a lot of aggression built up within him. More I'm afraid than Jared. It could become a problem. But when you're around it all seems to wash away. If I were to tell him something different than you, I know in my gut that he'd believe you, even when presented with facts backing my case."

"You sound so confident."

Bea grinned, keeping her eyes fixated on the approaching supplies bunker. "I have to be. Mine's the mercenary, remember."

The gangly Tolan, Vigdis Stornoway waited for her guests at the base of the shuttle's passenger ramp. Had Guile gone with Newby's cover, he never would have set foot on the rocky surface of Horde. Instead, he and his companions would have walked into an Alcon trap fifty kilometers above the surface. There, awaiting a shuttle that would never arrive was the Valiant and an impatient captain.

The group needed no introductions. He had informed them of the new route they were to take. As for Stornoway, being a telepath gave her the edge of knowing each of them with a slight twinge of the skin along her head. It was disturbing to have another being read his thoughts, but he had become used to it.

Another to expect her mental breeze was Stead. He was less than exuberant to see her. He followed Guile closely, fighting his own mind to place a wall behind himself and her meddling. He had never cared for her abilities and it shown in his concentration. Stornoway seemed amused with his weak attempts and broke through his barriers as he passed her.

The rest of the crew paid her intrusion no mind as they fanned out between their shuttle and the nearby maintenance transport. Stornoway's personal guards escorted them the rest of the way to the transport and out of sight.

Stornoway gave Guile what passed for a grin among the Tolan. "Word has spread that you have paid a most unpleasant visit to Newby."

"I see that rumor runs faster then the shipping lanes."

"Then the rumor is false."

"No," Guile smiled. "Before you chastise me about interfering with everyone's business this way you should know the reasons behind it. As I saw it, he was going to turn me over to the Empire to alleviate two headaches from his life."

"He gave you a fixed schedule," she assumed.

Guile nodded. "One that did exactly what I told him I wanted. Had he truly set up a good cover and given me a route that led to level four Imperial access I would have had no choice but to board an Imperial ship. He was simply feeding me what I wanted to hear."

"You can be sure that I am not feeding you what you want to hear. From here you will be boarding a supply freighter that is due to re-supply the Blackhawk tomorrow. It's the most direct route I could find."

It was more than he had expected. The corners of his mouth rising above his facial wraps were evident enough that he was pleased. "You're a gem, Vigdis. I don't know how to repay you."

Stornoway waved to the shuttle they had arrived in. "This is payment enough for the cover, but I need a bonus. I need you to tell me that you will drop your contract with the Alliance once your job is done."

"It's already done. I gave my contract to someone else."

"Then you are on your own after this?"

She was reading his thoughts. "You know I'm not."

With her long reach she rested a hand on his shoulder. "Stay away from the Vengeance, Jared. It can only bring you trouble."

Why was she so concerned with his personal mission? It had nothing to do with the Alliance yet she tied the two together. "I won't promise you anything, but I'll consider what you've said. The last thing I want is additional heat."

"Good," she smiled. "Then I take my leave of you." Stornoway looked to the transport. The skin on the back of her head twitched as she sent out a mental message to her guards. "Take care, Jared. I wish I had more time, but I have a rendezvous I must make."

As ever, Stornoway was surrounded by mystery. Her talents gave her an edge over everyone other than Tolan. That lopsidedness in thought took away the weight her words had. He wondered how much of what she spoke was from her mind or his.

Chapter Twenty-Three

A seven-hour star flight jump to an imminent battle with two squadrons of kids should have been the worst of Bea's problems. Despite hours spent in simulated attacks on destroyers she was not entirely confident that any of the pilots of Blue and Gray would survive the encounter. She even doubted that the four experienced pilots would make it out alive. A hard rattling behind her head and erratic status displays simply worsened her outlook.

Bea should have realized her fighter was unfit when she lifted off the flight deck. The flight controls were sluggish and the Star Flight initiator failed on the initial jump order. The Companion confirmed a faulty circuit, but reassured her that all systems were running smoothly. Somehow, with the countdown dropping below one minute, she doubted the accuracy of the unit's report.

Starlight flared up around her and rotated back into points of distant light. Because of the failed first jump attempt, the rest of Gray squadron had already arrived. Pre-briefing had prepared the squadron and they were forming up into three diamond shaped formations as Bea slowed. She need only pass in front of the squadron and assume the lead. She appreciated their discipline in not needed her to order maneuvers.

A second set of fighters sped into the star system from an opposite direction. They too slowed, then formed up into three groups. The fighters of Blue squadron came to a crawl far enough so that only their running lights could be seen. Both groups were now in position on either side on the flight path between two navigation probes. This was the best spot for an ambush as most heavier freighters had to make the normal flight transition from one star flight lane to another.

"Blue leader to Gray leader," Shadle said. "We're in position."

"Copy Blue leader. We're ready here."

"All fighters switch to inter squad channels and secure your com lines. Five minutes to contact."

Five minutes. Bea sighed. More than enough time to build up her reservations about the mission and throw out any confidence she had in their success. She longed for the days when Devil jumped into battle with the backing of an Imperial Star Cruiser. She may have despised everything they stood for, but she did admire the strength of the navy. Strength she was about to face.

The nova's proximity alarms sounded and fifteen blips appeared on the targeting screen. Long-range sensors marked three threats encircling twelve neutral targets. Visually it was easy to tell the difference between the two types of targets. The destroyers were the same odd-looking masses with their dual heavy weapons turrets. The freighter haulers on the other hand were three times bigger than their escorts with thick bodies and rounded bows.

"They're ahead of schedule," Shadle said.

So much the better. Bea thought to herself. "Punch it up," she ordered Gray squadron. "Group two, you have the lead destroyer. One and three, concentrate fire on the trailer."

Engines flared up and twelve nova fighters accelerated towards the convoy. From a distance, twelve more fighters became clearly visible as they too pushed towards the destroyers and freighters. Compared to previous raids she had been involved with, this was well organized and heavily armed. Had the targets been commercial and not Imperial Bea might have had the confidence she desperately needed.

Bea armed her missiles and switched weapons over to the warhead launchers. Her targeting reticule centered against the destroyer trailing the convoy and a distance to target lock began to scroll down. Sensor screens projected by the escort destroyers prevented the use of the navigational probes as a targeting system. As expected, the two groups of fighters had to do it the hard way.

Bea already knew she would not get close enough before she would have to break off her approach. What she did not know was that the lead freighter held no cargo. Instead the belly of the beast opened and released two squadrons of bi-wing fighters. Defensive alarms sounded all through the cockpit. She pulled out of her attack without a moment's thought. As Barger had predicted, they would not have a chance.

"Group two, continue your attack. One and three form up and defend them until their last missiles are released."

"Lead, I've got multiple missile lock."

The voice was not familiar but a recognition system built into the com system identified the pilot and displayed her name.

"Break off and evade, ten." Bea shook the lock on her and pulled back into formation. "Keep your heads and hold tight. You should be able to shake a lock long enough to reach the Bi-wings. Take them one-to-one from there."

Thick pulses of amber streaked out from the lead destroyer. Simultaneous blasts caught the lead fighter of group two and incinerated it.

"Break your angled attack and level off with the bow plane. Hold your course tight with the front of the destroyer and you won't provide it with an easy target."

"Lead, break hard right."

Bea did not question the young voice that warned her. She pulled the stick back and to the right rolling the nova over the right wing. Bright amber laser bolts seared

Chapter Twenty-Three

close to the belly of the fighter. They barely registered on the fighter's shields as they blasted off into the distance. She continued the roll out until she leveled off with the attacking bi-wings. The fighter that had fired on her was directly in front of her, but before she could return fire it disappeared behind a cloud of shattered metal and secondary explosions.

"Thanks, three."

The assisting nova pulled up alongside her with the pilot giving her a thumbs up. Bea smiled. Maybe the situation was not as bad as she had anticipated. The younger pilots were evolving quickly into a tight fighting unit. A far cry from six months ago before Guile and Barger had started training them.

Threats sounded, but not from missile lock. Amber lasers splashed against her forward shields throwing out cyan sparks from the invisible shell. Bea kicked up the nova's engines and closed the gap on the attacking bi-wing, dodging to the right and left all the while. She could not see the Imperial fighter behind the pulses of energy. Her only response was a short burst of unaimed fire from her guns.

Bea's nova cried out from a direct hit to the aft quarter. A mad shaking marked the end of her aft shields and damage to the hull. She could only guess at the extent of the abuse. The damage report scrolled across the tactical screen. She cared not to look. The thought towards the stability of her craft was only rhetorical.

"All missiles away," the lead pilot from group two said.

"Shields down. She's listing."

Bea rolled over long enough to see a large breach in the destroyer's hull just ahead of the engine housing. A bright red glow from inside the tear clearly displayed the extent of the damage to the engine core. If the crew were lucky, half of them would reach their escape pods before the core went critical.

"Group one pull out and engage fighter defenses. Group two, commence attack on destroyer number three."

Bea threw her fighter into two tight rolls to the right and found herself behind a bi-wing. It wasn't the same fighter that fired upon her, but at this point a target was a target. She acquired missile tone and released a pair of thermals. At a hundred meters the pilot had no time to break. The fighter took both missiles in the aft quarter and broke apart. In the last second as the power core gave way and erupted the pilot ejected away. Depending on who won he would either spend a week in the infirmary or years in a cell.

"Break hard left!"

Bea rolled to port then pulled both herself and the nova into a tight bank to the left. A pair of thermal missiles skimmed far too close to her canopy as did the under side of another nova. She cursed initially from surprise, regaining her composure only after her Companion confirmed her pursuer was nothing more than debris.

"Thanks, eleven."

"Two minutes before they jump again," Shadle said.

Bea looked down to her chronometer with her eyes gapping. Five minutes had already passed her by in what felt like a split second.

"I've already lost three fighters, Bea. We've lost."

Responding on its own the Companion spat out her squadron's stats. She was down four fighters with two ejects and three others heavily damaged.

"I'm not looking good either. We have to pull back before they finish us off."

"Negative resistance squadrons. You are covered."

Bea looked out both sides of her canopy in a vein effort to find who had breached her secured channel.

"Lead I have positive tone. Request permission to fire."

The enthusiastic voice that rang out from her headset was unfamiliar in that the Companion could not identify him. The only other question was whether the new threat was targeting her squadron or the destroyers. If the question were answered either way an entirely new set of questions would arise.

"Permission granted, two. Take 'em out group."

The targeting screen registered five new smaller targets, possibly fighters, and three transports. A series of bright targets lit up around the neutral threats on a direct line for the two remaining destroyers. Her Companion identified the warhead targets as fusion missiles with advanced guidance systems. The newer guidance system allowed the missiles to determine the best line of entry based on the targets defensive capabilities, thus inflicting the most damage.

Bea rolled only her right wing so that she had a clear view of the impacts. She already had a picture in her mind of what the missiles could do. The actual impact shattered all her thoughts. The missiles split up towards the two destroyers. The leading warheads struck the aft shields, with the invisible shell erupting outward. The trailing set slammed into the engine housing with full force.

Each destroyer immediately began to list to one side from a sudden loss in guidance and propulsion. The entire engine housing bubbled with secondary internal explosions. Each bubble burst and spewed fire once the armor had withstood as much as it could. Tertiary explosions ripped forward and pressed out through the weakest points in the armor, the gun turrets. Each emplacement exploded out into space.

"They're dead, lead."

"Very good."

For the first time the fighters came into view. They looked somewhat similar to that of the Nova. Almost like they were pieced together with Nova parts. As the lead fighter closed she could make out the finer details. It was then that she recognized them as Scraps. The organization of her assisting fighters and the craftsmanship of the spare parts gave off the impression of a planetary militia, but the markings were strikingly pirate.

"Resistance strike force this is Arlast Raider intercept team two. Are your squadrons in need of further assistance?"

Bea caught the flash of a Bi-wing as two novas poured fire into it. "We're doing fine, intercept lead. I do have a question for you though."

"I'm sure you do, Resistance lead. Shall we complete the task at hand first?"

Chapter Twenty-Three

"Gladly. Narra."

"I'm listening, Bea."

"Order the freighters to slave to your squadrons' Companions then let's get out of here. Arlast lead, prepare to receive rendezvous coordinates."

"No need Resistance lead. We already have a boarding team waiting at your jump coordinates. We'll meet you there."

Who in the world could have given away their assault plans? It was a serious breach of both security and morality. To hand over sensitive mission data to a well-known pirate organization was suicidal for the party involved and treacherous for their leaders. Jared, she conceded. This has to be Jared's doing.

Minutes later the convoy group dropped out of star flight in an empty system with a dead star. The only navigation probe within reach was under Alliance control and only activated if a prior coded signal was sent. It was the perfect location for what was about to take place. A rapid transfer of supplies from Imperial ships to independent freighters.

All but one freighter was stripped of its goods. The remaining ship fell under Arlast control, much to the dislike of Shadle. The moment she discovered that an Arlast transport had docked with the lone ship she landed in its bay. It was the last move Bea would have recommended. Given that she was rear guard during the jump there was little she could do to stop it from happening though.

The freighter the Arlast Raiders chose to take was the same that had held the bi-wings. As Bea passed through an opening in the rear of the ship she could see the lifts used to bring the fighters out of storage for launch. This was necessary as the bay was just large enough for two fighters or a single shuttle.

Bea slid down from the cockpit. Her boots hit the deck, but not loud enough to drown out the sound of a very upset pilot. She looked towards Shadle's fighter and saw her standing in front of a bulkhead door with her back towards her. She was visibly arguing with someone with a heavy rifle. Her sudden burst into a run was understandable.

"...no right to interfere in our dealings," Shadle ranted.

Bea slid up next to her and grabbed her shoulders. She looked over the heavily armed man standing in front of the two, sizing him up for a confrontation. He had no look about him that would lead her to believe Shadle was in danger of getting killed. The size of the weapon and notoriously heated temper of the Phalnx did worry her. If she pushed the wrong button they both could end up floating home.

"I'm sorry, sir. Narra has a tendency to over react when she's rescued by strangers."

Shadle shook off her grip. "That's not the point. Our mission was clear. Either we take the whole convoy or none at all."

"You were not aware that we were sent as assistance?" A female asked from behind the bulky Altass. Altaff stepped into view from around him. "Then you would also not know of our deal with the Alliance."

Shadle did not recognize her, but Bea did. "Please forgive me, Malane. As I stated about my partner here she can over react at times. Could you please inform us as to the nature of this deal?"

"Before he disappeared, Jared Guile contacted me about your situation. He stated that the convoy would not go without fighter defense and he assured me that you would need assistance. He also assured me that the freighter containing the fighter defense would have storage bays full of fighter supplies and hardware." She rested a hand on her brother's shoulder. "And he was right," she told him.

Shadle turned around and gritted her teeth. "I wish Jared would tell us about his deals."

"I'm surprised that your leader, Patron I believe his name was, had not informed you ahead of time that this was to take place. It was with him that we confirmed the exact time and location the attack would take place."

Bea gritted her teeth. "Something tells me that what you are going to say next is not going to sit well with either of us."

"Most likely. I will confirm with your thoughts. As you may have suspected Jared has turned over all future dealings with the Alliance to me. He clearly stated that he could not maintain the supplies that you require."

"Did he say if this meant his affiliation with us was over?"

"I will not answer yes or no to that particular question. As is the case in my line of work, such a disclosure could endanger my valued business relationship with him. It will be unethical of me to betray his trust after he gave this most valuable contract to me without asking for much in return."

"What did he ask?" Asked Shadle.

Altaff's answer was directed at Bea. "Your life."

"It wasn't his to save. Or yours for that matter. You should have turned him down."

Altass grinned behind his sister. "You think us the fools with such a remark."

A simple gesture with her hands silenced her brother's harsh response. "I will allow you your anger towards this arrangement. I have studied the reasons behind the formation of the Sutherlin Alliance and can sympathize with your purity. I only ask that you awaken and understand that your purity can only go so far. Dealing with people like me or Jared is a necessity unless you have the power of the Alcon to take what you will."

"I don't need a lecture in how the galaxy works and I don't need excuses. The blood we've spilled has cleared us of the purity label long ago." Bea spun on a heel and stormed back to her fighter.

Shadle watched her leave then giggled nervously. "Maybe I should apologize for her this time."

"No need," Altaff said. "She just learned that Jared loves her as much as she loves him and she doesn't know how to take it."

Chapter Twenty-Four

Fallon appeared bored to the bridge officers and he was. The search for Jared Guile and the resistance had slowed drastically. Information that normally flowed in from the smuggler and trade informants had stopped entirely, reducing leads to next to nothing. Even the leads he had stumbled across himself were drying up. Wherever he was, he was not leaving a trail behind him. Fallon did not believe for a moment that he had gone into hiding. The only other reason for the sudden change had to lie within the deals he had made.

S'Lendo twitched as a report scrolled across his screen. He wanted nothing more than to bury it behind other reports that Fallon usually ignored. That was impossible in this case. A messenger had been sent to Volana Three to find out why there was no more information coming back from Administrator Newby.

"Has scout team five reported in yet?" Fallon asked.

S'Lendo jumped in his seat. His commander had not seen the obvious concern so he proceeded as if nothing was wrong. "They have, sir."

"And?"

"They found the shuttle on the outskirts of the capital city. It had been stripped of all usable equipment and burned out. There was no trace of the messenger you sent, his escorts, or the shuttle's pilots."

The blank expression on Fallon's face did not change. "I grow weary of these reports, Forn. Before we left for Perditia I could smell Guile around the corner. Now his trail is just a painful memory in my side. It stops now."

"Orders, sir."

"Have the files from Devil been cleared yet?"

S'Lendo glanced to his data screen of assignments and shook his head. "No, sir, it has not. The central library said that our request has yet to clear."

Fallon closed his eyes. "What about my request for new fighters?"

"Nothing yet, sir. Admiral Ishat has not given an explanation why."

"What is Mister Gesh involved with at the moment?"

S'Lendo typed an inquiry and received an answer a moment later. "He is currently in contact with the Prime Dictate of Cadera Prime. Shall I ascertain the content of the conversation?"

Fallon reopened his eyes. "No need. When the minister is finished inform him that he will be returning to Volana Three to speak with the administrator personally."

"I'm sure he will find out what happen to the last envoy."

"Whether he knows or not I do not care. He will be guarded during his stay. You will send a detachment from the Dagger Unit to ensure his survival and the administrator's cooperation."

"And if Mister Newby refuses to answer any questions?"

Fallon slowly turned towards him. "Then Dagger Unit will enact what they were assembled for." He stood and moaned out his disappointment. "I'll be in my ready room should anything new come up."

With a long, slow stride Fallon left the bridge and entered his personal office. He was not sure if the lack of response from the fleet bothered him more than Guile's cold trail. The rebel mercenary had all but disappeared, as had the communiqués from Admiral Ishat. He had received the light carrier he had requested long before he returned to Perditia, but the additional fighters and light support had yet to grace his presence.

What further deepened his troubled brow was a cold silence from the Regent. Since his return to the outskirts of the Badlands, he had only received one message from the palace and it was the usual note of appreciation for seeing the Regent. It was more a subtle threat never to refuse her request, but he accepted it with a smile nonetheless.

Then there was the Nullify. As far as he knew, the devastator class cruiser was a mere five hours away, hidden under the umbrella of a binary star system. The idea was that the cruiser needed to charge off of a powerful system. The need for the ship to be at full charge when the main Alliance cell turned up was essential. Rather than leaving the Nullify undisturbed on the edge of the target system while it gathered enough power she would be ready to release a full pulse.

A chime from his comm panel shook him from his troubling thoughts. "Yes," he said as he opened the line.

"Sir, we may not have to send another envoy to Volana Three." Said S'Lendo

Fallon's eyes narrowed. He sat down in his thickly padded chair and leaned towards the speaker. "Explain."

"It appears that Mister Newby has been killed."

Eyes perking he sat back. "And how did you come about this startling revelation?"

"I'm not sure, sir. The thought just arose in my head."

Tolans, Fallon thought as he rolled his eyes. "Have we received any visitors?"

"Yes, sir. An outdated shuttle bearing old Imperial markings just arrived. I was prepared to detain the occupants for questioning."

"Is there a Tolan among them?"

Chapter Twenty-Four

"One moment." S'Lendo paused. "Yes there is. She says she needs to see you."

"I'm sure she does. Have her escorted here."

A Tolan in an old Imperial shuttle. Probably one of the first to have had the old Galactic Defense Fleet symbol replaced with the Alcon. He had an affinity for artifacts like that. Most run down craft were retired to scrap yards and eventually broken down for parts and sold off for shipping or re-engineered into new military hardware. To have a working piece of history would be a prize to a collection that consisted of fifty to a hundred year old hand weapons.

Fallon was one of a handful of admirals in what was known as the collector's society. Among the fifteen officers he had the smallest collection, but the most unique. In addition to the twelve weapons that adorned his boxlike home on Perditia he held two examples of extinct humanoid species in the Grand Museum. Though this may seem like a treasure that set him above the other collectors, it simply set him apart. After all, Fallon had been the cause of the extinction.

The door to Fallon's ready room parted ten minutes after the order was given. S'Lendo was the first to step through. "She says she used to be a pilot."

"A pilot," Fallon repeated. "The only Tolan pilot we ever had was..." S'Lendo stepped to the side and allowed a pair of long legs carry the Tolan into the light of the room. Fallon grinned from recognition as he finished. "...Vigdis Stornoway. As I was saying. This must be Vigdis."

Stornoway took just two steps to cross the room and sit down in front of the Admiral's desk. "A pleasure as always, Admiral Fallon."

Fallon waved S'Lendo out of the room never taking his eyes off the former Devil pilot. He waited long enough for the door to close. "What would bring you from the trade lanes to my ship?"

"A mutual annoyance and a business proposition."

"And what could you offer me that I don't already have?"

"Locations of all four Sutherlin Alliance bases and their strengths."

Fallon leaned back into his chair and folded his hands in his lap. He pursed his lips, attempting to determine whether she was telling him the truth. What it came down to was that his leads were all but dried up and this was as fresh and solid as any he ever had. "Captain," he called out.

S'Lendo re-entered the room. "Sir."

"Provide our friend here with suitable quarters and prepare a new set of deployment orders. We may be moving in sooner than expected."

Guile felt sick to his stomach. He knew he needed to get aboard the Blackhawk, but he did not have to like it. Each hour that passed drew the destroyer closer to the system he pictured in his mind, his old post. The pilot barracks, the fighter docking ports, the briefing room. More importantly, a heartless captain sitting in the center of the bridge and fiendish orders filtering down to Stead.

"All hands, destroyer in parking orbit."

He heard the announcement and filed it somewhere in his mind. The sight of the ten-year-old ship preoccupied his full attention. He was not expecting the kind of emotions seeing it would bring up. The churning of his last meal and the pounding in the back of his head. It was not unlike what he felt during star flight. It was however, intensified.

Stead walked up behind the troubled mercenary and rested a hand on his shoulder. "You ready?"

"I'm not sure. I don't know if I can do this."

Stead moved next to him and looked out the view port at the Blackhawk and the Nightwing. "You don't have much choice. None of us know where to go from here. You're the only one besides Barger who has any sense of what the rest of our mission is."

"I could put you in charge and let you figure it out." Guile turned away from the window. "I'm just making this up as I go."

Stead squinted out at the ship then looked to him. "You really are bothered by this, aren't you?"

"More than you know, Haggin. More than anyone seems to know."

"What is it that you know that the rest of us don't?"

Barger stepped into the small room, interrupting them. "Aeon has a shuttle ready in the maintenance bay."

"We're on our way." Stead grabbed Guile's shoulder and dragged him along. "We'll continue this later."

The small insurgence team departed the cargo freighter in a converted cargo hauler. The thin craft had four arms that dangled from the belly. Each held an umbilical line and mini tractor beam. The insides, normally filled with the magnetic generators that powered the tractor beams had been gutted to make room for its current passengers. The resulting passenger compartment was cramped but acceptable.

The makeshift shuttle slid into line with the four other cargo haulers that were in the process of ferrying supplies to the two destroyers. Close to the Blackhawk it broke off from the others and pulled alongside the portside docking hatch. Halash eased the small craft close to the moor enough for automated umbilicals to pull in the rest of the way. The hauler docked with the destroyer with no one the wiser.

Guile hacked into the docking controls from inside the hauler, ordering the hatch to release. In a calm rush Barger and Guile boarded the destroyer and sprinted down the darkened corridor to a main corridor that ran the length of the ship. Either way, the corridor was long and held few places to hide.

"Which way?" Guile asked under the bright lights.

Barger gave a glance down each direction before shooting a harsh smirk towards him. "You don't remember?"

"It's been awhile." He gave his companion a sour expression before leaning against an angled wall. "You have to remember that she was just a few months out of dock when I came aboard. Who can say how many modifications she's had since then?"

Chapter Twenty-Four

Barger grinned. "You can't imagine what an insult that is. She hasn't been touched in eight months and the last shot that hit her shields barely made a ripple. Dock engineers have done nothing more than verify that she was in top shape."

Guile looked down each direction again, retaining the confused look that bothered his scarf covered face. "I still don't know."

"Flight deck and no man's land," he said with his eyes pointing to the deck. "One deck down."

"They still call it no man's land?"

"Isn't that what it is?"

The two intruders remained in their grease-covered jumpsuits as they meandered aft down the corridor. They were twenty meters from the access corridor before they came across a vertical lift. The four by four deck was open aired and had simple handrails around the edges to prevent an accident against the magnetic plates that provided the lift with motion. Accidents were uncommon beyond stupid mistakes.

The lift touched down on the flight deck. Guile stepped into the bay that was open the width of the neck and ran the entire ninety-two meters back to the engine compartment. Barger was a bit more hesitant. The long and open bay was lined on one side with racked missiles, laser cannons, and replacement fuel pods. The opposite length had six seven by seven meter access hatches located above and to the side of the fighters mounted below.

Both had vivid memories of running down the center of the bay, stopping at the cylindrical personnel hatches leading to the fighter cockpits, and dropping down. The sounds of hard boots echoing along the decking rang clear in Barger's head down the silent bay. It was deafening in that there was no sound at all. He neither missed it nor hated to see it go. It was a better life, yet one that brought him pain.

A firm, gloved hand gripped his shoulder, bringing him back to reality. The slit in Guile's face wrap betrayed sympathetic eyes. A deeper pain rested there. Much deeper than Barger's. He wanted more than needed to ask what drew him away from this life of war and luxury. A want that he could not yet bring himself to face.

"I may have had time to forget the pleasantries, but the pain lingers," said Guile in a whisper. "Hang on to the good times as long as you can. They'll keep you sane until you can find a new outlet."

"Hey!" A faintly familiar woman's voice shouted a few meters down the bay.

Guile took no mind and ducked into the shadows between the lift and a corridor leading to the bow. Barger on the other hand lingered long enough to identify her. Chief Loma Cole was unmistakable in her black jumpsuit and red badge above her left breast. He on the other hand was more difficult to pick out under the layers of filth he had so carefully placed on himself.

"Is there a problem?" he said in a returning charm than he had not felt since his last day aboard.

Cole stopped a few steps from him. His voice had hit her like a solid wall and the gazed look in her eyes relayed a troubled thought running through her mind.

"Loma."

She took a step back, further decreasing her chances of identifying his features. There was a glimmer of hope behind her eyes. She was hoping that it was him, but hating the thought that it could be. He assumed that the official report released was that he was dead. Her continued anger at his intrusion solidified the hypothesis.

"You two don't belong down here. What are those, tug outfits? Did you come in on the freighter? You missed your check in by two sections and three decks."

Barger fully stepped from the lift, allowing the bay's lights to fully illuminate his face. The color may have been off from the grime, but the curves where the same. A longer response just added punch. "It's a freighter jumpsuit and I'm not here to check in."

Cole's right knee visibly buckled, dragging the right side of her body onto her hip. "Wes?"

He took another step. "Not dead I'm afraid."

Cole was just as beautiful as the last time he had seen her. Underneath the filthy, matted hair and her ratty, old jumpsuit she was the same woman that he had fallen for the day he arrived. Her age of one hundred thirty standard years and a vast engineering knowledge had never swayed his interest in her, and though she had never shown the affection he had for her, they remained close friends.

There was no mistaking her reaction that she thought he was dead. "My god," she gasped.

Barger relaxed into a half pompous, half comforting stance. "Which one?"

"All of them," Cole answered with growing relief. She took two steps forward and stopped a breath away from him. "Alder had told us you had been captured, then the official report came down that your body was found in the wreckage." She looked passed him at the stranger standing in the shadows. "Who's he?"

"A friend." He glanced back over his shoulder. "Someone you might know."

"His face was hidden." She ignored him and gripped both of Barger's shoulders. "What are you doing here?"

"Information. Sensitive information."

"You're dead, Wes. If intelligence even suspects that you're alive they'll hunt you down."

"They already are," Guile said out of view.

Cole's eyes narrowed. She searched the shadows for the stranger. "Then what are you doing back here? This is the last place you should be."

"I've got nowhere else to turn. I need Alder's help with something."

A realization struck her with his last words and she was not happy about it. "You're with the Alliance, aren't you? You're working for the murderers of loyal Imperial citizens."

Barger managed to work one shoulder away from her grip. "Now hold on, Loma. I haven't murdered anyone and the people I work for wouldn't have the stomach for it."

"Bold words, rebel."

Chapter Twenty-Four

"Hold on now," he said, finally breaking her tight grip. "When have you known me to fight the bad fight?"

Cole took a step back. "You shouldn't be here. You'd be killed and I'd be shot for treachery. Worse than that, one of these days you and your rebel friends will have to face Devil and you'll have to make the decision to kill us to save them. Now I don't know how that sits with you, but it doesn't work for me."

"Listen, Wes. You and I were good friends and now that I know you're alive I'd still like to consider you one. Leave here now and leave the Alliance before you have to face some tough choices. I won't think any worse of you for it."

"I couldn't live with that," he responded. "I've looked into the eyes of our future and I've seen nothing but death. Death for them, death for us, and death for the Empire. I won't stand here and tell you that Alcon will fall to these children, but he will not remain in power as long as our youth are willing to sacrifice themselves to protect their future."

"Noble sentiment," Guile said, beating her to the punch.

"Your friend doesn't hold your beliefs. Is it like this throughout the Alliance?"

Barger chuckled at the comment. She did not know how wrong and yet how right she was. "He simply doesn't trust the people involved. You wouldn't believe who is a part of this."

"I can take a guess just looking at you. I would go so far as to place Jared Guile at the top."

Guile caught himself from bursting out laughing, letting a simple snort escape his cupped hand.

Barger bowed his head and grinned. "You don't know how close you are."

"He supplies you?"

"No," he said. "You really don't know how close you are."

Cole leaned onto her left hip and folded her arms. "So what am I suppose to do with you?"

"Just let me see Alder and I'll leave you to your work. If he saw me taken, then he knows I wasn't in the wreckage. He'll respond accordingly."

She pursed her lips, trying to decide which direction to take. When she finally made her decision it was the one he had expected. Minutes later he and Guile were guided forward into no man's land and to Kirkland's new quarters aboard Blackhawk. As expected, they were Barger's old quarters and still bared the removed markings of his name. Kirkland's nameplate had still not been mounted even after this many weeks.

Cole slid past Barger on her way back to the bay. Guile snapped at her shoulder, gripping it as tight as he could. He gave her no explanation. It would simply be understood that he would not allow them to walk into a trap alone. She was to be the insurance that they would make it off the destroyer in one piece.

Barger chimed the door and stepped back. A second later the door slid back into the wall. Kirkland stood there with a blank expression on his face. He looked into

Sutherlin Alliance

Barger's eyes and the color in his face faded away. The recognition was there. His appreciation for Barger being alive was not.

"What are you doing here?" asked Kirkland softly.

Guile was in no mood to wait for an answer. Still holding onto Cole he pushed his way past the two and into the room. Barger shrugged and stepped passed Kirkland as well. He stepped across the small room and sat down on the bed that had been his. He waited and watched for Kirkland to say something. He continued to stand at the door even as it shut behind him.

"You can let go now," said Cole, sarcastically.

Guile let up a bit, but not enough for her to squirm free. "Dispense with your tough attitude, Loma. You're a mechanic, not a fighter."

"And how would you know?"

"Because he used to be a Devil," Kirkland said, breaking his silence.

Barger and Guile both shot a puzzled and concerned look in his direction.

Cole reached for his hand and broke Guile's hold. She stepped to the bed and sat down next to Barger. "How do you know?"

Kirkland leaned against the door, his eyes intent on the floor. "I made my own inquiries after the official report was released on Wes' death. I found out that Jared Guile was the pilot who had destroyed the station. I saw with my own eyes that Wes had not been killed. Rather, he had been picked up by Alliance fighters. The same fighters that helped Jared escape." He looked up at Barger. "I just put two and two together."

Cole's gaze fixated on Guile. "Jared?"

Guile reached for his face wraps and lowered them enough to expose the deep scars along his jaw. "Miss me?"

In one fluid swing she slugged his left leg. "Traitor," she blasted him.

Guile blew a kiss down to her and grinned. "I get that a lot."

Kirkland shook his head before returning his gaze to Barger. "You didn't tell me why you were here."

"For help," he answered bluntly. "Mister Guile here suspects that the Alliance is about to suffer a similar fate to that of Sutherlin."

"And I'm supposed to care."

"You did, or so I thought. You were the only person I could turn to."

"You thought wrong." He reached behind him and opened the door. "Now if you and your friend will please get out of here before you get me into trouble I would appreciate it. I have a flight schedule to prepare."

Barger folded his arms. "I'm not leaving until you help me. I'm just asking for information, not physical assistance."

"What kind of information?" Cole asked before Kirkland could ask them to leave again.

"Fleet deployment," Barger said while still looking at his former friend. "Particularly the deployment of Admiral Fallon's task force. I already know he just returned from Perditia, but what I don't know is where he plans to strike next."

Chapter Twenty-Four

"I don't know either. I only know that we are to receive additional ships from fleet command. Now if you'll please leave."

Barger shook his head. "I need more than what you know. I need access to the fleet registry."

Kirkland's tone deepened to an almost growl. "Why? So you can access battle group strengths and pick apart the task force one ship at a time?"

"So I can keep a group of kids from being murdered," he snapped in defense. "The Alliance is made up of more than just rebels. They have taken in political prisoners and the families of those that Emperor Alcon has singled out as threats. Citizens, mind you that have only committed the crime of speaking out against the destruction of the galactic congress and the creation of a dictatorship."

"The Sutherlin Alliance is a gathering of criminals," retorted Kirkland. "I may have been conscious of their plight in the past, but that was then and this is now." He shut the door and locked it. "Which is why you have to leave," he continued in a whisper.

Cole nudged Barger then directed his attention to the air vent in the ceiling.

"It's bad enough I had to mention his name in the open," Kirkland said with a wave of his hand towards Guile. "I don't want to say yours and give your situation additional attention. I don't know if you are aware of it but your head commands a hefty price."

Barger looked to Guile who nodded. "I do know, but that doesn't change things. Coming here was the last thing I wanted to do. Involving you and Loma ranked even lower than that. On the other hand, Jared agreed that this was the only way to get current and accurate information. If he had gone to his sources the deployment list would have already aged by at least a week."

"Listen, Alder. Believe me when I say this. You are the only person I can trust in the Empire. You were the only person I ever trusted besides Loma. I need your help. Not so much as to help myself or my new friends but because you helped me make a decision that changed my life for the better."

The remark drew considerable curiosity from Kirkland. Enough to have him kneel down and relax his guard. "How so?"

"All your talk about the Sutherlin Alliance and various other rebel uprisings. About how they were growing in frequency and why. Until you joined Devil and we were able to resume our friendship, I had been set in my path. I had laid out every promotion and every post I would have until the day I retired. The Empire was to be my life. The inside information you began to spout out about how battle groups like Captain Merrill's were ravaging peaceful worlds to command respect got me to thinking about where I was going. I found myself doubting my place in the Empire and even considering the Alliance position instead of hating it."

"That doubt about the Empire and open mindedness towards the rebels allowed me to accept an offer that either meant my life or my salvation." He tossed up his hands. "Call it a religious revelation or just a personal realization, but I was reborn on that Alliance cruiser. And now that I've spent time training and getting to know them, I have a new understanding about how the galaxy works. A new understanding as to why the last holdout realms refuse to bow down even under the Empire's heavy guns."

"Freedom, Alder. They fight for independence. A concept not heard of in the galaxy for over a hundred years, before the last empire dissolved into the autonomous realms governed by the galactic council. I know in my heart that what the Emperor wants is just, but he is going about it the wrong way. Pain and suffering is no way to unify a galaxy in turmoil."

Kirkland let his legs slip out from under him. "I never thought you were listening to me."

"I did more than listen. I converted."

"You rebelled."

"Is there a difference?"

"There isn't when it comes to the Alcon." Kirkland managed to work his left leg up underneath and prop himself up. "And I have a greater responsibility now. I have to respect the oath I took until the day I die."

"As did I. I took the oath and obeyed the Emperor until the day I was declared dead. Now I'm here to ask you to help out your deceased friend by giving his new spirit what it needs to survive."

"Under protest. If confronted I will admit only that I was helping under protest."

"Fine. Just tell them the truth. That Jared Guile held a knife under your throat until you provided us with the information we required."

Cole was nodding in agreement even before Kirkland looked to her for reassurance. "My data pad is under my pillow. I never changed my code."

Barger reached under the pillow and removed the small device. He activated it and typed in the code. He and Kirkland had shared each other's codes in the event that one was hung over and the other had to check in for him.

Guile looked over the pad and grinned. "High level access is restricted as I expected, but this gives me access to the back door like you said. Give me a few minutes." After a moment he glanced up to Barger. "The room is secure but there is a monitor just outside. The image scrambler you and I are wearing are enough to distort the recording. They'll know someone was here but they won't know who."

"Good enough for me. Break in and get what you can. Remember that we're on a time limit here."

Words did not come easy once Guile went to work. Cole and Kirkland updated Barger on where the destroyer had been since his disappearance. Barger returned the favor letting them in on what he's been doing with the Alliance. Both were surprised at the lack of experience the rebels had. What surprised them even more was how quickly the pilots he and Guile were training had advanced.

Before any of them knew it, a half hour passed. Guile's sudden gesture of shock and fear broke up a lighthearted discussion about academy practices and how they had changed over the years.

"What is it?" Kirkland asked.

Chapter Twenty-Four

"The Nullify."

"Excuse me," Barger said. "What is a Nullify?"

Guile looked up from the pad. "It's a devastator class star cruiser with enough fire power to wipe out all life from a planet in one shot."

Barger's eyes widened. "How's that possible?"

"I'm downloading her profile right now. I found everything under the fleet's registry. She was just assigned to Admiral Fallon's task force not long after he returned to the sector." A brief beep from the pad drew his attention back to the small display. "I have the final count for the Admiral's task force. He now has this new ship, his battle cruiser, two carriers, five medium cruisers, and ten destroyers. There's also something in here about new deployment orders."

"New orders?" Kirkland asked. "They must be fresh. We're running on orders given two weeks ago."

"They came in two hours ago. The task force is to break into four battle groups and make assaults in four systems. The new orders look to be a result of a skirmish resulting in the loss of three escort destroyers."

The convoy attack, Barger thought to himself. "Looks like Patron is going to have to hold off on the major strike he was planning."

Guile tossed the pad onto Barger's lap. "Look at the assault systems."

Picking up the pad he scrolled down the list. He stopped at the last and frowned. "Luikart."

"Where's that?" Cole asked.

Barger set the pad down. "That's the Alliance home base."

"I'm sure the other three match up our minor cells," said Guile. "The battle groups assigned to each target are scaled at least four to one in each case. However they got this information, it maps out our strengths in each system. We have to get this back to Patron so he can begin the evacuation."

"There isn't time." He tossed the pad back to Guile. "The time stamp for deployment is set for two days from now. By the time we get back there won't be enough time to evacuate the base."

"Then we have no choice. You have to get back and prepare them for a defensive strike. I'll get our team onto the Vengeance and see what we can do from there."

"Which ships are assigned to the Luikart strike?" Kirkland asked.

Guile answered before Barger could check. "Devil has been assigned as support."

Kirkland and Barger found each other's troubled looks. This is exactly what both had hoped to avoid. The Empire would not rest until the rebels were destroyed, and the Alliance would never give in. As was the case in many conflicts, two friends would be thrown against each other in the middle of it all.

"Don't say it," Kirkland gave in. "I won't shoot unless I have to. What I will do though is help you get out of here."

"No need," Guile interrupted. "We have a ride."

Barger stood. "Not for long. You need to stay here and I need something with star drive."

"What are we going to do with the hauler?"

"You're the mercenary, Jared. Find some way of using it to get aboard the Vengeance."

"May I interrupt?" Kirkland said as he stood. "If we have indeed been assigned to a multi-system strike then we won't be meeting up with the Vengeance. The battle groups will jump into the system in pairs within seconds of each other so that if there's an ambush, not all the ships will be pinned in."

"He's right," Barger told Guile. "Tactics changed a few months after you resigned due to the rising occurrence of pirate raids."

"Then I'll have to give Admiral Fallon a reason to come here. The only problem I see here is how you plan on getting back to Luikart."

Therein lay the ultimate question. By himself he did not stand a chance. Though the destroyer had at least one shuttle docked in the landing bay, he would have no access to it. His only alternative stared at him as if she knew what he was thinking, and he hated having to approach her with his outlandish idea.

Barger turned to Cole. "Can you prep a shuttle discreetly?"

Cole nodded. "Getting out of the bay will be another story. I'll have to drop the restriction field long enough for you to get out. That leaves me high and dry."

"We can't have that, now can we. I'll just have to find another way."

Cole shut her eyes, fighting her own fears of what she was feeling. "No!" She blasted out. "There is no other way. I have to drop the field...and leave with you." She stood and cupped his mouth before he could speak. "Don't refuse. You have no other alternative and if I drop the field and stay I'll be shot for treason. It's the only way."

Less than an hour later a firefight erupted in the landing bay. Two security guards were killed and Barger was hit in the side before Cole could drop the restriction field that prevented any craft from entering or leaving the bay. Fighting pain and a seeping wound Barger pushed one of the two shuttles off the deck at full power and blasted out of the bay. Three more guards were killed from the wash back created by the powerful engines.

A thousand meters off the port bow, moments before gunners had positive locks on the fleeing shuttle, the hauler erupted from placed charges, opening a ten-meter gash across the hull. The rush of escaping air pushed the destroyer over on its side, throwing off the weapon locks. Only one, un-targeted shot chased the fleeing craft. The shuttle jumped out of sight seconds later, leaving six stowaways onboard the damaged destroyer.

Chapter Twenty-Five

Guile could not have planned it any better. There she was. The Vengeance, clear as a stored image resting a hundred meters off the Blackhawk's starboard bow. And sitting at her command, Admiral Galt Fallon, believing that he was here simply to give assistance to an injured ship. He reached a safe parking distance and began to shuttle repair crews to the destroyer, unaware that on a return trip one of the transports would have additional passengers.

Who would have thought that a trap would have given him such a unique opportunity? Guile was handed the completion of his mission on a silver platter. Now all that remained was the follow through.

Guile turned to his three Alliance comrades with a large, yet understated grin. "Well, my friends. We have approached the den of the beast disguised as his allies. Now all that remains is to cripple him before he awakes. I've asked a lot of you, but now I'm going to ask a great deal more."

"Don't bother," Stead said. "We rode it out this far. We aren't backing down now." He stepped closer to the viewing window and moaned. "I just wish you'd told us ahead of time what we were getting into."

"By pure luck we've gotten this far. If I had told you we'd be breaking onto the Vengeance a week ago, I wouldn't have believed it myself, but here we are."

Vipryn and Aeon stepped from a changing room with Alcon naval uniforms on. Each looked incredibly uncomfortable and uneasy in their new attire.

"You look great."

"Hardly," Aeon growled. "I'd rather have stayed in the maintenance uniforms."

"Sorry, Aeon, but the Vengeance only has automated maintenance. There was no other way."

"You could have just shot me."

The humorous remark drew the appropriate response. Anxiety ran high and it showed in the restrained chuckles. Any more and any one of the team would have a heart attack.

The ship wide intercom crackled to life. "Repair crew seven report back to bay three for departure. Repair crew seven to bay three."

"That's us," Guile said.

"I wish it weren't," Aeon responded.

Stead stole one last glance out at the ship that seemed to take up the entire viewing window. "This is crazy. It may be a worthless effort, but at least in a fighter I would have some control. But this."

"Trust me, Haggin. You'll have more control than you ever thought you would. That ship is the last place the Empire would think to look for us. I'll give you nine to one odds that they'll believe we're on the Valiant if they think we're this gutsy at all."

"I'd take those odds if I weren't so petrified."

The group of imitation officers worked their way to docking bay and boarded the small transport. The filthy crewmembers paid them no mind as they too boarded the transport and found seats towards the back. As was customary, the officers sat along the forward benches. With everyone aboard, the transport lifted off the deck and exited the destroyer. In less than a minute the ship closed the gap to the Vengeance and landed in one of its ten bays.

Shadle could not have been in a better place to see the badly damaged shuttle appear on the horizon. She had already been on her way up to look out at the stars when the sensor probes at the edge of the system sent out an emergency signal. Bea and two other fighters blasted away from the planet on an intercept course, fully intent on bringing down the intruder, which was interpreted as an Imperial craft.

By the time Shadle had reached the observation bunker Bea relayed an all clear and called for emergency teams to be standing by for wounded. She still did not know who or what was coming. It was not until Bea called for Patron to be present at their arrival did she realize the team that had left was aboard.

"All hands clear the tarmac," a woman's voice announced from a speaker in the bunker wall. "Intercept fighters to land at fighter row. The shuttle will be landing just outside the medical ward. Emergency teams are standing by."

Shadle wanted desperately to know who exactly was on the shuttle and who was injured, though she knew in her heart who it was. Please let him be all right.

The three escort fighters followed in closely as the shuttle slowed. Damage was visible along the port side from what looked like cannon fire. Penetration into the shuttle was deep enough to expose a demolished battery pack. With the craft traveling in star flight the loss of even one pack reduced power to the passenger cabin drastically. At best the occupants would be on minimal life support with no lights and reduced heat.

This is where the harsh training of the Imperial academy would have to play a critical role. Shadle had not experienced what so many others had, but she knew what it entailed. Hours if not days were spent in nearly lifeless conditions to simulate power failure in space. Temperatures dropped below freezing at times. If the

Chapter Twenty-Five

injured man aboard had a mortal flesh wound these conditions could only benefit. Blood flow would slow and the wound would freeze.

As soon as the craft dropped into the hidden opening of the base, Shadle turned towards the lift and descended. The drop into the base seemed to take forever. Images in her mind of the damaged shuttle replaced those of layer after layer of passing rock.

The shuttle and fighters had already touched down when she reached the bottom. In a flurry, Shadle raced across the tarmac towards a group a people standing behind the shuttle. As she closed she made out a female in a grease-layered jumpsuit, Patron, and three white clad doctors standing over a hovering gurney. One was in the process of strapping a brace onto the patient as she approached.

"Wes," Shadle cried out from the front of the shuttle.

A hand reached up, beckoning the doctor pushing the gurney to stop. "Narra," Barger mumbled behind a thickly fatigued voice.

Shadle reached his side and gripped his extended hand. Bea caught up shortly after and joined the small group as they escorted him towards the infirmary. Along the way she took a closer look at Loma Cole and glanced back down to Barger. His lazy gaze up to the rocky ceiling told her not to ask.

"What happened?" Bea asked halfway to the infirmary.

Cole reached into one of several pockets, pulled out a data pad, and handed it to her. "All you need to know is on this. He recorded a message on the way back. I told him not to, but he insisted. He spent a lot of time looking over all the information Jared Guile downloaded."

"Then Jared's ok?" Patron asked.

"The whole team is fine. A full update is on the pad."

Shadle leaned closer to Barger and whispered into his ear. "Hang in there, Wes. I'm not going to let you die over your stubbornness."

Barger gave her a weak smile. "I'll be fine. I just need some rest. The hit I took wasn't a bad one."

Shadle looked up to the closest doctor who gave her a more complete diagnosis. "He appears to have several broken ribs and a deep burn. The temperature in the shuttle was just above freezing, which helped. It limited his blood loss to a minimum. He needs rest."

The doctor pushing the gurney held up a hand to stop the escorting group from following them into the infirmary. All but Bea watched through an open window as Barger was taken into an operating room.

"This doesn't seem like things turned out the way he planned," said Patron.

Cole leaned against the door leading to the infirmary. "He was hit during our escape. Apparently Jared wasn't as clean breaking into the fleet registry as he thought he was. A security team met us in the bay with less than cordial intent. Wes convinced them otherwise."

"And you are?"

She held out a hand. "Flight Chief Loma Cole." Shadle shook her hand briefly. "Until I assisted Wes on his escape, I ran the engineering crew for Devil squadron's flight one. I've had the honor of knowing both Jared and Wes during their tenure with the squad."

"So then you must know Bea."

Cole squinted as she looked her over. "Not really. I know the name, but I believe she was assigned to the Nightwing."

"Patron," Bea interrupted. She handed him the data pad. "You should see this."

Patron took the pad and glanced over the information displayed. His skin paled at the schematics displayed. "Alert all commands. Review and briefing in thirty minutes." He handed the pad to Shadle as Bea ran off. He addressed her directly. "I want all fighters and transports ready for liftoff immediately and have all pilots on standby."

Shadle wanted to ask why. She looked over the information and with eyes wide her questions were answered.

Guile stepped from his room into the spacious officer's lounge. It was not really a lounge by any means, but it was in itself larger than the enlisted quarters. He would have to thank Stornoway the next time he met up with her for making him an officer. Surrounded by enemies and buried within a complicated mission, it was nice to sit back and enjoy the luxuries of officer life.

"Ironic, isn't it?" Stead asked from the long couch opposite him.

Guile sidestepped and eased himself into a chair. "More than I thought it would be. Had we stayed we might have ended up in one of these rooms."

The door to the outside corridor slid into the wall and the rest of the insurgence team walked in. The two pilots sat down next to Stead. They were still not completely comfortable with the smugglers and it showed. It did not matter to Guile either way. As long as they worked together in a fight they could distrust one another as much as they wished.

Aeon took the chair next to Guile, leaving Vipryn to stand. The way she slithered in her officers uniform displayed her displeasure in wearing the groomed clothing. She was more at home in rags and stood in protest.

"How do we look?" Stead asked.

Aeon folded his arms. "Well, we're firmly entrenched behind enemy lines and our friends in the body armor have no clue we're here. If we chose, we could stay on board for months without suspicion."

"We won't be here more than a few days. Long enough to map out key locations and escape routes."

"Why so soon?" Savash asked.

Stead spoke up before Guile could. "The attack on the destroyer convoy stirred up more of a hornets nest than we had originally anticipated."

Guile's eyes narrowed. Stead had blatantly lied to his men for no reason that he could fathom. Even so he would go along with the misinformation. "Security has been tightened all around the Empire. If we don't move quickly we could be trapped here."

"What's the plan?"

"Jared," Stead said.

Guile leaned towards the central table and flipped open the display screen of a large data pad. The screen flickered on and a deck-by-deck layout of the cruiser appeared. "Before we left Horde I obtained a tactical layout of the Vengeance. Originally the idea was to transmit the plans to the Alliance, but with our time frame cut short it may come of more use to us."

Moving small cross hairs across the screen with the use of a touch pad, Guile highlighted an area in the large, forward section of the ship. "This is the secondary computer core. It serves no function other than to support the primary computer core in the event that it fails. Because of this it is lightly guarded by a single team and is manned by three operators. As fortune would have it, only one of the operators is human. The rest are automated. This is where we will cause the most trouble."

"How so?" Aeon asked.

"Halash is the best computer programmer here," Stead answered. "He can rewrite the most complicated base program in about a half hour."

"And Alcon programs are not that complicated as long as you can access the system," Guile added.

"We'd have two to three minutes at best before someone realized the system had been accessed," Aeon warned. "They'd shut us off and pump gas in and we'd be dead before a single string could be re-written."

"Not if the ship's system analysts think we're busy tracking down problems in the mainframe. Problems that aren't security risks, but major inconveniences on the command officers."

"Such as?"

"Reprogramming the toilets to pump instead of flush. Shutting down laundry maintenance. Reducing panel illumination by fifty percent. Petty problems that can cause a serious uprising within the pampered power structure."

"How long?" Halash asked.

Guile rolled his eyes towards the ceiling. "Say twenty minutes to break the low level codes to the maintenance protocols. Another ten minutes to change the variables. I'd give the officers another four or five hours to discover that their problems are related, then five minutes to clear the system. If I start in an hour you'd have two hours to break into the control room and another three hours to make the appropriate changes before you'd be noticed."

Halash nodded. "No problem. All I'll need is a base par to translate."

"You'll have it."

"What about security?" Vipryn asked.

"That's where I come in," Stead said. "Security will be too busy chasing down a ghost intruder through the lower decks to notice that a few of their own are missing from their posts for a few minutes. The most I can give you is a little bit of time though, because they will send a unit. You two will have to switch uniforms with the guards and display your acting abilities when asked what happened."

"I'll do it, but I won't like it."

"You don't have to like it. You only have to enjoy the healthy fee you'll receive for the added task."

Aeon lightly elbowed Vipryn in the ribs. "Bonuses. I told you we'd like this contract."

"You're going to like it even better when we get back," Guile said. "I'm going to give you a weapons contract good for three million credits over the next eleven months."

Aeon almost fell to the floor. "You treat us too well, Jared."

"The Alliance rewards its providers well," Stead said. "Now if you don't mind, I believe the four of you have some prep work to do."

Guile stood long enough for the two smugglers and two pilots to shuffle out of the room before he sat back down.

"Everyone has a full assignment except for you," Stead commented. "What are you planning that you aren't telling me?"

"A diversion."

"What kind of diversion?"

"One that will keep everyone busy for some time."

Stead's eyes narrowed. "You're going after Galt, aren't you?" He leaned forward and rested his elbows on his legs. "You're planning on killing him."

Guile nodded. "But not before I draw security away from the rest of you. I'm going to give you long enough to get off the ship before I slit his throat."

"You can't do this, Jared."

"Why not!" He snapped back. "He had slit the throats of countless innocents with the full support of the Alcon and galactic government. What is wrong with a fair amount of justice in this backward galaxy?"

"It's because he has full support that you can't murder him. You have to let this little war take its course. He has to die attacking the Alliance or a defenseless world for it to mean something for us. If you kill him now you make him a martyr within the Empire. You give them a chance to place a sign over our heads proclaiming the resistance a band of murderers and thieves. Our supporters will have no choice but to pull our backing and leave us out to dry."

"It can't wait, Haggin. If we pass up this opportunity and let him live he will never leave me alone. He will hunt us down and when he finds us, our hides will be hanging from a rod on the back of his bridge."

"What did you say?"

"I said our hides..."

"No," Stead stopped him. "You said that he would never leave you alone."

"You know what I meant."

Chapter Twenty-Five

"I know exactly what you meant. You found out that he was the captain of the Blackhawk while we were stationed there and you find him responsible for your discharge."

"Discharge," Guile shuddered. "What are you talking about?"

"Don't deny it, Jared. We all read your file after you left. In your own words you stated that you couldn't take the pressure as a member of the Empire's front line squadron so you were discharged dishonorably."

Guile shook his head. "I never said that. In fact I never made a statement. I simply filled out my discharge papers with an explanation for my request. It never included pressure as a reason for leaving and I was never given a dishonorable discharge."

"And you never swore under oath that the loss of three pilots during your last raid was your fault."

"What?" Guile blurted out. "Never would I admit to such a thing. Those boys died because of the orders given them by command."

Stead leaned back. "I'm confused. Your file never said that orders were given during the raid. We were under the impression that you were in command."

"I was never even offered command. I was told that each unit was under direct orders and was to carry them out at my prompting. If I had been in command that day, Haggin, we never would have left the ship."

"What did happen, Jared?"

Guile sank into his seat. A stabbing pain pierced his heart as the memories washed over him in a flood. "The Blackhawk and Nightwing jumped into the system after a distress call was sent by a scout ship. When they arrived the scout ship had already been destroyed and its attackers were fleeing back to the planet. Our arrival must have surprised them into panic and they altered course and made a run for a nav probe on the far side of the system. The alert squad was launched but they never caught up to them."

"In retribution, the Blackhawk went into orbit and bombarded the capital city and leveled it, but apparently it was not enough for the captain. He pulled records from the rubble and tracked down who the pilots were of the fighters that destroyed his scout ship. He identified their families and their villages and marked them as targets. That's when we came into play."

"Each of us received a strike package with marked armed targets and we were sent in to take them out. What we were not made aware of was that the three target villages were completely occupied by women and children who were defenseless and had no idea we were coming or why. We butchered them in their sleep, burning down their homes from a safe distance. Then, with the pre-notion that the women were the pilots we shot down the survivors in cold blood in revenge for our fallen comrades."

"I felt something was wrong from the beginning and against orders I stayed when the rest of you left. I searched the burned out huts and found blackened mothers holding their charred children. Unfortunately I stayed too long and fell under flash fire from a sweep team." Guile rubbed his damaged skin under his thin wrap. "That's when this happened."

"What about the pilots who died? They came under fire from the rebels."

Guile shook his head. "I did some digging after they patched me up. They found out during their raid on another village what was happening. When they tried to save a family they were caught in crossfire and killed by our own men. I thought you knew all of this."

"No," Stead said. He was pale from horror. "None of this came out in the official report or in your private logs. We had been told from the beginning that you were in charge of the mission and that you sent those pilots into a situation that you knew they'd get killed in."

"Never. From the start of the mission something did not feel right. My Companion detected no fighter emissions leading to the planet, indicating that the group that attacked the scout ship never returned to the surface. A power signature scan of the village also came up negative so I knew there were no weapons present. Even a hand blaster on standby would give off something. Instead these people were without any form of technology. At this point I didn't even believe that the pilots had come from the village. A latter report from the sweep team stating that they had detained a group of men coming into the area confirmed my feelings."

"I made several official inquiries, a few unofficial, and my only answer was to follow orders and leave the clean up work alone. At that point I had had enough and resigned my commission. I guess repercussions for the attack required a scapegoat and a resigned officer was the obvious target."

"You made a hell of a scapegoat," Stead said. "They had all of us believing that you had planned the attack. They also did a good job of covering up the slaughter. Until now I believed we had downed armed aggressors."

"Believe me, Haggin. You weren't the only one to fall for Imperial propaganda. For years I had believed that all the worlds the Empire attacked were hiding traitors and heavily armed rebels. It wasn't until that last raid that my eyes opened."

"So you think that because of this you have to kill Galt? He's no different than any of the other commanders."

"He's smart. Smarter than any other Alcon officer I have encountered and he has more ambition than the Regent herself. This makes him our most dangerous adversary and a threat to the resistance. If we let him continue than we risk losing it all."

"We?" Stead asked. "Since when has the resistance's cause become your cause?"

"Since I realized that I have friends out there in the cold of space. I never knew how much I missed the comfort of a group. The feeling that I belonged somewhere. That was my whole reason for joining the academy. I had no family to call my own. I didn't even have a race that the academy medical examiner could identify. I may have been raised on Telestia with Telestian parents, but I learned long ago that I had been taken in by them."

"I've often heard others speak of how your past dictates your future. They've wondered how an orphan, who no one knows where he came from would grow up.

Chapter Twenty-Five

It's always been a question that has affected me more than any other. My foster parents knew of my turmoil. They encouraged my enrollment into the academy in hopes that some of my problems would go away."

He looked away. "And they did until the day I learned the Empire was a lie. Then all my questions and anguish crashed back down upon me." Guile reached across, gripping Stead's knee. "My questions about how I would grow up were answered the day I completed my first contract. You can imagine my reaction when I placed the barrel of my blaster on the forehead of my first victim and pulled the trigger without hesitation."

Guile pulled his hand back and grinned. "If only my parents could have lived long enough to see what I've become. Maybe the shame would have placed enough guilt on their hearts so that they wished they would have looked harder into my true past."

"What would that have helped? If anyone should research your origins it should be you. Who else would have the resources and connections to find your birth parents and home world?"

"I've asked that of myself on many a lonely night."

"What answer did you give?"

"Only one. That either I remain alone and prosper in the hell that is my life or I give into what I truly want. The family that I had before Galt uncovered my eyes to the Imperial lie."

"You realize that by taking it upon yourself to remove Admiral Fallon from the equation that you risk losing everything. Even more so, you risk hurting your friends who are expecting you to return to them."

"That's a risk we all take."

"No it's not. When we risk it all it's as a unit where we can watch out for each other. What you're doing is removing the rest of us from the balance. I can't allow that for the others nor for myself."

"I hardly think you'd worry about me," Guile said. "If anything you should be glad to see me go."

"Quite the contrary. Although I feel a deep sense of competition when I'm around you I find you to be a valuable ally to the Alliance. I would hate to see you go. Besides," he grinned. "Who would I argue with if I didn't have you?"

"Trust me, Haggin. With your personality I can't imagine it would be hard for you to find someone to disagree with."

Stead stood, allowing Guile's attempt at humor to reach a part of him he normally kept closed. "I won't disagree with you on that point. Now I will leave you to think about what you want to do while I get ready. Knowing you, it will not take long to make up your mind." His voice trailed off as he left the room. "Keep in mind who your decisions affect."

Guile squeezed his eyes shut and gritted his teeth. The questions and the headache had returned. Though they helped him to choose his path, it tended to cloud his focus. The last thing he wanted to think about before a battle was the people he could hurt both by living and by dying. The outcome of his hostility was something he neither wanted to address nor face.

"Focus," he whispered to himself.

As his vision narrowed to the task at hand, a soft smile and a pair of crystal eyes crept in from the side he shook his head. Long ago, before his heart died, she had been with him in spirit before every fight. She was as much a part of Guile's focus as a pair of cross hairs and a trigger. That had all disappeared behind a blood red shower of hatred.

Now her soft voice and features returned. They seemed out of place now. He wanted them there more than anything else, but she did not fit into his plan. Her image had reminded him that he had someone to return to. Someone to live for. But his mind was set on not coming back this time. What he had planned, there was no escape.

"Please leave. Please let me protect you."

His pleas were answered with a whisper of love on a breeze of warmth. It may have come from the ventilation system; save it was as much a last act of desperation from what he knew of Bea. After it was done and he continued to wish her away, she waved. Bea may have been light years away and not the person he once knew, but she had to understand.

"Thank you." Guile chocked a tear back up inside of him before it could escape the corner of his sealed eye. "I have to do this."

The fleeting image of the woman he cared for more than any other blew him one last kiss before disappearing behind the bright red haze of his undying rage.

Chapter Twenty-Six

Pilots, support crews, transport crews, and command officers slowly crammed themselves into the small briefing room. The officers, mainly Imperial defectors and ex-planetary militia, showed their experience with passive expressions and hard strides. The youth and the majority of the pilots on the other hand radiated their anxiety with brisk paces and narrow eyes. They searched the three tactical screens for signs that the mission ahead would be a smooth one.

To wide-eyed surprise, their mission objective was less than satisfactory. Right there on the center screen in bold letters. A death mark for the small band of warriors. One that few would return from and had little chance of success. Their final objective was clear. The destruction of a battle cruiser.

The pilots sat in the first six rows with Ghost assuming the last two. Unlike standard mission briefings Ghost's commanding officers were not present. Instead the Patron himself stood behind the podium with his laser guild in hand. This was unusual and a bit intimidating. It displayed the importance of the mission to have him directly briefing the group. Hardly a morale booster by any means.

"Please be seated."

The group took their seats, though uneasily.

"By the request of the Sovereign our target has been selected. We are to attack and destroy the Devastator class star cruiser the Nullify."

"Devastator class?" An officer from the back asked.

"This is a secret, though not new, class star cruiser with enough fire power to permanently remove all life on a planet. She was commissioned some time ago and in that time she has successfully fired her main weapon on three separate occasions. One of her targets was the planet Sutherlin." Harsh murmurs erupted around the room, mostly from the surviving Sutherlin that were present. He continued before the mumbling had a chance to die down. "Her next target is here. Tracking places the Nullify within primary firing range, but the base will not be in direct line for another hour and a half. Many of you have noticed that we began evacuation proceedings a day ago. As you all are well aware of though, this leaves us no time to complete the task."

Dead silence replaced the anger and confusion, allowing his words to echo. "If not for an insurgence team that is currently operating on a star cruiser we would not have known it was heading towards us. Without this team and for the bravery of one man, we would also have no clue as to how to stop this ship."

Patron stepped away from the podium. The lights dimmed and the center screen faded out. It was shortly replaced with a port side elevation view of the Nullify. Animation showed the ship as its two halves spread apart. At their maximum separation, the charge of energy began to build between the two halves and the primary weapon fired. The view quickly shifted to the first test firing images and the destruction of the surface of a planet.

The nest image to appear on the screen was a wire frame diagram of the cruiser with Barger as narrator. "Good afternoon. As you have just seen this cruiser is the most powerful weapon the Empire has unleashed on the galaxy, and as luck would have it is headed your way. With all its power though, it does have flaws."

The view zoomed into the nose of the cruiser and two openings. "These two ports are the particle intact tubes for the main power core. They lead directly to the reactor and the power regulators. If two of the four regulators were disabled the reactor would overload and the cruiser would destroy itself. Unfortunately the intake track is coated in argon and will not allow any weapons to lock on."

The cruiser rotated to the left so that the pilots could view straight down the tubes. "Each intake opening is roughly three times the size of your fighters." The animated camera followed along the port side tube as he spoke. "This will allow a single fighter to enter a tube and follow the course straight back to the regulators." The animation stopped at a mildly open area with a single sphere with large conduits leading to its four conduits. The view zoomed into one of the conduits and onto a round port, which was highlighted. "Once there you will have to fire a pair of fusion missiles and hit a three meter coolant port without the benefit of a weapons lock. After you've knocked out the regulators, turn around and get outta there."

Patron returned to his place behind the podium. "The Nullify has no fighter protection and limited defensive capabilities, which is where I add another level of difficulty to the task at hand." The image of the cruiser faded and was replaced by that of the Vengeance and a pair of destroyers. "This is what stands between you and your mission goal. The pride of the Alcon fleet with its own fighter squadrons, seventy weapon batteries, and Devil squadron in support."

"Three squadrons against a full battle group?" A pilot interrupted.

"We will fire two shots from each proton cannon to weaken the Vengeance's shields before you get close enough to engage. Your principle concern will be the fighters. It is imperative that you give Ghost the time it needs to destroy the Nullify."

"I don't mean to sound withdrawn from the idea, sir, but even with weakened shields she can still pack a serious wallop. And how are we to take on Devil?"

Chapter Twenty-Six

"I understand your concerns. That is why a plan has already been put into effect to inflict additional damage to the Vengeance once she's been hit initially."

"Per design and program specifications given to me by Mister Barger before he returned, all of your Companions have been upgraded to handle additional tasks. It is both our hopes that with added intelligence handling problems you will be free to take on your opposition. With that, I will bid you good luck, success and a safe return."

"Attention!" An officer close by ordered of the room.

Officers and pilots stood to attention and saluted. Patron returned to salute with a loose wrist before solemnly walking from the room. Once gone the room burst into the expected concerned conversations. One of which revolved entirely around Ghost. Do to the lack of time though, each smaller group filed out of the three doors and continued their worried mumbling outside of the building.

The pilots of Ghost were on their way to the flight deck in three separate lifts. The drivers wasted no time getting their important passengers to their fighters. The less experienced pilots of Blue and Grey squadrons were shuttled to the far end of the spread out landing area to the newer Novas. The veterans of countless battles were given to the older Novas. As was said on many occasions though, it wasn't the hardware so much as it was the pilot behind the hardware.

Shadle and Bea hopped from the hovering lift in front of their novas. Ground crews were climbing over the fighters in a frantic rush to prep them for battle. The missile pods were in the process of being loaded with the ever-deadly fusion missiles. They blended against the body and were nearly impossible to notice beyond the launch opening in the front. The sight of the ground crews, verifying the stability of each missile before loading, brought slight relief to the two pilots.

Bea turned towards the extended ladder of her Nova only to have a gloved hand grab her shoulder. She turned towards Shadle. "Not now."

"I have to or I'll regret it."

She shook off his hand. "This won't be the last time we're going up."

"You're all fired up, ma'am!" The ground crew chief shouted from Shadle's cockpit.

"Just a minute!" She shouted back. Shadle lowered her eyes, not able to look her in the eyes. "With Jared and Haggin gone and Wes in the infirmary this is going to be tough."

"They have their problems, but they're exactly where they need to be. The fact that they are on the Vengeance gives me all the confidence in the galaxy that everything will turn out. We will succeed. Now get up there and let's kick some Alcon ass. We have some kill records to beat today."

Shadle grinned. "Are we placing bets?"

"Only if you want to. I have to remind you that I have the advantage of several years. Maybe I should give you a handicap."

"You do and you'll have one for real. Just stay outta my way."

Bea slapped her on the back and waited as she turned and climbed the ladder to her fighter. As she watched her, satisfied that she had renewed what little faith Shadle had, she wondered if she could convince herself of the same. Everyone in the squadron felt the same as she did about not having Stead in the lead. And the fact that Guile or Barger could have been with the squadron as well did not sit well with her.

Bea hopped up onto the third rung of the ladder and bounced the rest of the way up. At the top she was greeted by the crew chief. He held her helmet with care and displayed a smile across his face. He had been her crew chief for two years and took pride in taking good care of her and her fighters. Today would be no exception.

"How are we looking today chief?" Bea asked as she sank into her seat.

"We've locked down the problem you had during your last mission. Actually your new companion found the problem and fixed everything itself."

Bea looked over the effected status lights. Each displayed green as did their backup lights. Satisfied, she poked the crew chief in the side. "You sound disappointed."

The crew chief assisted her as she strapped herself in. "These new companions are cutting edge. I just don't want to lose my job."

"Don't worry, chief. As long as I keep jumping into combat I'll always need a good pair of hands to bandage my wounds. A little box can't do everything."

"Don't try telling them that." The chief snapped the data and air lines to her helmet and slipped it over her head. Carefully he snapped it to her flight suit and closed the air seal. "Good luck, Commander."

Commander had a good ring to it. She knew the promotion was only honorary until Stead returned. Bea planned on making the command last as long as she could though. In her heart Ghost should have been hers.

"Do me a favor, chief. Pack your gear and keep your crew on standby in case this isn't successful."

"As ordered, Commander, but it won't be necessary. With you in the lead I expect to live a long time."

"I appreciate the compliment, chief. I hope you're right."

The crew chief flipped her a short salute before sliding down to the deck.

Bea slipped down the clear face shield of her helmet and blew into the boom microphone. The speakers in the helmet cracked to life. "Online," she said.

Her new Companion responded positive with a chirp.

Bea tilted her head. That's new, she thought to herself. "Give me green across the board then release gravity locks."

The Nova revved up above the whine of engine standby. Every indicator, save weapons status, turned green. Three thumps from the three landing struts rumbled through the cockpit followed by a slight jump a half a meter off the deck.

"Line open to the tower." The nova's communications lit up as the canopy slid shut. "Tower, this is Ghost lead."

Chapter Twenty-Six

"Lead, this is tower. You are cleared for lift off. Imperial task force one thirty to firing range."

"Copy that, tower."

The flight deck filled with the high whine of thirty screaming fighters. The nova's canopy slowly sealed, closing out the ear-piercing sound and locking her into the mission. At this point there was no turning back. She had an hour and thirty minutes to intercept the Alcon task force to prevent it from destroying the heart of the Alliance. If she thought any harder on the subject she might drive herself insane.

The last of Admiral Fallon's battle group appeared in the system, drawing a sigh of relief from S'Lendo. A last minute message from the Blackhawk had warned of additional damage caused by the hauler explosion. There had been worry that this would have impeded the ship's ability to join the group. All those thoughts were put to rest when two blips appeared on screen and not just one.

"All ships accounted for," S'Lendo proudly said.

Fallon rotated his chair to face forward. "Bring weapons and shields to standby and prepare for counterattack. Pull the Violator close enough to mask her from long range scans. I want her squadrons to be a surprise."

"Can I ask you a personal question, sir?" S'Lendo asked.

Fallon chose not to turn when addressing him. "If you wish."

"Should we not deploy our advance screen and lock down the ship?"

"I do not see the need, Captain. Our guest has assured me that this particular resistance cell does not have the capabilities to dispatch a boarding party. If I am not mistaken, her report also states that the majority of their pilots have neither the experience nor the will to openly assault the group. Should they find the will, our alert fighters will provide more than enough cover."

"I understand that, sir. My worry lays more in our slow approach. We have no idea what long-range defenses the Alliance may have procured in the time since they hired Mister Guile. Should they inflict damage at this distance, even the most inexperienced boarding party and fighter squadron can pose a serious threat."

The folds on the back of Fallon's head ruffled momentarily. "I have considered all options, Captain, but if it will put your mind at ease you may seal the inner bulkheads and release the alert fighters."

Colonel Wells stepped onto the bridge behind a pair of parting doors. His presence was announced with a puzzled look on S'Lendo's face. Fallon noted the look he had not seen before and turned to investigate. He too found cause for concern upon seeing the respected officer with wet pant legs.

Fallon folded his hands in his laps. "Might I ask why you step onto my bridge in such a condition, Colonel?"

"My apologies, Admiral. It could not be helped. For an unexplained reason the environmental controls in my quarters are not functioning correctly. This unfortunately is the least offensive of my uniforms."

"I will have to back the Colonel, sir." S'Lendo admitted. "I awoke this morning to a mild flood."

Fallon closed his eyes. He sat on the bridge of the most powerful cruiser in the fleet and he was confronted with uncontrollable maintenance problems. "Shut down waste and water lines to the senior officers' quarters and conduct a diagnostics of the basic maintenance protocols. I refuse to face such difficulties on a day of triumph."

"Trajectory plotted," helm announced.

Fallon turned back around and looked over the tactical display. "Time to firing."

"Adjusting, sir. We projected the coordinates of the resistance base and have plotted it on the far side of the target planet. The Nullify will need to be in direct line of the base for the attack to succeed."

"Very well. Estimate time to fire then relay tactical data to my station."

The time had come. The Regent had predicted it, as had Admiral Ishat. The fate of the Sutherlin Alliance lay in front of him on a dead world. It was a pity that the full force of the Nullify could not be used to lay waste to a lush world. Instead his vengeance against the resistance would be directed to the base itself and he would have what he so long desired.

For another Alcon officer the situation provoked an entirely different emotional response. For a brief moment as the Blackhawk's alarms sounded, Kirkland thought that he would be excluded from the coming battle. The destroyer lurching into hyperspace minutes later shattered that hope in a crash of spinning starlight.

He walked slowly from the pilot barracks and into the long fighter supply bay. Ahead of him stood Vallejo and the other four pilots of one flight. For them the feeling was of anticipation and hope. They knew that a harsh fight was coming and it could only mean glory for them. Reports that the Alliance consisted of academy washouts and young, inexperienced pilots gave them a confidence they had not displayed before. It was if they knew they were flying into a shooting gallery.

"I'm pleased you could join us," Vallejo said smugly.

Kirkland stopped in front of him. "You seem happy. I thought killing your fellow Sutherlin would turn your stomach."

"Quite the contrary," he leered. "This is my chance to repay them for their treachery. What better way to honor my species than to avenge the innocent and punish the guilty?"

"Funny you should put it that way."

There was something in the way the Captain spoke that raised suspicion in his heart. Vallejo was hiding something. He knew more than he led on and it had to have something to do with Barger's visit.

"Have no worry about the Alliance, Alder. They will soon be erased as a threat."

"I'm not worried about our success, Captain." Kirkland looked around the bay. He saw the ghosts of the dead and the missing walking amongst the current crew and

Chapter Twenty-Six

pilots. He saw Barger and Cole chatting as they once had. Behind them he saw Guile preparing himself for his last flight in a Devil uniform.

Vallejo had turned and walked away when he finished. "It's theirs."

Chapter Twenty-Seven

Guile looked to his timer for what must have been the tenth time in the last five minutes. The crucial team had exactly three minutes to complete their task before Alcon security would discover the lack of a trained response. So far, Stead's tinkering had distracted normal security sweeps, but it would not last. Unless they finished soon, he would have to take matters into his own hands and that usually meant someone would die.

As if timing was against him, the ship's normal corridor lights dimmed and red tracer lights flooded his sight with flashing amber. Ships' horns sounded with three short bursts shortly followed by a brief whistle from the intercom.

"All hands red alert. Enemy task force in sight. Battle stations."

Guile glanced back to his timer. They were early, which meant Fallon had stepped up the timetable. He was out of time and down on luck. His only other option was suicide, but he had little choice at this point. For the assault to succeed he had to accomplish his objective. The Vengeance must be disabled.

Officers and crew alike began to run down the corridors in varied directions. Not caring to be choosy, he pulled his side arm from its holster and picked out a random officer. In his clearest voice he shouted, "Up with the resistance," and he fired twice into the officer's back. The current situation outside being what it was, the outcome could have been predicted. All armed personnel drew weapons and ran after him.

A stray blast caught his blaster pistol and stripped it from his hand. Guile turned away from his attackers and sprinted for an adjoining corridor. The heavy body armor he had under the officers uniform he wore kept him from the speed he knew he had. The blaster rifle under his coat did not help much either. The combined impedance made him an easy target. He may as well have just painted a bull's-eye on his back.

Three shots from three different weapons converged on the small of his back and sent him flying. He slammed into the corridor wall and rolled to the deck. In the same instant he unlatched the rifle from his coat and threw himself into a tight tuck and roll. The bounce off the wall brought him up against the facing wall and at a slight angle to the three gunmen. He released four short bursts and the crewmen were engulfed in blue pulses of energy. All were forced back and onto the deck. They would not get up again.

"Intruder, section eighteen," the overhead speaker spouted out.

Lifts to the command deck would be secured. The only other way up was through the access tunnels. Guile turned away from the pervious action and squinted down the corridor. If memory served him correctly, there were ladder tunnels two sections aft. It might as well have been a week's journey in his armor. Despite the obvious problems his armor made though, he could not ignore the sorry state his body would have been in right now without it.

While running he activated a scrambled squad channel. "Give me an update, guys. I'm running into trouble here."

"Security is tight in here," Halash responded. "I don't know if this is going to work."

"Keep trying," Stead shot back. "I don't plan on risking my butt for a failed plan."

"Where are you now?" Guile asked.

"You know better than that, Jared. I won't say if you won't."

He must have been close to one of the several security armories located around the ship. "Understood, Haggin. Hang in there."

"You too."

Guile made the sectional trek aft in less than five minutes, pausing momentarily at cross-corridors. He was not about to be taken by surprise from behind. Funny how all the precaution in the world can do you no good in a strange environment. A body length from a hatch in the corridor wall, a strong pulse slammed into his body armor, burning away his coat and lifting him off the deck.

A collision was coming and it would not be a pretty one. Guile ducked his head and placed the rifle out ahead of him. The rifle, his arms, then the rest of his body slammed into the access hatch with the force of a vehicle slamming into a solid wall. The hatch locks gave way and exploded into the tunnel. Both the hatch panel and Guile slammed against the opposite side of the vertical tunnel and dropped straight down. Much as he would have liked to see where he was going Guile blacked out from the collision.

Three flights of fighters led by one scrap and two new novas quickly left the planet far behind, leaving a distant dull reflection. Too far for conventional weapons, but close enough to fall under the firing arc of the Nullify. The Alcon battle group was at the edge of the system. Long-range probes displayed one mass approaching at a higher rate than any normal craft on entry. Bea knew far too well that the single mass was really two cruisers with total destruction their intent.

The group of thirty fighters spread out in a broken formation to give off the appearance of many more targets. The tactic was sound, as it would force an exaggerated response and a lack of positive missile locks. It not only aided the chance for near misses, but it added hope that the flights would close the gap to the cruisers before their missile launch tubes could reload.

"All flights check in," Bea requested.

"Green squadron standing by."

"Blue squadron standing by."

"Release safeties and arm all weapons," she ordered.

The last planet in the system came up quickly. Its blue haze of clouds glowed from the light of the distant star system.

"Escort flight to assault group."

Bea checked her tactical screen. She picked up the small group of transports forming up around the moon of the planet. "Assault group, copy."

"We're standing by for our run."

"Roger that, escort. Hold back until positive targets are acquired."

"Coming up," Shadle said.

The three squadrons rounded the southern equator of the planet and emerged into open space. Spearing the darkness directly ahead of them arose four cruisers of differing design and two destroyers. The Vengeance obscured the view with its overwhelming size, but the sleek Valiant and the flat edged fighter carrier were clearly visible.

Bea jerked the fighter momentarily to the right from surprise. She regained control. "Control this is Ghost lead. We have visual sighting of the Imperial battle group. I can identify three star cruisers. Repeat, I have a visual identification of three star cruisers."

Patron stepped back from the tactical board.

"I concur, sir," a controller said from behind Patron. "Long range probes now read three star cruisers, two destroyers, and the Nullify on approach."

"Can you get a tag on the third cruiser?" Patron asked calmly.

"It's a carrier," Shadle said from the overhead speaker.

"That means there are at least thirty bi-wing squadrons awaiting them," an officer in the back of the small control room said.

"What do we do now?" The controller asked.

"We're committed, sir," Bea said. "I could break off the assault and make a run for it, but that won't do you any good. We have to see this through."

"Fighters!" A frantic pilot shouted.

Fallon folded his hands in his lap. The battle he had been anticipating for months was at hand and he had more than enough firepower to see it all end here. He had the galaxy's most powerful weapon to port, Captain Merrill's cruiser to starboard, a fighter carrier in the lead, and Devil squadron as support. What more could he need to end the Alliance once and for all? He needed only to wait for inevitable victory.

"Squadrons one through eight have launched. Resistance fighters will be in range in two minutes."

Sutherlin Alliance

"Very well," Fallon answered. "Send the Violator to point to draw off the initial attack then move the Nullify between us until it is within firing range of the planet."

The chief security officer approached the captain and stood at attention at his side. "Internal report, sir."

Fallon's eyes narrowed as he turned towards the officer. "Internal report?"

"Yes, sir. I have received two separate security breach reports. One from the officer's quarters and one from system section eight."

"And?"

"I can report that both breaches have been secured and we have at least four intruders apprehended from one of the scenes. It appears as though they were trying to sabotage the reserve computer core, but were unsuccessful."

"One of the scenes?" Fallon asked. "What of the other intruder?"

"No definite report as of yet, sir, but one of my guards hit him with a pulse rifle and he dropped through an access shaft. He is believed to be dead."

Jared, Fallon thought to himself. "I want visual confirmation before you make that assumption and I want you to personally conduct the search."

"Shall I double your security, sir?"

"No need." He swiveled forward. "This intruder will never make it up this far. Triple protection along all access lifts and tubes to the command deck."

"Sir." The officer turned on one heel and proceeded aft.

Fallon looked to the tactical screens, but stared beyond them. So, Mister Guile. You grace me with your presence. In a flush of surprise he thought him to be foolish. Why would a man of his reputation dare board a star cruiser and attempt to sabotage it? Then he fell into the realization that Guile was more to the Alliance than a simple supplier.

"You'll regret becoming part of them, Jared."

"Sir?" S'Lendo asked.

"Reset internal sensors to the Telestian anatomy."

"Incoming!" the chief weapons officer declared. "I'm reading four...no six long range photon tracks from the target planet."

S'Lendo looked to Fallon, who did not acknowledge his Captain's foresight. "Increase forward shields two hundred percent. Drop aft shields to compensate."

Fallon closed his eyes. S'Lendo's effort was sound but futile. He could only wait to see how much damage the attack would inflict.

"Contact!" Bea shouted as she released the first on what would be many flashes of fire.

The lead bi-wing was split by her quad burst, crushing the command pod and leaving the wings spinning away. The lead fighter's trailing wingmen broke off away from the debris, giving her no clear shot. She picked up speed a notch and blasted through the fire flash and spit out another quad burst. Two streaks blew harmlessly beyond another trio of fighters. The right two clipped a second bi-wing

Chapter Twenty-Seven

between its starboard wing and engine. Both the wing and command pod spun into each other and exploded.

"Ghost group break up and engage the first wave."

"Here they come," Shadle mumbled from behind.

Six brilliant orange blasts of energy, each larger in diameter than the fighters, lit up the darkened attacked craft as they passed. A single bi-wing was unable to break its course and was devoured by the first proton blast. Unlike with aggressive particle weapons, the fighter remained intact. As in passing through an ion storm though, every system aboard the fighter fused together and burned out. The pilot was still alive after the attack, but would not be for long if not recovered before the air recycling system failed as well.

The six streaks of electrical nightmare continued on, passing along the port side of the carrier Violator. Each struck the Vengeance's shields above a bald spot in the bow of the ship. The combined force of the proton energy attack had created its own ion storm under the shields. Blue fire danced down from the shields, raining across the hull. The electrical lighting burned into the armor, leaving behind harsh, black scars.

The primary computer core had been the target and the accuracy and intension bared fruit. Lights dimmed around the impact points followed by a wave of blinking portholes slowly flowing aft. The failure of system after system had reached almost to the engines and bridge when the secondary computer core came on line and took up the duties of it's fallen predecessor. Lights flashed back on as quickly as they had failed.

From a distance the failed, then recovered lights were clearly visible. Bea had tensed her grip, hoping that they had been successful. With the quick recovery it was evident that Guile's team had failed. The Vengeance was still a threat.

"Ghost lead to base."

"We see it lead," the Luikart base controller responded.

"It appears we have a more serious problem," interrupted Patron. "I suggest you jump out as soon as possible."

The temporary loss of communication with the flagship and subsequent disorder among the bi-wings ended, dragging Bea back into the battle. "I can't do that, sir. If we leave you now we'll lose everything. We're in this fight till the end."

"Understood, lead. Good luck. And thank you."

"Don't thank me yet, Patron. We have a long way to go."

"Ghost group, pour it on!" Shadle cried out.

Bea followed with short orders. "Blue and Grey pull up and out and engage the next wave of fighters. Assault team, hold back and wait for an opening. This might take awhile." Come on, Jared. Help me out here.

Chapter Twenty-Eight

Guile found himself on a catwalk overlooking a large bay. An intense pain throbbed in his side where he had landed on his rifle. Not even the flexible armor could have cushioned the blow. He judged the drop to have been about fifteen meters. The large, body-shaped dent in the deck next to him alluded to a possible bounce when he hit. The growing pressure in his ribs seemed to agree.

He eased himself towards the railing and looked over. Two deck levels below crews worked busily around row after row of cargo, moving containers into open spaces. This was not in any way a military bay, but rather the storage area for ship supplies. If he had to land somewhere, this was as good a place as any. He was less likely to run into heavy security here.

Nevertheless, he had to press forward. Swiftly, he ran across the catwalk and turned into a corridor. It was dark, but short, angling slightly to the left. It appeared to open to a larger room. He gripped a heavy rifle firmly at his side he jogged down the corridor and stopped at the end.

A brighter light filtered in from the adjoining room. Guile peeked around the corner. The room dropped down two meters from the corridor. Across the room, beyond two columns that ran to the ceiling, was a longer corridor. Standing in his way though were a pair of guards facing away from him. The corridor that they faced was a good ten meters long and there were undoubtedly more guards around the corner.

Quietly, Guile lowered himself to the room floor and crept behind one of the columns. He knew there was no way to take both guards down with his knife without either of them sounding the alarm. He would have to take both of them out cleanly and recover in time to catch any reinforcements that may round the corner. It was chancy, but what other choice did he have? The only other way out was back the way he came, which meant a fifteen-meter climb up a slick shaft.

Rifle in the lead, he stepped from behind the column and fired once into the nearest guard. The blue pulse of energy ripped from the barrel and engulfed the guard's upper body. Though only a mere fraction of the exaggerated blast had any effect, it was enough to penetrate his armor and take him down. If the circumstances for firing the weapon for the first time were any better, he might have enjoyed the light show.

Guile fired again as the second guard turned in surprise. The force of the energy blast threw him from his feet and slammed him against the wall. The impact might have been painful if he had lived long enough to feel it. Both his armor and chest were burned away an instant before he hit. A light gray residue covered them both.

The sound of the heavy weapon was more than enough to fill the corridor with loud cracks. From around the corner, three guards sprinted. They were shaken to see two of their comrades down, giving Guile all the advantage he needed. He switched his weapon to rapid fire with the flick of his thumb, and he unleashed a barrage of blue pulses after them. All three were burned down in the blink of an eye.

Guile was poised for another attack. Neither to his surprise nor joy did more guards round the corner. Instead, he relaxed his grip on his rifle and jogged to the turn. He had no idea what to expect when he rounded the corner. The coast could be clear or there could be an entire unit aimed and ready to burn him down. He simply had to trust his luck and jump into the thick of it. His options were limited.

With guns flaring he jumped into the opening. A single, heavily armored guard stood six meters from him with his hand blaster pulled from it's holster. Guile wasted no time firing several pulses down the corridor and into his chest. With some resistance he dropped to the deck. A second guard with standard armor appeared from an adjoining corridor and fired blindly past him. He fell sharply from his rushed mistake.

This too was a short corridor, which ended in a docking port waiting room. Half the distance to the left was a two-meter indentation that marked a blast door and possibly a secure room. The corridor the second guard had sprung from was close to the waiting room and very inviting. After he cleared the room, he would have to take that path.

So that his back was covered, he stepped into the opening of the adjoining corridor. At the far end he found another heavy guard approaching him. The guard disappeared behind a pounding of blaster fire and fell into the large room he had come from. Satisfied with the kill, he backtracked to the blast door and readied himself for an impending onslaught of resistance.

Guile released the lock to the doors and stepped back. The heavy doors parted, revealing three heavy guards and four regulars. A firefight broke out immediately with the heaviest of blasts coming from Guile. It was an impressive light show by any standards and a loud one.

Guile dropped the three heavy guards first with two near misses as their only answer. One of the regulars managed to clip his shoulder armor as he and the other three dove for cover. He no longer had clear shots at any of them and with no cover of his own, it wouldn't take them long to recover and pick him off.

His answer was simple enough. He dropped his rifle to the deck and reached for the weapon at his side. It was small and resembled a hand blaster. Appearances can

Chapter Twenty-Eight

be deceiving though and Guile proved it. With one squeeze of the trigger, he fired a single projectile behind the columns the guards were using for cover. A ball of fire erupted from the point of impact, devouring all four of them in a cloud or burning red.

Guile slipped a new round into the handheld launcher and slipped it back into its holster. He picked his rifle back up, turned, and ran back out of the room. He left the blast doors to shut behind him and he worked his way towards the as yet untouched room. Once there he found more trouble and few places of cover.

The room was large and had a guard tower up to his right. Guile dropped to one knee, dodging aimed fire from the heavy guard positioned there. Still on the one knee, he unleashed a series of pulses into the position, tearing apart the deck, walls, and guard. A good portion of the supporting structure collapsed from lack of substance and entire tower fell to the floor.

A thin blaster pulse clipped Guile's left thigh, spinning him around. Two more heavy guards had emerged from behind a guard post with yet a third staying behind to defend his position. Guile dove back into the corridor and pressed his back against the wall. Periodically, he stuck his body around the corner to take pot shots at the two guards who were working their way towards him. He gained the advantage as both popped up from the last bit of cover that lay the distance. He spotted this and rolled from his protection. He fired heavily at both and dropped them from the action.

The last guard would have been a problem if Guile had not had a large number of projectiles with him. He set his rifle onto the deck and removed the rocket pistol. He kept low to the ground, just under the guard's line of fire and timed his shots. When he was confident that he could pop up and fire, he did so and a thin streak of smoke rocketed across the room. In the blink of the eye the guard post exploded and was reduced to burning pieces of metal.

As he walked across the room, Guile heard heavy footsteps from the far side of the room. Curious and eager not to be taken by surprise, he raised his rifle and ran to the far end of the room. Sure enough, there was an open door behind the guard post. With a grin on his face he stepped threw the doorway, turned, and caught six heavy guards by surprise. They didn't stand a chance. The hard pounding from the blue energy charges dropped all six.

Guile walked back into the room and turned towards a blast door that looked promising. He stepped towards it and stopped. Standard naval procedure when a ship was boarded was to have a heavy guard stationed behind all blast doors of secured access. Again he had the advantage as he opened the door firing. The guard had no time to assess the situation and fell dead to the deck.

The blast doors hid an access lift to the upper decks. Using an access card from one of the guards Guile entered the lift and rode it up as far as it would go. In a stroke of luck the maintenance bay was dedicated to waste management, which was where the lift led. Far above the dedicated lift were the control center and the waste redirection hold for the command decks.

By the time he reached its highest level, the secured alarm sounded on the deceased guard's belt. The alarm was designed to alert the cruiser's security force to an intruder without alarming all aboard. From appearances Guile could not tell whether the alarm would give his current position or the location he had just been. Either way he had far too little time to remain idle.

Guile stepped from the lift into the refuse control room. Across the room from him were six waste management men and three guards. Though only the guards were armed any of them could sound the alarm, and an alert only twelve decks below the command levels was an all-ship alert. That meant a quick end to the raid and his bid to end Fallon's life.

Salvation came in the form of a pressure release line and valve close to the waste team. He took aim and pumped two shots into the valve. The valve exploded and took all nine men with it under a strong stream of fresh water. A flood control channel in the center of the room immediately opened to keep the room from flooding and the water began to flow beyond a pressure door.

A status board close to where the management team had displayed an escape path for the water. It ran down a corridor towards the garbage and waste disposal bay, past a waste tube that came directly down from the command levels, which was located next to a guard post. He needed to get past the post and climb up the tube to avoid any serious resistance.

Guile dropped into the knee high water and reached a control panel. From there he released the pressure door and opened up the dark corridor that marked his path. Guards were already working their way towards him from the post and he found himself under heavy fire. He pushed forward against them, returning fire blindly down the winding corridor.

Opposition mounted faster and heavier than he had predicted and his path became marred from blinding light flashes. Three shots to his armor further shook his concentration and pushed him back first into the flowing water. His rifle fell from his grip and washed away from him. Guile scrambled in the water for the weapon, but a fourth shot to the square of his back forced him under water. The rush of the current dragged him along the bottom and towards the disposal units.

Guile counted eight armed guards and waste management personnel before he dropped. At the rate he was moving with the water, he would reach them and die in less then thirty seconds. His only option lay in his holster. Fighting the current, he slipped the launcher far enough out of the holster to fire a rocket towards a wall. The rocket swayed a bit from the force of the water but found a surface to detonate into.

The pull of water shifted drastically and Guile found himself being pulled towards the new opening. He passed through the opening and instantly dropped seven meters into a refuse processing bay. He sank his head below the surface of the wastewater before rebounding off the bottom and jutting up. Despite the horrible stench, he took in his first breath since going under in the corridor.

Guile's second breath of rotten air came as he looked up to the hole he had created. A steady flow of fresh water poured through the opening, keeping the armed

Chapter Twenty-Eight

men above from spotting him. More importantly, they could not fire at him. He figured he had less than five minutes before they worked their way to an access hatch and caught up with him.

With that thought in mind, he reloaded the small rocket launcher and waded towards a dark tunnel. The level in the tunnel was shallow as the floor rose closer to meet the ceiling. By the time he reached the opening, the waste was only ankle high.

Guile closed on an access hatch and none too soon as far as he was concerned. Not only was the smell more than he could bear, but the waste was burning the injuries left from the blaster hits. His armor had stopped most of the laser impact, but not all. As the thin plating around his body began to fail each blast tore into his flesh.

The access hatch opened to steps that led back to the corridor. Cautiously Guile climbed the steps and peered both directions. The water level was beginning to recede, leaving him to believe that the guards were going to try to catch him from behind. The sounds of boots sloshing in the tunnel behind him solidified this feeling. Once more he had the upper hand and he aimed the launcher behind him. With one explosive rocket the tunnel collapsed in on itself.

Something heavy banged up against Guile's shin as he stepped into the flow of water. He looked down and graciously accepted the gift of an Imperial rifle. He slipped his launcher back into its holster and brought the rifle up to his side. The weapon was not even close to the strength of his lost rifle, but it would do. Anything was better than a weapon that could kill its holder if used on an object that was too close.

Guile turned down the soaked corridor and jogged the remainder of the distance. He found no resistance on his way to the guard post. Once there, he accessed the waste tubes from the command decks. Using the same codes that had given him control of the maintenance regulators, he took command of the waste management system and shut down one of the tubes. Taking a deep breath, he climbed into one of the two-meter tubes, magnetized his boots, then started up.

A cool hand grazed the surface of Barger's forehead, bringing him back to consciousness. The damage to his rib cage had been severe enough to keep him from the raging battle, but in his heart he was with each of the pilots. Many of them had come to him in the hours before the final flight briefing and he had talked with them in length. The reassurance that he laid on their minds relieved his troubled mind from foreseeing the worst.

The time he took with the young warriors was more than his wounds would allow though. He had missed the briefing that had been displayed in his room and had no idea what the three squadrons were up against. A worried Loma Cole had debated whether or not to even tell him. But there she was, standing over him with a data card in hand and a pair of narrow eyes. Her age and experience shown through her young skin for the first time.

"It's worse than expected, isn't it?" He received no answer. "The carrier joined the task force after all, didn't it?"

Cole carefully laid the data card on his covering sheet. "It was the first to drop into the system. She released her first wave as soon as our fighters came up from behind the last planet. That's ten to one odds against a vastly inexperienced group of pilots. We're already taking heavy losses to Blue and Grey."

Barger fought fatigue and pain to sit up straight. A streak of fire rose up from his right side almost forcing him back down. He could feel each cracked rib creak from the pressure supplied by his brace. Too much movement could damage his bones further.

"Where are you going?"

"Up there," he answered with a look to the ceiling. "They're gonna need help, so don't try to stop me."

"I wouldn't dream of it. I know you too well."

"Then what are you really doing here?"

She leaned over and tapped the data card with her index finger. "This is all the current data on the task force. I've grounded your fighter and dropped your companion into another. I took the liberty of making a few modifications so don't be surprised when you see her."

"A few?" He asked with a warm smile. She was famous for her minor modifications. The simplest that he had seen consisted of a pair of gravity bomb launchers mounted to the outside of a bi-wing's wing panels and a medium cruiser cannon in place of the standard quad guns. If she had done any less he would have been surprised.

Her grin matched his "No more than usual. Now get up and let me strap your side down so you don't tear out your brace. I can't promise that the torque won't tear up the strap, but it should give you some relief until it breaks."

"Thanks, Loma."

"Just come back in one piece."

"On your six!" Came the shout over the com system.

Shadle pulled hard to her right and rolled the nova on its starboard wing. Dual pulses of quad cannon fire grazed the underside of her shields on their way to the wrong target. The bi-wing she had pursued took all but one of the eight beams of energy and disintegrated. In the rush to avoid that fate, she dropped power and drifted off course until the fire and debris dissipated.

"On your port," the same pilot informed.

Punching engine power to maximum, Shadle rolled back on her left wing and dove across her previous course. In her savior's direction she let loose a quad burst and caught the starboard panels of a passing bi-wing. The full force of the laser fire split the wing apart and sent the surviving bulk of the fighter spinning away. The second bi-wing who had sought her death suffered a similar fate as her wingman dropped a dual burst into its port engine.

Chapter Twenty-Eight

Mentally Shadle chocked up another kill for herself. Openly she gave direction to the blue pilot. "Thanks for the assist. Kick it up and help me punch a hole in the line."

"As ordered."

Tactical was a mass of Imperial fighters, but visually Shadle could see a weakness in the line. Heavy losses from the carrier Bi-wings were being filled from the Vengeance and the Valiant. The time it took the reinforcements to move into position however gave her a clear shot. Six fighters, loosely spaced in the center of the battle line, were still in the process of filling in an even larger gap. Should she take the advantage now, the first attack run on the Nullify could commence.

"Ghost six, prepare for your attack run," she ordered.

Taking her lead, her Blue wingman closed up under her port wing. Shadle pushed her engines as hard as they would go. She momentarily switched control to her missiles and fired a pair with a soft lock. Lasers flashed green as she switched back. A quad burst jumped from her cannons, shortly followed by two missiles and a quad burst from the Blue pilot.

Two of the six bi-wings rolled out to avoid the missiles. A third dropped to elude Shadle's laser fire. The pilot pulled back up into the second quad burst and caught two of the energy bolts through the command module.

"The last three are yours," Shadle said before pulling up and to the right.

The two dodging bi-wings broke towards her. The lead spun in close enough to take a shot. Shadle nudged her control stick enough to alter course a degree. She missed the first onslaught of fire before letting a smile crease the corners of her mouth.

Shadle had turned enough to edge across the pass of the circling missiles she had fired. As she passed she picked up the missiles out of the corner of her eye. Taking precautions, she dumped a portion of her laser energy into the engines and sped up out of the warheads' flight path. The lead and trailing bi-wing were not as fortunate. The first was clipped by the leading missile and lost altitude control. The clipping was sufficient to detonate the warhead. Proximity alone was enough for the powerful device to crush the starboard panels of the fighter and send it spinning away. The second missile found the trailing bi-wing dead on.

Heavy sweat streamed down the right side of Ghost six's face. The dogfight with the bi-wings had taken much from his stamina. So much so that when a break in line appeared he had lost all desire to start his assault run. Duty and fear rode up on him in the form of the two other novas of his flight, spurring him to commit to the task at hand.

"Check in."

"Ghost twelve standing by."

"Eleven ready and willing."

Six pushed out his chest. He let go of his throttle long enough to clear the moisture from his check. "We have our hole. Break the line then push shields forward to maximum. You might as well loose guns."

"Copy that," said eleven and twelve in unison.

A blaze of cannon fire from the three ghosts and the escorting Blue split two bi-wings in half. The fire line created by a dozen bi-wing squadrons broke enough to allow the novas to pass. In the few seconds it took additional fighters to plug the hole the three ghosts were through and the Blue was swinging around to attack the line from the rear. Like a ring of hurling asteroids the massive bi-wing wall held its ground better than could have been expected.

"Damage," requested six.

"We're both fine," answered twelve. "Our escort has broken back and is tearing the hell out of a couple of bi-wings."

Six shook his head in disbelief. Before Barger and Guile had joined the alliance, those rookies could not even complete the simplest of simulator runs. Now they were fighting incredible odds and surviving. Strict training and easy targets were playing a huge role in the battle. The tight grouping of the bi-wing flights was allowing even unaimed shots to score hits.

"Arm your warheads. Set the countdown at a thousand meters."

The thin form of the carrier caught the corner of his eye. From his tactical count she still held at least half her fighters in the hold. At any moment she could spew a few more to intercept his flight. He chose the dissipating seconds before they reached the start of their run to ease between twelve and eleven and the carrier. He reduced his cannon recharge rate to zero and transferred that energy to his port screen.

As he had predicted two bi-wings leaped from the carrier's bay, screaming towards them. Six flinched, almost missing the start of the run. "One thousand and scrolling. Watch your port, twelve. We just picked up a pair of tails. Eleven, watch the bow of the lead cruiser for return fire. Call out threats."

Neither bi-wing had the optional missile pods mounted to the wings. That gave him four or five more seconds before they would be in laser fire range. At their present angle of attack they would sweep in behind the formation of novas, forcing six to switch his port screens to aft. He also let off the throttle long enough to fall behind his flight.

"I've got the tails. Eleven, if you pick up fire from the cruiser I expect you to take the hits for us. Sorry twelve, but our target is all yours."

The first of the fire from the bi-wings caught up to six and pecked at his aft shields. He refused to shake a single shot rather than allow one of them to pass and take down another nova. Instead he sent all available power and shield energy aft and began a slow dance back and forth. The hits were cut in half, but the intensity increased with each meter the bi-wings gained.

Eleven had the toughest job of the three. The first blast from the distant Vengeance grazed his shields and sent him into a single roll. Not only would the cruiser

Chapter Twenty-Eight

bring its medium guns to bear on them, but also their heavy, ship to ship batteries. One direct blast from one of those and no amount of shield power could save him.

"I've got range to the intake ports," twelve said.

"All power to engines," six snapped. "I can't hold them much longer."

"Down to fifty percent," eleven said as a flash of shield sparks drew six's attention ahead and to his right. "I..."

Two medium batteries caught up with him and shattered his shields at the cockpit. The surviving laser energy pierced the canopy and blew out the bottom of the fighter. Still intact, the remainder of the pilotless hull drifted off course. A final cannon fire blew through the rear of the fighter a moment later.

"You're running out of time, twelve. Punch it up."

A quad burst from both bi-wings caught six's starboard wing during a loose roll to the left. The shields were gone in a wisp of amber and all eight laser lights stripped away the wing and cannon entirely. He fought to keep the fighter in line against his own aching muscles and the sudden loss of power from his right side.

A brilliant flash of light grabbed his attention from his controls long enough to see the remnants of several medium cannon blasts tear apart Twelve's port wing, engines, and aft quarter. Despite it all, the nova remained on course, though it lacked power and most likely a live pilot. Seconds later the fuel cells erupted from internal fires and the nova was reduced to hurling chunks of burning debris.

Six gave into the fighter's need to bank to the right. Feeling no more resolve, he thrust what was left of his shields in his port engines and pulled as tight a starboard turn as he could muster. One of the two bi-wings broke clear in a steep dive. The second rolled hard to the left. It was not enough. The nova slammed into the Imperial fighter and both flared out in a single burst of flame and energy.

Chapter Twenty-Nine

Fallon stepped through the door to his ready room confident that the resistance cell was about to crumble before him. Everything that could go wrong was going right, without the assistance of the promised reinforcements. He couldn't understand why he had been so worried about the limited resistance that he knew was out there. Maybe all the waiting and wondering was more than the depths of his mind could take. The sight of just three squadrons and a handful of medium sized ships was enough to boost his confidence.

The first reports were beginning to come in from the three other battle groups. There was still no word whether they were victorious in catching the Alliance off guard. In his heart he had no worries either way. In the time it would take to finish of the fighters ahead of his ship, the three bases would be occupied by Imperial garrisons.

His renewed sense of power came to an abrupt stop as his ears flooded with the faint sound of a high-pitched whine. The sound made only by a hand held blaster charging to full power. The only sound that could have diverted his attention from his coming victory. The additional sound of the closing door being locked fueled a sudden burst of anxiety in the admiral. No guard would have gone to such lengths to protect him without his request.

"Pleased to meet you at last Admiral Fallon of Arlast."

Fallon had never heard the voice before, but a deep desire to find him told him exactly who it was. "You grace me with you presence." He turned to face Guile who was standing in front of the sealed door. "Though I am disappointed that I could not hunt you down myself."

Guile held the weapon at his side, displaying his confidence that he had total control of the situation. Fallon trusted him in that respect. A man such as this would never lower a weapon on a target unless he truly had control, which meant the nearby guards were dead. The mere fact that the mercenary had made it all the way to the bridge without gapping holes in his body solidified this.

"It's hard to chase a rat with a lift. You need to dirty your hands."

Fallon grinned. "An interesting analogy for yourself. I could not have used a better one." A stench filtered its way to him, turning his stomach. "I see you've made good use of our waste facilities."

"Unfortunately yes. I have had a hard time getting permissions to see you. Now if you will. Have a seat, sir."

Sir? Fallon turned his back to him, for a moment thinking he would end up with a hole in his back. He sat down behind his desk, ridged from a mild sense of fear. "So you are the intruder. I thought you had been caught."

Guile casually approached the desk and sat down. "It's true I was the reason the intruder alert had been sounded, but I wasn't the one your security teams captured."

"You used a diversion? But you work alone."

"I'm here alone, and don't think my companions are any concern of mine. They came of their own free will to complete their own mission. My goal is much different."

"You think you can silence this task force by silencing me," Fallon presumed. "It won't work."

"But it will set the Badlands task force back more than a year from finding the rest of the resistance cells. You may have found this one, but you will never live long enough to find the rest."

It was funny how he saw things differently, given the information he possessed. "How can you, an obviously intelligent individual, assume that by killing one admiral you can topple the chain of command? You show more confidence in me than I deserve."

"I know more about you than you would care to admit. The Arlast are an unknown race beyond the Alcon upper command, the secured traders association, and a very prominent smuggling organization. You are a strong, intelligent, very resourceful race whose tenacity is greater than that of even the Tolan. No other being could have uncovered rocks to find a virtually invisible mercenary who has few friends and trusts even less."

"No, sir, you are the reason the resistance cell was uncovered, and you are the reason I have not had a decent night's sleep in months. I have had to dispose of once-good connections because of you and it will take me years to gain new ones. That alone prompted this visit."

"But you are here for more than just your own quest for vindication."

"As much as I'd hate to admit it I have found a cause I can support. My years of being a mercenary and a smuggler can never equal what the Alliance is doing. They may be sacrificing themselves in great numbers, but they are fighting for what they believe in instead of running from it. Instead of hiding in the shadows and picking the pockets of the Empire."

"They will fail," Fallon said with a strong confidence. "They will die under the Emperor's boot."

"They will die in defiance and they will inflict damage that will echo throughout the galaxy. Already there are loyal star systems that are sending their young to join

Chapter Twenty-Nine

the Alliance. The dismantling of the uniform government was the attention getter and this battle will be the catalyst. The Alcon will never be able to silence the uprising because while the fathers and mothers openly support it the sons and daughters are secretly fighting it."

"It's a dream. A fantasy of a confused and misguided ex-Imperial pilot."

"It's the dream of the Alliance and a nightmare for you. Admit it, Admiral. If this small band of rebels that is attacking your ship now had not been here, you would be all the way across the galaxy fighting to expand the Empire. Instead, one of the Alcon's brightest commanders is stuck uncovering stones in the wastelands of the galaxy. The resistance may not win, but it will be a constant reminder that you will never be able to rest and rule with absolute power and control."

"I admit nothing. Especially when I stand to die before this battle ends."

"You aren't going to die, Admiral. You will spend the rest of your life in an Alliance prison cell on some distant world. You will end your days knowing that they got the best of you."

"Some punishment," Fallon laughed. "Why not initiate one of my interrogations. Torture me for a few years until I die of pain."

"A life in a four by four cell is more than enough to break someone who needs a challenge in his life to continue. Someone whose ambition drives him to never rest and challenge all odds. No, sir, you will remain alone, confined, and without any diversion for that active mind of yours. Your life will be pain."

The fold of skin on the back of Fallon's head twitched uncomfortably. The mercenary was right. He could never survive long under such conditions. Better to face one of his own tortures and at least have something to occupy his mind.

"Tell me, Jared. How do you come about all this personal information?"

"One simple truth, Admiral. We are a lot alike."

A chime sounded at the door drawing Guile's attention long enough for Fallon to trip a silent alarm. He turned back around with an angry expression across his face. He must have realized the moment he turned that he had made a mistake. The look of anger deepened further as the chime sounded again, this time with a hard banging on the door. Whoever was at the door was part of the security force and was alerted the instant the alarm was set.

"Yes we are. We both know when we've made fatal mistakes." Guile raised his weapon and lined up the barrel with Fallon's chest. "I should kill you now."

"You do and you lose your only chance for escape."

"At this point I have no need to escape."

"Sir!" A voice demanded from beyond the door. "Are you alright, sir?"

"I'm fine! I have a prisoner! Prepare my shuttle for immediate departure!"

"In your dreams," Guile said softly. "Or should I say nightmares."

Guile kept the smaller weapon aimed at Fallon. In a single, fluid motion he slipped the warhead launcher from it's holster and raised it close enough to the door to trip the sensor release. "Unlock," he calmly said as the warhead charged to life. The door slammed open, surprising the three guards outside. Without hesitation

Guile unleashed a single charged round into the first guard. One blinding flash of light later and all three were scattered along the corridor.

"Perhaps we are much alike," Fallon said as Guile looked back.

"Your shuttle. Where is it?"

"Why not kill me now and save yourself the trouble?"

"Because as you so boldly put, you are my only chance for escape." He stepped closer and jabbed the barrel in Fallon's chest. "Now move."

The sight of the modified Nova was more than he could take. Barger gazed over the shoulder of his driver at the two boosters mounted on the outside of the upper engines and the large fuel tanks mounted outside the lower engines. Behind the cockpit on the main body, between the wings and the shield generators, were two disposable pods with four warheads apiece. Each warhead bore the unmistakable markings of plasma torpedoes typically mounted to Imperial heavy bombers.

The driver stopped and rounded the front of the vehicle. He eased Barger down and limped him to the extended ladder. With even greater care he used his arms to brace the pilot's back during the slow climb to the cockpit. Once he was certain that the injured Barger was safely at the top and slowly sliding inside he saluted and backed away.

"Sadler," he called to his companion. "Before you even say a word I know what the displacement must be like. Just compensate and help me up before the fighting ends."

Sadler chirped a positive.

"Thanks, buddy."

Barger left the simple startups to Sadler while he focused on raising the nova up from the planet's surface. All across his board his systems flashed green. The one he was most concerned with was the added panel to his right. Both lights slowly faded into the green. The delay worried him, but not enough to keep him from using the boosters. The fate of his students weighed heavier on his heart.

"Barger to control. All systems go."

"Copy that, sir. Good hunting."

"Wish us luck, Sadler."

Barger closed his eyes and reached for two switches that were mounted to the added control panel. With trembling fingers, he flipped both switches and gritted his teeth. Both boosters flared up in three short burns before igniting with full force. In two bright blue flames the nova vanished with blinding speed.

Guile and Fallon reached the Admiral's escape module amidst the steady bursts against the Vengeance's shields. The Alliance pilots were putting up a valiant fight, throwing everything they had against her, but it was evident the shields were holding. Any longer and the assaulting group would fail and the resistance would fall in one, devastating blast.

Chapter Twenty-Nine

There was nothing Guile could do beyond bringing what was left of the Alliance the man who would be their doom. It would be little consolation for such a tragic defeat. On the other hand, the capture of an important and influential figure in the empire would go a long way to obtaining whatever goal a shattered resistance might have.

Fallon entered his access code to the docking hatch of the module without a fight. He stepped to one side and let the pressure door pull back into the wall. Guile squinted through the steam and was taken aback by the presence of three figures moving about inside. Two of the unshapely forms were slightly shorter than he was, but the third was more than recognizable. Although he could not identify him or her he knew it was a Tolan.

"Vigdis," he said. He was not sure if he had it right, but the guess was a valid one.

The gangly form stopped. The Tolan turned as the steam dissipated and it indeed was Stornoway.

"What are you doing here?" He asked of her.

Her bodyguards faded from view, leaving their employer. "I should ask the same of you." Stornoway passed the distance along the docking corridor in two steps. She stopped in front of Guile and looked to Fallon. "I would have thought you a wiser man and taken my advice."

"That's why you're here, Vigdis."

Guile shot a glance to Fallon. It was only at the sight of his devilish grin that he realized his mistake. His question to Stornoway should have answered itself as soon as it was asked.

She removed the weapon from Guile's grasp with a quick, fluid swipe. "I apologize, Jared, but my loyalties were always to the Empire and Admiral Fallon. I merely work for him under contract now."

"Which was why you lost your contract with the Alliance," a voice echoed down a side corridor.

A single blaster round pierced the air and shattered the weapon from Stornoway's hands. From around the corner Stead stepped with a heavy rifle in one hand and a side arm in the other. He flipped the smaller weapon into the air from which Guile gratefully took it. Stead walked closer to the three with his rifle trained solely on Stornoway. Guile held two fingers close to his tattered pants, indicating that there were two more foes waiting for them.

"I assumed you would be dead now," Fallon said. "I was informed that the second insurgence had been contained."

"It had been. I was the third team."

"Where were you?" Guile asked.

"I had to rescue team one after I finished my chores."

"Chores?"

Stead shook his head.

"Scare tactics." Fallon grinned. "It won't work. As you have seen to it I no longer have control of my ship."

Stornoway twitched and the two bodyguards jumped into the corridor. With one long arm she grabbed Fallon and with the other she gripped the exposed portion of the hatch and pulled both of them out of the way. Timing was of the essence, which always worked to the advantage of a telepathic Tolan. She and Fallon were clear as the first salvo of fire spread out along the access hatch and ship corridor.

What was left of Guile's body armor took two hits and split apart before he was propelled back on onto the deck. Stead spun to his side and pressed himself against the corridor wall. Several bolts passed close to his back, but none struck. Guile on the other hand lay flat and motionless on the deck.

Both of Stornoway's bodyguards crept into the access corridor and slid against the walls. Stead had few options. He looked down to his fallen comrade and discovered an additional choice that only a mercenary could provide. Strapped to his belt and visible because of the fall was the warhead launcher with a single round loaded and ready to fire.

Stead checked for Stornoway and Fallon. As expected they were long gone. Putting the loss out of his mind he focused on the approaching attackers and the launcher. At best he would have a second of confusion if he fired wildly down the corridor. He figured it would take at least three seconds to reach the weapon, unlatch it, and then fire. The risk of releasing an unaimed shot and severely damaging the escape module were additional drawbacks.

The sound of heavy boots running in the distance told Stead he was out of time. Pausing only for a deep breath, he released several pulses down the corridor then he dove for Guile. The two bodyguards recovered quickly and jumped into the clear. Each had solid draws on Stead's head as slid across the deck. By all rights he was dead. He let his eyes shut and he came to a stop at Guile. There was nothing left for him to do.

Stead flinched at the sound of two pulses firing. He felt no pain. Only the heavy beating of his heart remained. Maybe it was the adrenaline or maybe it was his fear, but he never realized that the pulses fired were too close to have been from the bodyguards. What set him off was the grip of a gloved hand on his shoulder. He opened his eyes and looked to his right.

"We're even," Guile said. The mercenary tried to smile, but was in too much pain.

Stead stood up then offered a hand to him. "We're far from even." He stained, supporting a great deal of Guile's weight. "I still owe you much more."

Guile slung one arm over his shoulder and allowed his argumentative friend to help him to the escape module. "You can repay it by telling me what happened to the others."

"I didn't arrive in time to save Halash. The rest took a shuttle and left. I stayed so that I could find you. Considering the trouble I was running into I figured you'd have more problems up here."

Chapter Twenty-Nine

"Where were you?"

Stead chuckled. "Engineering."

Bea dropped in under the wing of a Nova, hiding her from the younger pilot's attackers but giving her a clear shot at them. The dual bi-wings that approached from straight ahead opened up on the Nova. Taking heavy hits to his forward shields, the pilot pulled out. Both Bi-wings followed his sweeping roll out. Neither saw the Nova that had them lined up. Three quick combined bursts disintegrated the lead Bi-wing. The second attempted to roll out. He failed.

Bea pushed through the flaming wreckage of the Bi-wing and pulled up and to the right. Just over her canopy she saw the nova returning to its previous course towards the Nullify. Neither the experienced nor the inexperienced pilot saw the three missiles tracking from the Vengeance. In order, the missiles exploded in the shields of the Nova. The first was more than enough to knock down the already weakened protection. The second blew the entire fighter apart. The last was simply insurance.

"I can't believe this!" Bea shouted into the microphone that hung by her cheek. She rolled off course to avoid the blinding laser blasts from the class two star cruiser. "We can't get close enough."

"On your port," Shadle calmly informed.

Bea banked up and to the right, allowing another Nova to pick apart a bi-wing that had been trailing her.

"We've lost all but Blue lead and five and are down to six fighters from Grey. Ghost has lost the first run."

"It won't matter, Narra. By the time we knock down the fighter defense, the cruiser will have picked us apart. The proton blasts just weren't enough. She just switched to her backup systems."

"Fighter alert!" a desperate pilot shouted.

Bea looked on in disgust as the carrier prepared to field her remaining six squadrons.

The Admiral's escape module exploded from the rear of ship and curved out away from the long tail. Its surviving occupants braced themselves against the turbulent ride of a ship that was designed to push the cruiser's captain safely away during her destruction. It was never intended for fleeing intruders.

Guile fought the controls to level the escape. All the while he watched the distance indicator.

"How soon?" Stead asked.

Sweat beads streaming down his face he mentally counted down. "A thousand."

Stead stroked the only button on his detonator. "Not much further or we'll be out of range."

"You...never told me there...was a range." Guile choked up, saving his breath. "Do it now."

Stead depressed the button and gripped his seat.

A white flame tore through the tail of the Vengeance, lighting up the darkness surrounding the massive ship. Bea rolled out to one side. For a moment she could not see past her faceplate. Quickly, the blast shield inside her helmet lowered to ease the brightness. Her eyes adjusted enough to see where she was going. On impulse she pulled up out of her dive and watched in awe at the rippling explosions along the cruiser's hull.

All along the engine housing of the tail, the hull blew from the frame in red and yellow explosions. Larger blasts ripped entire decks away as each of the twelve power cores erupted in white light. An unfortunate bi-wing returning to his hanger with damage was greeted by a rolling flame that incinerated the flight deck. Another landing bay exploded outward, visibly sending sections of fighters out into space. Fresh fighters that the Alliance would undoubtedly have faced after a short time.

A ring of explosions split the engine housing cleanly from the other half of the tail. It drifted away still rippling with smaller blasts. The heavily damaged section floated the length of the cruiser away before the engine core blew. There were no indications it was coming. In one fire ball, the remaining housing exploded, sending three shockwaves out in different directions. The second of the powerful waves of energy washed over the Vengeance, forcing it to list to one side. Desperately the gunners along the forward arcs fired out at the fighters, but with a list they found no targets.

"She's dead!" Bea shouted out triumphantly. "Escort flight you are cleared to engage the cruiser."

Chapter Thirty

Both boosters cut out. They and the added fuel tanks that supplied them with propellant tore from the nova's wings with micro explosions, leaving them behind as the fighter continued on towards the battle.

"Bring shields to maximum," Barger told his companion.

Directly ahead of him was the carrier. From her port side bays, he could see bi-wings lifting off the deck where they had been placed from hot storage. In moments an additional twelve fighters would launch from the port side and another twelve from the starboard.

Barger's active board located the Alliance fighters engaged heavily a thousand meters off the port bow of the listing Vengeance. Coming up quickly from behind was the Valiant, which had yet to release the majority of her fighters. The same was true for Devil squadron from the two destroyers beginning up the rear. They would be the last to launch should the tide turn in the Alliance favor.

Though he did not want to face Devil he was about to turn the tide in his favor. With the nearest detectable enemy unable to respond, the carrier had dropped its port and starboard shields to allow the quickest fighter launch possible. Barger was the undetectable allowance. The distortion field provided by another of Cole's little modifications gave his fighter the appearance of an intermittent energy wave, one that could have been produced naturally from any number of anomalies. With their attention drawn to the battle, the carrier's sensor operators would not have the time or the notion to make a more in depth scan of him.

"Arm one through four," said Barger as he released the safeties to the plasma torpedoes.

He lined up his targeting reticule with the portside landing bay of the carrier and accelerated to attack speed. The outline flashed green within range and he pulled the trigger. Four quick pulses of blue rocketed past the right side, reflected off his canopy, and spread out ten meters away from each other.

Barger switched over to missiles and brought the nose of the nova slightly to the right. The targeting computer locked onto a bi-wing that had left the bay ahead of his torpedoes and flashed green. He snapped off two missiles from the nose launchers and switched to cannons. The reticule faded red and would not flash green again until he closed enough for the cannons to effectively track a target.

The missiles passed the torpedoes a hundred meters away from the carrier and broke off to the right. They tracked in on the lead bi-wing and struck without so much as a flinch from the Alcon pilot. The fighter disintegrated inside the billowing explosion and was gone as the fireball dissipated.

The approach of the torpedoes was noticed as soon as the fighter was destroyed. The port and starboard shields sparked to life just as a second fighter passed through the shield perimeter. The thick energy wave cut the fighter in half. The resulting decompression of the cockpit blew out both halves of the command pod and sent the sliced wings spinning away.

Unfortunately for the crew and remaining pilots, the shields came up a second too late. The torpedoes were already inside the shield perimeter and passing into the bay. Just inside, they broke off in four directions with one heading aft and one turning towards the bay. The vast internal fighter bay provided the torpedoes another two seconds of flight time before all four hit within milliseconds of one another.

The forward torpedo tore a gash along the portside nose of the carrier, first bubbling out the armor then exploding with a single burst of flame. The fact that the explosion had to tear through two bulkheads before it finally erupted out into space demonstrated the power of the two-meter long weapon.

The warheads that turned towards the base and upper decks of the carrier hit simultaneously. A wave of fire swept through the bay and threatened the atmospheric shield that kept it from decompressing. Instead, the field reflected the energy back inward, causing further damage to the occupants and fighters inside. If the first blast hadn't killed everyone on the flight deck the second two surely did.

The last warhead took the longest to reach its target. The result was better than expected. The single bulkhead that separated the landing bay from the engine compartment blew inward, allowing the ball of fire to spread out through the engine room and engulf the core. All four coolant tanks shattered under the pressure and rising temperatures. The unchecked heat from the core itself did more damage than the torpedo ever could have, rising a thousand degrees above specifications in seconds.

The first escape pod rocketed away from a location close the bridge when the primary engine core went critical. With the engine room destroyed and the controls fried, the breach went without impedance. There was no visible warning and no surviving. The aft third of the carrier was simply engulfed by fire and debris hurtling in every direction faster than the eye could track. Both fire and material rolled section by section towards the bow, splintering the armor and incinerating interior decks and bulkheads. The wave of unrelenting destruction came to an end just short of the nose

Chapter Thirty

and bridge of the vessel, allowing the lifeless remains to drift away. A silent tomb for the dead that were not consumed by fire.

The Valiant seemed stunned by the abrupt destruction of the carrier, giving Barger one shot. He switched back to the torpedoes and released the last four with a soft lock. The last had barely cleared its tube before he flipped over to missiles and scrolled through his target selection until it came up on the starboard shield generators. Six missiles were away before he reverted to guns and locked his gaze on the first available bi-wing.

"Assault group," he called out. "Your path is clear to the Valiant. Ghost group, break into assault formation and engage the Nullify."

At first Shadle could not believe that the carrier had been destroyed. Between rolls she had seen the first of many more fighters to leave the bay. The next thing she was able to see was that same fighter torn apart by a pair of thermals. Then all hell broke loose. She had just finished off a bi-wing and had banked to the left to engage any more fighters coming from the carrier when the core went critical.

Barger's voice answered all her questions. The sight of the familiar blue trails of the plasma torpedoes bearing down on the Valiant with six thermals speeding on ahead was both welcoming and reassuring. The cruiser had just reached firing range of the fighter battle and was preparing to launch her fighters. With the assault transports still two minutes out, the Alliance would have lost its remaining numbers to medium cruiser cannon fire alone.

All six thermals erupted against the cruiser's starboard shields above the dual shield generation domes, hurling out sparks of particle energy. The combined force of the projectiles weakened and dispersed the defensive screen long enough for the four torpedoes to pass harmlessly through the perimeter and strike the two domes. The forward of the two cracked like and egg and splashed debris in a halo around its remains. The aft dome absorbed the warheads and exploded inward, creating dozens of fires on several decks.

The missile strikes were enough to force Captain Merrill to grip the back of his chief weapons officer's chair. The ripping impact of the torpedoes jerked him back and forced him to the deck. The back of his head slammed against the hard metal and cracked open in two places, leaving him disoriented and bleeding. He was not about to let his personal pain interfere with the job at hand though.

Gripping his wounds to prevent further bleeding he staggered to his feet and barked out, "damage!"

"Hull breach at number one and two starboard emitters. Field strength at zero. I have six fires raging on the lower decks and the secondary weapons grid is ablaze. If we don't get that fire out we'll lose all backup power to the starboard batteries."

"How far can we spread out the remaining emitters to cover the starboard side?"

"Not enough to encase the entire ship. I can give you full bow protection."

"Very well. Fire control to the weapons grid. Helm, bring us about ninety degrees to starboard and bring up the port guns. Put us in direct line to the fighting and keep us there. If the battle moves you move with it."

"Sir," communications said. "I've received word from the Vengeance. The bridge and all primary systems are offline. They still have power to her bow batteries and navigation, but they have lost all shields and main engines."

"I can see that for myself." He had witnessed the total destruction of the engines as they tore free from the ship. "Tell me something useful."

"At best maneuvering speed they could clear the ship from the system in six hours."

"Has anyone located Admiral Fallon?"

"No, sir. Security teams note that the captain's pod is missing, but that isn't saying much. Most of that part of the ship is gone."

"Fine," he snapped. "Commander, note that at this time I am taking command of this task force under article six of fleet regulations. Order Vengeance to evacuate the ship and scuttle her if possible." As if that were necessary at this point. "Launch all fighters before what happens to the Violator happens to us and order Devil to launch immediately. I want a full screen and I want it now."

"Impact five seconds!" An officer shouted out.

Damn. The transports.

Twenty torpedoes in total struck the gaping holes where the starboard shield domes had been. The resulting chain of explosions pushed hard into the interior of the cruiser. The power grid of the starboard half of the ship collapsed altogether with lights blinking out and gun turrets falling silent.

That's it. "Commander," he said back to his first officer. "It appears we have underestimated the Alliance and their capabilities. We still have a job to do and I intend to see it through. Helm, close our distance to the Nullify and place our starboard side as close to her hull as possible. We will defend her until she destroys the Alliance in one final blast."

"She's breaking off," Bea said with some joy.

"Not quite," Barger responded. He knew what Merrill was up to and there was nothing he could do to stop it. Half the transports had already been destroyed the moment the bi-wings knew they were there. The others had barely enough time to release their torpedoes before they had to break off and return to the planet. With no defensive weapons they would have joined their colleagues as floating debris.

"More fighters," said Shadle in a rush. "Valiant got off seven before her fighter bay went up. I read twelve more coming up from behind her."

"That would be devil," Barger said solemnly. "You two better group up for your run. I'll hold them as long as I can."

"Copy that," Bea said.

"Copy that," Shadle said. "Wes, I want to buy you a drink when this is over."

"It's a date, Narra." A real one this time.

Chapter Thirty

Kirkland was the last to drop from the Blackhawk, having been ordered to bring up the last flight. Somehow word had spread that he had met with the intruder before the destroyer had been damaged and he was deemed a risk. The rest of the squadron had tried to back him up, but there was no convincing Captain Vallejo. The bond between Kirkland and Barger had been a visibly strong one and though he had no proof, Vallejo knew that the intruder had been Barger.

"Two is away," he mumbled loud enough to be received.

The battle was well under way and he had observed it from his cockpit. The shock of losing both the Vengeance and the Violator had long since worn out. His only concern now was in destroying the Alliance fighters before they could inflict damage to the Nullify. The thought of facing his friend in combat lingered in his mind, but his loyalty to the Empire was overpowering. No matter how he felt about their methods.

"Two flight, form up on my port then break into your attack groups. Stay with your wingmen." Let's make this as quick and painless as possible.

Barger pulled up alongside Scio and Nyssa, giving their fighters a brief once over. Both had taken a few hits, but were well enough for the coming fight. He needed them as badly as they needed him. More so because they showed the most promise when it came to the one on one fight.

"Give me your signs," he said.

"Three," Nyssa responded.

"Five," said Scio.

"Alright you two. Long range shots at point. The first Devil flight should break at the sight, but you can be sure they won't go down. Break and take them one on two. If they stick to Devil protocols they will stay in pairs to cover each other. That may give you an advantage in the first few moments. Take it when you get it and don't be afraid to waste a few warheads."

"Copy that, lead."

Lead. There was a stretch. He was acting as lead against his former commander and distant friend. Which one are you, Alder.

"Contact," he told them. "Soft lock and fire."

Three missiles streaked out from the novas. Without a hard lock, none of Devil's first flight was sure who the missiles were after. As such they broke off in three pairs. In sync, Barger and his wingmen split off to pursue the groups of two.

Much to his surprise, Barger caught a hard tone on the trailing of the first pair. Rookie mistake. Must be my replacement. Wasting no time he fired a pair. With much restraint the trailer allowed Devil lead to dictate the evasive maneuver and he followed. There must have been some confusion. Both missiles converged from apposing directions and tore the bi-wing from existence.

Devil lead turned sharply to port and came up nose to nose with Barger. There was no doubt that this was Vallejo and the Captain cared nothing for his wingman.

The intent in the way he piloted his fighter betrayed his true feelings. He wanted blood and he wanted Barger's.

Whether he gave himself away with the quick kill or he was under observation from his first torpedo launch, Vallejo had him singled out. This was long in coming and both pilots were anxious to engage. Laser fire was traded on the first pass, neither craft taking a single hit. For Vallejo's unshielded fighter, that was more of a necessity.

Nyssa fought the force of a hard bank up and to the left in a desperate effort to stay behind the more agile bi-wings. Only once had he acquired a soft lock on the trailing fighter, but lost it when both dove out of a climb. His companion continued to shout at him that the second flight was closing fast and would be within firing range in thirty seconds. By the way his targets kept trying to pull to the right, it was apparent they were trying to set up an assisted kill for the approaching fighters.

"Five."

Scio answered behind grunts and groans, both from himself and his fighter. "You in trouble, three?"

"I will be soon. We're about to be boxed in. How you doing back there?"

"I've nicked one of 'em and he's losing power, but I can't let off and engage him to finish him."

Nyssa gave his tactical display quick glances between slight flight adjustments. "Open up to port and force 'em towards me. If I can get a clean shot maybe we can switch pursuits."

"Copy that, three. Here goes."

As suggested, a flurry of quad cannon fire lit up out of Nyssa's starboard wing. Two dark blotches turned towards him. In response, he lit up to port on his targets, easing them in Scio's direction. Nyssa kept the trigger pulled tight against the flight stick, filling space with shards of energy, while Scio did the same.

The Devil pilots realized all too late what was coming. All four crossed each other's path then directly into the firing arc of the novas. The injured bi-wing escaped unscathed, but his lead was not so fortunate. Two streaks from a quad blast caught the fighter's port wing and shattered the panels. A harsh power drop off forced him into an abrupt port roll.

Nyssa's targets found all four of Scio's quad burst, with the lead taking two through the starboard engine. The trailing bi-wing took the remaining two bolts through the canopy, effectively removing its controlling factor. As the lead fought to stabilize his flight path his wingman's bi-wing drifted off into the distance.

"Give it up, Captain," said Barger over an open comm channel. He was doing his best to fight the pain in his side and limitations of the nova's maneuverability to stay close to Devil lead.

"Sorry, Lieutenant. I have too much respect for myself to simply give up."

"Splash one, lead," said Nyssa. "We'll have two more in a moment."

Chapter Thirty

"Watch for the second flight you two."

The shock of losing pilots to anyone other than Barger distracted Vallejo enough for a single burst to shatter a panel at the back of his port wing. The splash of sparks brought him back to his senses. He noted a slight power drop off to his port guns and filed it away in the back of his mind. At the rate this fight was going, he was not going to get off a single shot against his pursuer. Much as it left a vile taste in his mouth, he was going to need assistance.

"Two this is lead. I have a tail that refuses to shake."

"On my way, lead. Two flight break up and engage."

Barger paid the order no mind and sent forward shield power into the engines. Should he pick up a tail it would simply give him the benefit of shield splash across the rear of his fighter. He knew that for the assisting bi-wing to get a clean shot, Vallejo would have to ease up on his harsh maneuvers. That would mean instant death under a quad burst. The odds were slightly in his favor, but not by much.

"Ghost seven and eight pull in for your attack run," Shadle said amidst a heavy panting. "Ghost four you are clear for lead."

Two novas burst past her canopy in a pale flash. They gave quick chase to Ghost four who was lining up with the intake ports of the Nullify. Behind and to the left of her was ten. Ahead and to the right was Bea. They kept a safe distance outside the reach of the injured Valiant and ahead of the raging fighter battle.

It was clear that the remainder of Blue and Grey would not last much longer. The survivors were mounting a valiant defense to buy Ghost enough time to kill Nullify. There was only so much that eight young pilots could do against thirty seasoned bi-wings. Missiles nearly exhausted and shields dwindling, the Alcon fighters would soon finish them off and turn their attention on both Ghost flights.

"Ordinance check of Blue and Grey squadrons," Shadle requested of her Companion. A quick list of what was remaining of the warheads scrolled up. "Greys, form into pairs and give Blue as much cover as you can. Blue leader, target bi-wing leads and fire on red only. Take down as many flight commanders as you can."

"Roger."

Removing flight commanders would not help enough to ultimately save their lives, but it would slow down their ruin. It might even disorientate the bi-pilots enough to score a few more kills before the fight would end.

Heavy fire rained down across the nose of Ghost four as he led the way. Still a thousand meters out from the Nullify, he was able to maneuver a bit off course to avoid the thick blasts of energy. The distance scrolled down faster and faster though, and his margin for error was shrinking. Should he stray too far, he could easily slam into the hull of the target craft instead of passing through the opening to the intake shaft.

At five hundred meters he leveled off. As a precaution, he poured all available power into the forward shields and braced himself. Right off he took a direct hit that sent him into a straight-line spin. The mounting pressure from the high force spin sparked fierce resistance from his muscles. They wanted to give in and relax against the base of the cockpit. A hard will and even stronger resolve prevailed and he was able to level out the wings.

"You ok, five?"

"Fine, seven."

"I've had it!" The female pilot in Ghost eight shouted out.

Five didn't have to see it to know what was coming. A blast of energy from a medium gun emplacement tracked in several meters to his right and lit up the side of his canopy. The light disappeared behind him only to be replaced by an even greater burst. Burning debris and a light shockwave rained over the rear of the Nova, causing minor damage to the hull.

"Loosen up, seven. I don't want both of us flaming out on the next hit. Take the left port. I've got the right."

At a hundred meters yet another cannon blast found its mark, hitting ghost seven at an angle. The failing shields had no chance to deflect even a part of the two meter in diameter streak of light. The full force impacted and disintegrated the nova. No scream, no explosion. Just the unrelenting wave that came from a heavy cannon. It was a miracle shot from a weapon designed to fire upon slower, less maneuverable vassals. Even if the nova's shields had been at maximum the chances of survival were slim.

"Going in," ghost five said.

Anything that could be seen by the naked eye vanished as the nova rocketed through the right intake port and into complete darkness. Two running lights mounted on the inside of the warhead tubes flared to life and illuminated the smooth interior of the tunnel. For as far as ghost five could see down the intake tube, it kept the same diameter and failed to veer off in any direction.

The only error that came about his choice of the intakes came half the distance to the reactor core. A blockage was coming up fast with no visible avenues of escape. At his speed, he had no time to slow and with limited maneuvering space, he had nowhere to turn. His death came quickly.

"Ghost five, to lead. Do not take the port intake. I repeat, do not ta..."

Static filled the secured comm channel of Ghost five. Another pilot had died in the defense of the Sutherlin Alliance. Three more Grey squadron fighters had also died on the latest attack run of the Nullify. The kill ratio was high with the Alliance pilots, having taken another ten bi-wings with them, but one loss was too many. Five fighters from the ruckus and three more Devil bi-wings were on an intercept course.

Chapter Thirty

"We've already accomplished more than anyone could have expected here today," Patron said with pride. "But our chances are all but gone. Commander, I ask that you take your pilots and continue the fight another day."

Bea closed her eyes. His order was tempting to say the least. She had seen more death this day than she had seen in her entire life. Although the Alcon had suffered the worst, if the Nullify was given the only shot it needed the Sutherlin Alliance would die and the Empire would be the victors of the day.

"No sir." Bea opened her eyes. "We entered this fight with less of a chance than we have now. Tighten up," Bea told her group of three. "Accelerate full throttle and dump all available weapons power and aft shields into your engines."

Her wingmen knew what that meant. The Nullify was two thousand meters out and at that speed they would not be able to adjust their flight path in the slightest. If the Valiant's gunners were at all as good as they were supposed to be, all three fighters would be easy prey. The only benefit would be in reaching the Nullify before the fighters could close to weapons range.

Chapter Thirty-One

Barger heard the order and knew what was at stake. This would be the last run against the Nullify before the planet's rotation would bring the Alliance base into a direct firing line. At that point, the cruiser's main weapon would pound straight through the narrow opening to the base and destroy half the planet from the inside out. More so, the Alliance would be all but crushed.

"Sadler, open a secured channel to Alder."

The overworked companion chirped a negative along with a few other harsh beeps.

"I know he's the enemy, Sadler, but he's also a friend. Just do it."

Sadler gave him one last belligerent whine before obliging his request.

"...and hold off for a clean shot," said Kirkland.

"Thank you, Sadler. I'll make it up to you." Barger released the mute and spoke freely. "Alder."

"Wes? What the hell are you doing? I'm on your tail."

"I know, Alder. You can stay there all you want, but I need your help."

"Fat chance. I nearly lost my commission for speaking with you. Vallejo knows it was you who snuck onboard."

"All the more reason."

"No way, Wes."

Barger closed his eyes and released his controls. On Devil lead's next break he was clear of the nova's firing arc. The move also left Kirkland with the perfect kill. "Go on, Alder. The kill is yours. Any mishaps you've ever had can be righted right now."

"Think about your next choice. Before the day I was taken by the Alliance you yourself told me how you felt about the Empire. And in those drunken words I discovered what had been rooting inside of my brain for a long time. You have to feel the same way or you'd never have blurted out your discontent. Drunk or not."

"Look inside your heart, Alder. They're about to do to the Alliance what they did years ago at Sutherlin. Where millions of innocent lives were lost, their surviving sons and daughters are about to die for standing up for their parents' memories. The Empire is wrong. There is nothing more here than that simple fact. Don't help them kill the memory of Sutherlin. Don't let it all just end this way."

In the back of his mind he pictured four lasers converging on the tail of his fighter and ripping him apart. The thought stayed there even when the answer cracked back over the channel.

"You made your point. What do you need?"

Barger blew out a sigh of relief. "Call 'em off. Give us a chance."

Out of the corner of his eye Barger saw the charging light of Vallejo's bi-wing. He had completely swung around and was on his way back at top speed.

"Devil two to flight two. Break off and regroup at the Blackhawk. I repeat, disengage the enemy. For those of you that have even the shred of humanity I have seen, you will take flight one with you."

The moment of hesitation had come. The survivors of flight one paused in their maneuvering, stunned. The advantage dropped cleanly into the palms of Nyssa and Scio who vaped their pursuits.

"Lead to three and five. Pour 'em on and get back to the Nullify. We have friends that need our help."

Scio wasted no time releasing the last of his missiles at maximum range. Three were targeted in the center of the attacking bi-wings. The last two arced around the tail of the Valiant and streaked in between the injured cruiser and the Nullify. Half the distance to her bow, both missiles turned inward and struck meters inside where the aft shield dome had been. Lack of shielding and outer hull provided both warheads with the cleanest point of impact, allowing the entire force of the explosions to do the most damage.

Both he and Nyssa passed between the two cruisers at top sub-light speed, pouring everything they had into the gutted starboard side of the vessel. Small eruptions, followed by roaring internal fires blanketed each point of impact. The two fighters had done considerable damage to the already scarred hull by the time they reached her bow.

For some unknown reason, the Valiant had let up fire from her bow only to have the large blasts of energy replaced by smaller streaks of light. The bi-wings had closed the gap much quicker than expected and threatened to cut the novas off before they could breach the left intake. The order to abort and engage the fighters was on the tip of Bea's tongue when three of the Imperial fighters exploded in a serious of detonations.

The two survivors split up in front of two arcing novas. The distraction was enough to pull one of the bi-wings away from its duty. The other remained intent on its course of action. In response, both Bea and Shadle decelerated slightly against the possibility they might have to engage the determined bi-pilot. Ghost ten had other plans.

Chapter Thirty-One

"Break off!" Shouted Bea with grim determination.

There would be no reasoning with him though. Guns drained into the engines and shields all but gone from hits taken from the Valiant, he had only one weapon left. Altering course only to keep in line with the bi-wing, the nova impacted at its highest velocity. There could not have been a more spectacular explosion from the destruction of a pair of fighters. Like steel against glass the bi-wing shattered into uncountable fragments, while the nova erupted in a ball of fire that breeched the left intake port.

"You're clear," Scio said with some reluctance. The shock was there as it was in Bea's mind.

Bea and Shadle passed into the left intake port at maximum speed.

"That was the last mistake you'll ever make," Vallejo said over an open comm channel.

Since the order had been given two of Devil's pilots had broken. Almost as quickly, the other three turned on them and opened fire. One of them evaporated under the heavy fire. The survivor then began a hard series of maneuvers to avoid ending his life in a similar fashion.

"Forget Vallejo. Go save him."

Kirkland broke off his dodging of Vallejo and accelerated towards the loyal pilot who had followed his order. Barger on the other hand remained vigilant and slowed slightly to gain Vallejo's undivided attention. In the end he knew his former commander wanted him more than Kirkland. His second would only be a second place prize compared to the blue ribbon he would get for Barger's head.

"It's you and me, Vallejo," said Barger in disgust.

"I wouldn't have it any other way, Barger. I've waited a long time for my twelfth rebel kill."

A quad burst erupted from the bi-wing's guns just behind a painstaking roll out to the left. The brace that had held his ribs together was breaking down, making each turn feel ten times worse. He was not sure how much more pressure his side could take before he would collapse at the controls.

"There's only one rebel here, captain. And I intend to see...this through till the end."

Vallejo slapped single fire across the nova's port wing, reducing the shields to almost nothing. The recharge rate was down to five percent meaning that he would not have field protection for another half an hour. Pain aside, he would have to rely solely on maneuvering if he expected to survive the day.

"You're losing it, Barger. One more shot and you're mine."

Half the distance to the power core and the same blockage that had forced the end of Ghost five appeared before Bea. She was as good as dead had the Nullify not gone into its pre-fire conversion. The thick bulkhead that sealed off the intake slid away and fell below sight on its long journey to it's locking position. Although the disappearance of the bulkhead gave both fighters a clear avenue of attack it also meant that the planet was close to its primary firing angle.

"We're running out of time," Shadle said from behind.

"You don't have to remind me. Release safeties and prepare to fire. We may have to release early and forgo trying to get back out."

Bea's targeting screen lit up as a distant light down the tube grew larger. "I have range. Five seconds."

Her blast shield barely had enough time to darken as the nova burst out into the oversized power chamber. A single, blinding light radiated out from the central power core. The core itself read higher than the nova's power readings could detect, repulsing any weapons lock that could be generated. Instead, the targeting computer found a soft tone on the power regulators that kept the core in check.

Bea released the weapons lock and turned over firing to her own aim. She eased the fighter up slightly, lining the nose up with one of two coolant towers. Without a moment's hesitation she fired a pair of fusion missiles, then banked out hard to the right and entered the other intake tube. Behind her, Shadle mimicked her actions and followed her out. All four missiles struck, illuminating their exit vector in a fiery red.

Each turn became increasingly difficult and it was beginning to show. Vallejo's slap shots were closing in on him with each pass. Sadler warned him that if they were any closer he would not be around long enough to see the end of the battle.

"Inventory," he called out in too much pain to read the display.

Sadler answered him, signaling one warhead in the port tube and no power to the cannons.

"Arm the warhead for proximity impact and disengage all safeties."

Barger juked to port and caught a laser splash across his port wing. The heat sheared away a majority of the armor, leaving the two cannons at the end dangling by power cables. A hard turn to right and down snapped the cables giving the cannons their desired freedom.

"On my mark give it a half second. Burn then detonate on the half. Three...two...one...mark."

The last thermal missile blew out the port tube. Once out, the propulsion ceased and the missile drifted.

"Too bad, buddy," Vallejo shouted in triumph.

Thirty seconds after the missile spouted from the tube, Vallejo passed. He was a mere three meters away from the warhead when the timer elapsed and it exploded. The force of energy alone knocked the bi-wing off course. An added wave of shrapnel and fire shattered the port wing and split the port engine in half. Lack of stability sent the fighter into a long, right bank.

"All power to guns," Barger ordered Sadler.

He strained against the tightest turn he could muster, arcing the nova in hard. The bi-wing had already begun its off-course turn with its pilot frantically trying to stabi-

Chapter Thirty-One

lize the fighter enough to make a run for it. Power to the starboard cannons barely peaked out between red and yellow when the two turning angles crossed.

"Just the best slap shot you've ever seen, Captain." Barger slapped off a combined fire from the starboard cannons, piercing the bi-wing cockpit dead on. As the fighter rolled off pilotless into oblivion he relaxed. "If this had been a real engagement I would have just won the day."

"Increased power readings from the Nullify," one of only a few surviving bridge officers announced. "It looks like she's preparing to fire."

Merrill looked up to the tactical screen, fighting his body's desire for unconsciousness. He had lost a great deal of blood into the multitude of cloths the now dead chief physician had given him. Still, he preferred his present state to the alternative. If he had given in to the physician's request that he be taken to the infirmary, the ship's captain would have died with the rest of the overcrowded compartment's occupants when a utility conduit erupted energy plasma throughout the entire section.

"Recall all fighters from the firing line."

"Sir, said the replacement communications officer. "Fleet command has just relayed a status report from the other four battle groups."

"Route it to my station."

With expedience the junior officer transferred the entire update to the captain's console. Merrill leaned his woozy head over to look. It took but one scan of the eye to determine how the Badlands task force had fared this day. With a frown he leaned back in his chair and dropped the cloth to the deck. From the report he could find no reason to fight his body's need for eternal rest.

Energy readings from the power core were off the scale even beyond the scanning shield that kept the Nullify from appearing on energy scopes. The destruction of the coolant tower left the power buildup unchecked, sending more than what was required into the firing chamber. The horizontal firing plates were fifty percent open and still charging when the surge broke free of the power core and poured into the spider-web of power conduits running between the plates.

Beads of sweats built up around Bea's forehead intensifying the look of concentration. Her narrow view was set solely on passing out of the intake port and clearing a safe distance away from the cruiser. The seconds ticked down faster than her distance indicator.

At least the Alliance will be safe, she thought to herself.

Starlight came earlier than expected as her Nova blew out of the port in a blinding shot. Vapor trails of escaping gases spread out from the tips of her wings, giving her escape a bird-like form. Graceful, but fleeting.

Shadle was a hundred meters off her tail as the first web conduit ruptured from an excessive power build-up. In a vain attempt to release the charge before it destroyed the ship, her captain had ordered the weapon fired. It was too late. Half the conduits were caught up in the spreading rage of fire and pulses of blue lightning. The release of the full pulse with the horizontal halves not completely opened compounded the terminal result. Half the blast exited the firing chamber into the blocking slabs of steel. The rest of the energy expanded in a ring through the forward halves at the first contact of superheated gases.

Only a supernova could have rivaled such a spectacle. White light brighter than the brightest star engulfed both the Nullify and the crippled Valiant in a heavenly glow produced by hell itself. A bluish shockwave of energy and microscopic debris freed itself from the internal chaos, spreading outward in a vain attempt to reach throughout the galaxy.

Caught up in the rush of power, Bea's nova was knocked off its escape trajectory and thrown end over end. A surge of added power crawled over her controls like an arachnid made up of pure energy, frying every onboard system she had. Had she not strapped herself in firmly and kept a reserve air tank linked to her main air feed, she would not have been conscious to realize that she had not been the closest one to the devastation.

In the moments before she blacked out her fighter rolled parallel with the destruction. A glimmer in her eye reflected the star like presence of the destructive energy. A second, less powerful shockwave blew out from the now vaporized Nullify, spreading away from the galactic plane. Had she been around when the galaxy was born, Bea would have sworn that she had just witnessed the birth of heaven.

Chapter Thirty-Two

The celebrating was brief to say the least. Warm handshakes and swift pats to the back were followed by an informal medals ceremony for the seven warriors who returned. These were the first medals given within the Sutherlin Alliance and thanks to them they would not be the last. A victory greater than could be told in a thousand tales had been won against heavy odds.

But at a terrible cost.

Patron stood on a catwalk, cautiously observing the recreation below. Younger pilots not yet trained well enough to have joined the battle sat with eyes wide at Ogden Scio and Nyssa as they regaled them of the fierce battle. It would be a story beyond the reaches of embellishment. No amount of forgery could top the truth of what had taken place. The pain alone would outlast a lifetime of lies.

Mild celebration was felt all over the Sutherlin as she and a handful of freighters completed the evacuation of the temporary base on Luikart. Despite the defeat of the task force their location had been revealed. Word would spread quickly of the defeat and it would not be long before more ships would arrive. The hasty retreat further into the Badlands gave the rogue fleet both the chance to regroup and to rest.

The celebration seemed to fade towards the large view ports that gave the recreation room a spectacular view of rotating starlight. Alone and separated from the rest were Bea and Guile. They were no closer than a breath yet, no further away. They stood in silence. They stood in grief. The two had already witnessed a lifetime of fighting. Now they were beginning a new life where the fighting was that much more important.

Stead had long since given them the room they needed to be alone. The room they deserved. He had congratulated them and had accepted a returned gratitude. For the first time in their long time acquaintance, Guile held a warm smile across his face for his rival. The feeling was genuine on all sides and marked a turning point in Guile's life. It was a change he needed and one that would propel his long-awaited healing process.

Now he and Bea were by themselves in a room filled with smiles and laughter. They were reluctant to hold each other's hands or to offer condolences for the loss of all but four of the thirty-plus pilots who had left the surface. They were content in spending the moment close to one another, using the other's warmth of heart and soul to pass the time.

Several decks away the need for comfort was greater than anywhere else on the cruiser. Four occupants were still in the infirmary where Barger gained his first glimpse of life in the Sutherlin Alliance. It was here that he first met Narra Shadle. It was in her eyes that he gave up all hope of rejoining Devil squadron. It was in her words that he gave himself to the Alliance. His only wish was that he could have realized it long ago. Before he was faced with having to watch her in the very same bed he had been in some time past.

Two beds away Alder Kirkland and the Devil pilot he had rescued from the wrath of the rest of his squadron were silent. They had taken more than their share of damage from both laser fire and the shockwave from the Nullify. Their wounds in the defense of the Alliance were not as severe as Shadle's however. The damage done to her body was nearly as terrible as the harsh gashes that adorned her fighter.

Tight body wraps kept her from any movement. Her wounds had refused to heal. The purpose of the wraps were to hold her together long enough to bring aboard a specialist from another Alliance cell. She was still days away from the rendezvous though and the situation did not look good. Despite the pain in his side Barger was by her side, intent on seeing her through this.

At his request Loma Cole had stayed away to give him time with her. He had promised to share a drink with his injured friend and she had yet to regain consciousness since being picked up by the rescue shuttle. Barger was already in the infirmary when Bea escorted her into the room. She could not stay after an hour at the edge of the bed.

"Wes," Shadle said in a weak voice.

Barger looked down to her. "I'm here, Narra."

A tear built up at the corner of her closed eyes. "I can't see, Wes."

"Stay still. Your blast shield failed." He too felt moisture well up around his eyes. "The blast blinded you."

"Then we got her."

Shadle's strength surprised him. She must have known the condition she was in, yet she thought only of the Alliance and its safety. Barger had not until now realized what true devotion was.

"You got her, Narra. Bea's companion recorded the missile hits. Both of hers weakened the shielding around the coolant towers, but yours finished her off."

Shadle managed a pained smile at the corners of her mouth. Not even her facial muscles were spared the agony ailing her body. "I'm glad. Then none of...this was in vain."

Barger laid the back of his hand against her cheek. She was fighting to speak. "Try to rest. You'll be getting help soon enough."

Chapter Thirty-Two

In what seemed like a lifetime she slowly tilted her head against his hand and rubbed her soft skin against his. His heart welled up with her gesture of feeling. If he could have, he would have picked her up and blasted out of the cruiser to meet with the specialist. His thoughts were borne of pure passion. She would die without constant care. Care that he could not provide on his own.

"I'm dying," she whimpered.

Barger knelt down. "No you aren't."

"It's ok, Wes. I can die with...a clean conscience because I...can say that I truly lived. How many of us can say that?" She took what must have been the hardest swallow of air in her entire life. "Just tell me one thing. Can you trust me now?"

She knew the truth before she even asked. The Nullify was preparing to fire and Barger was close enough to make a run of his own. He chose to stay with his fight and let Bea and Shadle do the job with his full trust. Still, she needed to here it from him and he was more than happy to oblige. "With my very soul."

"I'm glad." She paused, her blind eyes searching beneath her swollen eyelids. "Where am I?"

Barger's lips parted to tell her the truth. He stopped short of facing reality and instead gave her what she wanted. "On the observation deck of the Sutherlin. We're outside the galactic plane, looking back into the stars."

"I can see it," she said with a growing smile. "It's beautiful. I can see all the stars winking at us. All our friends are standing beside us." Shadle's lips narrowed flat. "Tell me where you come from, Wes."

Barger's lips wavered. "I was born on the planet Eriam. It's a small planet with lush forests and deep oceans. It has little technology outside the major cities and has weeklong hiking trails that defy beauty. Each day begins with a startling orange sun rise, ending with..." He wanted nothing more than to take her there in person. As he told his life's story to her, he knew he would never get the chance.

About The Author

James Spix was born in California in 1974. This is his first published novel. He works as an engineering manager and graphics designer and lives with his wife in California.